Then, Again

Then, Again

A Novel

JACLYN YOUHANA GARVER

LAKE UNION
PUBLISHING

Text copyright © 2024 by Jaclyn Youhana Garver
All rights reserved.

Published by Lake Union Publishing, Seattle

www.apub.com

Amazon, the Amazon logo, and Lake Union are trademarks of Amazon.com, Inc., or its affiliates.

ISBN-13: 9781662519901 (paperback)
ISBN-13: 9781662519918 (digital)

Cover design by Jarrod Taylor
Cover image: © Dethan Punalur / Getty

Printed in the United States of America

To Stephanie, my BFF

A Light exists in Spring
Not present on the Year
At any other period—

—Emily Dickinson, from "A Light Exists In Spring"

Under the summer roses
When the flagrant crimson
Lurks in the dusk
Of the wild red leaves,
Love, with little hands,
Comes and touches you
With a thousand memories,
And asks you
Beautiful, unanswerable questions.

—Carl Sandburg, from "Under the Harvest Moon"

a wind has blown the rain away and blown
the sky away and all the leaves away,
and the trees stand. I think i too have known
autumn too long

    (and what have you to say,
wind wind wind—did you love somebody
and have you the petal of somewhere in your heart
pinched from dumb summer?

—E.E. Cummings, from "A Wind Has Blown
    the Rain Away and Blown"

AUTUMN (2017)

I have been staring at the front doors for fourteen minutes. Maura never stays past 3 p.m. It is now 3:14 . . . 3:15, and she hasn't left yet.

I am parked at the opposite end of the lot from her car. My music plays low, as though I'm afraid she'll hear. The tune is too upbeat, too poppy, and she would scowl to see me mouthing along when my thoughts should be focused on prayer and healing. *Forgive me, Father, for I have sinned* in lieu of Justin Timberlake's "SexyBack." It's a song of healing for me, but she wouldn't understand.

Maura steps from the swinging double doors of Pax Nursing & Rehabilitation ninety seconds later, and I hunker down in my seat. She doesn't look my way, but I still hold my breath until her car pulls out of the parking lot. I watch the "JESUS is my BEST FRIEND" sticker on her rear bumper as it turns out of view. I flick off my engine and all but run through the front doors. I hate being late to visit Charlie.

"Hey, Asha," Madison sings to me. They all know me by name. "She was waiting for you. You just missed her."

"I've been outside for fifteen minutes," I confess.

"You're terrible."

I give Madison a smile. I like her. I like that her phone is cased in neon pink with unicorns. I like that, when I'm speaking to her, it can buzz, and she won't look at it, doesn't even flinch. I like that even when Madison's not smiling, I can still see the faint shadow of a dimple, as though she is a human so endowed with happiness, it's always there, just below the surface, waiting to spread to anyone nearby who needs some joy. I envy that.

"Have you told her yet?" she asks, and I shake my head. "We can do it for you, if you want?"

I shake my head again. "I'll do it. Soon. I swear."

I used to get lost when I'd visit Pax. Now I know the halls and turns from muscle memory. Charlie's room is on the west end of the building. That's why I like to come at 3 p.m.: The sun is in its descent, and his room is flooded with cheer. Or as much cheer as you can put into a nursing home and rehabilitation center that specializes in adults in their prime. That's what the website said: "adults in their prime." It's still mainly old people. Old people and Charlie.

When I walk into his room, I sigh at the gloom. Maura always closes the curtains, as though to ensure the room is in a constant state of mourning, contemplation, and solitude.

"This has got to drive you insane," I say to Charlie as I fling open the curtains. "Don't you want to slap her across the face sometimes? Or is that only me?"

I light the cinnamon candle I brought from home—we're not supposed to have open flames, but everyone here seems to trust me. Besides, I can't *not* attempt to cover that sterile, medicinal smell, disinfectant trying, and failing, to mask the scent of blood and infection.

A blue straight-backed chair is in the corner, and I drag it closer so I can hold Charlie's hand while I sit with him.

"Guess what I just heard in the car?" I ask, and I sing a few lines, shimmy my shoulders to the tune. I kiss his hand and try not to think about dancing to the song at our wedding.

"Let's see, what's new, what's new . . ." I stare into space while I run the tips of my fingers slowly up his arm, reaching my hand into the loose short sleeve of his hospital gown, then back down until I hit the nail on his middle finger, up and down, up and down, not massaging so much as reminding myself what his skin feels like.

"I'm going to Florida next month. Dad says hi. He wanted to visit but . . ." I trail off. "I'm looking forward to it. Haven't been in forever. I think the last time we went was last Labor Day. Or was it the year before that? Huh. I'm staying for a week. You'll miss me, right?"

I pause, giving Charlie time to respond: *Of course, Asha. I don't know what I'll do without you, with only Bible-thumpin' Maura coming by every day to ask the Lord Jesus Christ to return me to her, but at least I have Madison's sponge baths to look forward to.*

"Madison is the *receptionist*," I say, teasing. "You and I both know Katherine is the one who bathes you. But if you keep your eyes closed and pretend it's Madison, I wouldn't blame you. She's way cuter."

I look at my husband, take in his now-gaunt body barely making a lump in the hospital bed. His face is sunken, nearly gray. He's hooked up to wires and machines, faint beeps, whines, and whirs forming the soundtrack to our weekly date. Some studies show that people in comas can hear. But after a year of looking up studies online, I've learned that studies know nothing—especially not what it's like to kiss your lifeless husband and understand, in your heart and in your brain, that he's gone, that everything that made him *Charlie* has left this room, this planet, this dimension.

But I keep rambling anyway.

"I talked to Jada this morning. Had my review. She's really happy with my work, said I can keep working from home. She did want to know if I thought I'd ever come back into the office full-time. I said I wasn't sure, but come on. You know I'm never going back there."

I write copy for a small ad agency in Cincinnati, Valentine & Vine. The work, for me, is mindless, which makes it perfect.

As I ramble, I pause mid-line. Something's missing from Charlie's table. I'd left it right by the candle.

"Where'd the dates go?" I ask him. The last time I visited, I brought a plastic container of dates I'd picked up from Kroger. Not as good as the batch from the Middle Eastern grocery, but passable. I'd left a note for the aides, told them to help themselves.

But it was a big container—surely they're not all gone.

One guess, I heard in my brain from Charlie.

I turn around to peer in the trash can behind me. Bingo. My nearly full container of dates.

Maura.

"What a cunt," I say, but I'm not surprised. "Sorry," I tell him. Not for calling his sister a name, but for the wasted dates.

I ramble for another twenty minutes, and it's pushing 4 p.m. when my phone buzzes. I need coffee. You at Pax?

There's a Starbucks down the street. I say I'll be there in ten minutes.

I stand up and place my flat hand gently on the side of Charlie's face, turning him to me so I can press my mouth against his. I refuse to stop kissing him goodbye, even though I don't feel him there, even though I know he is no longer of this world. He may be only a shell, but he's *my* shell, and I can't quite give up hope that wherever he is, whatever he's doing, he feels the weight of my mouth, the pressure and moisture and taste of his wife.

I blow out the candle and, at the door, I stop and look around. It took me months to treat Charlie's room like my room, too, to feel like I belong here and am not intruding on . . . on what? On his coma? On his quiet? I blow him another kiss and make an effort to walk away at a normal pace; I had run into Pax, yes, but whenever I leave, I want to run away as fast as I can, too.

Bridget is waiting for me at Starbucks when I arrive, and she holds up my coffee.

"House blend, two sugars, splash of cream?" I ask, though I already know the answer. I take my coffee, a sip, and a seat.

"How is he?" she asks.

I shrug my shoulders once, and she nods.

"I ran into Jason Kapaglia last night."

I freeze. I absolutely freeze. The noise around us seems to grow louder—the baby trying out his voice at a table nearby, the whirring of the coffee machines and blenders, the too-chipper singsong of the drive-through barista. It's so loud, I am deaf.

"Why are you telling me this?"

"He asked about you."

"OK, but why are you . . . wait, what?" I think I'm smiling. I can't help it.

"Me and Alfie saw him at dinner. He was there *alone*. Can you believe it?"

"No Simone?"

"I didn't ask. But I did notice a distinct lack of a wedding ring."

"Shut up."

"I know." She sees my brain working and nods. "I already googled it. Divorce was finalized last month. He's back in town."

"Where?"

"Here. His house."

"HIS house?"

"His mom never left. Isn't that wild?" I flash to the first time I ever set foot in Jason's childhood home. I was thirteen years old. It was more than twenty years ago. "But we're missing the point here: He asked about you. Asked if you were still in town. How you were doing. I said you were fine. He asked me to give you his number."

"You said I was fine?"

"You think I'm going to try and explain your mess?"

I stare at her and don't realize I'm crying until she hands me a small package of tissues from her purse. "This could be a good thing," she says. "I haven't seen you smile like that in ages. I miss it."

So do I, and I immediately feel guilty—for the smile, for its reason. Right now, my husband is my lifeline to anything that remotely feels like *me*, and that tether is frayed, the knots drooping. When Bridget said Jason's name, for a flash, I felt that *home*. That's why I smiled, and that's why I'm crying now. That feeling of home makes me feel guilty. And that guilt makes me feel like trash. And I am desperately sick of feeling like trash.

Bridget nods like she had listened to and understood my thought process. "I know, babe."

This Starbucks is L-shaped, and we are seated in the longer portion of the space, near the bar, against a window. We can see most of the coffee shop, except for a small alcove in the back, the bottom portion of the L. After I mop up my tears, I raise my head and immediately catch eyes with the woman I'd cowered from in my car that afternoon. She steps around the corner and into view. This woman always seems to pop up and surprise me.

It's Maura, Charlie's sister.

SPRING (1996)

It takes retrospect to divide a life into its various seasons. A girl doesn't know for sure that childhood has ended until a few years into that next chapter. She doesn't know she's left behind the awkwardness of young adulthood until she's firmly entrenched in Grown-Up Land. And she doesn't know Phase II of Grown-Up Land has kicked in until she can flip through the calendar and wonder where the hell the months and years have gone.

I can say with certainty that I left my childhood behind the summer before eighth grade, when my father and I moved from Hillsboro Beach, the Florida town where I grew up, to West Chester, Ohio, the town where I became *me*. I once read somewhere that who we are in eighth grade is basically the same person we are as adults. I think about that a lot.

We moved because my dad had accepted a job teaching in the Middle Eastern Studies Department at the University of Cincinnati.

"You are lucky to be a new girl in 1996," my dad told me. "When I was the new boy, students were not very nice to me."

Granted, Dad had been "the new boy" from a city in Iran no one had heard of, while I was the new girl from the Atlantic coast of Florida, where a percentage of my classmates would go during the next half dozen years of spring breaks.

If arriving in West Chester marked my first step outside of childhood, the second step on that list occurred minutes after we pulled into the driveway. That's when I met Bridget. She lived a few doors down, and she rode her bike in circles around the street in front of the new house until I called out, "Hi." We've basically been inseparable ever since.

Step three occurred thanks in part to the Olympics, which Atlanta hosted that summer. It was the year Gail Devers won the gold in the 100-meter dash. I was obsessed with her and even picked her as the topic of my English project later that year. My dad ran track as a kid, and the stars lined up in that mysterious way of theirs to give me that urge to chase after nothing, too—just like my dad, just for the sake of the chase.

Before long, I started chasing after Bridget: She rode her bike around the neighborhood, and I jogged with her. I wasn't fast, but I never got tired, and she always rode slowly enough so she wouldn't leave me behind. Eventually, I started going for runs without her to chase. I liked it because it got me out of my head. Moving is scary, but I never wanted to freak out on my dad or make him feel badly for pulling me away from my grandparents in Florida or my friends Craig and Heather, who lived across the street from them. When I ran, all that disappeared. Sometimes I'd do nothing but listen to my shoes slapping on the sidewalk, or I'd count houses that I passed. One, two, three, four . . . twenty-nine, thirty, thirty-one . . . fifty-two, fifty-three, fifty-four . . .

Eighth grade was also, of course, when I met Jason Kapaglia, who was the fourth and final step out of childhood.

Even though I was the new kid, I'd heard rumors from the first day or two of school that some kid named Jason had a crush on me. Had he passed me in the hall? Seen me at lunch? He wasn't in any of my classes, but junior high is nothing if not a giant game of telephone, staffed by preteen operators who think who's dating whom is the most fascinating topic in the universe. At least, that's what it was like in the midnineties. I hope things are better now. Or maybe I don't.

Bridget pointed out Jason to me one afternoon at my locker. He stood across the hall with two boys, and they all kept staring at us.

"He's walking this way, oh my god," Bridget stage-whispered, slapping at my arm.

I looked over my shoulder and, for the first time, got a good look at Jason Kapaglia. My stomach fell to my sneakers. Good Lord, this boy was beautiful.

With my eyes, I traced the slope of his nose as it dipped toward his philtrum. I traced the outline of his mouth, his full lower lip. Jason had a strong chin even though he was only thirteen, and I followed his jawline up toward his ears. This close, I could spy a tiny scar next to his left ear and wondered where he'd gotten it, if it had hurt. His hair, to me, seemed golden, like he'd spent the summer outside, and the season had bleached each strand a different shade of sunny. He wore it a little long on top. I fought an urge to touch it, to brush it off his forehead so I could get a better sense of the shape of his eyebrows. His eyes were hazel—through the years, they'd sometimes look more brown, more gold, more green, depending on the light—and they crinkled when he smiled at me. He had short, stubby, dark eyelashes and a face smattered with freckles.

I made this inventory during the seconds it took him to walk across the hall to me, and the din of junior high seemed to drop a few decibels. Everyone, apparently, understood this conversation was going to happen even as it was still occurring to me.

We didn't bother to introduce ourselves—we each knew the other, in that rhythm of school days—and he didn't bother with small talk. Thirteen-year-olds don't do small talk. They're smart that way.

He stood across from me, and his voice was soft when he stammered, "I was sort of wondering . . . if you were . . . I mean, are you . . . aryouuointoehdancetomar?"

I shook my head, smiling a little. "What?"

Jason closed his eyes tightly, took a breath, and tried again, understandable this time, but still strung together: "Areyougoingtothedancetomorrow?"

"Yeah," I said, a little too loudly. "Me and Bridget." She still stood next to me, and I saw her wave in my periphery, but Jason's eyes didn't flicker from the path they traced from his shoes to my face, from my face to his shoes. I asked, "Are you going?"

"Yeah," he said, shuffling his feet. "Since we'll both be there, would you maybe wanna dance with me?"

I became very aware of my pulse, and I couldn't hear anything but the blood in my veins thumping in my ears. I wasn't sure I'd be able to speak, so I nodded instead. He smiled at me, and I again fought an urge: I desperately wanted to kiss this strange boy I could hardly speak to, right there at my locker. But I didn't. Not to say there wouldn't be a hundred locker kisses in our future, but not on that day.

After, he rushed back to his friends, who I'd later learn were Dan and Edward. Dan had a buzz cut, close-set eyes, and ruddy, blotchy skin. He chewed with his mouth open and thought it was hilarious to pull out a seat someone was about to sit in. Edward had the blackest skin I'd ever seen, and he wore his hair in tiny braids. His art projects always won regional and state contests, straight through high school. As Jason approached them after inviting me to dance, Edward grinned and held up his hand for a high five. Dan seemed pissed, which I'd eventually learn was just the way his face looked.

The next night, Dad dropped off Bridget and me at the school for the dance, the two of us accidentally clad in similar brown dresses scattered with a tiny floral print. They were as bad as they sound, but it was the style there for a minute.

We walked into the gym, and it hardly looked like our school. The overhead lights were off, and strobe lights were set up along the walls. The bottom two sets of bleachers were pulled out to give students a spot to sit. Just outside the gym's double doors, long cafeteria tables were covered with bowls of punch and pretzels and soda.

Most of the gym floor was open for dancing, and Bridget and I staked out our spots right up front, by the DJ, with Bridget's friends

María and Kendra. I'd met them only once or twice over the summer—did that mean they were my friends, too?

As song bled into song, we danced harder and wilder, jumping and shouting and waving our hands above our heads. I remember this clearly, the feel of the thumping music under my skin, the strobe lights turning my classmates' faces into colorful puzzle pieces, bouncing works of art. Even though we were awkward, fumbling children, we thought we were such hotties. I love that about us.

I hadn't seen Jason the whole dance—had been pretending like I wasn't looking for him every ninety seconds—but as soon as the first slow song came on, Jason appeared at my side.

"Should we dance?" he asked.

"I didn't think you'd want to," I said, having convinced myself in the waiting that he'd changed his mind. In response, he brought his closed fists up close to his face and twisted them, wiggling and flapping his arms, his entire body, in a way that utterly did not match the opening chords of the slow song coming from the speakers. *He's a weirdo*, I thought, surprised. "You're a weirdo," I said, loving it. He stopped abruptly, grinned a little, and moved to grab my waist as I reached for his. Then we both reached for one another's shoulders.

"How about this?" Jason said, setting my hands on his shoulders. He placed his hands on my waist. He was only an inch or two taller than me, and if I looked straight at him, the eye contact was too much, too heavy. I focused instead somewhere over his right shoulder.

"You look really pretty tonight," he said. "I mean, you always look really pretty."

When we're thirteen, we should all have tiny hype men like Jason Kapaglia. Junior high is a time of horrible self-confidence, especially for girls. For the most part, though, I never struggled with confidence. Yes, it's pathetic to get your self-confidence from a boy, and eventually, it existed on its own, outside him. But I cannot overstate Jason's influence. Because during the years when girls notoriously hate their looks—too much acne and/or bad hair and/or growth spurt and/or why am I still short? and/or bad clothes and/or boobs are too big and/or what boobs? and/or why is this boob so much bigger than that boob? and/or a whole lot about boobs—this boy I adored told me constantly how glorious I was.

Throughout the song, Jason tugged me closer and closer until he'd wrapped his arms almost completely around me. Eventually we realized we were each humming along with the tune.

I pulled back to look at him, and before I could say anything, he sang along with Mr. Tony Rich, lyrics about loving someone for a million years.

Inside my head, I screamed, *A boy is serenading me at the dance, oh my god oh my god oh my goooood.* Over his shoulder, I saw Bridget pointing us out to María and Kendra. I widened my eyes at them, trying to convey the depth of my *OH MY GOD*, and waved.

"What is it?" Jason asked, and he turned to look at my friends, his cheek brushing mine. I leaned my face into his, and I felt him tense. He didn't move away, though. I was acutely aware of the parts of his skin that pressed against mine. Slowly, slowly, I moved my hands up his shoulders until my fingers rested lightly against the back of his neck. He shuddered a little, then nuzzled me. "That feels nice," he whispered. We danced the rest of the song that way, humming along, swaying, enjoying the feel of the other's weight.

When the song ended, I pulled away reluctantly. I wasn't sure what had happened, but I wasn't ready for it to be over. Tony Rich transitioned into the oh-so-romantic "Boom Boom Boom" by The Outhere Brothers. I expected Jason to walk off the floor, but he started again with that same weirdo wiggle from a few minutes before. I matched his moves, then *whoop*ed loudly and spun around as fast as I could. I waved my friends over like an air traffic controller.

The five of us spent the rest of the dance together. When slow songs came on, María, Kendra, and Bridget swayed next to us, their arms around each other, moving in a giggly unit while Jason and I held each other tightly.

"Last dance!" the DJ called. It seemed like only moments had passed, and I could taste disappointment on my tongue; I wasn't ready to leave. I didn't want to go home.

"Asha?" Jason said. He was holding me tightly, and I had to pull away to look at him while he spoke. "Do you think . . . maybe . . . I mean . . . Doyawannabemigirlfren?"

I didn't need to ask him to repeat it; even though he'd mumbled, even though he'd sped through the question, I knew exactly what he had asked.

"OK," I said. Then I surprised us both when I leaned forward and gave Jason a kiss on the cheek. On the middle of the dance floor. In front of everyone.

A few people catcalled and whistled. I heard Bridget shout a "WOOOO!" from over my shoulder somewhere. But the sound seemed to come through a fog. The only clear thing was the expression on Jason's face. His eyes had lit up, and he looked at me like I was the most perfect thing. For a moment, I felt like I was.

AUTUMN (2017)

In the days after Charlie's coma, Maura chopped all her gorgeous blonde hair into this severe little razor-sharp bob. It is always perfectly flat-ironed, not a strand or flyaway out of place. She doesn't wear much makeup, but it's not as if she needs any. Hers is the kind of natural beauty that makes strangers stare: large, wide-set, sparkly eyes so blue, I swear, some light makes them look purple. A peaches-and-cream complexion with a tiny, pert nose. A little bow tie of a mouth. When she smiles, it takes up her entire face.

But I haven't seen her smile, really smile, in a long time.

Which makes *this* grin extra special—in that way that it's special when the tiger at the zoo catches you looking at it, and it slowly stands up and stalks quietly toward you. You watch the muscles clench in her jaw, and you see the way her silky body slinks forward. This cat is beautiful, but this cat will also eat your face. Thank god it's behind glass.

There is no glass between Maura and me.

She rushes to the table and wraps me in a hug. I have not stood up, so she's bent over me, and I'm enveloped in her slim arms and torso. I hear her iced coffee slosh in its plastic cup next to my ear, and Bridget and I stare at each other over Maura's shoulder.

She straightens up and eyeballs Bridget's drink. "What's that?" Before Bridget can answer, Maura continues, "I drink so much plain iced coffee, my followers must think I have an addiction. Can I take a pic?"

In an instant, Maura has her phone in hand. Without waiting for a response, she snaps a photo of Bridget's drink, peers at the image, and says, "There's a weird glare. Let me . . ." and she reaches for the drink to move it farther from the window. She shuffles behind me and shifts my purse from the empty seat to take another photo of the drink, which is topped with whipped cream, caramel drizzle, and chocolate shavings.

"Almost got it . . ." she says, and she reaches into the large straw hole at the top of Bridget's domed lid. "Those clumps don't look great," she says, using a single fingernail to separate a larger chocolate shaving into two smaller ones. She sucks the chocolate off her finger, pushes the cup back to its original spot, and snaps a few more photos.

"That is perfect," she says to herself, tapping the phone a few more times with the short, sleek coral manicure that was just inside my friend's beverage. "I'll post this tomorrow," she says, finally addressing us. She slides her phone in her bag and continues as if that didn't just happen. "I was waiting for you at Pax. I wanted to invite you to prayer group this weekend. We're dedicating it to Charlie."

"That's sweet, Maura, thanks," I say, my mind racing for something, anything, to say I must do instead.

"She's busy," Bridget cuts in. "We're going shopping."

Maura's cheer is replaced by a flash of irritation, but only for a moment. "Well, maybe you two can reschedule? Melody has put together a special rosary service for Charlie. She's Catholic, and she promised to teach it to me. Her family recited one like it every day for a week, and her sister's baby got to go home from the NICU. Poor thing was born seven weeks early, can you imagine? Our God is a miracle worker. He heard their prayers. I know it will work with Charlie. I had a dream last night about him, and Charlie told me he heard my prayers, and they made him stronger. Isn't that the most beautiful thing you have ever heard? What does Charlie say to you in your dreams? I wonder if he ever visits us at the same time?"

I feel my face fall, as though every muscle has given out. "I've never had a dream about Charlie," I say, and Maura does not try to hide this second, ugly flash across her face, across her whole body, as though my slumped limbs and features have given strength to hers. Tight lips, chin raised, shoulders back: Maura is the picture of smugness.

"We can add you to the intentions of our prayer group," she promises, "but it would be much more effective if you would join us. Bridget can come, too."

"No, she can't," Bridget says. She does not pour on the sweetness here, nor does her voice get a sharp, nasty edge. Her tone is in no way impolite, but she offers no further explanation.

Maura sighs, and she turns to me. "I think, if you tried a little harder, this might all be over already, and I'd have my Charlie back."

My body tenses, and I want to scream that he's my *husband*, that our bond is stronger, more meaningful, more intimate, more passionate than anything a person can share with a *sibling*. *What do you even need me for?* I want to say. *Like your prayers aren't enough?* or *So if this doesn't work, does this mean Jesus doesn't love you?* Or, worst of all, *If you'd bothered to attend Charlie's care-planning meetings, you'd know what was going on and the total futility of what you're doing. You'd know what I did.*

But no, not yet. I need to be emotionally ready for *that* conversation. It's not something you throw at a person to hurt her, even when that person enjoys her feelings of superiority over your filthy, heathen heart.

Bridget is watching my face as my brain cycles through these responses, and she chimes in again. "Great running into you, Maura," she says. "I'm sure we'll talk soon. Bye-bye."

Maura stands at our table, unsure what to do. She is not ready to leave. She has more to say, more guilt to pour upon me, more insistence that my prayers can do more than the dozens and hundreds of doctorate degrees that have been devoted to cases like Charlie's. But Maura has been dismissed, and Bridget stares at her, smiling, silent, until Maura walks uncertainly away.

At the door, she spins around and hisses too loudly, "Tell *Francis* I said hi, you slut."

A duo of teens nearby watch her leave, then turn to me. "Dude," one says. I fling my hands in the air and shake my head, the picture of *Tell me about it*, then turn to Bridget to voice a fear that's lived in my guts for months: "Do you think she told her folks?"

"About Francis?" Bridget asks, and I nod. "You said they aren't close."

"They're not."

"So maybe not."

"It seems like something she'd do," I say, and Bridget gives me a small smile. As much as I'd love for my best friend to reassure me that my fear is unfounded—that of course Maura has not told her parents, a.k.a. my in-laws, about the most shameful thing I've done—I knew she wouldn't do it. But sometimes, especially when we flounder, we ask questions we know we won't get answers to. Or questions we won't like the answers to.

One of the reasons I love Bridget is her honesty. She wears it kindly when so often, so many use it as a mask to hide cruelty, the crew who start sentences with, "No offense, but . . ."

Bridget and I stare at each other in silence, and I ask, "What the hell were we talking about again?"

"We'll finish later," Bridget says as I remember and say simultaneously, "Jason Kapaglia."

"You still want to hear this?" she asks, and I nod. She eyeballs her drink as she might a small snake that's gotten into her living room. "Let's go to your house. I am *not* drinking that." At the exit, she drops the full drink into the trash. "That bitch owes me six bucks."

SPRING (1996)

After the dance, it seemed like overnight everyone heard I was dating Jason Kapaglia. Girls who'd never before talked to me would say hi as though, by having a boyfriend, I had suddenly become interesting. On the bus home, everyone tried to sit by me, and when I wouldn't give up my seat with Bridget, they'd sit in front of us, behind us, listening to our conversation, laughing at everything I said.

"What is going on?" I asked Bridget.

"You're popular," she said simply. "I hate you."

"Shut up, I'm not."

"Jason is, like, the hottest guy in school. Everyone wants to be you."

I liked it better before, when I could walk to class without everyone greeting me. In the bathroom, girls would ask me what I thought of their new shoes, their new lipstick. I didn't even wear lipstick.

Jason started calling me after school, and we'd talk on the phone until Dad called from downstairs that it was dinnertime.

"You have been spending a lot of time on the phone lately," my dad said one night over burgers. "There is a boy who calls you a lot. It is always the same boy?"

"Oh my gosh, yes! Just one boy, Dad."

"Is he a respectful boy?"

"He is very respectful, Dad."

"Hmm," Dad said.

The next week, Dad asked me if I wanted to invite my boy over to dinner. That's what he called Jason—"Your boy"—as in, "I would like to meet your boy. He has been taking up so much of my daughter's time."

"He's coming over *tomorrow?*" Bridget squealed the next day at school. "Aren't you *nervous?*"

Of course I was. I hadn't ever even seen my boyfriend outside of that very building, and now he was about to set foot in my house.

"I'm jealous," she said, but she was grinning. "I wish someone wanted to make out with *me* all the time."

"Shut up!" I whispered. "We've never made out! I kiss him on the cheek!"

"But you want to," she said matter-of-factly. "And he wants to. You're going to soon, right?"

I didn't know. Bridget was right—I *did* want to—but . . . how? Where? Would I be any good at it? Oh, god, what if I was terrible? Sometimes I would fold my tongue over on itself and try to imagine what it felt like to french-kiss someone. What the heck did you *do* with two tongues in your mouth at the same time?

That night when Jason called, I told him for the hundredth time to be at my house at 5:30 Saturday.

"So, I have a kind of weird question," I said, trying to ease into it. "Have you ever, like, kissed someone before? Like, *kissed* kissed? Like *really* kissed?"

"Oh," he sounded surprised. "Well. Not really. You're my first kiss, I guess."

"Good," I said. "Is that bad? That I'm glad?"

"No," he said. He sounded very serious. He got that way, sometimes, when we talked about us. "I'm glad, too. I'm glad you're my first kiss. And I'm glad I'm yours. Do you, like, think about that?"

"I . . . yeah, I think about it sometimes."

"I do, too."

At 5:32 Saturday—I knew the exact time because I was sitting by the window, staring at my watch—Jason's mom dropped him off. I was surprised when she didn't get out of the car. I'd never met her.

I opened the front door before Jason could knock, and I gave him a quick hug before my dad could come around the corner.

"Here," Jason said, and he handed me a red rose. "Mom tried to make me get a whole bouquet, but I liked this." It was the first flower a boy had ever gotten me, and I thought it had the prettiest smell in the world.

My dad stepped into the hall as I buried my nose in the soft petals and inhaled.

"Hello, Jason," my dad said, sticking out his hand. I was surprised to see Dad standing exceptionally straight, his shoulders pushed back and his gaze narrowed at Jason, even as he smiled and welcomed him to our house.

During dinner Dad peppered Jason with questions about himself and his childhood. Was he from West Chester? Did he have any siblings? What was his favorite basketball team? Did he like school? What was his favorite subject?

Jason had been born and raised here—he still lived in his babyhood home—and he had an older sister, Gaby. He said they were close, but I knew Gaby annoyed him; whenever I called, if she answered the phone, she always made fun of him for having "a little girlfriend," as she called me. He rooted for the Bulls, got As and Bs in school, and loved science class.

"Astronomy's my favorite. For my science report, I'm going to write about Alpha Centauri. It's part of a three-star system and is the second-closest star to Earth, after the sun. It's four-point-three-seven light-years away. That's the same as about five-point-nine trillion miles."

I was totally impressed and, though I didn't recognize then what it was, a little turned on—I loved his memory, how smart he was. I was so smitten, though, he could have said, *I'm going to do a book report about*

how often my dog relieves himself between the hours of six and nine p.m.,
and I would have thought it was the most brilliant thing I'd ever heard.

"Do you play any sports?" Dad asked. "What do you think of track?
Asha is an excellent runner."

"She is?"

"She did not tell you?" Dad said. "She watched the Atlanta
Olympics all summer, and she said, 'Dad, I'm going to be like Gail
Devers.' She won the gold medal."

"That's who you're researching for English," Jason said. "Are you
gonna go out for the track team? Maybe I can, too."

I shook my head. I ran for me. The idea of doing it with a team, *for*
a team? Ugh, that sounded horrible.

For dessert, my dad pulled out a small container he'd tucked into
the cabinet. Halvah.

"Maybe Jason would like to try an excellent Middle Eastern treat?"
my dad asked, slicing off a couple cubes of the crumbly dessert made
with tahini, honey, and flavors like pistachio, our favorite.

"Sure," Jason said, seeming eager enough. But the smile on his face
fell right off after he took a bite. "Oh."

"You don't have to eat it. It's OK. I know it's weird," I said, and felt
bad about the words the moment they left my mouth. It wasn't weird,
not even a little.

"No, no, I . . . I like it," he said, taking another bite and grimacing.

Halvah's texture is dry. It almost disintegrates on the tongue. I'm
not sure there's an equivalent American dessert. Maybe cotton candy,
which also dissolves, though cotton candy is also *candy*, lemonade pink
and sweet as a toothache. Halvah's a confection, but it doesn't taste
sweet the way Americans are used to sweet. I love it.

"Maybe a chocolate pop instead," my dad offered. "You can split
one while I walk?"

Every night after dinner, my dad circled the neighborhood. He
hadn't been a runner for some time, but he still enjoyed the solitude
and ritual of it, same as me. Sometimes I went with him, but he didn't

ask tonight. In fact, I couldn't believe he was going at all; I'd assumed he wouldn't leave us alone.

Dad kissed me goodbye and said he'd drive Jason home when he got back. After the door latched behind him, Jason and I looked at each other, eyes wide. Neither of us had expected this to happen.

"Um . . . do you want to watch some TV?" Jason asked at the same time I said, "Should we eat a Popsicle?"

As I dug in the freezer, Jason spied an open pack of basketball cards on the counter. I'd gotten them that afternoon and hadn't had a chance to put them in my collection yet.

"Can I see?" he asked, reaching for them. I handed him half of my chocolate pop as he shuffled through the players. "You like basketball?"

"The Miami Heat," I said. "My dad's favorite team. Mine, too."

When Dad was the new kid, I explained, he used to watch NBA games to improve his English. When Miami got a team back in the eighties, my dad was ecstatic. I was only five or six, but I can remember what a big deal he made out of those first seasons: Every game day was a party, and our neighbors would walk into and out of our house to sit for a quarter, have a handful of pretzels, chat with my dad.

See how graceful, he'd say, pointing out his favorite NBA players to me—Magic Johnson, Glen Rice, and his all-time favorite, George Gervin. Gervin retired from the NBA when I was a toddler, and Dad used to talk about how much he wished I could have seen the way the Iceman shot the ball, *Like a cloud off his fingertips.* Now Dad sends me highlight clips every finals season. *No one will ever play like Gervin,* he insists.

Jason flipped through my basketball cards, and I could tell he didn't know who most of the players were, but his face lit up when he got to an MJ. He studied the card, an image of Michael Jordan stuffing the ball on some poor schmuck from the Knicks. He flipped it over and read the stats. "He went to North Carolina, cool."

"You can keep it, if you want," I offered.

Jason looked surprised. "I can't take this from you."

"I have two, it's OK."

"You already have two Michael Jordan cards?"

"No, I have two of THAT Michael Jordan card. I've got about two dozen Jordans."

He flushed a little as he pulled out his wallet and slid the card into the photo slot where his driver's license would one day go. I'd never given a gift to a boy before. The action felt like bravery, somehow.

The basketball conversation over, our Popsicles finished, we lapsed into silence.

"TV?" he tried again and followed me into the family room. We sat next to each other on the couch. I stared straight ahead as I flipped through the channels, not really sure what I was looking for, not really seeing anything on the screen. I became hyperaware of my skin, and of the heat coming off his.

I settled on MTV and set the remote control on the coffee table in front of me. I turned to Jason and jumped when I saw he was barely an inch away from me. I faced the TV again, and I felt my body stiffen when he grabbed my hand.

After a few minutes, I still hadn't turned toward him, so Jason tried a different tactic: He got off the couch and got on his knees in front of me. He looked in my eyes, and I felt terror as I looked back into his. But not, like, scared terror. More like *I don't know what I'm doing I'm going to be bad at it but I really want to but I've never done this before and oh my god what do I do now help?*

"Is it OK . . . ?" he asked, whispering so softly I could barely hear him. "CanIkissyou?"

I nodded my head a budge, nearly imperceptibly. Jason closed his eyes and brought his face close to mine. My heart thudded. I thought I might faint. I closed my eyes, too.

Then, suddenly, Jason's lips were against mine, firm and tightly closed. He gave me a closemouthed peck with a loud SMACK, then pulled away. He looked at me with wide eyes and hopped back on the couch, next to me.

I turned toward him as "Nobody Knows" came on, that song we'd hummed to each other at the dance. I stood and held out my hand to him. He smiled at me and in recognition of the song. This, we could handle. This, we were comfortable with.

We wrapped our arms around each other and began to sway in that familiar way.

"Jason," I whispered.

"Yeah?"

"Kiss me again?"

He brought his mouth to mine, quickly, and we mashed teeth. We both exhaled a giggle before trying a third time. This time his mouth wasn't pursed so hard, and it fit neatly against mine. His lips were soft, and some foreign but innate part of me pulled his bottom lip lightly into my mouth. I heard Jason make a funny noise. Tentatively, the tip of his tongue made its way into my mouth, and I sucked on that a little, too. Jason hugged me tighter to him, and I felt something against my hip that made me start.

I pulled away from the kiss abruptly and looked at him, wide eyed. He had the same look on his face, and we blinked at each other for a moment. How long had we been kissing?

"Wow," he whispered, and we heard my dad open the front door. We bolted to the couch and were intently watching a commercial for juice boxes when my dad walked into the room.

It was time for Dad to take Jason home, and when I started to put my shoes on, Dad said, "Why don't you stay here, *bratti*? Let us have a little talk, man-to-man?"

Dad took a moment longer than necessary to get his keys from the hook in the hall, I think to give us some privacy to say goodbye.

"Thanks for coming over," I told him, and I snuck him a quick but soft kiss on his mouth.

When I heard the car pull out of the driveway, I grabbed the phone and punched in Bridget's number.

"Oh my god how'd it go tell me everything."

"We kissed!"

"Hallelujah! How was it?"

"It was awesome. And . . . I think I felt his thing!"

"Ewwwww, how?"

"We were slow dancing, and we started kissing—"

"—tongue?"

"Yes. And he was hugging me really tight, and it was just, like, there!"

"How big was it?"

"Oh my god, I don't know, Bridget!"

"Are you gonna kiss him again?"

"Definitely."

"I hate you so bad. I want to kiss a boy!"

Bridget would go on to have her first kiss two months later, with Jason's friend Edward, the nice one. She had a birthday party and invited me and Jason, Edward and Dan, María and Kendra, plus a few other people from school I didn't know very well.

For the party, Bridget and I decorated the basement with rainbow streamers, and we blew up what seemed like a hundred balloons. We let them bounce around on the floor, and Dan kept grabbing them to rub on everyone's heads, to make their hair all static clingy. Bridget's basement was made for parties, complete with a pool table and stereo system and stacks and stacks of CDs.

Bridget was the only one of us who knew how to play pool, but the rest of us pretended like we knew what we were doing. Whenever I would go to hit a ball, Jason would come up behind me, wrapping his body against mine, placing his hands over mine as I pulled back the stick and tried to hit the cue ball. I felt his thing again, and I whispered to Bridget about it when we went upstairs for more chips.

"THAT'S IT!" she stage-whispered.

When we got back downstairs, she shouted, "EDWARD! DANCE WITH ME!"

By the end of the song, their arms were wrapped around each other, and they looked like they were trying to eat each other's faces. Jason watched them, laughing, before he pulled me over, moving his head and arms in that weirdo way from the dance, and kissed me. It was no longer awkward; now, it was just good, it was just sweet, it was just everything and all I could think about. If I wasn't currently wrapped up in Jason's arms, I wanted to be.

Jason and his friends were the last to leave the party. He kissed me goodbye, a good, long kiss, broken up by Dan calling from the top of the stairs, "Come ON, dickhead, my mom's outside." Jason pressed his mouth against mine for a beat longer, then bolted up the stairs, shouting happy birthday to Bridget over his shoulder.

Bridget and I set up our sleeping bags in the living room. We combed through the pantry for the snacks we hadn't already eaten, pulling out pretzels, chips, cookies, popcorn—all the major food groups. She put in a movie we had watched together a million times and dimmed the lights. For a few minutes, the only sounds were Bridget chomping on popcorn and the smack of my mouth as I sucked cheesy salt from my fingers.

"So what do you think about Edward?" she asked.

"He's nice. Much better than Dan. You picked the right friend."

"I did," she agreed. "His mouth tasted like mints. I think I saw him eat like a whole thing of Tic Tacs."

"Jason said he had three packs of them in his pocket. He's been wanting to hit on you forever. Before they came over, he said Edward was super nervous. He did push-ups in your front yard."

"Shut up."

"I'm serious. Edward said his dad gave him the advice. Said it helped calm nerves."

"That's the dumbest thing I ever heard." But Bridget looked pleased. "So how far have you gone with Jason?"

"You know we've kissed."

"Is that all?"

"Yes, that's all! I don't want to do anything else."

"Didn't look that way tonight. He's pretty handsy."

She was right. When he wasn't in the room with me, when I was only *Asha* and not *Jason's girlfriend, Asha*, I didn't want anything more than kissing. But when I was with him, when his hands were rubbing my back, when he nuzzled the side of my face with his nose, I forgot all about that.

Why does your brain do that? Why does it want two completely different things at completely different times? It was like it was trying to play a trick on me, like I was two different people. Why would my own brain want to trick me? It made no sense.

"You're just horny," Bridget said, and I threw the bag of Twizzlers at her head.

SUMMER (2005)

After college Bridget and I rented a house together in Northside, a neighborhood a few miles north of UC, our shiny new alma mater. She found a job planning events for an old, local theater that regularly hosted community groups and fundraisers, and I found the gig at Valentine & Vine.

We painted the living room pale pink and bought purple throw pillows for our blue couch. In the kitchen, she painted swirling vines on the doors of the cabinets. We had two steady incomes, and we figured, Who cares if we never got our deposit back on the place? In the bathroom she painted words of encouragement around the oval mirror above the sink:

THERE IS BEAUTY IN YOU.

YOU SHINE.

SEXY AS HELL.

We invited our families to Thanksgiving—my dad and her parents and little brother—and we thought we were so hip, so grown-up. We went to Goodwill and found china plates to use instead of our plastic dishware, but we ruined the china when we put it in the dishwasher. We didn't even have the good sense to be mad about it.

We decided we would host the biggest New Year's Eve party ever. We invited everyone we knew—friends from high school, from college, from work, from down the street. We told them to bring their friends, and their friends' friends.

"Black tie!" we shouted. "It's a black-tie party!" We found discount prom dresses and picked out each other's gowns for the night: I picked a short, black, sparkly party dress that twirled when Bridget spun. For me, she chose a floor-length, strapless, cherry-red dress with a V cut out of the top, revealing a bit of my breasts. As we got ready that night, I dusted a soft touch of shimmer in my cleavage and hoped I'd find someone to kiss at midnight who'd appreciate it.

By 9 p.m., our house was packed, overflowing with laughter and alcohol and people we'd never met. We drank too much and danced too hard, and when midnight hit, I found myself sucking on the tongue of a man whose name I didn't remember. Two hours later I dragged him into my room and discovered that, yes, he appreciated my shimmer.

The next morning, before I opened my eyes, I said a little prayer that the mystery man would no longer be next to me, that he would have done the honorable thing and slipped out before I'd awoken.

I squinted open my eyes and scowled when I saw the body still in my bed. He was flat on his back, arms loose at his sides. He faced upward, not even turned on his cheek. I studied his shoulders, which were slim but muscular. His hair was long, sprawled on my pillow. I tugged the blanket down until I spied a pair of striped briefs, and I couldn't help it: I chuckled.

The man sniffled back a yawn and stretched. I watched the lean muscles in his chest ripple and said a silent thank-you that my prayer had not been answered.

He turned his face toward me and caught me watching him.

"Good morning, Asha," he said, and I balked that he knew my name. "Aren't you going to say good morning?"

I buried my face in my hands and peeked through my fingers.

"Good morning . . . Joe?" I asked, and the nearly naked man in my bed laughed hard and purely. My heart trilled. "Good morning . . . Dustin? Bob? Tutankhamen?"

He reached over and pulled me close to him. He put his face to my ear and said, "My name is Charlie, but you can call me Tutankhamen anytime you want, Asha Khoury."

Then he kissed my earlobe, and I felt a shock travel through my body and out my toes.

"Oh, what the hell," I thought, and I let Charlie Somebody make love to me.

Three hundred sixty-four days later, on Sunday, December 31, 2006, Charlie and I went to another New Year's Eve party: our wedding.

AUTUMN (2017)

"So do you want to see him?" Bridget asks. We've nearly finished a bottle of wine—which has, at no point, contained my sister-in-law's fingers—and are sprawled out in my family room.

"I don't know," I say.

"This isn't a betrayal," she promises. "It isn't."

"Are you allowed to date when your husband's in a coma?"

"Ash—" Bridget starts, and I cut her off.

"I know. I know. But I keep repeating ''Til death do we part.' And then I go, 'Well, he's brain-dead.' And then I go, 'He still deserves better.'"

"And then I go, 'And so do you,'" Bridget says. I am silent for a moment, and Bridget asks, "OK, be honest: How much of this has to do with Maura?"

"None of it. All of it. She's right."

"About what?"

"I don't know."

"You visit him, what, every week?"

"She's there every day."

"Do you *want* to go every day?"

"No. But Maura . . ." *But Maura what?*

"Don't go there. She's not worth it."

Listen to your friend. She's right. "So why does Jason want me to call him?"

"He's lonely? He misses you? He's curious?"

"He said that?"

"We didn't exactly get into explicit detail. He told me to tell you that you should call him."

I have to smile at that. Passing messages between friends is about as junior high as it gets—which, I suppose, fits us well.

I have made precisely no decisions when Bridget leaves twenty minutes later. After a shower, I put on a pair of worn pajama bottoms and one of Charlie's old Boy Scouts T-shirts. As I curl up on the sofa, I spy a folded slip of paper next to Bridget's empty wineglass: *555-2035,* I think without thinking. I used to call that number daily; surely Jason's mom doesn't still have the same number?

I open the paper. There are two numbers: One is, I figure, his cell, and the other . . . well, it turns out that not only do I still have Jason Kapaglia's phone number memorized (or, rather, his mother's, I suppose), but I recognize the handwriting as if it were my own. Jason used to write me letters: I know what a piece of lined notebook paper looks like when it is full of his promises. He wrote exclusively in mechanical pencil. His letters were small, and he used thin strokes. Apparently these are all still true statements.

I take the slip of paper into my office and have a seat at my laptop. It's time to turn to Google. I type in "Can you date when your husband is in a coma?" That feels presumptuous—I have no idea if Jason wants to date me—but I figure I'll start with the worst-case scenario. The best-case scenario. The most awkward–case scenario.

The first hit I get is an advice column from an Episcopal pastor. This should be good:

> My husband has been in a coma for the past two years. He shows no signs of recovery, and doctors say it is only a matter of time before he passes. I visit him often, but lately, I have been having . . . let's call them "stirrings." Is it wrong if I were to sleep with another man? Signed, Desperate

Pastor Von says the answer to that depends on my—excuse me, on Desperate's—ethical standing:

> Some people will be sensitive to and understanding of your needs while others will not. Do not focus on others' opinions. The only thoughts that matter are your husband's and yours. It is up to you to conclude what your husband would want for you under these circumstances. It may be helpful to ponder the question, What if the situation was reversed? If you were the one in the coma, what would you want for your husband?

Do I even *have* stirrings anymore? I close my eyes and think about the last time Charlie and I were *together*. It was two days before it all happened, in the morning. I woke up before him, turned toward him, studied him. I used to do this a lot. He slept on his back, arms to his side, completely open and vulnerable to the world. I loved this about him. I snuggled up close to his body and rested my hand lightly on his briefs. I left it there for a moment, and then I nuzzled the side of his face softly with my nose. I gently took his ear in my mouth and . . .

Yeah, OK, I still have stirrings.

So what would Charlie want?

I want you to be happy. His voice sounds in my brain before I can even finish thinking the question.

But what if what would make me happy is another man?

I want you to be happy, he insists.

Well, then.

Now what if the positions were reversed? I try to imagine Charlie with someone else. It's tough. Not because I feel jealousy at the thought of him with another woman, but because Charlie was always exceptionally *mine*. We fell in love fast and hard. Neither of us brought any baggage from old relationships. Yes, my Jason baggage had been heavy, but I'd unloaded it all before Charlie came into the picture. It's one of the many reasons why we were able to sync up so well, so quickly.

Bridget sometimes jokes with Alfie that, if he ever cheated on her, she'd get a pet dog so she could sprinkle Alfie's diced penis on top of the kibble. But my situation isn't cheating, is it? Can you cheat on another person when that other person has no higher brain function?

And what about Maura?

My sister-in-law is never going to like me again. After Charlie's accident, I inadvertently doused my relationship with Maura in kerosene and lit a bonfire. She won't ever forgive me. Sometimes I don't blame her. But not always. We can make stupid choices in the best of times—why should we be forced to marinate in guilt and regret for the choices we make when we're broken and raw?

Next, I google Jason. I know what I'll find—I've searched for him periodically over the years—but I do it anyway. He's never kept up with social media, but in the rows of Google Image photos that pop up when I search "Jason Kapaglia," I spy a few photos of *my* Jason Kapaglia. I count them off on my fingers:

(one)
This image was taken a few years after the last time I saw him. He is in college. He wears a sweatshirt with Greek letters on it, and he is passing an oversize check to a pretty girl with Down syndrome. In another pic from college,

(two)
he's all sweaty after a track meet, his lanky arms slung around the necks of the other guys on his track team. They each have a medal hanging against their jerseys, but the photo's black and white, and I can't tell what place they earned. A few images down,

(three)
there he is wearing a tie and seated at a slick metal desk. He studied business in college, and I think he worked for a bank in London. His wife, Simone—rather, his ex-wife, I guess—works for some kind of

consulting group, and her company transferred her overseas a few years back. I wonder whether he has an accent now. I've never been overseas.

I study the photo of him at the desk. His hair is shorter than it had been when he was a teenager; it doesn't hang in his eyes anymore. *You moron,* I admonish myself. *Why do you think time stood still for him after you were no longer part of his life? It didn't for you.* He wears a huge, bushy beard I don't like because it hides his philtrum. The first time I pressed the tip of my pointer to it, he grabbed my hand and kissed the pad of my finger. It was the first time *he* kissed *me*, a gesture made at my locker the week after the dance.

These memories and our shared history feel like a balm on my frayed ends, a soft spot to rest my nerves, which have been at attention for nearly a year. I imagine them, my nerves, with the bloodshot eyes of a cartoon character after twenty-four hours without sleep, hands shaking, a cigarette's ash flicking into coffee that slops all over the table. Thinking of Jason lets my nerves exhale, and I realize, this is the first time I've felt anything resembling peace since before the coma. That's not nothing.

I realize, no matter how this ends up, I want to reach out. I love these thrills I've had today on account of Jason. Maybe that's just me using him to feel good, but hell, he divorced his wife and then found a way to get in touch with me. I think we're trying to use each other. Aren't we?

As I sit at my desk, a small smile plays on my lips, and it's not long before my old buddy Guilt knocks its miserable knock on my brain. I do think all healthy, curious humans occasionally internet stalk their exes; however, it still feels like a betrayal to have a happy, healthy, fulfilling relationship with your husband and remember an old love vividly, fondly. Though how happy or fulfilling can a marriage be when one spouse is in a coma?

Once, Charlie and I were reading in the backyard. It was a sunny spring afternoon right after we'd bought the house from his cousin, after we'd put up a tall fence and painted the inside of it lavender. We listened to the rustle of squirrels chasing each other, the whir of a distant lawn mower, and we each had a huge, sweating glass of iced tea. Jason was nowhere to be found in my thoughts.

Until he was.

"Listen to this," Charlie said, his nose buried in *The Unbearable Lightness of Being*. He read aloud: *"The brain appears to possess a special area which we might call poetic memory and which records everything that charms or touches us, that makes our lives beautiful. From the time he met Tereza, no woman had the right to leave the slightest impression on that part of his brain."* He paused, took a sip of tea, and I watched condensation drip onto the open page. "Isn't that beautiful?"

He continued reading quietly, droplets of water *drip drip drip*ping on the page. I watched him getting lost in the story, lost in the idea of one person, one soulmate, writing to our poetic memories for all time. I wondered if I was that person for him, but I couldn't bring myself to ask. Because what if he turned the question around on me? And the answer to that question—*Did I write to your poetic memory, Asha?*—was, unequivocally, no.

Because Jason had gotten there first.

I wondered, Was the writing something permanent, beyond my control? And despite my choices—I chose Charlie and would always choose Charlie—did it simply not matter? Was I doomed to keep Jason tucked away not because I wanted to keep him there but because he was stuck there, welded to the folds of my brain, an inorganic but nonetheless necessary part of functioning, like a metal piece in a knee replacement or a plastic stent keeping a heart valve open so the blood can flow, so the heart can pump, can work, can live?

After a few moments, without lifting his head from the book, Charlie said, "It sounds torturous, having no say in who writes to your poetic memory. What if that person is a serial killer?"

"Or a politician," I said.

"A flat-earther."

"An anti-vaxxer."

"A Nazi sympathizer."

"A vegan."

"What if it was someone who thought the moon landing was fake?" he whispered, horrified, wiping the bottom of his sweaty glass on the open page.

"Or someone who wipes their drinks on a poor, defenseless book?" I jumped out of my seat and wrestled *The Unbearable Lightness of Being* from his hands. Charlie often poked fun at the way I read—I never break a binding, never make a mark in the margins. God forbid I drop a book and dent a corner or crinkle anything. I blew on Charlie's open page. "You poor, poor baby," I murmured.

When I looked up, my husband held my book in his hands. He eyeballed me as he dipped a finger into his tea—"Stop it," I warned—and moved his hand slowly, slowly to an open page—"You wouldn't dare"—and pressed the tip of his finger to the corner.

I pounced on him again, and we wrestled and shouted, cackled and kissed. After, both our books were creased and dented.

"That fence sure is going to come in handy," he said, planting a kiss at the top of my cleavage.

"You're a monster," I informed him, flushed from making out like a teenager.

I smile at the memory. My god, I loved that man. Loved his mind, his way, his being.

Wait . . . no, I LOVE that man. LOVE his mind, his way, his being. Present tense. LOVE. Jesus. *Did* I love it all or *do* I still? Are those essences of Charlie still there? Where does love go when its object disappears? Is it allowed to wonder about something new? Or, in this case, something old, something that came first and pressed its permanence into poetic memory more than twenty years ago?

I open the top drawer of the desk and fish out Charlie's phone, tapping on the *notes* icon. About three months after Charlie's coma, I finally poked around a bit on his cell. He never kept it locked—ridiculously trusting, my husband is . . . was . . . is—so I snooped. He didn't have many apps, but I was surprised to find the notes app full with dozens of lists, each saved by date. The lists contained information of seemingly no importance. The one titled 5/20/10 had nearly a hundred movie quotes, highlighting lines from flicks including *Ghostbusters*, *Predator*, and something called *The Good Dinosaur*. List 12/20/15 was a ranking of Denzel Washington movies. His favorite was *The Taking of Pelham 123*. His least? *John Q.*

They weren't all movie themed, of course. List 11/24/12 was a list of restaurants he liked and favorite meals or drinks at each: wurstplatte at Hofbräuhaus, Goetta hash at Taste of Belgium, the Gunslinger Sprawl at Cujo's.

Since discovering this trove of Charlie, I've begun making occasional lists in my head, too. Not all the time. Not compulsively. But enough to feel like the new habit connects me to my husband.

Tonight I'm not merely browsing his lists. I know exactly what I want, and I select the 1/1/06 note—the morning of our non-one-night stand. It includes a single item: Asha Khoury.

I want you to be happy, I hear Charlie say again in my head, and I look at the scrap of paper with Jason's phone number.

I pick up the phone.

SPRING (1996)

Jason had been my boyfriend for nearly four months when he invited me to his family's Christmas party.

I wore a new sparkly red sweater and put small gold hoops into my earlobes. I pulled half of my hair back, leaving the rest down around my shoulders, the way I knew Jason liked.

I came downstairs and found Dad on his knees in front of the Christmas tree. When he stood, he held a small present in his hands, and he handed it to me.

"It's not Christmas yet," I said, but I tore into the dark-green-and-silver paper anyway. Inside a white gift box, I found a slim gold necklace with a delicate, twisted chain. A small charm hung from the center, the evil eye, and it had a tiny, bright-red stone, a ruby, my birthstone, in the center.

"To protect you." I gingerly unhooked the necklace and put it on. Dad smiled, nodded. "That will keep the bad things away."

"Dad, Jason is not a bad thing."

"He is a teenager. Of course he is a bad thing." His face softened, then, and he got the expression he always wore when he was thinking about my mother. "I wish Ma was here to see how happy you are, *bratti*." I still love when he calls me that. It's a term of affection: "my daughter" in Assyrian.

On the drive to Jason's, my dad told me a story I'd heard dozens of times, though I never got sick of it: He talked about the night I was born. He said how my mother was the prettiest, glowingest pregnant woman in the world, and how I was the most wanted baby in the world. He told me that my mom labored with me for only a moment, that she gave a little hiccup and POP, there I was. He said I came into the world smiling, curious, happy. I never cried, he said, and as my mom nursed me, I kept breaking the latch because I was trying to look around.

"I know newborn babies can't really see, but I swear on your life, you could see," he told me. That was how I knew he was super serious: He'd swear on my life.

He always stopped the story before the machines started to beep, before the doctors rushed my mom away to surgery. Even though it was such an easy birth, something had gone wrong. He wouldn't tell me until I was older what it was: postpartum bleeding caused by a lack of thrombin. After I was born, my mom's blood wouldn't clot. She died less than a day later.

When we pulled into Jason's driveway, the radio softly played Christmas music, and a light snow seemed to fall in slow motion. There was no wind, only the glitter of pinprick snowflakes. It was a night for magic, I thought.

The bushes in front of Jason's house were covered in twinkling lights, and all the windows had been outlined in flashing strands of red, green, blue, and yellow. A small electronic Santa stood next to the door, slowly bending at the waist to greet us.

Before I could knock, Jason opened the door. His face was flushed, like he'd been running, and he wore a red button-up shirt with a green tie.

"Hey, we match!" he greeted us, tugging on the sleeve of my red sweater. "Hi, Mr. Khoury. Thanks for letting Asha come to the party." He raised his voice then and shouted over his shoulder. "Asha and her dad are here!"

"Your mother can't find her punch bowl," Jason's dad said, stepping up behind his son. I grinned at his Santa hat. "Asha, good to see you!"

It was only the second time I'd met his dad, who extended his hand to my father. "Keith Kapaglia, good to meet you."

"Adam Khoury," my father said properly, if a little stiffly. "Thank you for inviting my daughter into your home."

"Would you like to stay? Have a glass of wine, or join us for dinner."

I looked at my dad with pleading eyes.

"No, I think I will let Asha have her fun. I think she will not talk to me for a week if I stay."

Jason had an enormous family. He held my hand the whole night, tugging me around, introducing me to aunts and uncles, cousins, neighbors. I finally met his mother, who was a tiny woman with the biggest chest I had ever seen. She had neat, curly brown hair that fell just above her shoulders, and she fidgeted with it as she talked to me.

"It's good to finally meet you, dear," she said, pulling me into an awkward side hug. "You're all Jason talks about, you know."

Before I could respond, Jason had me by the hand again, dragging me away.

Dinner wasn't a sit-down affair; people milled around the kitchen and ate standing up. Others sat at the dining room table or balanced their plates on their laps on a huge overstuffed sofa. Jason and I ate on barstools set up at the kitchen island—salad with tiny pieces of chopped-up salami and pepperoni, the biggest platter of olives and peppers I'd ever seen, homemade pizza with buttery garlic crust.

"Check it out," Jason said. He took a big bite and pulled the pizza away from his face, dragging stringy cheese out to the length of his arm.

"You are disgusting," his sister, Gaby, said as she entered the kitchen for more salad.

"I love you, too," Jason said through his mouthful of pizza.

I had barely finished eating before Jason hopped up and grabbed my hand again. "Let's go to my room," he said, and he wound me through the kitchen, down the hall and to the stairs. I paused at the foot as he sprinted up.

"Is it OK?" I asked, peering into the family room. "We shouldn't . . ."

"I gotta talk to you. It's cool. Come on."

He turned a corner at the landing, and I looked around, half expecting and half hoping for his mom to drag us back to the party. No one seemed to mind, and I followed him.

"Jay?" I called.

"In here," I heard from a room toward the end of the hall.

I poked my head in the entryway and was introduced to Jason's bedroom. The walls were covered in a blue plaid paper, and a desk was pushed up against the corner. He had a denim comforter on his bed, and a faded poster of Michael Jordan hung above the headboard. Next to it, smaller but newer, was a computer printout of the Miami Heat logo. I tried to hide my smile when I pointed to it.

"Yeah." Jason's eyes darted around the room. "I've had that up for like ever. Since last month. No, I mean last year, or something." I loved what a terrible liar he was.

I studied the bulletin board on his wall, which showed snapshots of him and Gaby when they were kids, a few of Jason's old school pictures, and a more recent photo of him with Edward and Dan.

"I need one of us to put up there," he said. "Come here."

He pulled a camera from the top drawer of his desk. I leaned over his shoulder as he stretched his arm back, the lens facing us, a selfie before the term existed.

"Hope I don't cut off our heads," he said, and I laughed as he hit the shutter.

"My eyes were closed, take another one!"

I put my arms around his neck, and he tilted his head toward mine. My eyes were open this time when he hit the button.

"What'd you want to talk about?" I asked, straightening up, looking around. I didn't know where to sit. He was in the only chair in the room, and I certainly wasn't going to sit on his bed. I picked a spot next to the desk on the floor and leaned against the wall.

"Um . . ." He was suddenly nervous. "How'd you do on that English paper?"

I babbled about school and noticed Jason was only half listening. "You OK?"

He tried to smile at me, but it looked like a grimace. "So the thing is . . ." And he trailed off. He looked around the room, like he forgot something and was trying to figure out the answer. He sighed hard and ran his hands through his hair, messing up his neat side part. I liked it better this way, messy. "This isn't right at all," he said, muttering. He reached into another desk drawer and pulled out a small gift bag. He thrust it at me. "Merry Christmas, Asha."

"Oh," I said, immediately feeling terrible. "I didn't know we were doing this. Gifts. I don't have anything for you." How did I not even consider that we'd exchange gifts?

"Just open it."

I pulled out a tuft of glittery tissue paper and saw two things inside: a small cloth drawstring bag and a CD. I pulled that out first, the single to the Tony Rich Project's "Nobody Knows," which contained four versions of the song—the one I knew from the radio, two remixes, and an instrumental version.

"I thought it could be our song," Jason said, flushing a little pink.

I couldn't wipe the smile from my face. "I love it," I said, and I did. Earlier that week, in the car with my dad, he'd been flipping through the radio. When "Nobody Knows" came on, I screamed so loud my dad pulled his hand back from the radio like it had grown teeth. "I just really like that song," I'd said, settling into my seat and letting memories from the dance and our first real kiss wash over me.

Inside the drawstring bag, my second gift, I found a bracelet with dark-brown beads. Each bead was super shiny, with stripes of lighter brown that shimmered and danced as I twisted the bracelet in my hands.

"Look how pretty," I said, holding it up to the light.

"Do you like it?" he asked. "They're called tiger's eye. Gaby helped me pick it out. Is it OK? If you hate it, I can take it back and kill her."

"No, no, I love it." I slid the bracelet on my wrist. "Thank you." He slipped off his chair to sit next to me, and his eyes kept darting between the bracelet and my face, back and forth, back and forth, until I asked, "What is it?"

"I thought it was perfect, especially for you."

"Why?"

He grinned, and he wiped his hands on his legs. "It sort of, you know, reminded me of you. It's the same color as your eyes. At least, I thought it was. Your eyes are darker. I should have found something better. It's that, your eyes, they're amazing. They were the first thing I loved about you."

Why could we always turn silence into something loud? It was as though the air was rushing in my head, through it, making me think I'd never hear anything clearly again. Somehow biology had failed me, and my heart had left its home in my chest to take up residency in my ears.

"The first thing?" I whispered into my lap.

Jason reached over to my chin and turned it gently toward him. His hand shook. I felt terrified as I looked at him.

"I love you," he said.

After the silence had stretched out for a year, he asked, "Are you . . . aren't you going to say anything back?"

"I don't . . . I mean, I'm not . . . I'm not sure . . . I don't know," I said. This was too big, too much, too soon. "I think we should go downstairs, maybe?"

I saw a look on his face that I'd never seen before, and it would not be the last time I saw it: When Jason was sad, when he felt crushed, his face crumpled, as though each muscle had stopped working. Everything frowned, not only his mouth. His eyes fell; his nose fell. I swear, even the tiny scar by his ear fell.

We didn't have much to say to each other the rest of the night, and I was glad when, as promised, my dad rang the doorbell at exactly 10 p.m.

Jason walked me to the door, and I gave him a little wave.

"Thank you for the bracelet and CD," I said, and I tried to smile.

He tried to smile, too. "Merry Christmas, Asha."

"Call me tomorrow?"

He nodded, and he closed the door softly behind us.

I listened to all four versions of our song no fewer than six times that night, and I wore my bracelet to sleep. Jason loved me—wasn't that good news? Shouldn't that make me feel happy?

So why was I crying? I pressed the pillow to my face to muffle the sounds, and I felt my body tremble like a storm. It was the first time I ever cried over Jason Kapaglia. It would be nowhere near the last.

"That is so romantic," Bridget said when I talked to her the next day. "Did you say it back?"

"No."

"What is wrong with you? Why not?"

"I don't know. I wasn't ready."

"How'd he take it?"

"He didn't really talk to me for the rest of the night."

"Asha, what is wrong with you?" she repeated.

"I don't know." My voice had gotten shrill, and I felt dangerously close to crying again. That morning when I'd looked in the mirror, my eyelids were puffy from the previous night's tears.

Jason didn't call me at all that day, or the next. Christmas passed without a word from my boyfriend. Two days later, Kendra, one of the girls we'd hung out with at the dance and Bridget's birthday party, called me instead. She had never done that before.

"Bridget told me what happened. Are you guys going to break up?"

"What? No. Why would we break up?"

"I can call and find out if you want? Jason's in my English class. We're friends. Want me to find out what's going on?"

I thought that was the nicest thing anyone had ever offered to do for me.

"I like him a lot," I told Kendra.

"I know you do. Everyone knows. You guys are, like, the cutest couple. Didn't you see all the girls staring at you at the dance?"

"They were?" I hadn't noticed—I was too nervous and too happy to be dancing with Jason. It was like we were in our own little bubble. Wasn't that what it was supposed to be like?

"They all have crushes on Jason."

"They do?"

"I tell everyone, 'That's Ash's guy. Find someone else.'"

I didn't know Kendra and I had such a close friendship. I felt like I barely knew her, but I was grateful. "Thanks for helping me out. I want to call him myself, but I feel dumb. He said he'd call me when I left his house after the party, but—"

"You went to his house?"

"For the Christmas party. I thought Bridget told you?"

"She told me you were fighting, that you didn't say you loved him when he poured his heart out to you. Were you guys, like, doin' stuff?"

Well, that was a weird question.

"Um. It wasn't like that. His parents had a Christmas party, and we had a really good time. Then Jason dragged me upstairs, and—"

"Ooooooo."

"No, no, we didn't do anything. We took some pictures, and we hugged a little. I love it when I can hug him. He gave me a really sweet present. And then he told me he loved me. And I didn't know what to say back. I know I should call him and talk to him about it, but when I think about it, I get so nervous I want to puke."

"Let me see what I can find out."

"Make sure he knows how much I like him. And call me right back, as soon as you hang up, OK?"

I thought Kendra would call back in ten minutes. It took an hour and a half. I didn't even say "Hello?" when the phone rang, only "What did he tell you?"

"Well, he's pretty upset."

"But WHY?"

"He's not sure he wants to date someone who doesn't love him."

"But you told him how much I like him, right?"

"I really tried, but he kept saying, 'I just don't know. I just don't know.'"

"And then what?"

"That was about it."

I should have asked how that had taken ninety minutes, but I was too crushed.

"Thanks for trying, Kendra," I told her. "You're a really good friend."

SUMMER (2006)

My first "I love you" from Charlie was considerably different.

After that first night together, when we rang in the new year—twice, I thought—I didn't hear from Charlie for nearly a week.

Par for the course, I figured, and, honestly, it didn't bother me. I'd had zero expectations, by design. I found that when I had expectations, I only set myself up for disappointments.

The naivety of that thought—that I knew anything about disappointment and grief—makes me feel tender and frustrated toward the younger woman I was then. That woman didn't know anything.

On the sixth day after New Year's Eve, the phone rang. Bridget picked it up, listened, then smirked. She handed me the phone. "Charlie Watters. Isn't he that guy from New Year's?" I made big round "WOW" eyes and took the phone from her.

The first words Charlie spoke were, "I'm sorry."

"For what?"

"It was wrong to leave you hanging like that. I'm an idiot."

"It's OK."

"It's not. If you don't call a new girl after a week, that makes you a prick."

"You're not a prick. Don't worry about it."

"Can this prick take you out tonight?"

"Tonight?" I caught Bridget's eye, and she nodded emphatically. "Um . . . yeah, tonight's OK."

Charlie offered to pick me up, but I told him I'd meet him. We settled on Cujo's, my favorite bar in Cincinnati. The walls were covered with posters from a bunch of fantasy and horror novels, and the menu boasted related drink specials: Alice's Drink Me Potion and Dandelion Wine are favorites, but I, like Charlie—at least according to that note on his phone—prefer the Gunslinger Sprawl, a bourbon cocktail with mashed cherries, orange liqueur, and a splash of rose water. A small stack of the sort of worn and torn paperbacks you can find in any used bookstore for ninety-nine cents acted as centerpieces at each small, scarred wood table.

I arrived ten minutes early, but Charlie was already there, at a table in the back, paging through one of the volumes of *The Green Mile*.

"The single-most-depressing King story in all of King-dom," I said, sliding in across from him.

"Nah, that's *Bag of Bones*," he said.

I watched him place the slim book on the top of the pile, making sure to line up the spines just so. "Type A much?"

"Guilty." He rattled through the proof. "The books on my shelves are arranged by size. I'm never late. I get my hair cut every six weeks. I've got appointments made through, like, 2009."

"And yet you'll let a girl wait a whole week to hear back from you," I tsked at him, then immediately regretted my teasing when his face fell. I reached across the table and lightly held on to his wrist. It felt remarkably intimate; it was only the second time I had met him. Though we were kind of past feeling uncomfortable touching each other, weren't we? "I'm kidding. I didn't think I'd hear from you again, that's all. I'm glad I was wrong. Who are you, anyway?"

It was the right thing to say; his face broke into the kind of smile that can weaken knees. I suspected that, if I'd turned around, every human in the bar who was attracted to men would have been looking furtively over at my date. His teeth were like a toothpaste ad, and he wore a short, full beard. He had chocolatey eyes and long, dark lashes.

His hair was brown, and he wore it in a low ponytail at the nape of his neck.

"Tutankhamen, don't you remember?"

"Yes, King Tut, I remember. But why were you at our party? My roommate said she didn't know you. Did you totally crash our New Year's Eve hoping to get laid?"

"No?" he said, and it was more of a question. "Your landlord is my cousin."

"Zach's your cousin?"

"He invited me over for New Year's. It was supposed to be a low-key night. When I got there, he said there was this raging party next door, and did I want to go. I didn't, but then I saw you come to the front door, and you had on that dress."

"It was a little slutty."

"Nope. No. No one means good things when they say 'slutty.' Your dress was not slutty. Your dress was . . . sweetheart, it was perfect."

"My roommate picked it out."

"Your roommate should pick out all your clothes."

"What, you don't like my T-shirt?"

I pushed my shoulders back and puffed out my chest, and he laughed again. I liked making him laugh.

"I'm really glad you wanted to meet up tonight. I'm sorry I didn't call sooner. My dad was in the hospital, and—"

"Charlie, Jesus!"

"No, no, he's fine. But I had to be there, and—"

"I cannot believe you let me give you a hard time for not calling. Is he OK?"

"He's fine. Had a low-level heart attack. My mom and sister were a mess. I felt bad leaving the house."

"They live nearby?"

"Newport, same as me. I grew up there. Went to Miami for college and got a job in town."

That night, I learned that Charlie had

(one)
studied engineering and,
(two)
like me, graduated in May. He'd
(three)
started work at P&G that summer and
(four)
was a Boy Scout. Not like "he was really polite, and he helped feeble people cross the street," but he was actually *in* the Boy Scouts.

In turn, he learned that I had studied marketing at UC, where I roomed with Bridget, and that I worked at an ad agency he'd never heard of.

"Why advertising?"

"It was easy. I never found, you know, a passion. I liked my marketing class in college, and then I took more."

When had he switched seats? We had started out across the table from one another, but somewhere in this getting-to-know-you conversation, he had slid into the seat next to me.

"Did I pass?" he asked.

"Excuse me?"

"You wouldn't let me pick you up. You wouldn't let me take you to dinner. We had to meet at this bar. Now that you've actually met me"—and here he spoke sotto voce—"and not only in a biblical sense, did I pass?"

I looked at Charlie Watters. I watched him chew the straw in his drink in a way that should have been feminine but simply turned me on. I looked at his lean, muscular arms and remembered how they'd looked in my bed, my turquoise comforter tangled around his legs, his hair splayed over my pillow. I remembered how he felt under my palms as he moved his body over mine.

I pulled him to me and kissed him deeply. I threaded my fingers through his ponytail and tugged his face back a little. "You passed."

I'd dated in college after Jason, but there wasn't anyone who excited me or challenged me. My dates were cute, or they were fun to talk to. But I hadn't had that kind of inexplicable connection to a guy since Jay. I'd started to wonder if maybe it wasn't possible. Maybe you get that kind of clicking only once in your life, and I'd had to go and click when I was a stupid kid, before I knew anything.

But me and Charlie, we clicked. Thank god you get more than one. After Cujo's he asked if I wanted to go play some darts at another bar, down the street.

"Not really," I said. "Bridget is spending the weekend at her folks'. You should come over."

"I'm not expecting—" He cut himself off, shaking his head.

"Don't be such a Boy Scout," I interrupted, slipping my arm around his waist and resting my hand on the top of his ass. "And you don't have to come over if you don't want."

"Well, no, I mean . . . I didn't say that . . ."

Twenty-five minutes later, Charlie had me pressed against our front door—we'd barely made it inside—as we worked to pull off each other's pants. It's *hard* to take off another person's pants when you're attached at the mouth. We laughed as we knocked our elbows into the wall, when he almost fell back onto the staircase behind him. But then he had his hand between my legs, guiding himself inside me, and suddenly nothing was funny anymore.

It sounds absurd, but the first time Charlie made love to me—actually *made love* to me, where it was more than sex—we were pressed up against my front door. I wouldn't have thought it was possible to make love standing up in the entryway of a house, but somehow the world slowed down and our focus narrowed. We kept our eyes open as he moved against me, strong and a little rough. When I came, a bead of sweat trailed down my cheek. He used the tip of his tongue to lick it off, and he finished a few moments after me.

We stayed upright for what felt like an hour, or maybe merely a second, our arms wrapped around the other, panting. He stepped back—I was still pinned to the door—and I took my shirt off and unhooked my bra.

"We're doing that again," I said, taking the stairs two at a time to my bedroom.

Two hours later he raided the kitchen and brought up a pint of my favorite chocolate chip ice cream, some pretzel rods, and a container of dates.

"What are those?" he asked, tearing off the top of the ice cream and digging in.

"Dates," I said, and confusion crossed his face. I took a bite of one and held the other end to his mouth. "It's a fruit. I grew up on them. Middle Eastern thing. Try one."

He looked down his nose at the bite, studying it with a furrowed brow. He made a loud chomping sound when he put his mouth around both the date and my fingers. As he chewed, his expression changed from curiosity to utter glee.

"Good, right?"

He shoved the ice cream at me and took the dates from my lap, eating half the container while I asked about his parents, what his childhood was like. He told me about how he became a Boy Scout and about his little sister, Maura, who was a senior in high school. The best vacation he'd ever been on had been hiking in the Adirondacks with his dad when he was fifteen years old. It was the only time he'd ever been on an airplane. He loved Guinness beer, LEGOs—"LEGOs?" I asked, and he said, "Shut up, I'm being vulnerable"—and volleyball, which he'd played in college. He said he'd never been in love.

"Yeah, right."

"I mean, I've had girlfriends. My high school prom date said she loved me, and I said it back, but it wasn't the right thing to do."

The sting of memory drew my eyebrows together. "I promise," I said, "it was the right thing to do. Even if you weren't sure. There's only one appropriate thing to say to 'I love you.' Even if you don't mean it, you say it and figure it out later."

"You'd think. When I broke it off that summer, she lost it. Threw lots of 'But you said you loved me!' in my face. I learned my lesson. Don't say it unless you mean it." He grew quiet for a moment, then fed me a spoonful of ice cream. "What about you? Any old boyfriends I should know about?"

I'd never told any other guy I'd dated about Jason.

"Here and there," I said, and he smirked. "I've really only had one serious boyfriend before. I dated around in college, but . . ." I shrugged. "No one interesting."

The next morning, when I woke up, Charlie was already dressed.

"Where you going?" I asked, sitting up, wiping the sleep from my eyes. "What time is it?"

"It's early. Six thirty."

I lay back down with a PLOP. "No. Too soon. Back to bed. You. Sleep."

He sat on the edge of the bed. "Would you believe I found my underwear in the kitchen?"

"How'd they get there?"

"I have no idea. I must have thrown them there in a fit of glee last night trying to get in your pants."

"It's not like you had to make much of an effort. I kind of gave you open access."

"Listen, I gotta go. Dad's getting out of the hospital this morning, and I want to go pick him up with Mom and Maura. Go back to sleep. But I wanted to tell you something, OK? And I want to say it and then leave so you don't feel any pressure to say anything. I don't want you to say anything, OK? OK. Asha, I'm falling in love with you."

He kissed the top of my head before he walked out of the room and closed my bedroom door softly behind him. I heard the front door click and a car engine start, then grow fainter as he drove away.

Well . . . how about that?

SPRING (1997)

After Kendra called Jason over Christmas break, he was sullen toward me. Toward everyone, really. When I saw him in the halls with Edward and Dan, they were the only two speaking.

At school, he'd still meet me at my locker between classes, but he barely glanced at me the whole time. One lunch period, I was so upset, I couldn't even set foot in that huge cafeteria full of people who'd wonder why the new girl—was I still the new girl after five months?—was weepy. I ate instead on the stairs off a side hallway alone, and I promised myself I would talk to Jason, that I would *make him* talk to me, that afternoon.

I'd volunteered to stay after school to tutor some people who were struggling in my chemistry class, so when Jason walked past my locker after the final bell, I wasn't rushing away to catch the bus. I called after him, and he walked slowly back, silent. The hall was nearly empty.

"I don't want to make you late for your bus," I stammered, and Jason shrugged, like he didn't care if he missed it. "Jason, you have to talk to me. I hate this. I hate that we're fighting. I'm sorry. Jason, please don't be mad at me."

I couldn't stop the tears, and I tried to wipe at them as fast as they fell from my eyes. Unfortunately, it is not possible for the boy who is breaking your heart to not see the physical evidence of your heartbreak when he is standing right in front of you. Especially when you're thirteen.

"Itheeweshubreup."

"What?"

I hadn't understood him, truly. But I knew what he said, even if his words didn't sound like American English when he mumbled like that.

"I think . . . we should . . ." Then he stopped looking me in the eye. He dropped his head, like he was uncomfortable. Or, maybe, like he was sad. ". . . break up."

In the months following this exchange, I replayed every way I might have responded:

I'm sorry I wasn't ready to say that I loved you yet. I know that I do, but that's scary, and you're my first boyfriend, and my first kiss, and my first, well, love, and I've never done this before.

or

Please don't take my silence on this "love" thing to mean that I don't.

or

I don't want to break up with you.

Or, perhaps simplest of all: *But I love you, too.*

I did. Of course I did. Why did it take him mumbling those hateful words to me to realize it? Why did something terrible and crushing have to happen for me to see what was obvious? Was this how it always was with new experiences? If so, this growing-up thing was garbage.

I didn't say any of those options, though. Instead, I ran away. I skipped my tutoring session and hid in the bathroom. Bridget had stayed after school, too, for art club, and found me after she ran into my dad looking for me in the hallway. Rather, she heard me. She stopped in to use the bathroom, and before she left, I let out a little hiccup—I was trying to be quiet—and she called out, "Asha?"

"In here."

"What happened?" she asked, pushing open the door to the handicap stall. She saw my face and rushed to the toilet—I'd closed the top and was sitting there, blowing my nose into toilet paper. "Ash, what is it?"

"He dumped me," I said through the sobs, and she gave me the biggest hug. She didn't say anything mean about Jason, and she didn't tell me I'd be all right. She only put her arms around me and let me cry on her.

"Your dad's here. I'll tell him you're still tutoring. My mom's picking me up soon. She'll take you home, OK?"

Twenty minutes later, I crawled into the back seat of Bridget's mom's car. Mrs. Casey took one look at my face and said, "That asshole dumped you, didn't he?"

"MOM!" Bridget scolded her, but I nodded.

I think Mrs. Casey always felt bad for me. This was mom stuff I was going through, you know? What teen girl talks to her dad about her first broken heart?

"Here's what we're going to do," Mrs. Casey said, handing me a box of tissues she'd taken out of the glove box. "We're going to go to our house, and you're going to pull yourself together enough to call your dad. Tell him I want to take you and Bridge for dinner and that you'll come home after. Is that OK?"

I blew my nose, then whispered, "Thank you."

That week at school? Torture. Junior high girls who get dumped should be allowed to take a week off school. Because if you rank all the mean people you're ever likely to meet—like, actually *meet*, we're not talking Hitler or Mussolini or anything—junior high girls are the meanest. I think all those hormones mess up their brains so badly that they can't remember how *not* to be a group of gross, nasty twats.

Remember all those girls who wouldn't leave me alone when I'd started dating Jason? All those girls I'd wanted to leave me alone, the ones Kendra had said were staring at Jason and me at the dance? Instead of waving to me in the hallways or telling me they liked my necklace, they stared me down and whispered to their friends behind cupped hands. They made these faux-concerned faces and clucked at me, feigning sympathy. One girl actually skipped up to me—she skipped!—with her arms flapping at her sides like she was a four-year-old playing ring-around-the-rosy.

"How's Jason?" she squealed, then ran off to a group of laughing girls down the hall.

After a month or so, things abated a little. I wore Jason's bracelet every day, and sometimes in the hall, he and I would even talk.

"That algebra test sucked yesterday. How do you think you did?" Or "Did you see the new Puff Daddy music video? I think that's my new favorite song." Anything except "I miss you. Can I be your girl-friend again?"

On Valentine's Day, the school sold dollar carnations we could send to our friends. I thought about giving one to Jason, but I was too embarrassed. Instead, I sent a pink one to Bridget and another to Kendra. I wrote the same thing on both of them: *Happy Valentine's Day! BFF, Asha*

I wondered if I'd get any carnations, and when the secretary of the student council came into homeroom to hand out the flowers, she made a beeline right for me, holding two carnations, the same shade of red as the rose Jason had given me when he came over that night for dinner. I felt my heart leap, then sink when she handed the flowers to the two girls behind me.

I passed Jason in the hallway after that class. He was practically run-ning, and he didn't look at me. He held his arm down at his side, away from me, but it didn't matter—I still saw the red flower in his hand.

I thought I was going to be sick. Who'd he gotten *that* from?

I spent the rest of the day convincing myself it was nothing. It was a mistake. Or they were friend carnations. Jason couldn't have another girlfriend. He was still in love with me. Wasn't he? You don't get over *loving someone* in the snap of a finger or the time it takes to dump your girlfriend at her locker. That's not how love worked. Was it? I had no idea, but I was learning that, however it worked, it completely sucked.

When I got home that day after school, I took a deep breath, and I called Jason. I had memorized his home phone number, and I dialed it as fast as I could before I chickened out.

His mom answered the phone.

"Is Jason there?"

"He went over to Kendra's house. Can I give him a message?"

What?

"Um . . . no, it's OK. I can try again later. Tha—"

But she'd hung up.

He was . . . where? Today? On . . . Valentine's Day?

I called Bridget.

"Have you talked to Kendra?" I shrieked.

She sighed. The girl was in eighth grade, but she sounded like an old lady with the wisdom of the ages when she sighed like that.

"I just found out."

"What is there to find out? Is she, like, his *girlfriend*? Did she send him that flower? Are they together on *Valentine's Day*?"

"Yes."

"To which part?"

"All of it."

"That *bitch*." Rage had turned my voice into little more than a high-pitched screech. "What is he doing at her house?"

"She said he was coming over for homework."

"On a Friday? Yeah, right. Skank."

"She said she let him get to second base last weekend."

My anger flashed to misery, then back to anger. Then back to misery. Bridget and I talked for an hour about how my friend could do that to me, what a terrible person she was, and how she was probably going to die one day from ghona-herpe-syphil-AIDS, an amalgam of all the dirty STD things you could get from being a skanky little skank. It was the nastiest thing we could think to say about a person.

When we finally hung up the phone, I curled up on my twin bed and sobbed into the *Space Jam* pillow my dad had gotten me for Christmas. As I lay there, I tried to figure out what Jason saw in Kendra, and, for the first time in my life, I started to compare myself to other girls. Kendra's hair was dark, like mine, but more brown than black. And it was curly. When she wore it up in a ponytail, short tendrils curled around her face like the teenagers in *Seventeen* magazine. When I wore my hair in a ponytail, the short, wispy pieces of hair around my face stuck out like I'd been electrocuted.

Kendra had had boobs for a whole year—of *course* Jason wanted to touch them—and, instead of being one of the junior high girls who sulked around in baggy sweatshirts with crappy posture in an effort to hide them, Kendra flaunted her chest. She always wore fitted white or pale-pink baby tees—once I even saw her with a belly chain—and she walked with her shoulders back and her chin up. At thirteen she had the posture and confidence of a CEO.

The more I thought about her, the worse I felt about myself and the angrier I got. So I did something I never would have thought I'd have the guts to do: I called Kendra. I didn't even care whether Jason was still over there.

"Hello?" Her stupid voice.

"It's Asha."

"Oh. Um. Hey."

"You are pathetic. I thought you should know."

"I'm really sorry."

"I do *not* forgive you. How could you do that? I thought we were friends."

"I didn't think he'd listen to me. I had no idea he'd actually break up with you."

"You *told* him to break up with me?"

Kendra had started crying. "He invited me to his house over Christmas break."

"We were still boyfriend-girlfriend then."

"I know."

"And you *went?*"

"I don't know. I'm sorry. I still want to be your friend."

"I don't want to be your friend. I'm not friends with bitches."

And I hung up the phone on her. My heart was racing, and my hands trembled. But I was proud that I'd stood up for myself like that.

It wasn't until years later that I realized—it wasn't *just* Kendra, you know? Jason was involved, too. When you're a teen and you're figuring out boys and girls and love and all that, it's easy to put those first loves on a pedestal. Why do we do that? Why, when something like this happens in a hetero relationship, do we always point the finger at the girl? Why did I only tell off Kendra? Why did I never tell off Jason?

I think it was because I was blindsided by it all. Kendra had been so devious, and I didn't understand it. I was too naive to know how to hurt another person like that. Though I had no problem calling her a whore every time her name came up in conversation for the next year, so what do I know?

I sometimes wonder how this all would have gone today. Cell phones didn't exist yet, at least not in the world of junior high school. When I wanted to talk to my friends or my boyfriend, I had to call their *home phones*. I had to risk talking to their *parents*. If the Valentine's Day mess had taken place in the twenty-first century, I would have texted Jason; I never would have called his house and accidentally gotten the truth from his mom. I never would have called Kendra or had to hear her voice while I told her what I thought about her.

Even as an adult, I admire the child who did that.

AUTUMN (2017)

"Hello?" *His voice.*

"Hi, um. Jason, it's—"

"Asha," we say together. *It's been how long? And he still says my name the same way. Once, he told me my name was an exhale, a happy sigh.*

"Yeah. Um. Hi."

"I didn't think you'd call," he says.

"Bridget told me you wanted me to, and I thought—"

"No, I'm happy you did. It's . . . Hi. It's good to hear your voice."

"It is?" *What a moronic thing to say.* "Yeah, I mean. Yours, too. Um . . . how are you?" *"How are you?" Are you kidding?*

"Back at home. Right now, actually, I am sitting on my childhood bed."

"Are the walls still plaid?"

"Would you believe me if I said yes? My mom never bothered to change my room. The house looks almost exactly like it did when we . . . when we used to . . . when I was little."

And what about you? Are you still the same? I'm sure as hell not. I ask, "How long are you in town?"

"Undetermined. I'm trying to figure out what to do next. Is that pathetic? Thirtysomething and starting over. Simone and I . . . we split."

"Oh. I'm sorry." *I really am. How about that?* "How did you . . . what happened? God, that's personal. I'm sorry. That's none of my—"

"It's OK. We weren't happy. She, um . . . she cheated on me?"

"Jason, that's awful. I'm sorry. Again, I guess." *I don't know what to say to him.*

"I don't want you to think, I mean, that's not why I'm calling. I was in town. And I was wondering how you—"

"I called you."

"What?"

"You said, 'That's not why I'm calling,' but you're not calling. I called you." *I'm such an idiot.*

"Oh. Right. I mean, that's not why I gave Bridget my number."

"I still knew it."

"What?"

"Your phone number. I still knew it."

"555-4137."

"That was mine." *He still knows it, too.*

Neither of us speaks for a moment. It isn't one of those companionable silences. It's drawn out, uncomfortable. Takes a hundred years.

"How are you?" he offers.

"Good. I mean, my husband's in a coma, and he's never gonna wake up from it. But good, I guess."

"Wait, what? Asha, what?"

"Yeah, um. It's been, like, a year? I visit him. It's . . . I don't know."

He says nothing. *He doesn't know what to say.* Then, "I always hoped you'd find happiness."

The hell am I supposed to say to that?

"God, that was bad," he says softly, as though he'd heard my brain.

"It was."

"I've never said those words in my life."

"You probably shouldn't ever say them again."

He sighs. "This is weird."

"Yeah."

"I've spent the whole day staring at the phone, hoping you'd call. I haven't done that in years. I wondered what we'd talk about. If I'd have the courage to say anything. And your husband's in a coma."

Charlie would have said, "If I had the balls to say anything." He'd have never said "courage." And I don't want to talk about comas.

"It's ten p.m.," I point out.

"What?"

"You said you spent the whole day staring at the phone."

"I've been staring a long time." He laughs. *Oh, I forgot his laugh.* "Do you want to go to dinner with me?" I say nothing. "Asha?"

My name.

"I thought that—"

I cut him off. "Yes."

"Yes?"

"Yes. Um. Dinner. Let's go."

"Oh. OK. Great. What are you doing Friday?"

Drinking wine and wearing my comatose husband's pajamas. Netflix and chilling all by myself, which I think is code for "masturbating while I zone out to some garbage I've seen a hundred times before."

"I think I'm free."

"Great. Can I . . . Do you want to meet there? Or should I pick you up, or . . . ?"

"Um."

"I'll pick you up?"

Shit.

"OK." I give him my address.

"So . . ." *He wants me to say more. I have forgotten how to hold up my end of a conversation. Dinner's gonna suck.* "I'll be there at seven." *I still can't speak.* "Bye, Asha." *My name.* "I . . ." He trails off, considering. "I can't wait to see you."

He hangs up before I not-talk any more.

SPRING (1997)

By the end of February, Jason and Kendra had split up, though I continued to avoid her as much as I could. It wasn't always easy—we ran with the same group of friends, which she tried to use to her advantage: She invited Bridget to her house over and over, and it started to become weird when Bridget kept turning her down.

I managed to successfully ignore Jason's ex until María's slumber party birthday, when Kendra finally ambushed me outside the bathroom. When I stepped out, she blurted, "I'm sorry. Can we talk?" and she corralled me back inside. She closed the door behind her, and we were both silent for what felt like a million hours. Finally, I spoke first.

"Why did you do that?" I asked her.

"I don't know." Her voice was barely above a whisper. "I ripped up all the photos I had of him, though."

"You weren't even together that long."

"We took a lot of photos. I thought they'd make us more 'official.'"

"That's dumb."

"I know it is. But, I'm sure you know this, he never wanted to do anything but talk about kissing and stuff."

I cracked a smile. "I know."

She jumped on that smile. "He's, like, obsessed."

"Totally obsessed."

To my surprise, I liked joking with Kendra, but a part of me was still sad because I wanted Jason to think about kissing me and only me.

I wouldn't ever actually trust Kendra again, and I'd still refer to her as a bitch in casual conversation with Bridget, but things were a little better after that bathroom confessional. That was what we called it. Even after junior high, when Kendra's family moved an hour away, she'd sometimes write me letters and sign them, "Love, your Bathroom Confessional Buddy!"

I eventually got good at ignoring Jason, and I pretended that I didn't like him for so long that it became truth. At some point I stopped wearing my tiger's eye bracelet. I didn't throw it out, but I kept it with Jason's school picture in an old jewelry box that had been my mom's. It was dark wood with a red velvet–lined tray set into the top. Inside the lid was a small, oval-shaped mirror, and when I tilted the lid back on its hinges, I could see my eyes. It made me wonder if my mom had ever looked in the mirror like that, if it could be a glassy porthole into the years before I was born. Wouldn't it be cool if I could get a glimpse of her? A shadow of a memory, an instant of eye contact to let me know she was in there somehow, that she was watching me. That she was rooting for me. That she loved me.

And when I shut up my bracelet and Jason's photo in the jewelry box, I liked to think of my mom in there, telling off Jason for being such a dick.

Campbell Junior High hosted its last dance of the school year the Saturday before our finals. Bridget and María came over before the dance to get ready.

"What about this?" I asked, swiping some dark-blue glitter on my eyelids.

"So, so pretty." María nodded, adding a third coat of sticky pink lip gloss to her mouth.

"You guys are such dorks," Bridget said, rolling her eyes. Sometime over the last school year, she'd stopped using glittery or shiny makeup. I, meanwhile, had started to use it. So while me and the rest of the girls in our grade pored through teen magazines for beauty tips, Bridget now paged through her mother's magazines, where the makeup tutorials actually taught you how to use *real* makeup, not stuff packaged in neon with bubblegum letters. Today she and I look through pictures from that time and shake our heads. There's Bridget, in clothing that she might wear today—a little provocative, but ultimately flattering, utterly timeless. Then there's me and the rest of our friends. Our T-shirts could either fit three people at once, with short sleeves grazing our elbows, or they appeared to be no bigger than a hand towel, with belly buttons everywhere. There was that week I thought knee-highs and suspenders were too cool. And, oh man, I had this crushed velvet vest you couldn't have bought off me for front-row tickets to a Boyz II Men concert.

The three of us went down the stairs like a herd of wildebeests, wild animals more concerned with where their next meal would come from than keeping their hair just so. María bumped into me, slamming my shoulder into the wall; and I fell back into Bridget, making her sit hard on the step, her head thrown back in laughter as she reached for María's leg and tugged; and we wound up in a heap of skinny limbs and hairspray. A secret, ancient nook in my mind registered then that, maybe, this was the last time we would act this way. That my friends and I were transitioning further into teenagers, with a capital *T*, and Teenagers were much too serious to roughhouse like wildebeests.

My dad stood at the foot of the stairs, and he snapped a photo of us like that, in a knot on the stairs, joyful tears streaking our makeup, our red faces camouflaging the Kiss of Rose blush we'd applied to the apples of our cheeks.

"DAD!" I admonished, not remotely upset. "Take a good one!"

We squeezed our skinny butts on a single step, our arms slung around each other's necks, and our smiles contained a hint of the mania from before, and we showed too many teeth, not enough eyes. When my dad developed the roll of film and printed extra copies for my friends, I was embarrassed to pass them along: We didn't look *pretty*. We looked a mess. Today, however, I keep those photos in a double frame in my office. When I sit there and do my grown-up things—pay bills, call the cable company, deal with insurance companies for my comatose husband—the photos are a totem for me. They take me back to that sacred place of my youth, on the stairs in the house that watched me grow up.

Walking into the dance, the final group outing of eighth grade, was a stark contrast to my first dance of the year, back when I'd first met Jason, when I'd spent the evening waiting for him, wanting to dance with him, wishing he'd ask me to be his girlfriend.

This time, I don't remember thinking about anything. My brain was not involved—I was only muscle and body and movement. I danced for two hours straight, and when slow songs came on, I threw my arms around María and, once, even Kendra. I hugged Bridget tightly and sang to her at the top of my lungs as she sang right back. We were two additional Spice Girls needing a little love.

I saw Jason only once that night. In the cafeteria, while I gulped down punch, I caught him staring at me. He was in the middle of a group of friends, and some girl I didn't recognize was hanging on him as though he was a piece of playground equipment. She was a little taller than he was, and she looked much older than us. At one point, I saw her tongue flick out and poke his earlobe, and she giggled. Ew. He, on the other hand, looked miserable.

We caught eyes for a moment, for a lifetime, and I blinked, threw out my empty cup, and walked back into the gym. As I passed Jason and his group, he was still staring at me. I surprised us both by blowing him a kiss. I barely registered the surprise on his face as the gym swallowed me up again.

SUMMER (2006)

The "fallout," if you can call it that, from Charlie telling me he was falling in love with me was considerably different from the fallout from Jason's "I love you."

In short: There was no fallout. And I knew exactly how to react this time.

When I got out of bed that morning, I saw that Charlie had left a note on the refrigerator: *Thanks for an excellent night. I never knew ghost-and-murder bars could be romantic. Love, Charlie,* and he'd written his phone number below his name. The second boy in my life had said he loved me, and he did it before I even knew his phone number.

That afternoon I called him. "What are you doing tomorrow night?"

"Would it be too hopeful to say, 'Seeing you'?"

"It would not. Come over for dinner."

"Are you going to cook for me?"

"I hope you like Assyrian food."

"Never had it. What time should I be there?"

I had until 6:30 the following evening to turn my house into a restaurant. I spent that evening scrubbing everything—yes, my *Saturday* evening—and I went to the grocery store at 10 p.m. You know who goes to the grocery store at 10 p.m. on a Saturday? No one. I had the place to myself and twirled in circles down the frozen-foods aisle just to give anyone monitoring security cameras something to watch.

I don't make Assyrian food often because it takes forever. But this seemed like the right occasion for kipteh, one of my favorites. It's essentially a giant meatball in an oniony tomato broth. Except the meatball is made with a grated onion. It's not the most *romantic* of dishes—seriously: a *grated onion*—but it's delicious, not too difficult to master, and seriously impressive. For my salad, I mashed up an avocado and mixed romaine with olive oil, garlic salt, Parmesan cheese, and halved cherry tomatoes. I had bought a raspberry-red tablecloth and a few long taper candles.

The next day when I set the table, my kipteh on the stove, Bridget watched, leaning against the wall.

"He told you he loved you already?"

"Yup."

"And he's only the second guy to . . ."

"Yup."

"Since . . ."

"Yes."

"And you're not freaking out."

I turned toward her and gestured with the salad tongs, splattering olive oil on the kitchen floor.

"I am not thirteen years old anymore. Besides, before he said it, he told me I didn't have to say it back."

"Do you?"

"Do I what?"

"Do you love him?"

"No. We've only hung out, like, twice."

"But you're going through all this trouble."

"He's special. I can tell. I don't love him yet. But I think I could. I don't want to tell him before I'm ready. But I also don't want him to . . . you know . . ."

"Go feel up Kendra Perkins in the meantime?"

"Something like that, yes."

I've known since junior high how lucky I am to have Bridget in my life. Not every girl gets that kind of friend, that sisterly bond, that family-you-choose closeness. It was why I didn't feel bad telling her, "You know you can't come out of your room during dinner."

And it was why I knew her reaction would be, "I know."

It was also why I'd made extra of everything—if I was going to exile her for the night, the least I could do was feed her.

I set her a place at the tableclothed-and-candled kitchen table, poured her some white wine, and served her dinner an hour before Charlie was due.

"You know this is my favorite," she said, cutting into the kipteh and delighting at the hard-boiled egg inside; she's always loved that part.

"You're not as good of a lay as Charlie," I said, shrugging a shoulder and heaping some salad on her plate.

By the time Charlie came over, I had cleaned Bridget's dishes, lit the rest of the candles, and set a stack of CDs next to the stereo system in the corner of our family room, starting with Foo Fighters' *In Your Honor*. I'd changed into some bootcut jeans and this sparkly teal top that Bridget said made me look like I had actual boobs if I used one of those magic, padded, push-up bras—my chest wasn't much bigger than it had been in junior high, sadly.

When I opened the door, Charlie held out a bunch of daisies. You can't keep from grinning at the sight of daisies; they're an actual bouquet of happiness. He grinned in return, stepped inside, placed his hand on my waist, and dropped a kiss on my nose. "You're welcome," he said.

He spied the set table over my shoulder and dropped another kiss, this time on my mouth. I took his hand and walked him to the table. "Sit," I instructed, and he set the flowers next to him. "Before we eat, I want to get this out so I can shake off the nerves. I've got a bottle of white. Or would you rather have a mixed drink?"

"What do you got?"

"Full bar." It had been Bridget's parents' housewarming gift to us.

Two single girls need to be able to make any drink at a moment's notice, Mrs. Casey had said as she pulled bottles of brandy, vodka, tequila, bourbon, gin, and more from her grocery bags.

"May I?" Charlie asked, pointing to the liquor cabinet, and I nodded.

He filled the martini shaker with ice, squeezed three lime slices into the shaker, and set the husks to the side. He poured in more gin than I would have, less cranberry juice, and a splash of elderflower liqueur, which he had to open because we'd never used it, because we had no idea what it was. He capped the shaker and shook it over his shoulder with two hands. The ice made a sound like a maraca. He set out two martini glasses and ran another slice of lime around the rims.

"Sugar?" he asked, and I got him the shaker from the cabinet above the coffeepot. "Saucer?" he asked, and I retrieved one of those, too. He poured some sugar onto the plate and placed the upside-down martini glasses into it, twisting, sticking sugar onto the rim. The ice clinked against the tin shaker as he poured the drinks into each glass. He garnished each with a piece of lime rind he had expertly sliced off in a curlicue.

I took a sip. It was sweeter than I thought it'd be, but not too sweet. "Like it?"

I answered by taking another sip. "Where did you learn to do that?"

"I bartended in college. When all the college girls started ordering cosmopolitans like *Sex and the City,* my boss asked me to make a few variations. This was everyone's favorite. It's called a Bradshaw." He sat at the kitchen table and held up his glass. "Cheers," he said, clinking his glass against mine.

"Khouboukh," I said, lifting my glass again. He looked at me quizzically, and I answered, "'To good health,' in Assyrian, for when you're toasting a man. When you toast me back, you say *khoubakh* for a woman, or *khoubokhen* if it's a group."

"Hoboken," he tried, which was exactly how I used to say it when I was a kid.

We each took a sip, and, before I set down the glass, I took one more. I sat across from him and placed my hands flat on the table. I took a deep breath. "So here's the thing . . . the thing is . . . about the thing . . ."

He sat silently, sipping his drink, waiting for me to figure out the thing.

"You're only, like, the second person to tell me that?" I started. "The first time, it was bad. We were young, and he was my first boy-friend, and I didn't know what I was doing. And I didn't say it back, because it was too soon, and I was young. Seriously. Really young. And he didn't know what *he* was doing, either, and it was this awful thing. And it ended up OK, eventually. But it really freaked me out, which really freaked *him* out, and it was really bad there for, like, a long time. So I've never said it to anyone else, only that one guy, later on. But I thought I'd never told anyone else because I was afraid to, because of how bad it was that first time. But maybe that wasn't it. I haven't said it to anyone else because I haven't, you know, *loved* anyone else. And this is pretty quick, with you. It's too quick. But . . . that's not bad. I mean, you know . . . I'm glad you told me. I really am. I'm happy. But I'm not, you know, quite there yet. It's not to say I won't be. Give me a little longer than a week. And don't think I'm not into you because I'm not saying it back right now. Because I am. Into you. Like, a lot. I really like you, Charlie. And I'm not dating anyone else. And I don't want to, I'm not looking to. So I can't give you, you know, *that word* yet. But if you wanted to, sort of . . ."

He waited a beat to see if I would finish. When I still couldn't find the words, he asked, smirking a little, "Go steady?"

"Yeah. Yeah, if you wanted to 'go steady,' I guess I'd be OK with that."

"You guess?"

My laughter had a nervous, manic tinge. "I haven't had a boyfriend in a really long time."

"Hm. Well, sure. I'll be your boyfriend."

After dinner we messed around in the kitchen until Bridget called from the staircase, "Is it safe to come down yet?"

The following weekend I visited my dad. Periodically after college, I would go home for a few nights at a time because dinners once a week weren't enough. I'd arrive after work on Friday, we'd watch a movie that night, eat some tea and cheese for breakfast the next morning, spend the day together or do our own thing, dinner, share a beer, finish the night with rummy or another movie.

I had to work late that Friday and didn't show up until nearly eleven. He waited for me to start the movie, *War of the Worlds* with Tom Cruise. We clinked our mugs of tea and hit play.

The next morning I found Dad already heating pita straight on the burner. When I say "pita," I don't mean the fluffy Greek shell you're thinking. This is a soft, thin bread Dad found only at the specialty grocer in Clifton. For breakfast he liked to heat it straight on the burner—no pan—until it crisped, then fold in fresh feta. We'd roll it up and eat it with Earl Grey. And there you have it: Wheaties for Assyrians, the breakfast of Persian champions.

"I want you to invite Charlie for dinner tonight," he said right after I took a huge bite.

"What?" I asked, choking. I'd hardly mentioned him.

"He is the first boy you've told me about in a wery long time," he said. I smiled; there was no V sound in Assyrian, and as fluent as my father is, when he's tired, he sometimes slips—we didn't get to bed 'til after one last night. "He must be special."

"We just started dating," I said.

"So he is not special?" he asked, and I felt my face flush. "Invite him. We'll make dolma. Or is he a picky eater? We can grill chicken."

I flashed to Charlie's delight at the dates, at the kipteh. *He's going to think we cook like this all the time.*

"Dolma would be great."

Most people associate dolma—sometimes called dolmade—with Mediterranean or Greek cuisine. But I grew up with it as an Assyrian

78

dish. My dad swears on my life it's the first solid food he ever gave me. You can make it with cabbage leaves, but that's the trash version. No, dolma requires large, hearty, deep-green grape leaves. Most of ours come from Jungle Jim's, but a few years back, Dad found some wild grape leaves in the woods behind our house. There's never enough for a full batch, but he likes adding the handpicked leaves to the brined jar leaves we get from the grocery.

That morning, in addition to grape leaves, we picked up fresh parsley and dill, ground beef, rice, leeks, an onion, plain yogurt, and a can of tomato sauce from Jungle Jim's, which is more of a food warehouse than a grocery store. Concrete floor. Such a collection of fresh and exotic foods that it smells unlike anything I've encountered before or since, this strange aroma of green and, somehow, foul. Not that anything is rotten, it's just a mixture of so much, it overwhelms. Like pulling chocolate chip cookies out of the oven, next to a man in good but strong cologne, while a cucumber-melon candle burns beside a bouquet of fresh roses. Separately, the scents are delightful; together . . . no.

First, Dad washed the herbs and rice, letting each soak in a cool water bath in the sink. It didn't take long for the kitchen to smell of dill, which always lingers in the air and on our hands for hours.

Meanwhile, I diced four large cloves of garlic—I take it back, making dolma makes my hands smell like dill *and* garlic for hours—and stirred them into the yogurt, refrigerating the container until dinnertime.

Dad dried the herbs, and we fell into a rhythm pulling the broad, curled leaves off the parsley and the soft, piney needles from the dill, discarding the tough stems, our hands a whirl. Each parsley leaf separated with a soft *pop*; the dill fell away silently.

I chopped the leeks into large square pieces while Dad set up the food processor. He scooped in handfuls of the herbs and leeks, then pulsed the machine until everything was finely chopped. I pulled small bits of what, at that point, was a finely diced salad and popped it in my mouth. The mixture was crunchy, a little dry, exceedingly flavorful.

To this day, this stage of dolma tastes like my grandmother's kitchen, where I first learned the recipe. It's notes of sunshine, a warm hand at the back of my neck, the flavors of safety and that certainty of love you feel as a kid, if you're lucky.

I mixed the chopped herbs and veggies with the raw ground beef, cleaned rice, salt, pepper, and paprika. We pinched off pieces of the mixture, a bit smaller than a golf ball, and set them in the center of a flat grape leaf. Spread out, a grape leaf is bigger than my hand, even bigger than my dad's. And every time we complete this step, my dad makes the same joke: "No smoking."

Order dolma out somewhere, and sometimes you'll be met with a dumpling that, for some inexplicable reason, is cigar shaped, like they rolled it up instead of tucking and folding the points of the leaves into a small round ball.

We layered the dolma into a large saucepan, then covered the dumplings with water, cooking the whole thing for an hour and a half.

Then I poured about two inches of vegetable oil into a smaller saucepan and set it to low heat. I diced the onion and sautéed it, then added tomato sauce; this and the garlic yogurt sauce in the fridge were dolma toppings.

"When I die, if heaven doesn't smell like this"—like herbs, garlic, sautéed onions—"I don't want it. I'll go to the other place and spend my time hunting with Dick Cheney." Dad says that every time we make dolma.

Charlie is now the second boy to have dinner with my dad and me like this. I couldn't help but flash to that first time, with Jason. Even though comparing Jason-the-child with Charlie-the-man is hardly fair, I remembered how hard Jason had tried to find something to talk about with my dad, how stiff Dad seemed, how Jason tried to eat the halvah, how much he disliked it.

This dinner was nothing like that.

Charlie dug into the meal like he'd been on a week-long hunger strike. After his first bite, he let out a groan that did not sound unlike the noises he'd made in bed a couple of nights prior.

As if in explanation, he said, "My family eats a lot of chicken." After another big bite, and another groan, he asked me, "Can we make this together sometime? I'd love to learn."

To my jaw-dropping surprise, my dad started to tell Charlie about my mom, who asked Nana to teach her how to make dolma when she and my dad were seventeen or eighteen. Nana got the ingredients and invited my mom over early one Sunday afternoon.

"Come on, learn with me, Adam," my mom apparently said, calling my dad into the kitchen.

"Aye!" my grandmother exclaimed. "No balls in the kitchen!"

To this day I cannot imagine my nana saying this, but Dad swears it was almost a cliché in his house growing up: Boys weren't allowed to help cook when he was a boy in Iran. Nana would shoo him out, much as other Assyrian woman shooed out the men, or balls, in the family.

When Nana said this to my mother, my mom apparently replied, "Well, there's balls in my kitchen."

And then he started in with stories from Iran. My dad isn't stingy with these instances of his childhood, but he guards them. He doesn't share them with just anyone. But there he was, telling Charlie how he and his dad used to fish in the Persian Gulf with dynamite. They'd row a couple of hundred feet out into the water, throw some sticks into the depths, wait for the BOOM, and collect the fish that floated to the top.

He shared how, one evening, he went hiking with Papa, and they got lost. A camp of Bedouins found them. Hospitality traditions compelled the Bedouins to take in the man and his son, and Papa and my dad slept in a large tent on thin sheets, armed guards stationed just outside.

The next morning, when my grandmother asked where they'd been all night, Papa said, "Don't worry about it."

"To this day, he will not say he got lost," my dad told a rapt Charlie. "He acts like spending the night with a camp of nomads and his seven-year-old son is precisely how he intended to spend the evening."

AUTUMN (2017)

After hanging up the phone with Jason, I cry it out for about ten minutes. There are many reasons for the tears, but the biggest is this: As much as I've wallowed in my misery and loneliness, as much as I've thought over how I'm feeling and why, as much as I've shrieked about what's happened to me and to Charlie, there are still new things to learn, apparently. And I have just learned that I'm not only lonely. I'm not only looking to get laid, and I'm not only interested in something superficial. What I want, what I desperately need, is to feel like a human again. I haven't since that morning I drove my husband to the hospital.

That awful conversation I just had with my first love made me feel like a person, like someone who wanted something real, something that mattered. My last year has not been a life. I used to have a life, sure, and, speaking to Jason, I realized that I might possibly . . . perhaps . . . maybe . . . one day have a life again.

Without my husband.

And isn't that terrifying?

Just as my sniffles subside, my phone rings. My stomach simultaneously leaps into my throat and falls down to my ankles. *Jason?* I think with both fear and joy, but my phone reads *Sonja*, a work friend who checks up on me every week or two.

If it were nearly anyone else, I would let it go to voicemail, but one of the reasons I love Sonja is her lack of small talk. She calls, asks how I'm doing, tries to get me to make lunch plans, tells me she misses me, and hangs up after five minutes, max. So I take a deep breath and answer the phone.

"Asha!" she nearly shouts. "Asha, how are you? I have a wonderful idea. What are you doing Friday?"

Going on a date with the first man I ever loved. Well, the first boy. Ew, that sounds gross. God, I can't wait to see him. But I can't tell Sonja that. Well, maybe I can, but I don't want to.

"I'm actually busy Friday. Why do—" Before I can finish my sentence, Sonja makes an exaggerated sigh into the phone. She's blunt, but not rude, so this takes me aback. "What?"

"No, you're not. You're not busy! Come on, come out with me and Marko!"

"You and—" *Marko?* "Your cousin?"

"He asks about you every time I talk to him. Every time. He's going to be in town. Let's go out!"

I count the years on my fingers and realize it's been something like a decade since I met my coworker's cousin, that *one* time. There is absolutely no way that he still asks about me, that he's ever asked about me.

"Sonja, seriously? That wasn't anything. We danced together."

"Oh, you two don't have to get married. But come on! I thought you'd want to get out there a little."

Get out there? I think. "Get out there?" I say.

"I don't know," she says, sounding defensive. "I mean, aren't you lonely?"

"I . . ." *Yes.*

"And when's the last time you got laid?"

"I—"

"It's just, I was sitting at work today, looking at your desk. Did I tell you the new intern sits there now? Chloe's seriously good, but she's annoying as hell. And I just remembered how much fun we used to have. I miss you. I haven't seen you in so long, and I thought how lonely you have to be. I mean, it's been like a year, right? The worst year ever. I thought, maybe, it's time for Asha to start dating again. That's not crazy, right? I read this thing on Facebook once about the stages of grief, and I figured you gotta be to acceptance now. Right? Or almost? And if not, well, maybe I can help. And I bet *Marko* can help. I bet *Marko* really wants to help."

One of the biggest misconceptions we have about grief is that it's linear. It's not. We don't cycle through the stages—denial, anger, bargaining, depression, acceptance—in order, and we can absolutely move backward. We can skip over stages, then return to where we started, all in the course of a week, or even a day. Admittedly, these days, I tend to be camped pretty firmly under depression's umbrella, but that rush of joy about Jason at the coffee shop? That's the closest to acceptance I've been in a year. And here I am, on the phone with Sonja, talking about some guy I met once like ten years ago, and I've spring-boarded back over depression and bargaining and landed right atop anger, that spicy bastard.

"Hello-oooo?" Sonja adds another syllable to the word. "Earth to Asha. Where'd you go, girl? What do you say? Want to come out Friday with me and Marko?"

"I can't," I say and, surprisingly, decide to be honest. "I . . . I have a date."

Sonja lets out a whoop that could wake the dead. *Hear that, Charlie?* And I swear, I hear him chuckle. She sings, "Hal-le-LU-jah, girl, hallelujah. Who is he? Is he fine? YUM, I bet he's fine."

"He's . . ." I don't know how to answer this. I haven't seen Jason in so long. But I just Google stalked him, right? And Bridget just *saw him* saw him. I practically sigh, "Yeah, he's fine."

"That's my girl. OK. Well, Marko will be *crushed*, I tell you, but I'll let him down easy. I'll call next week. You can tell me all about your date with Mr. Fine, babe. Miss you lots." She makes loud, kissing *smack*s into the phone before she hangs up.

I think back over our conversation and get hung up, again, at *I thought you'd want to get out there a little.* Is that what people think? It can't just be Sonja, right? Do people see me and pity this grieving, guilty blob? The timing of hearing these words paired with what I now think of as my "stirrings"—thanks, Pastor Von—feels . . . not serendipitous, but linked, somehow. I let myself sit with this, let my curiosity and eagerness to see Jason grow.

It feels weird. It feels wrong. It feels wonderful.

SPRING (1997)

On the first day of summer vacation, the telephone woke me up at nearly noon. I reached for the phone at my nightstand and said "Hello?" without opening my eyes.

"Asha."

"What?"

"It's Jason?"

He'd misunderstood my *What?* It had not meant, *Who is this?* but *Wait . . . what is happening right now? Why are you calling me?*

"I was thinking about you. How'd your finals go?"

Why is he asking me about finals? I thought, but said, "History was hard. Mr. Kelsey's really tough."

"I'm sure you got all As."

What is happening right now? "Thanks."

"First day of vacation. Big plans?" He sounded nervous.

Why does he sound nervous? "I think I'm gonna ride my bike with María to the pool," which was a few streets away, inside our neighborhood. Residents could go whenever it was open, but anyone else needed to visit with a resident.

"No Bridge?"

"She's on vacation with her family this week."

"I wish I had a pool I could go to this summer."

Does he want me to invite him? "Yeah. Um, I should probably go."

"Do you have to? I miss talking to you. Thought we could catch up or something. Can I call you later?"

"If you want."

"I'll call you later." He sounded happier, more upbeat. "Bye."

"Bye?"

I hung up and immediately called María.

"I really need to talk to you . . . Jason called me."

"*Jason* Jason? *Your* Jason?"

We met up twenty minutes later.

"So what did he say?" María asked as we stood in line for lunch at The Hut, the pool's concession stand.

"I think he wanted me to invite him here."

"You didn't, did you?" María asked, darting her head this way and that, looking around the busy patio for any sign of a boy we knew.

"No way," I said, trying to sound tough. "Why would I *ever* invite him here? After what he did to me?"

"Do you miss him?" she asked, completely disregarding my *Who gives a damn?* attitude.

"No," I said, and she raised her eyebrows at me. "Well. Maybe a little."

I try to imagine an adult man doing to me now what Jason the boy did to me then, and I can't do it. What kind of self-respecting human lets a one-time beloved

(one)

leave during an emotional upheaval,

(two)

hook up with a close friend,

(three)

call unexpectedly after nearly a half year, and then

(four)

act as though the aforementioned betrayals never occurred?

The answer: No kind.

This was only the start of the emotional push and pull of Jason, and even this first step embarrasses my heart and makes her cover up her eyes like she's watching *The Exorcist*. I try to counteract my headshaking with understanding, though; Asha with her first love didn't know what the hell she was doing. It can be hard to show our used-to-be selves tenderness, and—tough as it is to follow through—I know tenderness is exactly what that girl deserved.

At the pool, María and I ordered corn dogs, and I wrinkled my nose when I saw my friend mix up her ketchup and mustard in a goopy swirl. "Gross."

"It's good, try it," she said, dipping her corn dog in the mixture and sticking it in my face, trying to force me to take a bite.

We were struggling like this, giggling, when Edward stepped up and said, "Hi."

María immediately clammed up—she'd had a crush on Edward all year and had been devastated when he and Bridget had made out at Bridget's birthday party. We learned his family had moved to our neighborhood a few weeks earlier.

"Waterslides?" he asked. What made my neighborhood's pool better than most were its twin extra-long tube slides, the kind you could usually find only at water parks. We spent the rest of the afternoon waiting in line for the slides, squealing as we placed our legs in the whooshing water, taking turns racing each other down. The lifeguard, Lori, was my neighbor, and she'd babysat me a few times last summer. She let María and me go down tandem, pressing her finger to her lips in a *Don't tell!* gesture. I wrapped my legs around María's waist, and we squealed the entire ride down, splashing a huge arc of water as the slide dumped us into the teal-blue pool at the end. The next time, I shoved María at Edward, and they went down together in the same tangle of legs and arms and squeals.

This was the start of the final summer I'd act this way. I didn't know it then, but the same secret part of my brain that recognized the specialness of that dance from two weeks before pulsed. It twitched, it woke up, and it got to work; it stored this memory at the pool in an extra-special box, taped up with extra-strong tape. It used a scrawling, childish penmanship and red permanent marker to write across the top, FRAGILE.

When I got home late that afternoon, I was sunned and wet and exhausted. I remember walking into my room and sitting on my bed, and I thought, *I should dry my hair. It's dripping everywhere,* but I never made it. I passed out on top of my comforter and awoke two hours later as my dad's hand cradled the back of my head, his dry, pursed lips pressed gently to my forehead.

"Your mustache tickles."

"I am sorry, *bratti*, I did not mean to wake you. You had fun today at the pool, I see."

"It was awesome," I told him, stretching.

"Awesome," he parroted back to me, chuckling, and he looked at me sadly.

"What is it, *Baba*?" I didn't often use the Assyrian word for *dad,* but I threw it in here because I knew what his sad expression meant. He wore it whenever I was about to get a story about my mother.

"She loved to swim, you know," he said, lowering himself down next to me. "She was like that little monster in the movie, where you add the water and they go crazy? When she got near a pool, or a lake, or the ocean, she went crazy, yelling and happy and splashing. She was a little girl again."

He would know; Dad met my mom when they were kids. His family moved to America from Iran in the early seventies, settling in Hillsboro Beach, Florida. Dad was only ten. He thought he would make friends easily, he told me, because he spoke English well. He'd taken classes in Iran, and he thought he was going to walk into fifth grade and impress all his new friends.

He never got a chance to impress them that first day, though. Because that first day, there were no new friends at school. No one talked to him, even when he tried to talk to them. Everyone ignored him.

When he got off the bus at the end of the day, he was sad. Not because he hadn't made friends but because, when his mother asked, "How was the first day of your new school? Tell me all about your new friends," what could he say? She would be crushed.

As he trudged home, he heard a high, sweet voice: "Hey, you!" He looked up, and, he says, my mom was standing there like an angel in a navy school uniform, with skinned knees and a yellow braid down the middle of her back.

"Hello," he said, stopping in front of the small blue clapboard house three doors down from his small white clapboard house.

"I never seen you before," she said, and before he could respond, a large truck turned onto the road, playing music. "Ice cream!"

He watched as she ran up to the truck—"She always ran like a tornado," he told me. "If I didn't get out of the way, she would destroy me, kaboom!"—and asked him, "What do you want?"

"I do not understand," he said, approaching the truck carefully. The side of the truck was covered in pictures of ice pops and chocolate bars with sticks. One treat was shaped like a dog's head and another like a patriotic rocket.

She huffed and ordered, paying with coins she pulled from her pocket. As the truck drove off, my father asked, "What was that?"

"The ice-cream man!" When knowledge did not register on my poor dad's face, she huffed again. "You never seen the ice-cream man? He comes up and down the streets, and he sells ice cream, and he plays his little song. *All around the mulberry bush, the monkey chased the weasel. The monkey thought it was all in fun, POP GOES THE WEASEL.*" She shouted this last part, throwing her hands in the air and nearly dropping her treat.

"Ice cream in America comes on trucks?" my dad asked, puzzled.

"Want some?" the little girl asked. She tore open the white wrapper to reveal two slim chocolate bars stuck together at the middle. "Here, take one." My dad grabbed hold of one of the small wooden sticks while my mom held on to the other. She twisted her wrist, and the pop split in two.

She took a huge bite from her half, though my dad was more tentative with his. He brought it slowly to his lips and pressed his tongue to the tip of the pop. It was cold and creamy. He took a larger bite—still not as big a bite as my mom's; she was nearly done with her pop already—and smiled at the sweetness. Today they're still his favorite; we have a box in the freezer at all times.

"I'm Vicki," she announced, presenting her sticky hand for my father to grasp.

"Oh. Hello." He took her hand uncertainly. "I am Adam Khoury."

She misunderstood and tried as best as she could: "Hi, Ah Damkoor Ee." She thought it was all one name.

"VICKI!" a lady who'd stuck her head out the front door of the blue house called.

"I gotta go. See you tomorrow, Ah Damkoor Ee!" She ran off, her braid bouncing on her back.

"And I said back to this wonderful little girl, 'Goodbye, Wicki!'" I suppressed a giggle. As an adult, I never laughed at my father's *V*s, but as a girl, I couldn't help myself. He continued, "And now, when my mother asked about my first day at school in America, I could tell her all about my new friend with the loud voice and the yellow hair and the *POP goes the weasel*, my new friend named"—and here he paused for such a quick beat, I don't think anyone else would have noticed—"Vicki."

The next day, the ringing woke me up again, but Dad picked it up before I could. He poked his head in my room and asked, "You awake, *bratti*? There is a boy for you on the phone. I think it is Jason."

"You get up way too early," I said into the phone, yawning.

"It's 11:37."

"Yes. A.m. That means it's still in the morning. 'After morn . . .' No . . . What the heck does 'a.m.' stand for?"

"Ante meridiem," he answered immediately. "It's Latin for 'before midday.'"

"Why do you know that?"

"Just smart, I guess."

"You're humble." I propped the pillows against the headboard to sit up. It was nice to be able to talk to Jason with no nerves, no worries about whether he liked me. For not the first time, I thought how nice it'd be if we could be friends.

"So I hear you had a blast at the pool yesterday," Jason said.

"You did?"

"Edward called me."

"He's pretty fun."

"Edward's great."

"He's never really talked to me before. I've been missing out."

"Cause you're *my* girl."

"Which of course means no other boy can talk to me." His use of the present tense hadn't escaped me, but I chose to ignore it.

"So I was wondering. If I hung out with Edward this summer, and if he brought me to the pool, would you want to hang out?"

"Would you even talk to me?"

"Of course I'd talk to you. I miss you, Asha." This was *not* where I thought this conversation was going. "When I saw you at the dance, all I wanted to do was dance with you."

"What about that girl who was hanging all over you?"

"Tina. She's a friend."

"Looked like a little more than a friend."

"We broke up before school let out. I didn't want a girlfriend this summer."

"How many girls did you date this year?"

"Um . . . four."

"Four? Jason, wow."

"I missed you." As if that explained what he'd been doing. When I think of it now, maybe it did. "So if I come to the pool, will you talk to me?"

"I guess?" Was he trying to date me again? Of course he was, but at that time, I was a confused little girl who wanted this boy to simultaneously leave her alone and love her forever.

Dad saved me. "*Bratti!* You want some breakfast?" he called from the stairs, loudly.

"More like lunch," Jason said, and I heard the smile in his voice. "Can I tell you one more thing?"

"What is it?" Why did my stomach drop again? Why did he *always* do this to my stomach?

"It's just . . . I really miss hearing you say my name." I must have been quiet for a long time, because he said, "Asha?"

So I was honest: "Miss you, too. Igottagobye."

That day, I ran farther than I ever had before. Typically I jogged in circles around the block, but when I passed the turn that would take me back down the street to my house, my legs propelled me forward. I'd only ever been on that particular stretch of road in a car. Without the glass window separating me from everything, I noticed things I'd never seen before in this Midwestern slice of suburbia: This house had a flower garden full of magenta blooms. That house was shaped like an A, like our old house in Florida. In my room, the bed had been nestled under the point of the roof, and I remembered one time when my friend Heather spent the night, she hit her head on the ceiling. *What is that doing there?* she asked. *Ceilings are supposed to be over your head, not in front of it.*

It started to rain on the run, a light sprinkle. The sun stayed out the whole time, somehow, and I stopped at a corner and jogged in place, searching the sky for a rainbow.

I didn't want to go home yet—the rain felt good—so I turned left down a street I'd never been on at all, not even in a car, and I noticed the houses getting bigger. That one looked like a castle. It didn't take much to imagine it with flags sticking out from the various pointed roofs. That other one had a pond. I wondered if there were fish in it.

"Wouldn't that be an awesome way to keep a pet?" I asked Jason later that afternoon. To my surprise, I'd *wanted* to call him back. I wanted to tell him about all the new things I saw on my run.

"You could name your fish George and Gail."

George Gervin and Gail Devers, I thought. *He remembered.* "We'd have to heat it so they didn't turn into fish-sicles in the winter."

"Their own little spa. You could call it the Khoury Cave."

I liked that. "I even got caught in the rain. I've never run in the rain before. It was really cool."

"Did you see the rainbow?"

"I couldn't find it," I told him. "Was it awesome? I'm jealous."

"When I saw it, I wanted to call you to tell you to look at it."

I liked that, too.

AUTUMN (2017)

In the months since Charlie's coma, I've become something of a social media lurker. I have Facebook and Instagram accounts, but I never post. Instead, I lose hours scrolling. It's easier than facing life.

Like this morning. This morning I awaken and immediately marvel, *Last night, I agreed to see Jason Kapaglia. The hell was I thinking?* I pull up Instagram and, still in bed, in the dark, with a sliver or two of light peeking from around my dark curtains, I start to scroll.

The fourth photo in the feed is the drink Bridget threw out yesterday. Maura has captioned it: **Decided to treat myself this morning! I *never* order anything this sweet, but sometimes, a woman simply has to tell herself, "I'm worth it." You'll never regret going for the splurge.**

She posted it an hour ago, and it already has more than two hundred likes and nearly thirty comments: **OMG, that looks soooo good #yummy! . . . Coffee for lyfe! . . . If I was tiny like you, I'd have dessert for breakfast every day!**

Maura actually responded to that third one: **You are too sweet, @d.a.n.a.baby, but I know everything I have is thanks to Jesus. What gifts has he given you? It's important to be thankful!**

I don't know why I hate-follow Maura and the Instagram feed, @loveabides831, which she started in the weeks after Charlie's coma. Why do any of us hate-follow anything on social media? Her photos are beautiful in a crisp, sterile way: The lighting is always a little *too* bright, the colors somehow vivid but muted. It's all vanilla stuff, rooted in her faith without getting *too* preachy, usually.

Unbelievable, I hear Charlie say in my brain. *That wasn't even her drink. What a damn weird thing to lie about.*

"Your sister is bonkers," I murmur aloud.

That evening, while I'm waiting for my chili three-way to heat up in the microwave, I'm back at it on Instagram. Maura, aka @love-abides831, has posted again. This photo is a selfie. She looks down and to the side, showing off a small but precise copper-colored, winged eyeliner. Her lip gloss is tinged gold, and her contouring is subtle. You wouldn't suspect it's there unless you know what her face actually looks like: Instead of hard angles and edges, Maura has made her face fuller somehow. The effect is soft, almost ethereal.

The image's caption is lengthy:

> You know, friend, I've spent a lot of today thinking about Gifts (thanks to YOU, @d.a.n.a.baby!) We all have different Gifts—some of us are patient, some are wise. Some of us have beautiful smiles that light up the lives of those who love us, and some of us live to serve others. Me? My Greatest Gift is my bff Charlie, aka my big brother. Charlie has had my back since we were young. When my prom date stood me up, he got dressed up and took me to the dance. He even picked me up from my first @3C event! (That's "Christ and His Crusaders Conference," for the unfamiliar ones. A life-changing three days. Check it out!) I became overwhelmed by the abundance of Jesus I felt in that room. I was not lucky enough to grow up in a family of faith, and the sheer amount of it at 3C was overwhelming. I am not proud to share that I had a panic attack—so much love should never cause panic!—but Charlie didn't judge me. He never judges me. He only

loves me. #loveabides What are *your* greatest Gifts?
Let's have a sharing party!

I notice that there are additional photos with this post, and I swipe
to reveal them. Up pops Maura and Charlie as kids, propped on the sofa
that the Watterses now keep in their basement den. I've always loved
this photo: Charlie's got his skinny arm draped around Maura's neck,
and he's smiling like a goofball. He's in that stage of childhood where
he has a mixture of baby teeth and adult teeth. His front teeth are enormous, and all the rest are approximately the size of corn kernels. It gives
him a lopsided, goofy grin. Maura, a toddler, sits with a stuffed bear in
her lap, smiling straight at the camera like she's posing for one of those
photos that comes with the frame. I swipe again. This was taken a few
days before Charlie's coma. I know because I'm in the photo. Rather, I
should be; Maura has cropped the image to show only the two of them.
If you look closely, you can see a piece of my hand on Maura's shoulder.

Immediately, my head fills up—with pressure, with tears. The sobs
come instantaneously, as though some monster in my brain has flipped
on a switch. The photo swims before my eyes, turns wavy, unclear.
This used to happen all the time, this ambush of grief, and it's always
unpredictable. At Kroger once, I saw a bunch of Boy Scouts, and I
hyperventilated while deciding between Golden Grahams and Corn
Pops. Once, I was flipping through Charlie's copy of *The Da Vinci Code*
and found a doodle in the margins, a surprisingly lifelike face rolling
its eyes. I'd had no idea Charlie was that good of an artist, and my tears
smeared his ink, which made me cry even harder. What other things
did I never get to learn about my husband?

While sobbing during this particular grief blast, the microwave
beeps. I hold a tissue to my nose and get my dinner. I gasp as I stand
in front of the refrigerator, trying to catch my breath as I figure out
whether I want lemonade or milk. I pull in shaky lungfuls of air as I
reach for the lemonade, wipe my eyes as I pull down a cup from the

cabinet, emit a pitiful bray as I walk my chili and lemonade to the kitchen table.

At some point during dinner, while I consider this newest post, my sobbing subsides. I hardly even notice, I'm so focused on Maura. She thinks she's telling the world about her greatest gift—excuse me, her greatest Gift—but she conveniently forgot the fact that her dear BFF hasn't had brain waves for nearly a year. It's a fact she's left out since the beginning. Hers is an account ostensibly about her life—its beauty, its challenges, her faith—but in it, she lies about that life nearly every day.

It seems to work, though. She has close to five thousand followers. They heart and comment on her posts, and she's good at engaging with them, as she did with @d.a.n.a.baby and her Gifts.

Prom night. Good Lord, Charlie says to me in my mind. Maura boasts that her big brother took her to prom. In his version of the story, though, he's less the BFF in shining tuxedo and more the eye-rolling sibling who took pity on his sister—and not for prom, but for winter formal junior year. Maura *had* been stood up junior year—that was true. After waiting for an hour for a no-show Trevor Marshbaum, Charlie offered to take her. The thing is, he never thought she'd accept: Who the hell wants to turn up at a school dance with her *brother*?

Well, apparently, Maura did. She spent the night telling anyone who'd listen what that no-good Trevor Marshbaum had done. The following Monday she learned in their shared algebra class that Trevor would be out for a few more days because he'd gotten acute appendicitis on Saturday afternoon. *That's* why he stood her up: He was having surgery. Instead of visiting him during recovery, Maura acted like they'd never even made a date to attend the dance together. It's too bad—he's a Realtor in town, and I've seen his face on a few billboards. Dude's *gorgeous*.

After dinner, I'd planned to visit Burnet Woods Park, across from UC. After Charlie and I met, we learned it was a favorite haunt for each of us. We went there all the time, over the same period of time, and we had no idea. These days, it's where I go when I need to be with Charlie. I don't feel him in that sterile room at Pax. I've never said this aloud to anyone, not even Bridget, but Burnet Woods is where I plan to scatter his ashes.

I change my plans and go to Pax instead. Something about Maura cutting me out of that photo makes me want to hold my husband's hand. Or, rather, the hand that used to be my husband's.

Eight in the evening is a quiet time around Pax, and I'm not surprised to see Madison with her phone at the front desk. The unicorn case makes me laugh. She looks up and grins at me, a little sheepish, and tucks her phone away.

"I know I'm not supposed to be on here, but—"

I cut her off with a wave of my hand. "I bet it gets quiet around here. And creepy."

She laughs. "I'm not creeped out. But maybe a little bored. It's nice to see you again this week."

"I need to hold his hand a little. I saw . . . well, I needed to be here."

"Everything OK?"

It's probably petty of me to do this, but I can't help it: I show @ loveabides831 to Madison. She reads Maura's latest caption, shaking her head slowly as she does. Then she swipes through the photos.

"See that hand?" I say and point it out in that third image. "That's me."

"She cut you out," Madison mumbles, and she studies the photo further. Her eyes suddenly fill with tears, and she brushes them away with the back of her hand. "He's a handsome one, huh?"

I nod.

"That smile. Oof." She patters her hand on her chest above her heart.

I stay with Charlie for more than an hour. I don't chatter through the visit, like I typically do, and I don't sit and hold his hand, like I'd planned. Instead, I ease down next to him and lay my head on his shoulder. I close my eyes and try to pretend I'm in our bed, and it's 3 a.m., and I've had a nightmare, and the warmth of his body against mine helps chase away the terrors.

I've never been great at pretend, but it's all I have.

I want so much more.

SPRING (1997)

That summer I went to the pool with Jason one time. Because in late
June my dad asked whether I'd like to spend the rest of vacation in
Florida with his parents.

I have always been close to my grandparents, and though we visited
them two or three times this year, the trips were always too short. So
when my dad offered up a whole summer with them, I felt like he'd
offered me the moon.

I called Jason to tell him.

"Wow," he said. "All summer?"

"I can't wait. You're lucky. All your family lives nearby."

"When will you come home?"

"I think the week before school starts?"

"Will you visit?"

"Here?"

"You know, to see your dad or . . ."

"I'll be gone less than two months," I said, trying to sound reasonable
and silence the flutter in my chest. *You want me to visit* you, *don't you?*

"Maybe I can visit? I've never been to Florida."

"I don't think so . . ." The very thought of asking my dad if my
ex-boyfriend could visit me *out of state*, which would mean *he'd have to
stay the night*—it was terrifying.

"Well, then, I guess I'm going to have to visit Edward this weekend."

"That sounds fun."

"Do you think you could hang out?"

"I'm babysitting Saturday night," I said, and Jason groaned. "We'll figure something out. Maybe I'll get home early."

I didn't get home from babysitting until after eleven. My dad waited up for me, the TV flipped to an old black-and-white mummy movie. I finished watching it with him, curled up at his side, subconsciously fingering my Jason bracelet, which I had put on for the first time in months a few days prior. Five minutes into the movie, without taking his eyes from the screen, Dad handed me a date from the bowl on the table. Without looking away from the screen myself, I took it from him and started to nibble.

Dates were one of the dozens of holdovers from Iran that persisted for my dad, and now for me. When I was little, I didn't even like them. They're not nearly as sweet as a child wants a snack to be. But I liked the texture: gummy, with a little bit of grit, not unlike a gummy bear, if the bear was studded throughout with bitty seeds. Because that was the appeal to me—the texture—I didn't eat a date like a normal person, taking bites. Instead, I nibbled at them, eating the two-inch-long treat in a hundred bites instead of two.

When the movie ended, Dad tucked me in. I guess it should have made me feel like a baby, that he still tucked me in sometimes, but it made me feel safe, secure. Loved. When he kissed me, he smelled like a date, a mild, subtle aroma that will forever make me think of home. He shut the door softly behind him, and I clicked on my bedside lamp. I had just started Judy Blume's *Forever* . . .

An hour later I had read the same paragraph three times, where Michael tells Katherine he loves her. She doesn't say it back, but then, she also doesn't act like a psycho after. *Why couldn't I have not acted like a psycho, too?* I wondered.

At that moment, a flash of light through my window caught my eye. I stared at it, and then, again, there it was. The window was cracked, and as I approached it, I heard a stage whisper: *"Asha! Asha!"*

I opened the window the rest of the way and slid up the screen to lean out.

"What are you doing?" I whispered, trying to modulate my voice, to keep it low enough so I didn't wake my dad but loud enough that Jason and Edward below me could hear. "Where're your shirts?"

Edward held up a beach towel, and Jason whispered as loudly as he dared, "Let's go swimming!"

"María's meeting us there!" Edward added. I couldn't believe it. *María* was going? They had woken up goody-goody, in-bed-by-nine-every-school-night *María*? *She* was going to sneak out of her house?

"Be right down," I hissed.

I grabbed my bathing suit, a pair of shorts, and a towel, then ducked into my bathroom for my toothbrush and a dot of toothpaste. I tiptoed downstairs, then stopped in the guest bathroom off the kitchen to change into my swimsuit and brush my teeth. I left through the garage, which had a second door leading to the side of the house.

I snuck up on Jason, who was still staring at my window like I'd drop a rope and shimmy down. Edward was gone, and Jason heard my footsteps before I could scare him. His face broke into the biggest smile, the kind he had worn after I kissed his cheek the first time at the dance.

"I wasn't sure you'd come."

"Let's go," I said, grabbing his hand and tugging him around to the front of the house. We ran the entire way, holding hands the whole time. It wasn't hard to jump the short fence into the pool area. Edward and María were already there, taking turns jumping off the diving board.

"Whoa," I said, surveying the area. It always seemed huge to me when dozens of my neighbors were spread out on their towels, splashing in the kiddie pool, cannonballing off the side of the deep end. But this way, peaceful, in the dark, empty, I was struck by how tiny it all seemed. I turned to Jason to say something, but before I could open my mouth, he'd given me a shove.

SPLASH, right into the pool, and I hadn't even taken off my shorts yet. I surfaced, spitting water, prepared to shout at him, but he'd already jumped in next to me. I shimmied out of my shorts, tossed them on the pavement, and tried to chase him. I knew I'd never catch him, though; Jason was a strong swimmer, and I was only good enough to keep from drowning. For every stroke I took, he pulled ahead two body lengths. He finally slowed down enough to let me catch him. I was out of breath and reached for his back. He lightly grabbed ahold of my forearms and pulled them over his shoulders, effectively giving me a piggyback ride. Before I realized what I was doing, I'd wrapped my legs loosely around his waist, letting him carry me through the water.

It was a warm night, and the pool wasn't cold, but a shiver ran up my spine when he reached his arms behind him and locked them behind my back, hugging me close to him.

We ducked under the divider into the deep end, and I unwrapped my legs so we could swim together.

"Don't," he said softly. "I got you." He waded farther than I thought he could—when had he gotten that tall?—and swam with me on his back when he could no longer touch the bottom of the pool.

I let go reluctantly when we reached María and Edward, then scurried up the ladder to jump off the diving board, too.

Edward and Jason each tried to outdo the other, adding somersaults and backflips to their leaps. Even María threw a few twists into her jumps. But I never would; I had a very real fear of going into the water headfirst. I didn't tremble or freak out or anything; I just refused to do it.

"Come on," Jason told me, and we swam to the side of the pool. There, he spent twenty-five minutes teaching me how to dive. He stood on the tiny ledge level with the water, where all the babies and toddlers stood before jumping into the open arms of Mom or Dad. He squatted, so his knees nearly came level with his ears, and he told me to mimic him. He raised his arms over his head, the tips of his pointer fingers touching each other.

"You don't even have to jump," he said. "Just fall."

He demonstrated, tipping off the ledge. It looked almost like a belly flop, but a gentle one.

"Didn't that hurt?" I asked when he surfaced.

"It's nice," he said, gracefully pulling himself from the water to sit on the ledge next to where I was perched. "Your turn."

I mimicked his form, and when he repeated "Just fall," I tipped forward.

It was one of the least graceful things I've ever done. I felt my limbs splay—instead of keeping my arms up over my head like Jason had, they flopped out like the top half of an X. When my belly hit the water, it stung. I kept my knees bent the entire time, and I entered the water like a frog. When I popped up, brushing my hair from my eyes and sputtering, Jason was laughing a great big belly laugh. I should have felt embarrassed, but instead I felt a weird kind of pride that I had made him laugh that hard.

"Like that?" I asked, pulling myself up to sit next to him.

"Exactly," he said. I responded by mimicking his goofy wiggle dance: fists near the sides of my face, elbows twisting and flopping about. His eyes opened wide at my movements, and he smiled so huge I swear I could have counted his teeth.

Then he kissed me.

It was nothing like our other kisses, and yet it was exactly the same, like nothing had changed. Neither of us seemed nervous or unsure what to do. His lips didn't feel stiff. They were soft, full, and I responded to them. I leaned into the kiss, and when I felt the tip of his tongue lightly on my lower lip, I opened my mouth in response.

María broke the spell: "Jeez, guys."

I pulled away and looked at Jason. When had he wrapped his arms around me like that? When had I threaded my fingers through his hair like that? I smiled, dipping my head, and he pulled me close to him again and kissed my hair before he stood and jumped straight up and out from the ledge, his body a firework of arms and legs. He surfaced with a whoop. I squatted where I was, still on the ledge, and I raised my arms over my head.

And I fell.

The next morning was Sunday, the day my dad and I would fly out to my grandparents'. He would stay for two nights, and then he'd return home. And I'd spend the summer in Florida.

I was still excited, but a lot had happened in less than twenty-four hours. Jason was my boyfriend again. Wasn't he? I certainly didn't go around kissing people like that if they were only my friend. I wondered how long I'd have to wait to figure it out.

It wasn't long. That afternoon, as I finished packing, the doorbell rang. My heart seized up. It had no way of knowing it was Jason, and yet it knew. It always knew. How the hell did it do that?

"Ash, it's for you," my dad called up the stairs. I poked my head out of my room and stepped to the banister, looking down into the front hallway. In my memory, the expressions on their faces are hilarious, and I'm certain I remember it wrong: Jason is looking up at me, grinning that enormous grin from the previous night. My dad is looking at Jason with his patented eyebrow raise. When I was little, the eyebrow raise could make my knees shake. As I got older, as I recognized my dad for the softy he was, I only feigned fear when he gave me that look.

"You're leaving soon, right?" Jason asked. "I wanted to say bye. Can you hang out for a little bit?" This was one of the things I loved most about Jason: his spontaneity. This was the second time in as many days that he'd shown up my house unannounced. Today it was the door and last night, my window. If there was a hole in my home, he'd appear there at some point in search of me.

Dad and I weren't leaving for the airport for a few hours, so Jason and I went into my backyard and plopped on a pair of swings on the playset left over from the family who'd lived in our house before. Dad had wanted to take it down when we moved in, but I asked him to leave it—Bridget and I had turned the fort into our secret clubhouse last summer.

Jason and I swung gently, quietly, peeking at one another, then staring again at the grass.

"I'm kind of bummed you're leaving all summer," he said.

"I *was* really excited. But then . . ."

He looked at me hopefully, his small hazel eyes round. "Then?"

I shrugged a shoulder. "You, I guess. I mean . . ." I didn't want to say what was on my mind: that while I was gone, he was going to date *another* four girls and have *another* four first kisses, all while I pined after my first love.

My first love. Huh. That thought hadn't come to me that easily before. I suddenly felt exposed, like all my neighbors had their binoculars out, trained on Jason and me chatting awkwardly in my backyard.

I hopped off the swing and climbed the wood ladder up to the fort. It had always been my favorite part of the playset. Bridget and I had promised we'd never let any boys inside. Once, she and I took markers and signed our names above the opening to the twisty yellow slide, the All Girls Pact, we called it, and I thought of the promise as Jason followed me into the fort.

His eyes followed mine, and he traced his finger over our loopy signatures.

"I wanna be in the club."

"Too bad, no boys allowed." But I smiled as I said it.

We settled on the wood-planked floor, our backs against opposite sides of the fort, and grinned at each other. We didn't speak for a few beats, and Jason broke the silence.

"Asha?"

"Yeah?"

"Will you be my girlfriend again?"

"Yeah."

I peeked my head out from the fort to make sure my dad wasn't watering flowers or something. The coast was clear, and I plopped myself down in Jason's lap, wrapped my arms around his neck, and gave him a kiss like last night's. The kiss lasted a year. The kiss lasted a second. The kiss made me nervous. The kiss made me brave.

I pulled back, lightly pressed the tip of my finger to the curve in his upper lip, and said, "I love you, too."

That smile.

But softer. More serious. Then he raised his clenched fists next to his face and gave me a wiggle. My heart trilled, and I grabbed one of his fists and brought it to my mouth, softly kissing the pucker made by his curled pointer finger and thumb. A current passed between us, and I thought that was how you knew you loved a boy, the current. I expected it with other boys, other men. But it didn't happen like that. It couldn't, and eventually I figured it for a one-time thing, a one-*guy* thing.

Then I met Charlie. The current was there, but it was different. I don't like to say "less than" because that implies the current is quantitative. The "less than" with Charlie didn't mean I loved him less. I loved him more. But the current with him, it was less because it had to be. Adult love doesn't have the abandon, the newness, the immediacy of first love. It can't.

And that can be a good thing.

SUMMER (2006)

Charlie loved to camp, a love bred from his years as a Boy Scout. In fact, he'd stuck with the Scouts for so long he'd joined the Order of the Arrow.

"Is that like a coven?" I asked when he told me. "Are you in a secret archery society? Are you an assassin?"

As he explained it to me, the pride radiated from his face, dripping from each word. Boy Scout leaders had to approve the membership, and it meant he lived his life with integrity, following Scout Oath and Law.

"Scout Law?"

He recited: *"On my honor I will do my best to do my duty to God and my country and to obey the Scout Law; to help other people at all times; to keep myself physically strong, mentally awake, and morally straight."*

"One-night stands aren't very morally straight."

"Who had a one-night stand?" He blinked at me. The man had a point.

This is all to say, he was incredibly excited to take me camping.

"I'm not much of a nature girl," I said. "Do we have to sleep on the ground?"

"We can bring mattress pads. It'll be fun, I promise."

My face must have screamed *I don't believe you*, because he followed his promise with, "Or maybe, we can stay in a cabin, with beds."

"And running water?"

"And running water."

"Good. And what makes you think this will be my first time?"

"Have you been camping before?"

"Once." He waited for more, so I said, "And I slept on the ground and everything."

He booked us three nights at a spot in Butler, Kentucky. The drive took less than an hour, which had me convinced there would be a Starbucks across the street and a highway exit fifty yards down the road.

"We could have gone a *little* more rustic than this, Mr. Boy Scout."

Silly me.

The cabin grounds were right off the Licking River, and for the final twenty minutes of the drive, Charlie wound the car around hairpin turns and past thick woods. On the open stretches, he kept his speed to thirty-five miles an hour even though the posted limit was fifty.

"Hey, Grandpa, why you drivin' like this?"

"Deer."

As if summoned, a doe stepped from the tree line a few yards ahead of us, then thought better of crossing and disappeared back into the brush.

The cabin was made of pale-blond, raw wood. Matching Adirondack chairs connected by a small table sat on the front porch. It was easy to picture an old couple sipping iced tea, watching the sun set from those chairs.

The front door opened into the family room, which boasted mismatched love seats and, unexpectedly, a television, which we would never turn on.

There was a full kitchen stocked with a few pieces of silverware, dishes, pots and pans, glasses and mugs. I spied a Mr. Coffee and a rusty teapot in one of the cabinets.

The bathroom existed—sometimes, merely existing is enough— and the bedroom smelled of must. I pulled a strawberry-scented candle from my bag and lit it to try to mask the odor.

The sun set as we unpacked. It had been an unseasonably warm April, but the night was chilly. I wrapped a fleece blanket around myself and shuffled outside, where Charlie was stoking a popping fire.

I inhaled deeply. "I think that's my favorite scent in the world."

"Mine, too," he said, and then he was off, quiet, lost in his head as he stared into the flames licking the logs.

"What do you see in there?"

His eyes flickered up to me for a moment, and I saw a small smile flash on his face. "Nothing."

I felt a tingle then. Not a current like I had that night in the pool with Jason or countless nights after. But something, and it was something that hadn't happened to me in a long time.

So I fell.

"Charlie?"

"Yeah?"

"I love you, too."

We weren't children. I wasn't worried about my father or neighbors spying. Nothing and no one were around but chipmunks and spiders. I was cold, but more than that, I was excited. Not just sexually—that, too, sure—but no, I was excited because of the tingle.

"Stand up," I instructed him.

I placed a second blanket on the tree stump he had been seated on, and I tugged off his flannel pajama bottoms. I pulled off my sweatpants and thong, and I straddled his lap. He grabbed on to the blanket still draped around my shoulders, using it as a kind of hammock to keep me pressed to him. I moved on him quickly but deliberately. He used his teeth to tug on my nipples through my T-shirt, and I pressed my open mouth to his as he came.

"Charlie?"

"Yeah?"

I said it again.

An hour later, we each had a marshmallow on a branch, hovering over different parts of the bonfire. I placed mine near the top of the flames so I had to blow it out every time it caught fire. Charlie kept his close to the embers at the bottom of the firepit; it melted slowly and steadily, the logical and methodical tortoise to my racing, hurry-it-up hare. He never caught his marshmallow on fire and, when he pressed it between two graham crackers and a square of Hershey's chocolate, it oozed off the branch perfectly.

"Let me make your next one," I said, and I added a swipe of peanut butter to his graham cracker.

"You're killing the integrity of the s'more!" But then he took a bite and groaned. "Where did you learn that?" I had amazed my Order of the Arrow member.

"Delicious, right?" I asked around a mouthful of my own peanut butter s'more.

"I have a question for you," Charlie began.

"Uh-oh," I said, grinning as I wiped a smear of chocolate from my lip.

"Why me? Why now?"

I nodded, pondering the question as I finished my s'more, staring into the fire the way Charlie had been earlier, hoping the right words would appear. A part of me, a large part of me, whispered, *No, don't.* But I wanted to tell him. I hadn't wanted to six hours earlier, but now it felt OK.

"I've been in love once before," I told him.

"The guy who freaked out on you?"

I nodded. "We met when I was thirteen. The last time I saw him was my twentieth birthday, at like two in the morning when he dropped me off from a party. I guess that's the exact definition of teen love. He was . . . I was . . . we were everything to each other. And we dated and broke up so many times, but even when things were really bad, somehow I still knew it would work out.

"Things with Jason—that's the guy—were always big. Very over the top, very dramatic. Everything was passionate, and it was crazy, and we made each other crazy, and I thought, I really thought, that was how love was supposed to be. That if it wasn't all-encompassing and messy, then it wasn't real. But that gets exhausting, you know? I don't think I could be happy with that forever. It's exciting. And it's fun. But it's too much.

"I haven't had a boyfriend since. I've gone on dates and stuff. Had some flings. But no one serious. I didn't actively push it away, I don't think, but I never made an effort, either. Which"—*huh, I'd never considered this*—"is the same thing as actively pushing it away, I guess."

"You didn't push me away."

"I didn't think I had to. You were supposed to be a one-night stand, but you kind of kept coming back."

"What you're saying is, I wore you down?" He had a half grin on his face, but he was serious.

"It's not that. You're not pushy or persistent, which definitely works in your favor. You're easy to like, and I let myself like you because . . . well, how could I not? I mean, you make it easy. You're effortless. Being with you is effortless. We don't have to be this crazy passionate mess. We can be passionate without the crazy, without the drama. And then on top of that . . ."

I trailed off, and Charlie cocked his head at me.

"I don't know about you, but you're basically the best sex I've ever had in my life."

Charlie bowed his head in thanks, and a few locks of his hair fell in front of his face. God, I loved his hair.

"It's funny," I continued. "I haven't seen Jason for almost three years. It's really not that long, I guess, but it seems like it's been forever. I feel like that was a different me, the girl who loved him."

"How so?" he asked, and I wanted to touch him. I reached up and tucked that soft tendril behind his ear, tugging his earlobe as I lowered my hand.

"Everything is precious when you're a kid. The firsts are the most important things, the most special things. Your worldview isn't wide enough to realize that those firsts aren't unique, you know?"

"I don't know about that."

"I mean, the stuff that was the be-all, end-all of everything, it's not like I was the only one who went through them."

"But they're your experiences. That's what makes them special," he said. "It doesn't matter if millions of people on the planet fall in love every day—each falling is extraordinary. It's its own tiny macrocosm with its own life-forms and pulse."

I studied him. He'd given this a lot of thought. "I know you said 'no one,' but really, what was your first love like?"

"You mean you?"

"Come on."

"You *are*," he insisted, and I blinked at him. He seemed almost frustrated I didn't believe him. "Would you take that look off your face? It's not like I was virginal until we met. I've dated, and I've had a few girlfriends, even. And they were all great. But sort of . . ." He trailed off, then muttered, "Man, this is going to sound awful. They didn't have any fire. They went about their days. They loved their mothers. They went on hikes with me. They fussed with their hair. They sipped wine. They were pretty and nice, and one day they'll marry men who are pretty and nice and who'll give them babies, and they will all be the most beautiful babies in the world. I dated perfectly nice girls who will live perfectly nice lives. There was nothing wrong with any of them."

"But you didn't love them?"

"They were all missing something for me."

"What?"

He paused. I liked this about Charlie; when he answered a difficult question or one where the answer was foggy, he didn't blurt out the first thing that came to mind. He gave it thought and formed his words before he spoke. It's an exceedingly rare trait in a person.

"You make your own rules," he said finally. "You cook me dinner, and it's Assyrian food. I don't even know what that is. For our first date, we go to a horror-themed bar."

"You love me because I'm a weirdo?"

"Well, yes. And your heart. I watched you all New Year's Eve. You were the life of that party."

"I was hammered."

"Yeah, but you were such a considerate hostess. You kept checking in with everyone, even people you didn't seem to know, to see if they needed anything. You refilled the chip bowls before they went empty, and you passed out champagne at 11:55. Do you remember our first kiss?"

"At midnight."

"Yes, but what do you remember about the details?"

"Umm . . . that when I woke up in the morning, you were still there?"

"My dad's always taught me that when people drink, their true selves are revealed. Your true self is caring and fun loving. I knew I wanted to usher in 2006 with you. When everyone started counting down to midnight, I introduced myself."

"You what?"

"I said, 'Hi, I'm Charlie, and you're stunning. May I kiss you at midnight?'"

"You did not say that. Who the hell says that?"

"I did. And a few hours later, when you dragged me up to your room, you ripped off your dress, and I thought I'd gone to heaven. I left you in bed and got you some water, and when I came back, you were asleep. I got in next to you and fell asleep, too."

"Wait a minute. We had sex that night."

"No, we didn't."

"We didn't?"

"I mean, I wanted to. Clearly. But you were passed out."

"But you were supposed to be a one-night stand. You weren't even supposed to be there in the morning."

"If I hadn't been there in the morning, I still wouldn't have been a one-night stand. I'm sorry to break it to you, sweetheart."

I loved when he called me that. He never said it in the sleazy Italian-gangster way. It was romantic, the way men called women their sweethearts in black-and-white love stories.

It struck me, then, that Charlie had never pressured me to do anything, ever. We slept together for the first time when I initiated it, soberly. I said I loved him on my terms. Even when I wasn't thrilled about the idea of camping with him, he changed the trip around for me.

"Where did you come from?" I was only half joking.

"Well, my dad's sperm joined my mother's egg and—"

"Oh, god, stop."

He grinned. "It's cool, though, isn't it?"

I wrinkled my nose. "Your parents having sex?"

"That I was born. That any of us were born. If my dad had made a move five minutes sooner, I wouldn't be here. If someone had rung the doorbell and interrupted, I wouldn't be here. It'd have been a different sperm and a different egg. I might have been a woman or had male pattern baldness by the time I was sixteen. I might be in a wheelchair. Or gay. Or a scientist who discovers a cure for cancer."

"But God chose to make a Boy Scout."

"Do you believe that?" he asked. "That God made us all?"

It was the type of conversation crafted for a campfire, the big-picture stuff that can make us feel small and unimportant while simultaneously filling us up with a wave of *I'm not alone. There's someone like me.* I had no way of knowing this was about to turn into one of the most important conversations of my—and Charlie's—life. And that one day I'd fail him so spectacularly.

"You have to believe that, don't you?" I asked. "Don't they kick you out of Boy Scouts if you're not Christian?"

"Faith is important, and respect for others, but it's not necessarily a Christian thing. There's programs for a bunch of denominations." He ticked off his fingers. "There's an Islamic group and a Jewish one. There's a Buddhist committee and a Hindu one, and even Zoroastrian and Sikh."

"Are you a member of any?"

"I don't really believe any of the doctrine or dogma, not as it's written. Bits and pieces of a lot of religions make sense to me, but not all of any one. My parents raised me and my sister vaguely Christian, but they never made us go to church or anything. It resulted in me, who questions and wonders about everything, and my sister, who found a Bible group a few months ago, right after Dad's heart attack, and has become this ridiculously devout girl almost overnight. It seems so out of the blue. We don't have a clue where she came from. I think some people must be wired for that kind of belief."

"But not you."

He shook his head. "Like I said, a bunch of belief systems make sense to me. Did you know Jews have no concept of hell? And when a Buddhist monk dies, his brothers chop up the body and feed it to vultures?"

"Excuse me?"

"It's a sky burial. They believe the body is a vessel for our eternal spiritual life. Once you die, there's nothing left of you in this realm. They put the pieces of your vessel on top of a mountain, and the sky dancers—"

"—the vultures?" I interrupted.

"Right. They take the soul to heaven."

"That's kind of sweet."

"And, get this, Christian Scientists don't go to the doctor."

"I feel like I've heard that one before."

"I love that concept."

"You don't want to go to the doctor when you're sick?"

"Well, no, not like that, but when I think about getting old and being put in bed and force-fed medicine to stay alive. That's not really alive. I'd hate to live like that. Not able to hike and kiss and eat and work and make love. That's not living."

"When my mom died, it was pretty quickly after I was born—she definitely didn't linger. I think my dad was always a little relieved he didn't have to make any decisions about hooking her up to tubes or machines or letting her go. He knew what she would have wanted, but I can't imagine how impossible that would have been—to know you can keep someone you love around, but it's not really them. And to know that they wouldn't have *wanted* to be kept around? How agonizing."

"Where do you think she is?" he asked.

"Like, in heaven or something? I don't know. I feel her sometimes. I have this old jewelry box of hers, and when I was little, I used to look in the mirror inside and wish I could see her looking back at me. I haven't done that in forever, but if I close my eyes and think about her really hard, I get this wash over me. Like my chest gets fuller, like she's pushed her way inside to say hi. That's always been nice, whatever it is."

Neither of us spoke for a long time, and it was a thoughtful silence, a sensual one. Not sensual like romantic, but physical, tactile, of the senses: I watched the tips of the flames flicker and dance, orange and yellow at the top, red in the campfire's heart, deep black maroon in the embers. I took big, cleansing breaths, loving the flavor of the smoke on the air I pulled over my tongue. I imagined that the air tasted the same way it sounded, crackling and snapping, its own ancient conversation of clacks and sighs. The half of my body facing the fire was warm, flushed. I pressed my hand to my cheek, which seemed to be radiating heat, then moved my fingers to the back of my calf, so cool it felt like slipping my palm under a silk pillowcase or around to the dark side of the moon.

The next morning I woke up before Charlie, right as the sun was rising, and I laced up my running shoes. I'd noticed a trail behind the cabin the night before, and I wanted to see where it took me.

"Take my iPod," Charlie murmured from bed.

"It's OK."

"I don't know how you run without music," he said, then immediately drifted back off to sleep. I found his Shuffle on the kitchen counter, held it in my hand for a moment, then left it there.

I stretched in the pale yellow of dawn. The birds were awake, and they serenaded me as I touched my toes, stretched my shoulders, did a few jumping jacks.

The trail itself wound around and through the campgrounds. I spied about a half dozen other cabins through the skinny trees with tiny new leaves. I heard rustles all around, and once I scared a bunny as I turned a wide corner. It darted off through the trees, disappearing as it hopped over a rotting log, cotton tail flashing.

Charlie's and my conversation loomed loudly in my brain. God and hell, love and Mom, vultures and death. As I ran, I let Charlie's words marinate: *You make your own rules . . . If I hadn't been there in the morning, I still wouldn't have been a one-night stand . . . I might be in a wheelchair. Or gay. . . . Do you believe that? That God made us all?*

I didn't reach any conclusions on that run. That wasn't the point, though. It was the wondering I loved, that fed me. Looking back, 2006 might have been right in the center on that gravel track of conclusion-less questions. Because the mid-aughts were a strange time, a time of in-betweens and transitions. Most of us had or were getting cell phones, but they were mainly just phones, nothing smart about them. Most of us, like Charlie, had an iPod, this sliver of plastic that held thousands of songs, negating the need for all those CDs we'd hoarded in our bedrooms or slid into holders strapped to our car visors. It was a time when the things we used to love, the touchstones to the things that mattered to us, stopped being necessary, when we looked ahead and wondered what on earth was coming.

When Charlie and I got home, I dragged out the tower of CDs relegated to the back corner of my closet. Spice Girls, Boyz II Men, Natalie Imbruglia, Ja Rule, Blackstreet—all bands this year's crop of high school freshmen would likely not recognize were they to grace the cover of *Rolling Stone* or *Spin*. In the tower's top slot, the Slot of Honor, as I'd always thought of it, was the Tony Rich Project single from Jason. I hadn't listened to it in years.

I slid the CD from its home and used my hand to wipe off a not-so-thin layer of dust. I'd spent so many hours staring at that black-and-blue cover, I had every contour of Tony's face memorized, the drape of his ear, the crisp lines of his goatee. I couldn't have said why, but I opened the cardboard case, catching the disk before it fell, the plastic prongs that had once held it in place long broken. I popped the CD into the boom box I still kept on my dresser. I didn't even know if it still worked.

The strings, winds, and what I swore were bongos filled my room. I hadn't heard the song in years—they didn't really play it on the radio anymore, not even during those throwback lunch hours—and I wasn't expecting to feel a pang of missing Jason.

No, that's not right. I didn't *miss* Jason or long for him in any way. But the music served as something of a transporter, an H. G. Wells–designed machine to transform my twenty-two-year-old self into my thirteen-year-old self.

I let the song play out, smiling at the memory. It didn't hurt anyone. It was mine, and I cherished it. Then I shut off the boom box and went to see what my boyfriend was doing.

AUTUMN (2017)

Friday morning I wake up filled with a longing that seems to press me into the mattress like a weighted blanket—or maybe like the long, lean body of a man who loves me. I have just dreamed the millionth Jason dream of my life. The millionth and first. Beginning in the year after we broke up for good, I started to dream about Jason all the time. ALL OF THE GODDAMN TIME. I'm no shrink, but those dreams must say something about . . . What? My guilt? That would make sense, but if that's it, the guilt must be pretty deep-seated, because—and I cannot stress this enough—I don't feel guilty about anything Jason and I did. I don't. I loved him, same as ever, same as always. And, sure, sleeping together after he was already with Simone wasn't the *nicest* thing to do to her, but I'd argue that I didn't do anything to her, this girl I'd never actually met. He did. But then, we do always blame the girls, don't we? (Sorry, Kendra.)

Here is a partial list of the dreams I have had about Jason in the years since I last saw him:

(one)

I am at a crowded party. I can't find him anywhere, but I'm desperate to. I want to apologize. I'm searching every room, but each room is packed with people, packed so tightly I can barely squeeze in, let alone find him.

(two)

The same as the above, but I know Simone is around, too, and I am not only looking for Jason but also avoiding Simone.

(three)

The same as above, but I find him. And I try to talk to him, but he is furious with me. He can barely stand to look at me. I beg, but he stomps off, and I chase after him.

(four)

The same as above, except he wants to see me, too, and we try to find a room where we can be alone and talk. But this is impossible because, again, this is the most crowded party that has ever existed in the universe. In the dream, I wonder what will happen if we ever find that empty room. Will we kiss furiously? Will we make love? Will someone walk in? Would I even care if they do?

(five)

There is but one dream that diverges in theme and plot from this crowded party where I may or may not find Jason, where he may or may not want to find me: I am in his driveway. I have never been in this driveway—it is as unfamiliar to awake Asha as it is to sleeping Asha—but in my dream, I know it is his house. He is at a workbench in the garage. I approach him to say hello, and a small child toddles out to me. "You have a son?" I ask him, stupidly, then drop down to the boy's level. "Hi," I say. "I used to know your dad." The boy looks at me quietly, curiously, while Jason watches us from the garage. The boy doesn't smile, but he doesn't run away, either. He cocks his head at me, and I reach for him. I want to cuddle him. I feel I must cuddle him. By cuddling him, I will be able to convince Jason that *I've* forgiven *him*.

These dreams used to come weekly, twice a week. Sometimes, they were spaced further out, once a month, once every other month. This is the first time I've dreamed of Jason since Charlie's accident, though, and I wonder if the aftermath will be the same, which is this: No matter where I am in life, what I am doing, what my priorities are, how old I am, if I am dating someone or not, these dreams take over my day. If I don't actively think about them, then my subconscious is mulling them over; and I know this is happening, even on that unknowable level, because I'm irritable on the mornings after Jason dreams. I snap at my friends, at my dad—even Charlie.

Charlie knew all about Jason—his utter lack of jealousy is on my list of 101 Things That Make Charlie the Best—and once, I tried to explain the dreams. Talking things over made me feel better, but it didn't stop the dreams.

Another time, before Charlie and I met, I reached out to Jason to see if I could be proactive about making the dreams go away. A month or two after I graduated from college, I looked up his college email address, and, having no idea if he still used that account, I sent him a note.

I skipped the pleasantries and wrote that I was hoping he could help me with something. I told him I couldn't stop dreaming about him, and that I always woke up feeling terrible after the dreams. I thought maybe if I knew that he'd forgiven me, as though I was somehow to blame for how often he'd cheated on Simone, the dreams might stop.

He wrote back an hour later. Said he wasn't upset, that I shouldn't worry about it, that he didn't talk about me to Simone. That they hadn't spoken about me since he confessed that the last time he and I slept together was my twentieth birthday, after they'd been dating for years.

He swore she'd forgiven him, but I was dubious: So what if she knew we'd slept together after they started dating? That's just physical. Had he ever told her how our emotional relationship hardly changed after they began dating? I wanted to ask, *Did you keep photos of me? Do you still have your half of the necklace? Did she make you throw away everything of me? Did she insist that you dispose of me in front of her? Did she make sure you weren't keeping anything hidden, secret, safe? Did you keep those things hidden, secret, safe, anyway?* Instead, I said I was glad he wasn't upset with me.

The dreams decreased in frequency after that, for a time, but they never went away. No, it took my husband slipping into a coma from which he'd likely never wake for *that* to happen.

Until now.

Last night's dream introduced a new setup: I am at dinner in a large room, at a table with girls I haven't spoken to since junior high. When I look around the room to see who else is there, I see Dad at one table, Jason at another. Jason and I catch eyes, and he scowls at me. I turn quickly back to my table and engage in conversation, making sure to laugh heartily, hoping he's looking, knowing he is, hoping he's missing me, fearing he's not.

Then, in a blink, I am in the middle of the room, rolling around on the floor with Jason, kissing. Then, in a blink, we are standing up, and he is dragging me out the door by the hand. Or am *I* dragging *him* out the door?

Then, in a blink, we are in my room, but my room is over a garage, adjacent to a harbor. I make sure Jason sees there are two doors, make sure he knows he can use either door when he wants to visit me, and he doesn't even have to knock. We make love on the bed, and I never, ever open my eyes because, in my dream, I am aware I am dreaming, and I am desperate to stay asleep, to feel the weight of Jason atop me, to feel his mouth pressed against mine. I come twice, short, powerful bursts in my sleep that are nice but feel incomplete.

When the me in the dream opens her eyes, she is alone in the bed in her harbor-view bedroom, and she knows Jason will never come see her again. She is overcome by a crushing heft of sadness.

When I wake for real, in my bedroom that is hundreds of miles away from any sort of harbor, I masturbate and have a third orgasm. I know I can't wake up from this, and it feels more complete.

After, I pull on some leggings and a sweater, make a cup of tea, and prepare for my day. I check my work emails and review my to-dos. Even in the midst of listing copy ideas for a fine-dining restaurant opening downtown, I'm giving only 10 percent of my brain to the task. Sure, part of that is because I've worked for Valentine & Vine since I graduated from college, and I can complete my job on autopilot. But it's also because my brain waves are devoted to the rest of my dumpster fire of a life. Like Maura's voice. *What does Charlie say to you in your dreams?* She drowns any lingering sweetness from the previous evening's nocturnal fantasies.

And then there are my mental efforts to talk myself out of tonight's date. What on earth will I say to Jason Kapaglia? What could he possibly want to see me for?

I argue with myself: *Oh, you know why he wants to see you . . . It's the same reason he's always wanted to see you after one of his relationships goes south . . . No, that's not it. You have no idea . . . Fine, if you want to be delusional . . .*

The loudest voice is insistent: *There is no way this can end up any way but awful.* I am a married woman. I have spent a year grieving a man who has not actually died. Do I really want to go on a date (*it's not a date*) with someone new? Rather, with someone who is the very opposite of new? I may not know the man Jason has become, but he still is not a new person. He is an old person, my very first person.

I promise myself that I will come down with a stomach bug right after my 2 p.m. call into the office. *Jason, I am sorry*, I will say, sounding pitiful. *Can we reschedule? . . . I'm not sure when. Let me call you when I'm feeling better.*

And I will simply never feel better. Easy-peasy, case closed.

Twenty minutes before my work call that afternoon, my cell rings.

"Hi, Dad."

"*Bratti*, how's my little girl?"

A couple of years before Charlie got sick, my dad moved back to Florida. My grandparents were getting older, and he didn't like them living far away. He offered to move back after everything with Charlie, but I wouldn't let him.

I'm fine, I'd told him then. *Don't worry about me. I have Bridget. I'm fine.*

I think he'd been glad—he loves his job overseeing the Foreign Language Education Program at Florida International University. And he missed Florida during his time in Ohio. There he can swim every day of the week if he wants, and he's always made friends easily. He found a social circle at work immediately. I didn't realize it when I was a kid, but everyone loves my dad. He's thoughtful and polite. He's not chatty, but he's the kind of guy you want to invite to a party where a lot of people don't know one another. He is comfortable talking to strangers, asking them questions so, within ten minutes, they are long past chitchat about the weather or sports. Dad is naturally curious and moves straight for the questions that matter: dream jobs, life goals, secret fears.

I guess I shouldn't be surprised, then, by what he shares when I say I can't talk long.

"I will not keep you. But I wanted to tell you the news. We can talk about it more later, if you would like. *Bratti*, I have met someone."

"A new swimming partner?" I ask, not getting it.

"No." He pauses, and I hear him chewing. *Dates,* I think. "I have met a woman. Her name is Celine. She is my French teacher. Remember, I told you I was taking lessons?"

I do remember—my father loves languages. He is fluent in Assyrian, Farsi, English, Arabic, and soon, likely, French.

"We have gone on three dates. I would like for you to meet her. I swear on your life, I think you would like her very much. She is a retired librarian and has a daughter your age. She divorced her husband nine years ago, when she learned he was in love with another woman."

My father is always like this: direct and matter-of-fact. To him, he is simply sharing details about his life. How could he know I momentarily stopped breathing? To the best of my knowledge, my father has not been with any woman but my mother. Once, in college, I told him he should date, but he said what he always said when the subject came up: *I have loved a woman. I am a lucky man. I must not be greedy.*

So why was *now* the time to be greedy?

"Bratti," he says, taking a deep breath, and then he mutters something in Assyrian.

"Dad?"

"This is not easy to say. But I want to say it. It is very hard to love someone so much, to have this person, this everything." *Ewything,* he

128

said. "But like I have found Celine, I think you could find . . . not now. Not right away. But there is more, my darling. There is so much in this big, wide world."

First Sonja telling me to move the hell on and now my father? Jesus.

"Dad, that's really great," I say, hoping he doesn't hear the panic in my voice. "Listen, I gotta go. Meeting time. I'll call you back later."

I do not call him back after my work call, nor do I come down with a stomach bug and cancel on Jason, as planned.

Instead, I call Bridget.

"I need you to help me get dressed." She is silent. I flash to the weeks after the coma, after Maura and Fucking Francis, when I couldn't get off the couch. Once, Bridget physically walked me to the tub, helped me undress, gave me a sponge bath, and put clean clothes on my body because I had been in the same pajamas for six days. So she doesn't think *this* is like *that*, I clarify: "I need you to help me get dressed for a date."

She *whoops* loudly. "I'll be right over."

"Give me an hour. I'm gonna go visit Charlie first."

"Now?"

"Now."

"That means . . . girl, you're going to see Maura. You gonna tell her?"

I am. Finally.

SUMMER (2006)

The day Charlie and I got engaged, he was in the midst of a 102-degree fever.

The night before, he was supposed to go to a birthday party with me at The Lighthouse, a downtown pub.

"Go without me," he said, sounding miserable. "Save yourself."

"Want me to bring you dinner?"

"Maura made me a vat of chicken noodle soup."

Maura—who was still in high school and hadn't fully transitioned into the stringent, zealous adult she would become—lived downstairs, and Charlie lived above his parents' garage. He wasn't even ashamed of it. He moved in after he graduated from college to save some money, and the apartment was fully furnished. He had his own kitchen, his own bathroom, his own living space. Granted, the "bedroom" appeared when he tugged on his convertible couch, but his space was tidy and homey.

I didn't yet know Maura well, even after nine months with Charlie. She was shy—always polite to me, but quiet, like she didn't know what to say. When she'd made plans to go to prom a couple of months prior with a boy she'd met in Bible study, I prattled on and on about how much fun I had at mine, even though I went with Bridget in lieu of a date. I was desperate to make Maura respond, to grin, to say anything, but she never asked for more detail. She only sat there, hands folded in her lap.

You intimidate her, Charlie had told me later that night. I was sure I'd misheard him. *You're the first girl I've brought around my family. She doesn't know what to think of you. She says you're so pretty it makes her feel homely. Her word. Not mine.*

To fully understand the delusions of this girl, you have to know what this "homely" teenager looked like: She wore her golden hair super long, straight down her back, and she seemed to possess some of that innate fashion sense that teenage Bridget had had, too, though with the sex appeal toned down. While the rest of Maura's peers ran around in low-rise jeans that flashed the top inch of ass crack to the world, chunky belts further tugging their jeans toward the floor, with white eye shadow that even Hollywood makeup artists could not make attractive, there was my boyfriend's sister in jeans that fit without showing too much curve. She loved the gauzy top trend, but instead of making her into an amorphous gut with legs, these shirts flattered her figure. She forewent the chunky, plastic baubles and instead veered toward simple chain necklaces with small gemstones. She had them in every color.

And don't even get me started on those dimples. Plural. As in one per cheek. When I was little, I wanted dimples badly. I once spent a weekend walking around, sucking in my cheeks like I was a fish. Finally my dad asked what I was doing, and when I told him, to his credit, he didn't laugh at me. He calmly placed me on his lap and explained I could not actually *give* myself dimples, that they were made by a tear in the muscle and were doled out genetically, like a hitchhiker's thumb or the ability to curl a tongue.

I was crushed and have hated all dimpled goddesses since—except Teen Maura, who I desperately wanted to like me. She may have been shy, but she was sweet. Case in point: She voluntarily spent that weekend taking care of her sick big brother.

I arrived at The Lighthouse at seven, feeling stupendous. You know how some nights, you're getting ready, and it all *clicks*? How some nights, you have to try on five different outfits, and none of them feel right or good or beautiful? But this night was a beautiful night. This night was a confidence night.

Which is exactly how it should be when you're out for a night with the girls. I'm not sure hetero men understand it, but when women dress up, it's not for them. It's for ourselves, mainly, and, secondly, for our girlfriends. No one will appreciate a well-fitting shirt or some pretty purply lipstick like a girlfriend. Before I left the house, I sauntered for Bridget, who catcalled at my new jeans, which made my butt look great, even if I couldn't wear underwear because, again, holy low-rise, Batman. She gushed at my over-the-knee boots and my silky striped top that somehow made my flat chest look like it was at least trying. She reached behind her neck to remove the chunky silver chain she wore and added it to my ensemble.

I'd assumed my coworker's party would consist of a small group of friends with a few significant others scattered about. Instead, Sonja had apparently invited every person she'd ever known and rented out the entire pub. A row of food lined the side wall buffet-style: fried fish, hush puppies, shrimp. When people approached the bar, the bartender handed them a beer without being asked or paid. There was even a DJ and a small dance floor.

"ASHA, YOU MADE IT!" I heard from across the room. Sonja, decked out in a hot-pink birthday sash and pointy, askew party hat, rushed at me, crashed into me, and wrapped me up in a hug.

"Happy birthday, So," I said, handing her a card. "It's not enough. Look at this place!"

"It's not my birthday. It's my NAME day," she said, tugging on her sash, which proclaimed exactly that in her drawn-on letters: HAPPY NAME DAY.

Apparently, in Slavic countries—Sonja's parents emigrated from Croatia—a person's name day corresponds to a saint's day, and Catholics celebrate Saint Sonja Day on September 22. I have no idea whether other Croatian people celebrate name days like this, but it certainly fit Sonja.

I found a few other girls I knew from work talking to some of Sonja's cousins, and before I knew it, we were the first people dancing. Throughout the night, I had flashes to junior high, partying and sweating with my girlfriends, swaying with Jason, getting lost in the dark and the music. The only difference was Tony Rich had been replaced by Nelly Furtado and Justin Timberlake.

I took a breather for a beer, and as I leaned back on the bar to survey the room, a man next to me said, "When it comes on, you should let me teach you the folk dance."

I turned to him, and my breath caught. This guy had short, beautiful black hair, and he wore a two-day scruff that should have made him look homeless but instead turned him into the cover of a trashy romance novel. I have never been into beefy, muscular men—the guys I'm attracted to tend to run lean—but he looked like he could bench-press me. A tattoo peeked out from beneath one short sleeve of his polo shirt.

I wanted to say *no, thank you,* but instead, without deciding to, without wanting to, I giggled. I swear to you, it popped out, like when you think you're going to toot a little and it's actually more of a shart. The giggle was equally as wanted as a shart, too.

"Marko," he said, and looked at me, waiting. When I said nothing, he prompted, "And what is your name? How do you know my cousin?"

"We work together," I shouted over the music.

He waited again, and then he repeated, "What's your name?"

I said, "I'm Asha," as the oh-so-subtle "Buttons," courtesy of The Pussycat Dolls, transitioned over to something featuring a whole lot of plucked strings. A portion of the crowd—Sonja's family members, I assumed—bum-rushed the stage, pairing off into couples. I saw Sonja grab Gordon, one of the designers we worked with, by his sweatshirt hood to drag him to the center of the room.

"Come on," Marko said, and he took my hand. Before I knew it, I was participating in a choreographed dance no one had ever taught me. Luckily, a good chunk of the other dancers looked as clueless as I was.

Sometimes Marko and I faced each other, his right hand on my waist, my left hand on his shoulder. We held the other's remaining hand, and we sort of hopped around the dance floor, spinning as we went. After one spin, Marko released me and started a complicated series of foot stomps and hand claps. Gordon and I caught eyes and made *help me* faces at the other.

After, the DJ switched back to popular music—bless you, Shakira—and Marko groaned when I thanked him and walked off the dance floor.

"Those beers are too free," I told him. "I need some food."

He built a plate, too, and we found an empty tabletop to stand at while we ate. I learned he was in town for the party, and he was a banker in Louisville.

"Really?" I said, looking him over. Nothing about this guy said "banker" to me.

He seemed to read my mind. "I know. My parents' doing."

"You didn't want to be a banker?"

"It made them happy," he said, shrugging. "I don't mind. It's nice to have weekends off and work a normal schedule."

He asked what I did and what it was like to work with Sonja. We talked about college and how badly he hoped to travel to Croatia the following summer to see the village where his great-grandparents met. He asked about my hobbies and perked up when I said I liked to run. He wondered why I'd never run a marathon or even a 5K.

"The competition doesn't interest me," I said. He reacted as though I'd said, *I slit puppy throats on weekends.*

After an hour I realized how much I liked talking to him. I didn't want to take him home. I didn't even want to see him naked—well, not beyond the way you want to see any hot person naked. I was simply enjoying myself.

You are not doing anything wrong, I promised myself. At midnight, as the DJ announced last call and swapped to a Kelly Clarkson ballad, Marko asked me to dance.

It was a dance so chaste that, about halfway through the song, Sonja ducked beneath our arms and popped up in the middle. For a bit she placed her head on her cousin's shoulder, and the three of us danced, and then, for another bit, she spun around and wrapped her arms around my neck.

When the song ended, as I pulled out my phone to call a cab— Uber wouldn't be founded for another three years—Marko's phone was already in his hand. "Let me call for you," he said.

"I got it," I protested, but when the lights flickered on, I stumbled. Why do bars do that? You've got to bring on the lights *gradually*.

"Let me call you a cab," he repeated, holding on to my shoulder to steady me.

Ten minutes later, we stood outside the pub. His hotel was around the corner, but he insisted on waiting with me.

"It's midnight in the city. I'm not leaving you out here alone."

"I appreciate the chivalry, but I promise, it's OK. I'm fine."

"OK," he said, but he didn't leave.

While we waited, I stared at the bottom of the tattoo I could see on his arm, and he caught me looking. He raised the rest of his sleeve, and I let out a little gasp. "It's an evil eye."

"For protection," he said. "You're familiar with it?"

I fished the tiny gold necklace my father had given me years before from beneath Bridget's oversize necklace. "I never take it off."

He smiled at me as the cab pulled up. I knew that smile. I had smiled that smile. And now it was time to go.

"It was good to meet you, Marko," I said, sticking out my hand, making it very clear that this was the only goodbye I was willing to give.

Instead of shaking my hand, he brought it to his lips and kissed it softly.

"You too, Asha." And he walked away.

I got in the cab, buzzing. *Damn damn damnshit damn.* Instead of going home, I gave the driver Charlie's address. I tried to text him that I was on my way, but in my inebriation, I couldn't get the letters right. I'd had my Razr flip phone for two years by then, but I never did manage to get the hang of texting on the nine-button keypad. To type a *B*, for instance, I had to hit the "one" twice. For an *R*, the "six" three times.

Twenty minutes later, I silently let myself into his apartment—Charlie'd given me a key a month prior—and eased myself down on the corner of the convertible couch-bed to kiss my sick boyfriend hello.

Instead, I sat on Maura, who let out a squeak, like a kitten with a stepped-on tail. I jumped up, and she flicked on the lamp next to the couch.

"Charlie's in my room. I thought he should have a real bed. I'll go get him."

"No, no, Maura. Please, stay here. I can go to him."

"It's a twin bed."

"Or I can sleep on the floor. Maybe there's some stuffed animals I can cuddle with."

That got a smile out of her, at least, though not big enough to showcase those dimples. I made my way into the kitchen for a glass of water.

"You look really pretty," she said. "Were you at a party?"

"It was my friend's name day," I told her, avoiding eye contact. "Croatian custom. It was at a pub downtown."

"Did you drink?" she asked.

I looked up, and she stared at me, wide eyed. "Have you ever had alcohol, Maura?" She shook her head. "Would you like to try some?"

She paused for a moment, then nodded almost imperceptibly.

I opened Charlie's fridge, and . . . aha: a half bottle of rosé I'd opened for dinner two nights ago. I took down two wineglasses and filled each a quarter of the way.

"It's pretty sweet," I said as she chugged it down. "Take it easy!"

She swallowed and made a face. "That was gross."

"Want more?"

She held out her wineglass, and I filled it halfway this time. She sipped in silence for a few minutes before she blurted out, "Charlie really likes you."

"I really like him, too."

"He, like, loves you."

"I, like, love him, too."

She looked at me like she wanted to say more.

"Is that OK with you?" I asked gently. I was certain she was going to tell me I wasn't good enough for her big brother or that she hated me.

Instead, she whispered, "I think I love a boy."

Maura and I stayed up all night gossiping about Ritter, a cute boy in her math class. As soon as she got talking, she wouldn't stop. I think this was the first time she'd let herself verbalize any of her feelings; she was embarrassed to talk to her girlfriends about him.

"My friends are kind of mean. They make fun of me when I talk to him."

"Sounds like they're jealous."

"They'd never be jealous!" She looked horrified.

"Have any of *them* had boyfriends before?" She shook her head. "They're jealous. It's OK. They'll get over it. In the meantime, tell *me* about Ritter. I won't be jealous. I promise."

"Promise you won't tell Charlie?"

"Charlie who?" And she laughed. I liked making her laugh.

Maura had only one full glass of rosé, but she'd never had wine before and couldn't have weighed more than a hundred pounds. It didn't take long for her eyelids to droop and her conversation to turn straight confessional.

That was when things got a little dark.

"It's not just my friends. I'm afraid to like Ritter because the last time I kissed a boy it was my first kiss and my dad almost died."

To this day, I am proud of myself for not spit-taking my wine. My mouth formed the first sounds of *What?* but I was so confused I couldn't even make myself say the word.

"He had a heart attack, you know," she said.

"I remember. Charlie told me he's healing really well. The doctors said it was a mild one? And he'll be on some medicine for a while?"

Maura pursed her lips—an expression that would one day become her go-to face when I was around—and closed her eyes. Tears started to trickle down her cheeks, then flood. She inhaled a huge sob, and I hurried to the bathroom to get a box of tissues for her. I put my arm around her shoulder, and she ugly cried until it was all out.

"It was after lunch," she said after she could speak without gasping. "I knew Jonathan had a crush on me. He's cute, but I don't like him like *that*. He kept getting closer and closer to me. And I've never kissed anyone before, and I'm a *senior*, so I just reached up and kissed him. It was sort of fun, so when he kissed me again, we made out a little. Mr. Barnes came out and yelled at us, and we ran down the hall to world history. Jonathan sat behind me and kept playing with my hair all through class. The notes I took don't make any sense. I started sentences and didn't finish them. I usually color-code everything with different pens, and it's all in orange ink, so trying to study from it is totally impossible.

"On the bus ride home, I couldn't stop thinking about the kiss. I'd never looked at Jonathan like that before, but . . ." She stopped speaking here, and another sob escaped. ". . . but I *liked* it. And then I got home, and a few hours later, I started to make dinner because on Thursdays, Mom has to work late. She gets home even later than Dad. And I was so lost in thinking about that *stupid* kiss that I didn't even notice that Dad wasn't home yet, and Mom gets home, and she's like, 'Where's Dad?' and I didn't have any idea. She keeps her cell phone off at work, and she finally looked at it, and there were like a hundred missed calls, and he'd collapsed at work, and it was like right around the time I was kissing Jonathan, and I know it's my fault."

She said these final words from behind her hands, which she'd pressed flat to her face, and I tightened my hold on her shoulders while I tried to figure out what to say. That this was the most absurd thing I had ever heard would not be helpful, but I needed Maura to know that her kissing a boy had no bearing on her father's health. What on earth had made her think it had?

"People kiss each other all the time, and it doesn't make anyone ill," I said. "And people have heart attacks even if they don't have any kids, when there are no teenagers to get their first kisses." I paused. "Why do you think the two are connected?"

"In Bible study, we talked about how in Deuteronomy, we learn that we pay for the sins of our ancestors. I figured that means bad things happen to us because of what our family does."

"Charlie mentioned you'd started going to Bible study," I said, mainly because I had no idea how to respond to this.

"I started after Dad's heart attack. It was so scary. I just needed . . ." She shrugged a shoulder, looking down. "I needed something. It's been really helpful."

"That's great," I told her, "but—and I know that's not what it says in Deuteronomy—I promise, no matter what, it's not sinful to kiss people."

"How do you know?" she whispered. "I know you and Charlie kiss. I've seen you. Aren't you worried that something bad will happen?"

"Oh, Maura," I said, and I wrapped her up in my arms and hugged her tightly. "Kissing your brother is a really beautiful thing. I don't ever wonder that something bad will happen because of it."

"Is that because you're meant to be?"

"I don't think so."

"You're meant to be with someone else? Then why are you with Charlie?"

"No, there's no one else. I just don't really believe in that stuff."

She pulled away from my hug, truly stunned. She asked, "Charlie's not your soulmate?"

"That doesn't mean I don't love him. But I don't believe in soulmates. I think we fall in love and decide for ourselves if we want to commit to that love or not."

I eventually learned that Maura and I each walked away from that conversation with very different opinions of how things had gone. I thought we'd had our first meaningful conversation, that we'd maybe opened up the gates to be close to one another. For Maura, however, the first Asha Is a Slut seed had been planted. It didn't sprout right away. No, it was like a corpse flower, that famed flora that smells of rotting flesh and blooms once every seven to nine years. It takes forever, but when it finally opens, whoo—what a show.

The next morning my boyfriend woke me up. He wore a blanket draped on his head like a shawl, and his nose was red and dry. He found me and his sister sprawled in his pull-out bed, the empty bottle of rosé on its side on the floor, joined by a second bottle of white I'd found in the fridge.

"You got my sister drunk, you lush," he scolded me.

"I'm the worst," I murmured.

That evening I lounged in the same bed, this time with Charlie instead of his little sister, as he flipped through the channels mindlessly. He didn't notice that I was next to him, silently freaking out. Out of the blue, I blurted out my indiscretion from the previous night at the bar.

"And I'm so, so sorry," I finished.

"Wait . . . you're telling me you danced with some guy in front of a room full of people, most of them his family, and then he kissed your *hand*?" he asked. "And you're apologizing *why*?"

"Do you hate me?"

"For what?"

"I don't know. Aren't you mad?"

"Do you want me to beat him up?"

"Charlie, I'm serious!"

"OK, seriously. I don't love that he kissed your hand. But what do I have to be mad about? Is there more I'm missing? Did you guys do it in the bathroom? After he kissed your hand, did you stick it down his pants? Did you trade personal cell phone numbers to have crazy phone sex at three p.m. in your cubicle? Ash, don't worry about it."

My mind flashed to my childhood and to Craig, to how much unnecessary angst he had caused between Jason and me. Craig was my friend, and he was only ever my friend. But Jason held that friendship over my head dozens of times during our relationship.

Charlie, meanwhile, trusted me completely. He had a sweet little sister I was desperate to get to know, even if she had some bizarre thoughts on love and the Bible. He had the kind of relationship with his parents where he could live above their garage without being smothered by them. They gave him his space. Charlie was a Boy Scout, literally. We were compatible in so many ways. He never pushed me. He supported me. He was the kind of amazing in bed that I could be happy with forever.

I thought about protection. I thought about Marko's tattoo, and I fingered the small necklace against my collarbone. And I knew: Charlie would always, always safeguard my heart. Isn't that what's most important?

"What is going on in that head?" he asked.

"Do you want to marry me?"

"What?"

"Do you want to marry me?"

He looked at me completely confused for a moment, his eyes searching my face. Then he realized I meant it, and he flashed me that toothpaste smile.

"You're serious?"

"Yup."

"OK."

"OK?"

"Yeah. Yes. Yes," he said, and he kissed me. "Let's do it. Let's get married."

SPRING (1997)

My dad fell asleep within moments of the plane taking off, and I watched Cincinnati shrink before me. I watched the buildings become the size of toy blocks, the roads and highways like concrete-colored ribbons winding through deep green. I wondered where my house was, and I started counting swimming pools, small rectangles that stood out like aqua highway signs dotted on the shrinking landscape.

I pulled out the book I was reading and flipped to the front to look at a photo Jason had given me as he hugged me goodbye earlier that afternoon. It was the photo we had taken at his family's Christmas party, in his room. I stare into the camera with a wide smile. Jason faces forward, but he looks at me. His smile is not as large as mine, but it reaches his eyes. They're squinty and happy.

I didn't know that Dad had woken up, but I jumped when he said, "I see you are talking to Jason again."

"I think so."

Dad waited for me to continue, and I did not oblige. He asked, "Is there more?"

"More?"

"Is he your boyfriend again?" His face registered disdain when he said "boyfriend."

"Yeah. He's my boyfriend again."

"And this makes you happy?"

"Very. I really like him, Dad."

"He is nice to you? He wasn't very nice before. Did he apologize to you?"

He hadn't, actually. It hadn't even occurred to me that he *should*. Should he?

"He's being very nice now," I said instead.

"Mmm." I wasn't sure what that meant, and I didn't ask.

Dad stayed for a couple of nights at my grandparents' before heading home. Alone with my nana and papa, I saw a lazy summer stretched ahead of me. I had books, swimming (but still no diving), and my oldest friends, who'd lived across the street from my grandparents since I was little.

Craig and Heather were twins, with matching short, white-blond haircuts. Each tanned deeply in the summer sun, which made their gray eyes pop.

The three of us developed an easy routine that summer—they'd knock on my grandparents' door after lunch, and we'd walk down to the beach a few blocks away. Heather and I always loved to put our towels on the damp part of the sand, where the waves could periodically lap our toes and shins. Every so often, a larger wave would splash up to our waists or even up over our heads. I loved that surprise; Heather hated it.

Which was par for the course; Heather tended to hate everything I loved—music, movies, celebrities—and she looked forward to telling me so.

"You like the Spice Girls?" she asked, wrinkling her nose. She rolled her eyes and said the Fugees was the *only* band on the radio that didn't suck.

We talked about school, and she actually said something nice to me: that she liked my bracelet. It was my Jason bracelet, which I hadn't taken off since I got to Florida.

"My boyfriend gave it to me," I said, feeling the weight of the words *my boyfriend* in my mouth. I hadn't gotten to use those words since my dad asked me about it on the airplane, and it felt different than it had the first time Jason and I dated. Like it was more serious. Or I was more mature. Or *we* were more serious or mature. Or in love.

"You have a boyfriend?" That was mostly how she talked to me—repeating what I had said, but turning it into a question, as if doubting its veracity or mocking me. "Have you kissed him?"

"Kissed who?" Craig asked, plopping down next to me. He'd been building sandcastles with his young cousins, who were visiting.

"Asha's *boyfriend*."

"You have a boyfriend?" Craig's question lacked the meanness of his sister's tone. Instead, he looked curious.

"It's no big deal," I mumbled.

"Well, *I'm* hungry," Heather announced, standing and marching toward her parents and uncle, who had set up camp farther down the beach.

"Dad said we can rent a movie tonight," he said. "Want to come over and watch it with us after the cousins go to bed?"

"Think it'd be OK?" I asked, watching Heather as she dug through the cooler and pulled out a sandwich.

"Don't mind her. She's a total bitch."

"That's not very nice!" I couldn't believe he'd called his sister a bitch, but he was nonplussed.

"Neither is she. I wondered when you'd notice."

"You're together all the time."

"She's my best friend," he confirmed. "But that doesn't change anything: She's a bitch."

We went for a quick swim before joining Heather to get our lunch, too. I rushed ahead to grab his towel before he could get it.

"Give it back!" Craig pleaded, but I'd already wrapped it around me.

"Oops, did I use the wrong one?" I asked, peering down at his Miami Heat towel. "Here, use mine."

Craig sighed, then proceeded to towel off with the Barbie towel I'd used at my grandparents' since I was seven years old.

That night, we watched *Candyman*, and Craig laughed at me because I watched from behind a pillow.

"You're missing it. Take the pillow down!" he demanded, trying to wrestle it from me.

"This movie is for babies," Heather announced, but she brought her legs to her chest as Helen Lyle stood quietly in her bathroom, the score little more than a raspy exhale. When the silence was shattered by Candyman's hook smashing through the medicine cabinet, Heather jumped and nearly fell off the couch. Craig and I burst out laughing.

It wasn't mean-spirited, I swear. We were all jittery, and we'd all jumped. But Heather didn't like feeling like the butt of a joke, and she stomped away with a huffy "I'm tired. Good night."

Craig and I watched the rest of the movie alone, giggling nervously whenever we got scared, which was basically the whole rest of the movie.

The next day the phone rang.

"*Brated Nana*, it's for you. It's a boy." My grandmother handed me the phone, giving me a sassy look.

Why would Craig call me? He lived across the street.

Instead of saying *hello*, I said into the phone, in my scariest voice, "Be my victim," and was floored when Jason responded, after a beat, "Hi, Asha."

"Jason!" I nearly shouted, then said, softer, "Hold on . . . Nana, is it OK if I take this upstairs?"

She shooed me away, and I took the stairs two at a time. At the top of the stairs, I didn't take a big enough leap, and I smashed my big toe into the top stair, hard.

"Want me to kiss it and make it better?" Jason asked, sounding unusually serious.

"Ew, why would you want to kiss my feet?"

"I'd kiss your feet. I'd kiss all of you."

I wasn't sure I'd heard him right, but instead of asking for more detail, I changed the subject. "How'd you get my number here?"

"I asked your dad."

146

"You called him?"

"I knocked on the door."

"You went to my house?"

"I thought it'd be better than calling. I thought I'd hear from you."
It's only been a week, I thought.

"I felt funny asking my grandparents," I said, making something up on the spot, and then I switched to brutal honesty: "But I'm very happy you called me."

He told me about his summer. Gaby had gotten her first job, scooping ice cream at The Twist, and his dad had taken him and Daniel to a drive-in movie the previous night.

"I want to go to a drive-in," I said. "I've never been. What was it like?"

"It was cool. They show double features, and we were there really late. I wished you were there."

"You did?"

"I miss you a lot."

"I miss you, too," I said. "And I actually mean it."

"You sure you're not lying to me?" he said, teasing.

"That's weird for me," I protested. "I don't really miss people. Craig and Heather asked me if I missed them, and I didn't know what to say. It's like I almost forgot about them when I moved. Isn't that bad? But I think about you all the time, especially at the beach. I go with Craig and Heather, and I definitely wish you were there."

"Who's Craig?"

"He and Heather live across the street. They were my best friends before I moved."

"What's he like?"

"Craig's nice. A lot nicer than Heather. Heather's kind of a bitch," I whispered. "Even Craig says so, even though they're twins. Oh my god, we watched the scariest movie last night, *Candyman*. Heather chickened out halfway through, but me and Craig made it to the end. I thought it was him; that's why I answered the phone that way."

147

"You're friends with Craig?"

"I'm friends with them both. Heather's not all bad. We all hang out together."

"Do you think he's cute?"

"Who?"

"Craig."

"I guess? His hair's super, super blond. It's almost white, kind of like an old man's." It dawned on me what Jason was getting at. "Jason? Are you jealous?"

"No," he said quickly. "No, it sounds like you guys really get along."

"He's my friend," I said. "You're sweet."

"I'm not sweet."

"You are sweet," I protested, and I lowered my voice. I knew my grandparents were both downstairs, but I didn't want to risk being overheard. "I love you."

"You do?"

"I told you that."

He was silent, and I thought again that we'd never really talked about everything that had happened, and my dad's words from the plane echoed in my head: *He wasn't very nice before. Did he apologize to you?*

"I kind of want to talk to you about something," I said. "You were really mean to me. Before."

Jason said, so softly I could hardly hear him, "I know."

"That really hurt. You know how much you meant to me."

"I know," he said again.

"Why did you do that to me?"

"I don't know," he mumbled, and I repeated the question: "But why?"

"Ineverlovedanyoneelsebefore," he said quickly. I was getting good at deciphering his speed language, and his words made me smile.

"Me neither. That's why it took me a while. I've never felt this before. I didn't know what it was. I don't want you to be mean to me again if I don't know what to say to something. Or if I'm friends with a boy."

"I trust you," he said. "Do you trust me?"

"I think so. I want to."

"But you don't."

"I mean, I do. I just . . . I don't want it to happen like last time. And four girls is a lot."

"It's not like you and me were still together. And . . ."

"What?"

"I didn't like kissing them. I mean, it was fun, but—"

"I don't really want to hear this."

"—but I kept thinking about you."

"When you were kissing someone else?"

"Yeah. It felt wrong. I missed you."

I was silent. I had no idea how to process this. I didn't like thinking about Jason with other girls, but I didn't think I should be angry. And the idea that he hadn't even been thinking about them? Even when they owned the other pair of lips involved? I felt a little bad for them—and a lot . . . flattered? Giddy? Happy? Yes. I think I was simply *happy*. To learn that he'd missed me. To learn that other people didn't make him as happy as I did. I was *happy*.

"Do you remember that dance in your living room?" he asked. Of course I did. "I'd give anything to hold you like that, right now."

To an almost-fourteen-year-old girl, there is no more romantic sentiment in all the world.

The next day Craig, his dad, his cousins, and his uncle went on a fishing trip. Heather didn't want to go, and she called to see if I wanted to come over. Craig always knocked on the door, but Heather used the phone.

Her room seemed grown-up to me, and it made me feel like a little kid. She had pictures of guys she called "hotties" all over her wall: Rider Strong, Josh Hartnett, and my favorite, Jonathan Taylor Thomas. I still had posters from Disney movies on my walls at home.

"Let's play Truth or Dare," she said.

"Dare."

"No, you have to pick 'truth.'"

"But the game is called Truth or *Dare*."

"Fine, let's just play Truth. Are you a virgin?"

"Oh my god!" I didn't answer her for a few beats. She took my shock for reluctance.

"God, you're lucky. Is it awesome?"

"Is what awesome?"

"Sex!"

"I don't know! I've never *done it*."

"Oh." I swear, in my memory, she actually looked down her nose at me.

"Have you?"

"Well . . . sort of."

"How can you be sort of a virgin?"

"Me and my ex, Derek, we *almost* went all the way. He really wanted to. But we did other stuff."

"Like what?"

"I gave him a blow job once."

I was horrified. Or was I fascinated? "What was it like?"

"It was really slimy. And super skinny, like a hot dog."

I thought Heather was the absolute coolest. I mean, I had a friend who'd not just seen a dick but *put it in her mouth*. Clearly it didn't take much to impress me. But I didn't want to seem too eager, so all I said was, "Ew."

"Definitely ew. But he said it was amazing. He said it was the best one he ever got. And he would know. He's, like, the captain of the football team."

"Why'd you break up?"

"So if you have any questions about sex, I can help." She'd completely ignored my question.

When I got home, I asked my grandmother if Papa and I could go to the mall. I wanted to buy some stationery so I could write to Bridget.

Before my dad and I moved to Ohio, Papa always took me to the mall. When it was too hot outside to walk, Papa walked the mall, long before women in tight pants and sweatshirts started to meet outside department stores to pump their arms and raise their knees in unison. Our final stop was always Cinnabon, where we'd share a sweet, warm mess. Without fail, he gave me the center swirl, which was the softest, gooiest part. Papa's sweet tooth was legendary—he often ate dessert before his dinner—and as I grew older, I saw his insistence that I take the sweetest part of the roll as his "I love you."

We walked together around the first floor of the mall, making two laps in companionable silence.

"Can we go upstairs?" I asked him, pointing up.

He nodded. "Ya, ya. Let's go."

I raced up the winding stairs and waited for Papa at the top. He ambled up slowly, and he smiled when he caught me looking for him.

I stepped into G. Thanks and left my grandfather seated on the edge of a small fountain.

"Ten minutes," I promised him, holding up both my hands, fingers splayed. "Ten minutes."

I loved looking at the stationery. I liked to sift through the pretty paper, peek into envelopes with bright-blue or striped insides. I selected a lined set with little palm trees in the corner and pale-yellow envelopes. I pulled the plastic wallet from my denim purse and handed the cashier two five-dollar bills. He gave me my change.

As I walked out of the store, I held up the dollar bills to my grandfather.

"Cinnabon!" I announced, and he nodded. "I want to treat. I will pay."

He nodded again. He still didn't let me pay. And he ordered extra icing.

AUTUMN (2017)

I cannot explain why I've decided to tell Maura the news *now*, hours before going to a dinner I'd never tell her about. In fact, I'd sooner go to church with her every day for a month before I'd even hint at anything having to do with Jason. Am I possessed or something? Maybe it's the nice feeling of something new going on, something different, something curious. It's the feeling of *something*. I've been trapped in *nothing* for so long that I want to take advantage of this momentum.

When I pull into the parking lot and spot Maura's car, a vehicle I have actively hidden from weekly for something like ten months, I nearly balk.

Remember the girl who told off Kendra Perkins, I think. *Channel that little badass. You're still her. You're still a badass.*

I focus all my awareness on putting the car into park, turning it off. Unbuckling my seat belt. Opening the car door, locking it, closing the car door. Putting my right foot in front of my left, stepping over the curb, step by step by step through the double doors of Pax Nursing & Rehab.

Madison is working again. "Three times in one week?" she teases, then pauses. "You know she's in there."

"I know. If you hear screaming, call security." I am only half joking.

Maura doesn't see me at first. I stand in the doorway of the dim room and watch her. She is in my seat. She faces Charlie, clutches his hand with her left. With her right, she holds her phone, reads aloud from some kind of app or note:

"You shall not make for yourself an image in the form of anything in heaven above or on the earth beneath or in the waters below. You shall not bow down to them or worship them; for I, the Lord your God, am a jealous God, punishing the children for the sin of the parents to the third and fourth generation of those who hate me, but showing love to a thousand generations of those who love me and keep my commandments."

This does not surprise me; Maura believes, in her heart, that Charlie's coma is payment for his family's sins. For my sins. For the sins that I pray, if I prayed, she hasn't told her parents about.

I shift my purse onto my other arm, and the soft rustle startles Maura. Her head snaps up. She drops Charlie's hand and reaches for her throat, her fingers landing on the small silver cross Charlie and I gave her as a bridesmaid's gift when we got married.

"Oh," she exhales, stammers. "Asha, I . . ." She takes a deep breath, composes herself. "We were reciting Deuteronomy. Join us?"

"No, thank you. Charlie never liked that verse." Charlie and I have never talked about that verse, or any verse of any holy book, but there is no way he'd have agreed with the sentiment. A jealous god bequeathing punishment on the innocent? Please.

Maura inhales sharply, and I see her narrow body tense up.

"Maybe Proverbs will be more to your liking," she says, and she recites from memory, *"Trust in the Lord with all your heart and lean not on your own understanding; in all your ways submit to him, and he will make your paths straight."*

"How are you, Maura?"

"Every day is a gift."

"And Charlie's a pretty spectacular gift, isn't he?"

She grins, in spite of herself. "I knew you were a fan of Love Abides. I hope it gives you peace? Some comfort?"

I dodge her question and instead ask, "How are *you?*"

She looks at me, puzzled. "How can I be anything but joyful?"

"Well, I'm awful. I miss my husband."

"I'll pray for you," she says. She's so goddamned *earnest*. "Maybe if we prayed together, God might hear better?" She is smiling at me, incredibly hopeful. She thinks it will work. She thinks God is listening, that he will fix Charlie.

Remember Kendra Perkins, I repeat to myself, and I dive right in: "I got some news at Charlie's care plan meeting a couple weeks ago." Maura is invited to the meetings—all family members are—but she puts little faith in modern medicine, and his parents haven't shown up in ages. It's too hard for them. "He's been having some breathing episodes. It didn't happen often at first, but it's happening more now. He stops breathing for a few seconds at a time."

"This is an inappropriate time to discuss this," she says, placing her hands on either side of Charlie's head, covering his ears. Her face is pure worry, eyebrows knit together, corners of her mouth turned down. "Let's go get some coffees."

"No, Maura, we need to talk about this now. Charlie can't hear us."

"The doctors have always said he might be able to hear us." She believes doctors when it's good news. When it's bad news, they're nothing but charlatans and stooges. As far as defense mechanisms go, it certainly keeps her hopeful.

"Fine. If I'm wrong and he can, he'd be happy I'm telling you this." I untuck the bottom of Charlie's blanket and show Maura his feet. "Do you see that?"

She looks at his toes, and I rub my thumb over the nail on his big toe. I trim his nails every other week, and they're due. Maura asks, "What is that? Why are they purple?"

It first happens on the feet, his nurse told me, and then it travels up the legs. It happens because the heart is no longer able to effectively pump blood to Charlie's extremities. It doesn't hurt, but it means just one thing.

"It's called mottling. Maura, he's dying." I have no more tears left—when they told me at his care meeting, they showed me how to breathe through my cupped hands to ease my hyperventilating.

"When?"

"They don't know for sure. Soon."

"Why didn't you tell me before? I could have been doubling up on my prayers for him. Asha, it's like you don't even want him to get better." She has not raised her voice. She is not yelling at me. She's not even speaking through gritted teeth. She is all concern, all worry. She sincerely believes that by preventing her prayers, I have doomed my husband for more suffering. I don't even think he's suffering anymore. He's not in there. Like the Buddhist monks believe, it's only his vessel. Maybe I should chop him up and put him on a mountain. I stifle a grin and hear Charlie's laughter in my head.

I think of an idea once hotly debated in an intro to philosophy class: that living is suffering and surviving is, somehow, finding meaning in life. I'm not sure about the meaning of life, but I'm certain that suffering is for me, and it's for Maura—it's not for Charlie.

"I've added a 'do not resuscitate' to his file," I say.

"You can't do that." Her composure cracks, and her body starts trembling. It's how it always is with Maura—she doesn't ramp up or ease into her anger; she jumps from zero to Hulk in the time it takes to blink her eyes. I know what's coming next.

"I'm his next of kin," I say.

"You're a slut." *There it is.* Her voice is shrill, her eyes wild. She stands up. "This is your fault. This is your fault."

"I will remove you from the visitation list if you do not apologize."

"You wouldn't dare. *Slut.*"

"I would." I mean it. As Charlie's next of kin, I provide Pax with a list of approved visitors. I've thought long and hard about taking Maura's name off that list, but as much as I dislike her, as much as I disagree with her, as much as I know that she blames me for Charlie's coma, I can't do that to her. Charlie is more than Maura's brother; he's her Bridget. I think that's one of the reasons she hates me: Charlie might be Maura's best friend, but I was his. Am his. Was.

I ask again: "Apologize to me."

She closes her eyes and murmurs, "Dear God, please open my heart so that I might be filled with the forgiveness of the Holy Spirit. Please grant me the strength to love Asha despite her sins, the way you love us despite our sins. Please open Asha's mind and heart to your glory so she might know the power of your healing love." She slowly blinks, looks at me with tears shining in her eyes, and holds her hand out to me as she says, "Asha, I am incredibly sorry."

Funny, Maura has never apologized to me. I used to wish she would, used to think I would find some sort of solace in the words, in her recognition that, yes, maybe I was wrong, but she's not perfect, either.

Today the words have finally come, and I find that they are empty. They weigh nothing. They are nothing.

SPRING (1997)

One sunny weekday afternoon, my grandparents and I visited the
Hillsboro Inlet Lighthouse. Nana waited on the beach while Papa and
I climbed the stairs to the top. I felt like I could see all the way across
the ocean, to . . . what's straight across from southern Florida? Could
I go there someday?

When Papa and I stepped back out into the salty air a half hour
later, Nana reached for us from a bench facing the water.

"Come, sit by me, *brated Nana*." I sat to her right, and Papa to
her left. He put his arm around her and settled into the bench, staring
straight out into the ocean, as I had done from the top of the lighthouse.

"Do you know why this lighthouse is very important?" Nana asked,
and I shook my head. "Your father proposed to your mother up there."

"He did?"

They were nineteen years old. He had loved her since they shared
that ice pop nine years prior. Nana said before he proposed, he went to
Vicki's house and asked her father's permission. He would not give it.

"Your father was crushed. He did not know what to do. I told him,
'Adam, do you love this girl?' And he said yes, he loved her very much. I
said, 'Will you be a good husband to this girl?' And he said, 'She is my
ruhama,' his beloved. And I told him, 'Then you should be with her.
She should get to decide, *bruni*.'"

"He did not have very much money, but he was very smart." I
nodded. My dad always tried to get me to play Trivial Pursuit with

him. After twenty minutes, I wound up reading the questions to him one by one, the game board forgotten. "He could have gone to school anywhere, but he chose to study in Boca Raton to stay close to Vicki. She did not go to school. She found work as a typist for a law firm."

I had heard all this before, but the proposal was new, as was my other grandfather's refusal to give my dad his blessing. I had never met my mother's parents; whenever I asked about them, my father said, *We do not speak,* in the kind of voice that made it clear that there was no more to say about that.

"Adam and Vicki were on a date, and he took her to the top of the lighthouse. It was her favorite spot in town, she said, because she liked to look over the water and pretend to get in a boat and sail out to sea. Where would she land?"

I inhaled a sharp breath. *My mother and I shared an idea,* I thought, and I held it tenderly in my mind's palm. I promised myself I would find out: If I boarded a boat that could sail in both my world and hers, if we launched from the Hillsboro Inlet Lighthouse and headed due east, where would we end up?

"Your father said they both stood at the glass, staring into the ocean, and he took her hand. And he said, 'Vicki, will—' and she said, 'Yes, Adam, of course I will marry you.' He had no idea how she knew what he was going to say. He took a small gold band from his pocket, my mother's ring, and he placed it on her finger.

"'How did you know?' he asked.

"'My dad told me.' For one of the few times in his life, my son experienced anger. He said he wanted to march up to that man and shout at him. He wanted to call him horrible things. He wanted to call him racist and bigoted and small-minded. Instead, he said to his almost-bride, 'You still wish to marry me?'

"The very next day, they went to the Broward County courthouse. They invited Papa and me. I was very proud. I had loved Vicki since she was a little girl. Her mother came to the ceremony, but she was not happy. When she smiled, she did not smile with her eyes. Her father refused to attend."

"Weren't you sad Dad didn't have an Assyrian wedding like you and Papa?"

"A little sad, yes. But those were *our* traditions, and now he had the opportunity to make new traditions with your mother. My sister, Nadine, your great-aunt, she yelled at me when I called to tell her. She told me I was a fool, that the marriage would be cursed. She is very traditional, like our mother was. I told Nadine, 'No, this is not a cursed marriage. This is very beautiful. You do not understand.' And I hung up the phone on my sister! I have always wanted to do that—my sister is very bossy."

I looked over at my grandfather, who was still staring out into the sea. His English was limited, and I always wondered how much he understood of our conversations. It never seemed like much. Often, I would have to repeat what I'd said to him in a different order, with different words, or he'd give up and simply say, *Ask Nana.* Was he listening now?

"Your father tells me you have your first boyfriend."

I was surprised at the quick change in subject—I hadn't realized Nana's entire reason for the story was leading to this.

"Your father says your boyfriend is very handsome."

"He did?"

"He says he is tall, and that when you walk into a room, he smiles the way Adam used to smile when Vicki walked into a room."

"Wow."

"You will marry this boy?"

"Nana!"

"What? It is a good question. You are my only grandchild. I am curious. Tell Nana your secrets."

"I don't want to get married, Nana. I'm too little!"

"When your father proposed, he was only five or six years older than you are now. That is nothing."

I insisted, "He's just my boyfriend."

"Ah, I see. You do not love him?"

I felt my face flush and could not control the smile from tugging at the corners of my mouth.

"So you do love him. And he loves you?"

"He says he does," I said softly, into my lap, still blushing.

Again, Nana nodded. "When we get home, I will read your fortune. Let's see if this is a good boy for you."

At this, Papa snorted. He looked at me and rolled his eyes. That man, I realized later, heard everything. Nana smacked the top of his hand. He held tight to it and gave her a big noisy kiss on her wrist.

When we got home, Nana boiled water for Turkish coffee, setting out three small bone-white-china coffee cups rimmed in gold. Each sat in a matching saucer, important for the reading.

While the water warmed, she ground her coffee beans until the powder was as fine as table sugar. When the water boiled, she added tablespoonfuls of coffee, letting it float to the top, and she added the sugar. She closed the lid on the airtight canister, looked at me from the side of her eye, and popped open the top once more to add even more sugar.

"An extra scoop of sweet for my favorite granddaughter," she said.

As the grounds sank into the open pot, she stirred the coffee once, twice. When tiny bubbles began to form a ring on the surface of the coffee, she turned down the heat. She allowed the coffee to simmer for three minutes, keeping it barely below a boil.

She poured three cups of coffee and set them at the kitchen table. Papa took his into the family room, where he flipped on the television. It was only me and Nana, me and my seer. I watched the rivulets of steam dance above the coffee, and I inhaled the strong scent. It almost smelled burned, but in a good way. The scent will forever remind me of my childhood.

Each glass held three ounces of coffee, but that was all you needed. I didn't love the flavor yet—I wouldn't appreciate its thick richness until college—but I loved the ceremony. I loved watching Nana make the coffee, and I loved the tiny teacups. I loved sitting at the kitchen table, which was always set with a white lace tablecloth under a thick plastic cover with a bowl of fruit in the center.

When I finished my coffee, a thick, black tar-like goop coated the bottom of the cup. Nana instructed, "Now make a wish."

I closed my eyes and thought for a moment. What did I wish for? I thought about our talk at the lighthouse, and I was surprised at what came to mind. It was a little girl's wish, I know now, but at the time, it felt very grown-up. I thought the wish in my head. I saw the words pop up, as if written in smoke with a scripty, romantic hand.

"OK." I nodded to her.

"Now hold the cup and flip it toward you upside down into the saucer," she said, and she demonstrated, as if she hadn't read my fortune a half dozen times before.

We waited a few minutes for the sludge at the bottom of the cup to fully drip into the saucer, to drip down the sides of the cup.

"Now flip it again."

I turned my cup right side up, and the inside was coated with the murky coffee grounds. They made splotches up the sides of the cup. Thick sediment still coated the bottom, too, except for a few spots where the glass showed through. I handed Nana my cup.

She peered inside, studied it for a moment or two, and said, "There is a big party in your future. A big party. Everyone you love will be there. It's a celebration! You will meet new friends this summer, and you will take a trip! Someone is missing you, *brated Nana*. Someone is missing you very badly."

"What about my wish?"

Her face fell.

"Ah, your wish. *Brated Nana*, I am sorry, your wish will not come true."

I remember how disappointed I felt. It wasn't until she read my fortune once after I was engaged to Charlie that I realized something:

Nana's fortunes were always the same. A big party! Someone misses you! No wish fulfillment, *brated Nana*.

My sweet grandmother. She lives alone now. Papa died a few months before Charlie's coma. She still likes to read fortunes.

She looked at me over the table.

"You would like to call your boyfriend now?" I nodded. "Go, go. Give Nana kiss."

I wrapped my arms around her neck and kissed her cheek. For the first time in my life, I noticed how soft it was. I grabbed the phone and ran upstairs, and Papa came ambling into the kitchen. He held out his overturned cup and saucer toward her and said, in English, "Is my turn," the *R* trilling gruffly, beautifully from his mouth.

He sat at the kitchen table, and she peered inside his cup, speaking to him in Assyrian. After being in the house for nearly two months straight—and after spending as much time there as I did as a kid—you'd think I'd be bilingual. Alas, their Assyrian conversations and giggles— even the indecipherable interjections, *Zhee?* and *Ayii!*, their versions of *What?* and *Oh!*—were intimate times between them, completely foreign to their only granddaughter.

That night I told Jason all about the lighthouse trip with Nana and Papa and how my mother and I had both wondered: What's across there?

A week later, I got a letter.

> Dear Asha,
> I asked my dad to take me to the library today. He was proud of me. He thought I was studying over summer vacation. I guess I did have some studying to do: I had to learn something for you. It's always for you. It will always be for you. You should never forget that.
> These are the coordinates of your lighthouse, rounded to the second decimal point: 26.26 degrees north, 80.08 degrees west. 2-6-2-6, 8-0-0-8—isn't

that easy to remember? I printed out the map for you and drew the line. See? If you and your mom were to board that sailboat together and sail east, you'd eventually run into Western Sahara, a country in Africa, into a province called Boujdour.

Maybe we can go there someday?

I miss you. I wish I could kiss you right now.

Love, Jason

How easy, as an adult, to look back upon the loves of our youth with eye rolls and scorn. It's what happens when we use our intellectual grown-up brains to filter those events, which were fueled, for better or worse, by dogged emotion. Those brains make us forget the rush and all-encompassing devotion of teen-girl love. Because, let's be real: I had it *bad*. And so did he. I mean, come on . . . *look at that letter*. That is some romance. I don't think there's a grown-ass guy on the planet who'd write something like that to his partner.

And if there is, he definitely doesn't live in the Midwest.

SUMMER (2006)

Charlie and I ran down a list of all the different ways we could get married.

Traditional church ceremony? But neither of us was religious. On a beach sounded good to Charlie, but I didn't have a significant memory of us at the beach together.

"What about my parents' club?" Charlie asked, and I made gagging noises. "Have either of us ever, ever played golf?" He conceded that no, we hadn't.

"I wonder if we could rent out Cujo's?" I said aloud, almost by accident.

Charlie jumped up out of his chair. "The spot of our first date. Yes, yes. That's it."

"Well," I said, raising an eyebrow. "Doesn't New Year's count?"

"New Year's . . ." he murmured. He blinked at me, his motor working. "What if . . ." Then he opened his pantry door, rustled some things around, and stepped back with a phone book in his hand.

"How did you even know where you keep that?" I asked, but he ignored me, flipped through the book, grabbed his phone, dialed, and put the phone to his ear. "What are you doing?"

"It's ringing," he stage-whispered then said, a little louder, "Hello? Oh, hello! Can I speak to the owner, please? . . . Great. Do you let parties rent out the bar? . . . What if it were all night? With food and an open bar? . . . December 31 . . . When would you need to know for sure? . . . OK, let me call you back.

"If we invite no more than seventy-four people total—that's seventy-six with us—we can have Cujo's from any time we want to start December 31 until one a.m. January 1."

"You want to get married on New Year's Eve?"

"It's when we met, isn't it? Can you think of a better way to ring in 2007? . . . Asha?"

"Quiet, I'm thinking."

"What are you thinking?"

"How hilarious it's going to be to see my Assyrian grandparents in a horror-themed bar at midnight."

When I told Bridget, she squealed.

"That is the tackiest thing I have ever heard! I'm going to take care of everything. Can I? Can I handle all your decorations? If you're going to get married in a dive bar, it is going to be the most elegant dive bar you've ever seen in your life."

And it was. Bridget draped every table in the room with deep mulberry silk, topping half of them again with black embroidered net lace. I was certain she'd find the paperback books repugnant, replacing them all with gaudy, glittering centerpieces, but she kept them, adding sprigs of pine, burgundy amaryllis, and tea lights atop small mirrors.

She turned off the dingy bar lights and strung fairy lights everywhere: They draped from the ceiling, every other strand twinkling like magic. They bunched in fish bowls spaced along the bar and every other booth. They framed the windows and the deep mahogany bar, making its scars charming, romantic somehow. They surrounded a tower of cupcakes, red velvet with buttercream frosting and shimmering black sprinkles.

Bridget even matched her and Maura's dresses to the decor. Charlie and I didn't want a huge wedding party; we asked only my maid of honor and his best man. Best lady. Best gal. I don't think he ever settled on Maura's title, but she and Bridget walked down the aisle together in matching wine-colored silk and black capes for warmth—which was necessary because Charlie and I got married on the roof of Cujo's. This was a brave decision, I knew then. In retrospect, it wasn't brave so much as flaky: Who plans a wedding outside in December?

Tito, the owner of Cujo's, was happy to let us use the space, but every time we talked to him, he asked us if we were sure.

"Get married in the bar instead, yeah?" and "Why not go to the courthouse, man? Gonna freeze off your *bolas*."

"Our *bolas* will be fine, thank you for your concern," Bridget insisted.

She had rented a half dozen industrial outdoor heaters, which she used to frame the space around the ceremony and the rows where guests would sit. But I didn't know how she had decorated any of it until my dad opened the steel door to the roof before he walked me down the aisle.

I stepped out and nearly gasped: She'd mirrored the lights she'd hung downstairs, and strings of fairy twinkles crisscrossed the space. They hung low—not so low that guests hit their heads, but low enough to create an intimacy I hadn't thought possible on an open roof. She'd rolled out a satiny aisle, which she lined with heavy greenery. In lieu of flower petals, she'd sprinkled pine needles on the aisle, unwittingly creating my favorite sensory memory from the entire day: Until the day I die, when I smell deep, woodsy, earthy pine, it will transport me to December 31, 2006. To my hand clutching the crook of my father's arm, to his proud, handsome smile. To the beautiful man standing thirty feet away, staring at me, his perfect mouth and face and eyes. My Charlie. We locked eyes, unblinking, the entire way. Everyone else disappeared—my grandparents disappeared, Charlie's parents and Maura disappeared. My friends from work and Charlie's cousins—they all ceased to exist.

He is the rest of my life, I thought on that walk. *Lucky, lucky me.*

The day after I proposed, I told my dad. I'd never seen him that happy.

You're not mad that I asked? That I didn't wait for Charlie to ask?

On the contrary, he said, standing up, pulling a bottle of sparkling wine from the liquor cabinet. *You asked him. It means it is what you want. It is all I could want for my daughter.*

He repeated those words to me then, at the end of my wedding aisle, in a low voice so I was the only one who could hear: "Your happiness is all I could want for you."

The pastor kept the ceremony blessedly short. Pastor Mark was Charlie's parents' pastor, and they asked if Mark could marry us; he had married them, and *Wouldn't it be nice?* his mother, Joanie, asked. I had no complaints—it was not as though I'd had any other ideas who could officiate. Pastor Mark agreed to keep the ceremony secular, and, after, I was extra happy we'd chosen the holy man; it was as though, in spite of the lack of religion in our wedding, God approved of our union. I mean, he rolled his eyes at us, but he approved.

If that hadn't been enough to endear Mark to me, his joy at my grandmother's traditions would have. Unbeknownst to me, Bridget had been in touch with Nana after I'd mentioned offhandedly that it'd be cool if I could incorporate something from an Assyrian ceremony into the wedding, but I hadn't a clue what that could be.

As soon as the ceremony was over, after Charlie had placed a sweet kiss on my mouth that sent a shiver down the sides of both my arms, the pastor pulled his phone from his pocket and queued up an Assyrian tune I'd never heard. Two small speakers at the back of the roof blasted the song. To this day I have no idea what the singer sang, but it was clearly a party song, celebratory voices rising with glee, backed with cymbals and drums and something that sounded suspiciously like a recorder.

All the women in attendance—Bridget and my grandmother, Maura and Charlie's mom and her sisters, Mrs. Casey, Sonja from work, aunts and cousins and more—rushed to line the aisle. About two-thirds of the women remained on the roof, and the rest spaced themselves out on the stairs leading down into the bar. Each pulled a bright square of fabric from the folds of her coat, handkerchiefs lined with penny-size iridescent sequins that made a soft rustle-jangle. The women at my wedding waved their party kerchiefs over their heads as though Charlie and I were about to board a ship, bon voyage and farewell!

Without realizing it was exactly what we were supposed to do—but what else *could* we have done?—Charlie and I danced through the Assyrian Soul Train beneath shaking silks of fuchsia and orange, lavender and silver, gold and navy. After, my grandmother told me the tradition banished all the negativity from our marriage. Evil spirits and sadness fled in terror before the party sequins, assuring the bride and groom a happy, healthy, long life together.

What else could two newly married people possibly wish for?

Things got a little fuzzy after the ceremony. I was extra alert during the actual wedding, trying to record every detail: the curve of my grand-mother's thumb and her pretty maroon nail polish, the only color she ever wore, as she caressed the side of my face when I bent to hug her. My grandfather's sweet smile. The rough brush of my father's mustache as he kissed my cheek for the millionth time. How, every time I turned to Charlie, he was staring at me with a giddiness in his eyes I'd never before seen.

We'd hired a three-piece band that Tito had recommended, The Francis B. Trio. The week before the wedding, Charlie had asked if he could pick our first dance song.

"Is it cheesy if it was my parents' wedding song?"

I followed him down the stairs through the garage and into his parents' house. His parents sat at the kitchen table, each with their own crossword, sipping tea.

"I wanna play something for Asha," he said, opening the small cab-inet that stored stacks of records. He kept his back to me, and I couldn't see what he'd selected. He slid the album from its tan-colored sleeve and placed it gently on the turntable. The needle made that faint, pleasant, scratchy sound as it found the record's groove.

The music started, chimes and horns announcing the tune. As Al Green's buttery vocals filled the room, Charlie spun around, arms spread wide, fingers snapping to the beat, mouthing every I'm-so-in-love-with-you word as he sashayed slowly toward me.

I covered my face with my hands. His parents were my future in-laws, but I hardly knew them, and I felt mortified that they should see his silly display of affection, as much as I'd loved it.

I needn't have worried. When I peeked between my fingers, his father and mother were clutched in one another's arms, swaying in the kitchen, their crosswords and tea forgotten on the table.

"Awwww," I felt myself exhale as I watched them. I was surprised to feel tears prickle my eyes. My poor daddy.

Charlie wrapped his arms around my waist and swayed with me. "Like it?" he asked against my ear.

"It's perfect."

Francis B. himself sang our first song with gusto, somehow transitioning seamlessly into the song that would *actually* transport me back to our wedding forevermore, the eternal Justin Timberlake and Timbaland, the ridiculous and perfect "SexyBack."

Charlie sang along, holding me tightly. I knew what he was thinking. I could feel what he was thinking, and I danced as close to my husband as I could.

I had no idea it would be one of the few moments of my wedding reception that I would actually get to spend with Charlie. Throughout the night, people kept pulling us in different directions. Not only didn't we eat together, but we hardly ate at all. At one point I pushed my way through the group at the chocolate fountain. I caught Charlie's eye, and I motioned him over. I had plans to feed him a fudge-covered marshmallow, but before he could make it to me, my grandmother grabbed his arm, wrapped his face in her hands, said something to him. Then his aunt caught him, then some friends of mine from work. Bridget stepped up to me.

"You have chocolate right . . . here," she said, gesturing on the entire lower half of her face.

"Shut up," I said around a chocolate-covered strawberry, shoving Charlie's marshmallow in her mouth. I swallowed, wiped my face, and told her, "You done good, sister."

"I know," she said, and I gave her a big smooch on the cheek. A camera flashed, and that photo, of our faces spotted with chocolate, me kissing her cheek, her laughing so hard you can nearly count her teeth, is framed on my mantel.

At ten minutes to midnight, the bartender and four servers came out with huge trays of etched champagne flutes filled with cheap bubbly. They passed one out to every guest, and I made sure to hand one directly to Maura with a wink. Everyone grabbed a noisemaker—paper horns with plastic mouthpieces and streamers, rolled-up paper tubes that unfurled as you blew, or handheld tins that clicked louder the faster you swung them around.

"Thirty seconds!" Francis shouted into the mic, and moments later everyone in the room shouted: "TEN . . . NINE . . . EIGHT . . ."

At "SEVEN," I couldn't stand it—I downed my champagne; threw my noisemaker on the ground; shoved my way through the crowd, ignoring hands reaching for me and wishes of happiness and congratulations; and nearly tackled Charlie. I wrapped my arms around my husband's neck, and I kissed him on the mouth for the second time in front of all these people. But that first kiss, the roof kiss, had been sweet, like a church kiss. This one was not sweet. It was not church. It was passion and love and hope and wishes for the next seventy years of our lives.

When Francis B. and his band shouted "HAPPY NEW YEAR," the bar erupted into cheers and clinking glasses, horns and noisemakers, shouts and claps, and I squeezed Charlie even tighter.

This was forever.

I really believed it.

SPRING (1997)

"How's Craig?"

"He's *fine*, Jason."

"See him lately?"

"I see him a lot. You know that."

I took a deep breath, moving the receiver away from my mouth so Jason wouldn't hear. At first I'd found his jealousy kind of sweet. It meant he cared about me, I told myself, that he didn't want to lose me, that he thought I was valuable enough that I could be lost. But as his questions continued, on and on over the summer, I no longer found them sweet. They were annoying, and they pissed me off.

"Why don't you trust me?" I asked.

"I do."

"Why don't you act like it?"

Silence.

He always got quiet when I addressed the issue, and he spoke in clipped sentences. I kept waiting for us to get in a real argument, but it never happened; Jason *never* fought with me. He *never* yelled at me. I even asked him about it once, years later, and he told me, *I don't ever want to yell at you. I don't ever want to take you for granted.*

He was very big on that, on not taking me for granted. I never felt like he did, and I told him so, but it didn't abate his fear, and it didn't encourage him to yell at me. Sometimes I wanted to get into fights. I thought, if he yelled at me, finally, maybe we could stop having different versions of the same conversation over and over again—it was always about jealousy, always about him holding on to me a little too much, a little too tightly.

But that summer, I didn't know all that yet. That summer, I thought it was only about Craig.

"I can't wait to see you next week," he said quietly.

"Me too."

"Do you miss me?"

"I miss you a ton."

And I did. I'd studied the photo of us from Christmas and imagined that kiss in the pool a hundred times over the summer, a thousand times, and I didn't really understand the funny feeling it brought to my belly and my *down there*. When I would think about the kiss in bed sometimes, I'd feel a pressure between my legs, and it simultaneously scared and thrilled me.

I tentatively broached the topic with Heather once.

"Oh my *gawd*," she shrieked at me. "You've *never* had an *orgasm*?"

I felt my face flush red. I associated the word with making babies and hadn't before considered that it could be something enjoyable. Rather, I hadn't equated the vocabulary with the feeling. I knew something was going on in my underpants, but I didn't know what to call it.

I couldn't bring myself to discuss this with Heather anymore, so I called Bridget that night.

"You know when Jason and I went to the pool that night?"

"*Yes*, I know, you snuck out. I'm so *jealous*." She sounded mad, but it was mostly for show.

"I think about that a lot. And it kind of makes me feel . . . you know . . ."

"Does it turn you on, baby?" she said, trying her best to mimic Austin Powers, which was one of the hottest movies that summer. I saw it with Heather, but Bridget'd already seen it three times in the theaters.

"No! I mean . . . Maybe? That's sort of what I wanted to ask? Have you ever . . . ? I mean, do you ever . . . ?"

Her voice got very hushed then, and very excited. "Oh my god, Asha, do *you?*"

"Maybe? I mean . . ."

"Have you?"

"Have I what?"

"You know."

"Like . . . touched myself . . . down there?"

"Yes!"

"No. Not yet. I mean, I was thinking about it. But isn't it . . . ? I mean, *do you?*"

I heard her race across her bedroom and slam her bedroom door. I heard her mom shout, "BRIDGE!" and Bridget respond, "IT SLIPPED!" I heard her clomp back to her bed, land with a thump. She gasped, like she was out of breath. "I totally did it for the first time last week!"

"You did???" I was happy. Completely. Purely. Happy. I wasn't alone. It wasn't only me. I wasn't a freak. Or, if I was, then we were both freaks, and that was fine. Somehow, though, I knew we weren't.

"It was awesome," she whisper-shouted. "You totally have to try. You have to try."

"I will," I promised her. "But . . . like . . . how do you . . . *do it?*"

"You just do. You just know."

"What if it hurts?"

"It doesn't hurt."

"What if it does?"

"It won't. I promise. You have to do it. Then you have to tell me about it."

The next day, she called me right after breakfast.

"So did you do it?" she hissed.

I looked around the kitchen. Nana was upstairs, and Papa was watering his garden.

"I did!" We both started giggling manically, jumping up and down together, more than a thousand miles apart.

This preoccupation with masturbation, by the way? It has continued into our adult friendship. We talk about it. We joke about it. We can't pass an adult toy store without going in together. It bonded us, somehow, that conversation that summer. Bridget had been my closest friend before that, but after that? She was my Best Friend. Capital *B*. Capital *F*.

On my final day in Florida, at the end of the summer, Nana invited Heather and Craig over for dinner. Papa grilled my favorite, beef kebabs, and Nana made a soft, fluffy batch of saffron rice. In the big scoop on my plate, single grains stood out bright, canary yellow.

"What's that?" Heather asked, and Craig answered through a mouthful, "It's rice, stupid, eat it."

"*Ayii*, don't talk to your sister that way!" Nana scolded him while Papa, stifling a grin, wagged his finger at Craig, nodding.

Heather glared at her brother and took a tiny nibble. Then another nibble. "Told you," Craig chided her when she cleared her plate and asked my grandmother for more.

For dessert, I had helped Nana make a cake.

"What is your favorite kind?" she asked me. "We make pistachio cake or cake with strawberry filling or lemon cake with blueberries."

"Chocolate."

"What kind of filling?"

"No filling. Just chocolate."

"OK. No filling. What kind of frosting for *brated Nana*?"

"Chocolate."

"*Ayii!* You don't want anything else in the cake?"

"Chocolate chips?"

She shook her head at me, *tsk*ing, and took down a red box of cake mix. I measured out the water and oil, and she cracked in the eggs. She used a handheld mixer to whip the batter.

"Make sure you mix long enough time," she told me as the whirling beaters *clack-clack-clack*ed against the side of her glass mixing bowl. "Mix enough for a fluffy cake. You will love it."

She used a wide white spatula to spread the batter into a pan. After she put the cake in the oven, she gave me one beater and kept one for herself.

"*Khoubakh,*" she said, clicking her beater against mine and licking the tines.

"*Hoboken,*" I said back, a joke from when I was a girl and Dad tried to teach me different Assyrian phrases.

After Nana brought the cake to the table, I clapped when I saw two candles stuck in the top: a one and a four. My birthday wasn't for a few days, but I'd be home by then.

Nana began to sing, Heather and Craig joined in, and Papa smiled at me. When I blew out the two candles, he gave me a big kiss on the top of my head. I cut five huge pieces of cake, and after I took my first bite, Craig started to chuckle.

"What?" I asked, my mouth full.

"You have icing on your face," Heather said.

I wiped my mouth but must have missed. Craig, who was seated to my left, reached over and wiped it off carefully with his pointer finger.

"Are you fourteen or four?" he asked, licking the icing from his finger and digging back into his cake. The gesture felt oddly intimate, even though there hadn't been anything romantic or suggestive in his face or body. Regardless, I knew I wouldn't mention it to Jason.

After, Nana and Papa gave me a pretty set of pens and some barrettes for my hair. Heather gave me the Fugees CD—"Because *someone* has to teach you about good music," she said—but Craig's gift was my favorite.

"Hey, it's like yours," I said, standing up to display the full length of the towel boasting a flaming basketball dropping through the hoop, the Miami Heat logo.

We three sat on the front porch for a few minutes after dessert. My flight left early the next morning, and I still had to finish packing.

"I'm gonna miss you guys," I told them, a wave of sadness flooding my chest. I didn't know when I'd visit my grandparents again, and when I did, I knew we'd all be older. I could see their grown-up shapes looming in the horizon, fuzzy around the edges. I guess my grown-up shape was there, too. What were the chances that we'd all want to play together anymore? They would have dates or homework or other mature, nearly adult things I couldn't imagine.

"Yeah." Heather wouldn't look at me. She'd found a rock on the sidewalk, and she pressed the toe of her sneaker against it, dragging it along the pavement, scratching a faint white mark. She looked up at me quickly, gave me a loose hug, said, "Bye," and hurried down the driveway, wiping her eyes. I watched her as she jogged across the street, not looking back.

Craig shrugged. "She's a bitch," he said, not unkindly. "I'll miss you, too." His hug was firmer, longer. He smelled of boy and summer, a mixture of grass and sweat and a faint perfume from his deodorant or shampoo. I loved that smell.

"I—" But Craig interrupted me, placing a soft kiss against my mouth. He pulled away and studied my expression, unsure how I would respond. When I smiled, he kissed me again.

"Bye," he whispered, taking a step back. I waved. When he crossed the street, he looked back, and I waved again.

Definitely wouldn't be telling Jason about *that*.

In the midst of freshman year, I'd have told you the school year took *forever*, that it seemed like a *lifetime, oh my god*. In retrospect, it passed as quickly as a heartbeat, the flutter of a butterfly's wings.

And it started with orgasms.

Rather, talk about orgasms. Again. With Bridget.

"You're going to laugh at me," she said, the both of us seated on her bedroom floor.

"No, I won't."

"Promise?"

"I won't make fun of you, I swear."

"I use a squiggle pen."

"Like . . . the thing that writes all shaky? With those loopy letters?"

"Yeah."

I blinked at Bridget and thought it over. "That's brilliant. I use this big marker I accidentally stole from María's mom when we stayed after school last month to make football posters."

She thought that was hilarious, and when Mrs. Casey walked in, she found us red-faced and gasping.

"Excuse me, girls. Hey, Asha, can I talk to you for a moment?"

Bridget's room immediately fell silent. *Did she hear us? She must have heard. Oh, god, we're going to get in trouble. I hope Mrs. Casey doesn't tell my dad.*

I stood up to follow Bridget's mom, and when Bridget followed me, Mrs. Casey stopped her.

"Just me and Asha right now, sweetie. Go downstairs and watch TV with Ryan. We'll be right down."

Mrs. Casey took me into her office, which had a bright-teal armchair in the corner with a tall lamp behind it. I often saw her in that chair with a throw, a book, and a cup of coffee or wine. It was the image of sophistication to me for a long time. Hell, it still is—I have a similar armchair/lamp setup in my home, where I read and sip coffee.

She looked at me and must have seen the fear in my face.

"Sit down, sweetie. Don't worry, this is nothing bad."

I sat in the chair, and she eased herself into the roller chair she kept at her desk. She looked pointedly at me, and I looked at my hands clasped prayer-style between my knees.

Mrs. Casey reached into the top drawer of the desk and pulled out a familiar pale-yellow envelope. She opened one of the letters I had written to Bridget that summer and handed it to me.

I glanced down at it quickly, and key phrases jumped out at me. "Do you think Jason would want a blow job?" ". . . it's like a hot dog . . ." "I love Jason!"

My eyes filled up with tears, and Mrs. Casey reached over to take my hand.

"Oh, sweetie! Sweetie, don't. Don't cry! I'm not mad, I promise. You haven't done anything wrong!"

I cried harder.

"Oh, no." I heard Mrs. Casey sigh. "Hold on."

She left the room and came back a moment later with a glass of water and some tissues.

I wiped my nose, balling the tissue in my hand, and sipped the water. I stared at the glass in silence. It had a cartoon pig on it. I always drank my orange juice in the morning from this glass. I had come to think of it as *my* glass at the Caseys'.

"Honey, has your father talked to you at all about sex?"

"Um . . . I don't know."

"Do you know what sex is? Do you know how it works?"

"Yeah," I mumbled. "I mean, we had the sex talk in school in Florida. They made the boys leave, and Mrs. O'Neill talked all about periods and how you can get pregnant from pre-ejaculation and you should only have sex if you get married and only loose girls do it before then."

A pained look crossed Mrs. Casey's face, and she nodded.

"So I've talked to your father—"

"What??" *She told my dad about the letter? My dad knows I've thought about BJs and Jason??*

"I offered to talk to you for him. If he thought you might be more comfortable talking to a woman."

"You didn't show him . . ." I held up the letter.

"No, no, dear. I know how hard being fourteen can be. Your body is changing, and you're experiencing things and thoughts for the first time, and it's confusing. And I wanted to talk to you about this. You have a boyfriend, and that's exciting. First loves can be wonderful. They can also be scary."

"What did my dad say?"

"He seemed a little relieved, actually. He said he'd been trying to figure out how to bring it up with you since Jason first came around. When you broke up, he thought he could stall a little bit more. Then he came back, you left for the summer, and he . . . let's just say, he does not know about the letter, this is a private conversation between you and me, and I only wanted to know if you had any questions."

I nodded. My mind filtered back to that day in school a few years prior, to everything Mrs. O'Neill told us. There was a lot I wanted to ask Mrs. Casey. Was it really OK?

"What's it like?" I whispered.

"What is what like?"

"You know . . . sex? Like, how do you know you're ready?"

"That is a very good question, Asha. I think everyone is ready at different times. Sometimes people aren't ready until they get married, like your teacher said. And that is absolutely OK. Sex is a very big decision. It tells another person that you not only love them, but that you trust them with your body and with your heart.

"But sometimes a person decides she's ready for sex *before* she gets married, and that's a hundred percent OK, too."

I shook my head back and forth very quickly. "I wasn't even thinking it! Honest!" And I wasn't. It was too big, too scary. I wasn't ready. How could Mrs. Casey think I thought I was?

"Well, you were thinking about oral sex, right? That's a very big step, too, honey. You're both young. Sex doesn't have to be intercourse, you know, and any kind of sex is a grown-up act with grown-up feelings. I know you love Jason, and maybe one day you'll decide you trust and respect him enough to make that step. But there's nothing wrong with taking things a little slowly, too. Has he ever pressured you?"

I thought about it. Anytime we kissed, he usually initiated it, but I liked that. A little after I got back from my grandparents', I went to his house for dinner. We kissed a little in his room, and he'd tried to unhook my bra, but he stopped when I swatted his hand away. I knew that one day I wouldn't swat him away, and that when that time came, it'd be because I wanted him to touch me, too.

"No. He hasn't," I said, and Mrs. Casey nodded.

"Good. If he does, you tell someone, OK? If not your father, you call me. It is never OK for someone to touch you without your permission. Sex and relationships, it's supposed to leave us feeling happy and loved. When we love someone, it becomes natural that we want to express ourselves physically. It's why you like kissing him."

We talked for another twenty minutes, and at the end, I gave Mrs. Casey a big hug. She squeezed me in return. "This is hard to go through for any young girl. I want you to know you can come to me with anything if you don't feel comfortable talking to your dad, OK? And one more thing." I consider Mrs. Casey the coolest human on the planet for what she did next: She opened the sliding closet door, grabbed a pale-orange duffel bag, and lifted out an unopened box of condoms. "This is not me approving of you and Jason having sex," she instructed me, her finger in my face. "But if it gets to that point? Come in here and take one of these, OK? Bridget knows they're here, too. I know she doesn't have a boyfriend, but I don't want to become a grandmother before I'm fifty."

An image of my grandmother flashed in my mind, and I tried to reconcile her—baking cakes, reading coffee grounds, taking me to the lighthouse and sitting on the wooden bench instead of climbing the stairs to the top—with Mrs. Casey, who went to the salon every six weeks to get her highlights touched up; who favored big, sparkly earrings and boots with heels; who played tennis every weekend with her friend Mindy. Even her first name was youthful and vibrant: Sophie. For those six months when Charlie and I talked about having kids, I told him I'd always wanted a little girl named Sophie. He kissed me on the nose and said, *Then it shall be.*

Well.

When I got home the next morning, I gave my dad an extra-big hug.

"What is this?" he said, holding me in front of him by the shoulders, smiling big and pulling me in for another squeeze.

For the first time in my life, I considered that raising a daughter on his own wasn't what my dad had signed up for. He'd wanted a family with his wife. He'd wanted to co-parent. He'd wanted to be the father and *just* the father; what man also wants to have to be the mother? My sweet father with his neat mustache and proper grammar bought me pads every month. He never even asked if I needed them or when I needed them; the last weekend of each month, there they were with the groceries. When I first got my period, he bought three different kinds. He never asked which kind I liked best—he must have snooped in the cabinet under my sink to see what I'd used.

He loved me, but he was never overbearing. He understood how important it was for me to discover things on my own. I think that's because he moved to a new country when he was young. His parents didn't speak the language well; while they were there to support him, he was kind of on his own.

But still, even in my adulthood, I can't believe he said yes when I asked, the weekend before my final days as a freshman in high school, if I could go on an overnight camping trip with Jason and his family.

AUTUMN (2017)

Bridget is sitting in her car when I pull up in my driveway.

"How'd it go?" she asks.

"You know how it went."

"She call you a slut?"

"Yup."

"And now it's time to get ready for a date."

I laugh. I have to laugh. If I didn't laugh, I'd cry. I look down at my clothes. "I actually thought I'd go like this."

We're standing in my garage, and Bridget surveys my outfit.

"Gray leggings?"

"Check," I say, tugging at the too-thin fabric stretched over my thigh.

"No makeup?"

I rub my open palms on my eyes. "Not a stitch."

"So perfect."

"I figure I'll be less nervous if I'm comfortable."

"You could go on this date wrapped in a robe of Turkish cotton, accompanied by two personal massage therapists, and you're not going to be comfortable."

"You're right. Should I cancel?"

"You don't want to cancel," she says, and she holds up the two huge shopping bags in her hands. "Come on. I brought stuff. I don't know if it'll help, but it's here."

"Thank you." I wrap her in a tight hug. She drops the bags and hugs me back.

"Unnecessary. Happy to do it. But, to be clear . . . I want to know what we're dealing with here . . ." She trails off, and her eyes get wide. "You haven't gotten laid since . . ."

"Fucking Francis, yes." My bout of insanity after Charlie got sick.

She continues to stare at me, unblinking.

"Yes, Bridget, thank you for the reminder. It has been nearly a year since I've gotten laid. I appreciate that very much. You are being incredibly helpful. Now would you like to tell me about the amazing sex you have with Alfie?"

"I want to point out the obvious real quick here. You're sure you want the first time in decades—"

"Eleven months," I protest.

"—to be with Jason?"

I'm not going to sleep with him, I want to say, but I'm not sure if that's true. We stare at each other for a few beats. How do I tell her that, since Jason's and my awkward conversation a few days earlier, I have not been able to stop thinking about having sex with my ex-boyfriend? I've tried to imagine what he looks like, what he's been up to all these years. Had Simone made him happy? Did he ever—gulp—think about me?

We step into my kitchen, and she opens the cabinets where I keep the glasses. She pulls down two flutes.

"These are pretty," she says, admiring the etched glass design.

"Seriously? Champagne?"

"This is a time for celebrating. It's been a while. You deserve it." She pops the bottle in the freezer. "You see her latest post?"

"I haven't been on all day."

"It's from like fifteen minutes ago. Look." She hands me her phone, and @loveabides831 fills the screen.

The image shows a brief, looping video of a spring rainstorm. The sound soothes, and the raindrops glimmer in a way that's almost hypnotic. It hasn't rained here recently, and I figure this must be some sort of stock footage, but Maura doesn't mention that. The caption reads,

> Friends, I need your help. I wouldn't ask if it wasn't serious, if I hadn't tried everything I could and still fallen short. My heart is broken, and all my prayers don't seem to be helping. I know—I KNOW!—that God only gives us experiences to help us become the shape He wishes us to have, and I'm thankful for His guidance. "For everything there is a season, and a time for every matter under heaven," and this is my season of sorrow. But my sorrow is heavy. Do you think, maybe, you could find it in yourselves to offer up a small prayer for me? I wouldn't ask if it wasn't urgent. From the very bottom of my heart, I thank you. #prayerchain #prayerwarriors

"Wow."

"I can't even make fun of it," Bridget says.

"No way," I answer. Maura still doesn't say anything about what's going on with Charlie, but come on—this is huge.

I see Maura posted this plea less than fifteen minutes after I left Pax, and it's already one of the most popular posts on @loveabides831. **I'm on it! . . . Stay stronggg, Maura! Jesus's has you're back! . . . I'll tell my Bible Study tonite #yougotthis** More than one follower asks for her address. Whether they want to send a card or show up on her doorstep, who knows. But it must feel nice to have such a support system.

I look up, and Bridget is staring at me, eyebrows knit together. Maura's support system might work for her, but mine?

"You're awesome," I tell her, and she grins.

"I got something for you. We have time? Before . . ." She makes a clicking sound in her cheek, like she's calling a horse . . . or, you know, implying sex.

"I'm supposed to meet him in three hours."

"That's plenty of time for . . ." She digs into her purse and pulls out a pale-yellow envelope in surprisingly good condition for a twenty-year-old letter.

"What is that?" I demand, smiling, knowing exactly what it is.

Bridget removes the palm tree stationery and unfolds it from its intricate pattern, tugging on the little point, pulling apart the top and bottom, flipping the paper over and opening the trifold. She begins to read:

> Birdie,
> I thought we needed code names for the summer. You be Birdie, I'll be Sasha.
>
> What's up & down & all around?? Heather told me the craziest thing. She gave her boyfriend a blow job! Ew, right?! Do you think Jason would want a blow job? How do you even do it? I was going to ask Heather, but I was shocked she did that. She is *not* that type. Guess I was wrong.
>
> I wonder what it'd be like? Heather says a guy's thing is just like a hot dog, but slimy.

Bridget looks up from the letter. "Has that woman *ever* touched a dick?"

"She was married to a guy!"

"What if they never consummated it?"

"Oh, come on. Charlie and I went to her wedding."

When I saw Heather at the hotel the next morning, I asked her how Christopher's hot dog tasted. She turned bright pink. "I was a little inexperienced then . . . um. It's much better than a hot dog." She'd had the sweetest little grin on her face.

"They were actually really cute together. She was legit the most beautiful bride ever. Looked like the cover of *Brides* magazine."

"Ugh," Bridget says, rolling her eyes. Then she keeps reading:

> I told Jason I loved him before I left for the summer. I love Jason! Jason + Sasha = true love 4-ever and ever. Wouldn't it be cool if we went to prom together one day? Me and Jason and you and Leonardo DiCaprio can take a limo together. Wouldn't that be awesome??
>
> Don't miss me too bad! Tweet tweet!
> Love, Sasha

She looks up. "Tweet tweet?"

"You were Birdie," I remind her. "I can't believe you still have that letter. I thought your mom would have confiscated it."

"She did for a minute. But after she talked to you, she gave it back. She never did tell me what you talked about."

"Really?"

"Said it was private." She looks at me pointedly.

"You still want to know," I say, smirking.

She keeps her gaze.

"It was the sex talk. Didn't she have one with you?"

"I plugged my ears with my fingers and went, 'Na na na na na na na na.'"

"I ate it up. Which was probably good. No one should learn about sex from the likes of Heather Nilsen."

"Like a hot dog," Bridget says, shaking her head. She has never even tried to hide her jealousy over Heather. She hated that I was friends with her first, and Bridget loved to bring up any misstep Heather made. Today Heather is a once-divorced (from Christopher), happily married (to Amanda) accountant in Asheville,

North Carolina. She is a far cry from the girl who'd bragged to me about blow jobs she'd never given, but what the hell—old jealousies die hard, I suppose. I definitely don't have the heart to tell Bridget the champagne flute she'd just admired had been a gift from Heather a few Christmases ago.

"Cheers, my darling! Think of you often. Please come visit!" she'd written in the card, which had featured her and Amanda in matching Santa hats, posing with their two cats, Ani and Fiona.

Bridget tucks the note away in her purse and demands I go take a shower.

"My god, do I smell?" I ask, sniffing under one arm.

"When did you shower last?"

"I shower!" She stares at me, serious, and I know she's remembering the time she bathed me. "Fine, give me ten minutes."

"Make it twenty. When's the last time you shaved?"

I stop and consider the question. "Better make it twenty-five."

A half hour later, I wear a towel wrapped around my wet head like a turban and my ratty old robe when I step into the kitchen.

"Better?" she asks, looking up from a magazine. I see her eyes take in the small blood pricks on my legs, nicks from an old razor I haven't used in . . . well, a long time. "Jesus, Ash!"

"Shut up. It's been a while," I say.

She stands to retrieve the champagne from the freezer. The doorbell rings, and I shout, "GO AWAY."

"Easy there, Sasha," she says, handing me the bottle. "Here, pour this."

I stand in the middle of my kitchen, holding the bottle as if I'd never seen one before, and Bridget walks down the hall to answer the door for me. "You know I can't open these stupid things," I shout to her. It's an irrational fear of mine, like diving: I am certain if I open a bottle of champagne, the cork will pop out and take out my eye.

"Um . . . Asha?"

"It's *Sasha*. Stupid Birdie. Tell them to go away, and come help me with this damn thing," I shout to her, peeling the foil from the neck of the bottle and dropping the pieces to the floor as I walk across the kitchen and turn into the hallway. I stop dead about a quarter of the way to the door.

"Hey," Jason says. "Um, I can get that? If you want?"

SPRING (1998)

"How far away is this camping trip?"

"Mr. Kapaglia said it's a KOA campground near West Virginia."

"And he and Mrs. Kapaglia will be with you the whole time?"

"Absolutely. Jay's sister and her best friend are coming, too."

"And Jason did not want to take his best friend?"

"Jason says I'm his best friend."

"I see." My father, who was still holding the newspaper open in his hands, set the paper down, reached up, and removed his glasses.

"Do you know why I am going to let you go on this camping trip?"

"You are?" I jumped up, ran to the other side of the table, and hugged my dad, continuing to jump up and down.

He smiled at my glee, but warily. "I was younger than you when I met your mother."

"DAD, we want to go camping, not get married."

"Thank god for that." His grin was a little more relaxed this time. "I was very young when I fell in love with your mother. And that love has never wavered. And young love can feel very powerful. If I tell you no, you cannot go camping, you would be upset with me." He wasn't asking, but I nodded anyway. "And, if not camping, you would want to go to a movie with this boy. Soon this boy will have a driver's license, and he will take you on dates, where his mother and father will not be." The idea of being alone, truly alone, with Jason gave me a thrill. "I want you to feel like you can come to me with anything that happens. Do you feel that way?" He looked at me curiously, genuinely not knowing the answer.

"Definitely," I said without thought. Then I paused. "Well . . ."

"Ah, there is a 'Well.'"

"I mean, some things are kind of weird to talk about with your dad. And when Mrs. Casey talked to me . . ."

"She has spoken to you, then?"

"She said she told you about it."

"She did. I was very appreciative at her offer. But I didn't know it had occurred. Do you have any questions?"

"Oh, um. Well. No. I think she covered everything."

"I am pleased there is a woman in your life with whom you can be candid. But I hope you feel like you can talk to me, too. Please, don't ever be afraid to talk to me. I may not like what you have to say, but I will not blame you. We can't help who we love."

At the time, I of course had no idea how progressive this was for my Middle Eastern father, but here he was, paraphrasing "love is love" back in 1998. I've had conversations with friends and coworkers about how tough it is for them to discuss certain things with their ultraconservative parents, and I am grateful on the daily that this is one land mine of adulthood that I've never had to navigate.

Of course, in the moment, none of that "My dad's so hip and open-minded" came to mind as my father checked up on my feelings for Jason: "And you love this boy?"

My smile said more than any words could.

"And you have told him?"

"Yeah, we tell each other."

"I don't like that very much—"

"Dad!"

"—but I will not like any boy you bring home. Though I do like the smile he puts on your face, as unsettled as it makes me."

The following week, the Kapaglias picked me up, their SUV loaded down with tents and food and pots and cooking utensils. Dad stood in the front yard as Mr. Kapaglia fit my bag into a space in the back of the car.

"It'll be great," he said. "We'll get your girl back in one piece, I promise."

"Please do not bring her back in more than one piece," my father deadpanned, and Mr. Kapaglia threw his head back, like it was the funniest thing he had ever heard. Mrs. Kapaglia smiled a tight smile from inside the car.

Jason opened the back door for me. Gaby and her friend Dora were in the captain's seats behind Mr. and Mrs. Kapaglia, and Jason and I squeezed between the seats to our bench in the back. Gaby reared back and smacked Jason hard on the butt when he shimmied through, and he jerked around to punch her, also hard, on the shoulder.

"SLUT."

"DICK."

"GUYS!" Mrs. Kapaglia said, not even bothering to turn around.

Gaby gave me a cheeky grin as I sat down. "Hey, Asha. Glad it's you and not one of his dumb friends." She reached around her seat, took my wrist, and gave it a squeeze.

Jason immediately grabbed my hand and held it tightly. Dora, Gaby's friend, caught us and grinned.

"You guys are adorable."

When we pulled into the campgrounds four and a half hours later, I was surprised to see a big sign for mini golf right across the street.

"Hey, look!" I said, turning around in my seat to watch the sign fade away.

"It was fun when it was open," Mrs. Kapaglia said. "I used to go there all the time when I was little. It closed years ago. So sad. No one takes care of it anymore. It's all overgrown."

As soon as we got to our campsite, Mr. Kapaglia insisted we set up our tents. There would be three: one for Jason's parents, one for Jason, and one for Gaby, Dora, and me.

By the time we finished, the light was getting dusky. I gathered twigs and small sticks for kindling with Dora, Gaby, and Jason, who disappeared immediately.

"He's soooo lazy," Gaby said.

Soon we were all seated around the campfire, roasting marshmallows.

"I've never had a s'more before," I admitted to Jason, quietly. His mother heard me.

"Never had a s'more?! Come here, let me show you a secret. It'd be a lot easier if we hadn't forgotten the *lanterns*," she said pointedly at her husband.

"I swore I packed them." He shook his head, then scolded Jason: "Jay, give 'em a break, would you?" Jason was cracking his knuckles incessantly.

"Seriously, you're driving me crazy," Gaby said, and Jason moved close to her, shoved his hands in her face, and cracked the four knuckles on his left hand rapid fire—*crack-crack-crack-crack*. "How can you stand him?" Gaby asked me, pushing him away.

While I roasted my marshmallow—continually catching it on fire, blowing it out, and sticking it back in the flames—Mrs. Kapaglia assembled my s'more: two halves of a graham cracker with a square of chocolate in the middle and . . .

"What's that?" I asked.

"Peanut butter. It's the only way to eat them."

I added my charred marshmallow and took a bite, melty chocolate dropping onto my chin.

"Oh my god," I said, graham cracker crumbs spraying from my mouth. Before I even finished my s'more, I asked for another.

Slowly, everyone started to drift into tents: Mrs. Kapaglia first. Then Gaby and Dora. Jason's dad sat up with us as the fire burned down to embers. Soon the three of us retreated to our respective tents, too.

I fell asleep immediately but awoke after what seemed like only a moment had passed. Dora was whispering my name.

"What?" I asked, rubbing my eyes. "What time is it?"

"Look," she said, and I saw a flashlight strobe straight into the tent once, twice, three times. She poked her head out of the tent, turned to me, and said, smirking, "It's for you."

Jason was squatting in front of the tent with his flashlight—that thing had really turned into something of an Asha beacon, hadn't it?—and he whispered, "Come on!"

I ducked out of the tent, but Jason had already taken off. I scurried after him, not sure where we were going, not wanting to be left behind. I heard him before I saw him, cracking his knuckles again. When I caught up, he had turned onto the path leading to the camp entrance.

"Where are we g—" But he cut me off with a kiss, a deep and hungry one. God, he was good at that.

"Come on," he whispered, taking my hand, and we crossed the street, toward the abandoned mini golf course. As we approached, I realized it was much more than mini golf. I saw signs for go-karts ("NO U-TURNS"), concessions ("no running or pushing"), stables ("Pay here for Horses"), something called mallet pool ("4.00 per hr., maximum 4 People to a table, it's challenging!"), and Skee-Ball ("it's madness!").

"I love Skee-Ball," I whispered, stopping at the small structure with the sign. Jason shone his flashlight inside. I saw what looked like a shower curtain up to the left, partially hiding two Skee-Ball machines. There was a faded yellow towel, a container for a six-pack of soda, and a wrapped-up diaper.

As I continued to follow Jason through the fun park, we passed what I thought was a stuffed animal but was actually a pair of stuffed lips, still somehow bright red.

I was scared, but also a little thrilled. I was not this girl. I did not trespass with my boyfriend into scary fun parks, just like I did not break into neighborhood pools after hours. Except, it seemed, I did—and I loved it.

Jason flicked a nob on his flashlight, and it glowed brighter, covering a larger area. Everything looked different in the light. Scarier. No telling what could be around that corner, behind this turn, in that hut with white plastic hanging baskets out front, the bottoms broken out.

He led me off to the right, into one of the smaller brown huts.

"God, it's going to be disgusting in there," I said, and I stopped short when he opened the door for me.

Inside, a half dozen lanterns were scattered across the floor. Guess Mr. Kapaglia *hadn't* forgotten to pack them, after all. Jason flipped a switch on each—*click, click, click*—so that the room glowed. Four or five thick blankets were nested in the center.

"When did you do this?"

"I snuck over here when you guys were collecting stuff for the fire."

"Jason," I say, still whispering. "Jason, I'm not . . . I don't want to . . ."

"What?"

I couldn't believe I had to say it: "I'm not ready to have sex with you."

"Is that what you think?"

I gestured to the sex pit he'd created. "What else am I supposed to think?"

"I mean, I was kind of hoping we could kiss and stuff. But no, I'm not going to try and have sex with you. I think we should be married before we do that."

"You do?"

"My parents got married when they were twenty years old. They waited. That's what we're going to do."

"You think you're going to marry me?"

"I know I am." He was solemn, like he was already taking vows.

My heart picked up speed, and I thought it might break my rib cage.

"You're shaking," he said.

"Jay?"

"Yeah?"

"I don't want to have sex. But . . . some other things would be OK?"

He wrapped his arms around me tightly and kissed me so hard I could hardly breathe, but I didn't mind. We fell onto the blankets, and suddenly he pulled away. We were each on our sides—oh my god, I was lying next to Jason Kapaglia—and he stared at me for the longest moment. He began to trace his finger on my face: along the curve of my jaw, over each eyebrow, around my lower lip, where he paused.

"You are the most beautiful girl," he whispered, and he said what he'd told me a million times before, what I would never tire of hearing. "I love you."

"I love you, too."

In my head, this was romance. This was love. We could be silly together, and it was a part of our relationship that meant a lot to me, but I never felt silly when we got physical. Maybe it's because *he* took it all so seriously, and I followed his lead. I didn't have anything else to compare it to, so it seemed right to me.

What's weird is that with Charlie, none of this stuff was serious. Not to say it wasn't passionate, but we weren't so precious about it. At all. And maybe that's it: The firsts are precious, aren't they? And by the fourths or sixths or lasts, it's a part of life. Like dinner.

My god, I sound jaded. I need to get laid.

Anyway, back to the non-sex sex pit my first boyfriend built for us: I felt Jason press his hand to my chest above my sweatshirt, and I placed my palm atop his hand, brought it to my mouth, kissed his fingers. Then I placed it back. When did he slide it into my sweatshirt?

"Ow!"

"Are you OK?"

"Not that hard, Jay."

"Like this?"

"Maybe just use your thumb?"

I taught him how to touch my breasts that night. He taught me how to touch him, too; he placed my hand on his pajama bottoms, and I drew it back like I'd touched something hot. I didn't know it could get that hard.

"You don't have—" Jason started, and I interrupted.

"I want to." I reached for him again, pressing my hands tentatively to his groin. This was a penis? It didn't feel scary. Like I said, it was harder than I expected. Nothing like a hot dog, and it didn't seem remotely wet or slimy. (When I'd told Bridget what Heather had said that summer, we couldn't figure out if she was right. *Maybe it's bumpy, like a gravel road?* Bridget wondered, but that hadn't sounded right, either.) Without thinking about it, I slipped my hand beneath the waistband of his shorts. It felt perfectly dry and normal, like any other body part. When I moved my hand on it, clumsy, Jason exhaled hard.

"Asha," he whispered.

"Am I doing it wrong?"

He placed his hand atop mine, and together we stroked him, kind of like petting the back of a small dog, but firmer. After a few moments his body tensed, and he let loose a low moan.

"Oh my god," I said. "Did I give you a . . ." He smiled at me. "Really?"

"Why are you surprised?"

"I didn't think I could."

"You are very good at it."

We kissed for another hour. Only once did Jason try to touch me like I'd touched him.

"Not yet," I said, because I wanted him to so badly it scared me.

"OK," he said.

AUTUMN (2017)

Jason Kapaglia is walking down my hallway. Should I say hi? Do we hug? A kiss on the cheek? Not a handshake, surely? He avoids dealing with the appropriate way to greet me by taking the bottle of champagne from my hands, stepping into my kitchen, and opening my cabinets.

Bridget mouths a surprised *WOW* at me as she gives a small wave and quietly steps out of my house, inching the door shut behind her. I scream at her in my brain, *DO NOT LEAVE ME.* She must hear it. She must. I stare at the closed door. Maybe it will start to speak and tell me what to do next.

I hear my cabinet doors closing, one after the other, and I pull the towel from my head and throw it down the stairs into the family room, where it lands in a heap. The uncombed, wet-head look has to be a *little* better than the towel around my noggin, right?

"Ah," I hear Jason Kapaglia say. He makes a noise—*hmm*—in a tone I can't place. I turn. He is holding my wedding flutes, the etched gifts Charlie and I gave our guests. They read, "Charlie & Asha" and "Happy 2007" and "Staying together since 2006." That was supposed to be forever. I really thought it.

"There," I say, pointing to the kitchen table.

"What?" he says. Notices the other glasses, the ones from Heather. Then, "Oh."

Jason Kapaglia puts my wedding glasses back in the cabinet. He wraps one big hand around the neck of the bottle, uses the other to twist off the little metal cage. I have already peeled off the foil. It is on the hallway floor, where I dropped it when I heard his voice in person for the first time in thirteen years. *Um, I can get that? If you want.*

Pop. I jump a little. Jason Kapaglia pours the champagne into one flute, then the other. Hands me this second one.

"Bridget left?" Jason Kapaglia asks, and I nod.

Jason Kapaglia picks up his glass. Stares into it, watching the bubbles rise to the surface, dance on the meniscus.

"Meniscus," I say.

He looks at me, cocks his head.

"Meniscus," I say again. Cough. "The, uh. The curve of the top of the liquid. Where the bubbles are, where they gather there, at the top." I look into my glass, at my own meniscus. "I don't know why I said that."

"Cheers?" he asks, holding his glass to me.

I have never had champagne with Jason Kapaglia. He was my first in so much. So much. But not this. Nothing adult. Well. Something adult. I clink my glass against his. It is a dead sound. Not the happy kind that rings and reverberates long after one glass meets the other, that fades perfectly, and you don't even realize when you can't hear it anymore. Just *clink*. No life to that noise. No longevity.

Clink.

I burst into tears.

Our tender teen affair was admittedly more tumultuous than tender, so when the tenderness did appear, I clung to it, as the desperate in love tend to do. Here is one of those moments I held close: Once, when we were sixteen, we were doing our homework together on my deck in early spring; a bright sun kept the cool breeze from being *too* cool. I don't even remember if we were technically "dating" at that particular point. It never seemed to matter. Anyway, I was buried deep in a textbook, and Jason whispered, softly, "Asha . . . Asha . . . look."

I lifted my head, and he pointed off in the grass, beyond the swing set. A small bit of brown fluff nibbled the long blades missed by the mower, past the wooden post of the swing set. We watched the bunny hop and eat for what must have been twenty minutes. I remember the way his little nose twitched, and when I shifted to get a better view, he froze, one long ear cocked in our direction. I held my breath, willing him not to hop away. After fifteen seconds, twenty, he resumed his dinner.

We spotted our bunny throughout the summer and fall. I called him Giles, after my favorite character in *Buffy the Vampire Slayer*. I worried about Giles all winter, hoping he was warm. I'd see his little hop prints in the snow sometimes, and Jason loved to point them out to me.

"Giles was out again, look!" Sure enough, I'd see the little rabbit prints coming out of the woods near the tree line.

One January day, the footprints led toward a large evergreen that towered in the back corner of our house.

"Giles is on the move!" Jason said, and we stepped out the back door in our jeans, sweatshirts, and sneakers, and we followed the prints. There was not a second set of prints back to the woods, and I was convinced I'd get a close-up glimpse of my little pet.

"Oh, damn," Jason said, a few steps ahead of me.

"What?" I asked, coming alongside him.

Right between the tree and the house, there lay Giles, unmoving. A noise escaped my mouth, and I buried my face into Jason's chest. He wrapped his arms around me and said nothing. He didn't try to lead me inside or hush me. He stood with me in the snow, and he held me while I cried big, stupid, heaving tears. Stupid because it was only a rabbit, a wild animal. Wild animals freeze in the winter sometimes. It's OK. It's what they do.

Jason asked, "Do you have a towel or something?" He followed me into the garage, and I got him an old hand towel, something Dad used to wash the car in the summer. "Want some hot chocolate?"

I did. I went into the kitchen and filled the teapot with water. From the window above the sink, I saw Jason walking gingerly toward the tree line, the orange towel wrapped up and held in front of him. He walked a few feet into the woods, disappeared for a moment or two, and reappeared, the towel hanging empty from one hand.

He came in through the back door as I got two coffee mugs from the cabinet; then he wrapped me up in a hug from behind, giving me a soft kiss on the ear.

"Thank you," I said. He took the mugs from me and finished making the hot chocolate.

This Jason who is currently sitting across from me, this grown-up Jason, doesn't hug me as I cry. We haven't touched one another in nearly a decade and a half. It'd feel odd, like a stranger comforting me in my kitchen.

But he isn't a stranger. I may not know him as an adult, and he may not know *me* as an adult, but we share a history. We share memories. And that, combined with the physical fact of him across from me at my kitchen table, tells me it's enough. The memories belong to a different person—who of us stays the girls we were in youth?—but I don't particularly want to be the person I am right now, either. So all this is exactly right, and it actually feels good. Letting my tender heart rest after the year it's had—of course it feels good.

But it also feels like a betrayal.

"Why the hell . . . ?" Jason looks at his champagne glass as though he doesn't understand it, as though it does not fit, does not belong. He takes my flute from me and dumps the contents of each in the sink. I am still standing in the middle of my kitchen in my old bathrobe. "Sit," he instructs, and I obey.

He continues to open cabinets, shutting them. On the third try, he finds my hot chocolate packets. On the fourth, my coffee mugs. Instead of looking for my teakettle, he makes our hot chocolate in the microwave.

We are silent during the ninety seconds it takes for my mug to take a spin around the microwave and silent during the ninety seconds it takes for his to spin. Silence is relative, I suppose; we don't speak, but the air is punctuated by my sniffles, by the occasional crack of his knuckle. I smile. Not with my mouth, but I feel it in my brain, where the corners of my mental lips twitch a little. *Still,* I think.

He sets my cup in front of me, then sits in the chair across the table from me. He takes a small sip of his hot chocolate, sets the mug on the table, and, for the first time since he's arrived in my kitchen, Jason Kapaglia looks me in the eye.

Oh.

Definitely not a stranger.

This face, though older, is the same one I'd loved as a thirteen-year-old, as a nineteen-year-old. Same short fringe of eyelashes. Same freckles, though there aren't as many, and the same eyes that seem to change color. When I first watched him open the champagne bottle, those eyes looked brown. From close up, they are flecked with gold. The scar I'd loved to kiss now blends into faint wrinkles webbing out from the corners of his eyes. I can't see it, and I wonder, if I were to move closer, to press his skin beneath my fingertips, would I find it? I guess sometimes scars heal. Other times, we change, and the scars don't matter anymore. They disappear, lost among the spaces of the sixty dashes that wreath a clock. Time is linear, but sometimes we circle back again, don't we?

Jason's hair is still thick, still golden, though not as long and a little darker. He keeps it shorter on the sides, where I can see strands of gray. *He has more gray hair than me,* I think. He is clean shaven. He has the same eyebrows. I recognize his ears.

When I finish studying his face, I realize that he's studying mine, too, his eyes searching my hair, my cheeks, my mouth, my nose.

"What do you see?" escapes from my mouth before my brain gives the words permission to exit.

"You're beautiful," he says without pause, as though his words had escaped without permission, too. After a few beats, he confesses, "I don't want to go to dinner with you."

I feel my heart crumble a little. I had been scared, yes, but I didn't realize he hadn't wanted to see me. I am stunned at how crushed I feel.

Then he finishes his thought. "I thought it'd be weird seeing each other. I thought we shouldn't do that in public. Not at first. Also . . ." He opens and closes his mouth a couple of times like he's in an argument with himself: *Should I say it? Probably not. But I want to. But no.*

He ends up choosing to say it: "And I couldn't wait to see you."

I've imagined this meeting over the years, especially over the last year, when my brain wanted something else to think about, anything other than a husband who is slowly dying in a nursing home. When I thought of Jason, I thought maybe we'd be physically drawn to one another, and as soon as he walked in my house, he'd take me there in the hallway, unable to contain ourselves. I thought he might tell me, *I still love you. I've always loved you. I've never stopped loving you.* I thought maybe he'd be mad at me for that last time. Or maybe he'd ignore me entirely.

But he is not ignoring me; he is staring at me. He is not confessing love or anger. He has barely said anything since walking into my kitchen . . . *It's 3:45. He's only been here for ten minutes. This is the longest ten minutes of my life.* I try to suppress a smile.

He looks at me, a question.

"Remember how obsessed you were with time? You always talked about how it moved faster and slower at the wrong times."

"Faster when we were together. Slower when we weren't," he says.

"You've been here for ten . . . eleven minutes now."

"That's it?" He checks his watch.

"Longest. Ten minutes. Ever."

"No kidding," he says. Then, again, silence.

I wait one more beat, then . . . "Jason?"

"Yeah?"

"Why are you here?"

"I got divorced."

"I heard. I'm sorry. But why are you here?"

He nods, as though that answers my question.

He tells me how, when Simone told him one day, seemingly out of the blue, that she wasn't in love with him anymore, that she had fallen in love with someone else, he had cried.

Why are you crying? she'd asked him, not unkindly. *Are you in love with me anymore?*

"I realized I wasn't. I didn't even ask who the other guy was. I didn't care. I remember, I looked around, and I didn't see myself anywhere in our flat. She had decorated the whole thing. It was very modern. Straight lines. Lots of gray."

The walls in my kitchen are sunshine yellow. My curtains are turquoise and gold. The cushions on my kitchen chairs are royal blue. The clock on my wall is shaped like a cloud. He studies it while he says, "There was no life in that flat. It was lifeless."

He pauses.

"It wasn't always that way. I did love her. Once. I suppose I still must. Right? I mean, once you love someone, don't you always?"

I thought about Jason as a boy. How deeply I had loved. How fully he broke my heart and how much I wondered about him still, as an adult, always. I thought about Charlie, how much I missed him. How much I wanted him still. I thought about my grandmother. When Papa died, she told me how she had loved him since she was seventeen years old. And now she was eighty-two, and she did not know anything else, not even herself, without him.

I thought about my father, who grieved for my mother for my entire life. And just now, he had decided, it was time for companionship. Did he love this French teacher? This Celine? Maybe. Maybe not yet. Maybe soon.

"Yes," I say into my hot chocolate. And I force myself to look up, to say this next part to his face. "I think if you love someone, a part of you always does. It might look different. It has to look different and change. But it's always there, yes."

We both know what we have said to each other. We have said, *I still love you. I haven't ever stopped.* We said, *I moved on, sure, but I always wondered.* We said, *Maybe we could love each other again, in a new way.*

I want, suddenly, to be kissed. I want to be ravished. I want his tongue to greet every square inch of my skin.

He stands up. "I should go."

What? No. *No.*

Instead of saying this, I walk him to the door. He places his hand on the doorknob, opens it. I am about to tell him to wait, hold on, hug me goodbye, take-all-my-clothes-off goodbye. I want to reach out my hand for his back, but my hand won't move.

He turns around and looks at me. We stand close to one another. All he needs to do is bend at the waist, dip his head to put his mouth to mine. His lips are slightly parted, soft. I am staring at them, and I reach up on my toes, put my hands on his shoulders, and press my mouth to his. He doesn't kiss me back or deepen the kiss in any way. But he doesn't pull away at first, either. He doesn't touch me with his hands, but this is not a friend kiss. When he breaks the kiss, I'd been leaning into him. I have to take a step forward to keep from falling. He places his hands on my waist to steady me. The touch seems to press a button *on*, turning the lower half of my body into a magnet. It presses to his.

His thing, I think. *I gotta call Bridget.*

He smiles down at me. Steps back from me. Steps out my front door. Closes it softly behind him. *Why are you leaving again?* I want to shout after him. The door latches, and my body flushes with what I can only describe as a liquid ache. I feel it in the spot where my teeth meet my gums and rushing along the top of my arms. It trails on my neck and in my throat, and my face tingles with it. My brain demands that my body open the door, that it call to Jason, shout for his return so he can put his hands on me, but I am frozen.

I hear his car door slam, the engine start. He doesn't drive off immediately. He idles in front of my house, as though he's waiting for me to rush after him. I long to rush after him, but I am made of stone.

After thirty seconds, I listen to Jason pull away.

I consider calling Bridget to tell her about the visit, and perhaps about his thing, but I decide against it. I don't know how I feel about it, beyond the desperate need to feel him, and I suspect I won't figure it out in one night.

I need to clear my mind. I need to not dwell on the dull pangs that gently vibrate the small hairs on my arms and hands. I need to not pick apart what's just happened. Once, I was queen of picking apart everything about Jason; I am now too old for that garbage.

I leave the hot chocolate mugs on the table, flick on the TV in the family room, and wrap myself up in a fleece blanket from the trunk at the end of the couch. Mindless. No thinking. It is how I best figure myself out now that I don't run anymore. I haven't run since Charlie's accident.

Here are three true things I have learned today, three true things I did not know were true at 3 p.m. At 4 p.m., however, they entered the world's realm of facts:

(one)
I am still attracted to Jason Kapaglia.
(two)
Jason Kapaglia is still attracted to me.
(three)
I do, in fact, want to sleep with my ex-boyfriend.

And I wonder, is it him I want? Or just the sex? Or is it sex with him specifically? I think it's this last one. Is that good or bad? Lucky or unfortunate? Love or convenience? Whatever it is, this realization that I want *Jason* changes things. Doesn't it?

And what about him? He's not using me for sex, I don't think, but to help him handle his hurting over Simone. It's all sort of the same, isn't it?

But what about—

Nope, I promise myself again. *Not today. Not now. Later. One day at a time. One hour at a time.*

One hour at a time.

It is 4 p.m., and my dinner plans are no longer planned. At 5 p.m., I call Donato's and order a large pepperoni pizza.

At 6:05 p.m., my pizza arrives.

At 6:07 p.m., a memory of fighting with Charlie over the last piece of pepperoni Donato's appears in front of my eyes like a flashlight flicked *on,* and my first few bites of pizza are extra salty—would you like a side of tears, ma'am?

At 6:53 p.m., I take my dirty napkins, paper plate, and half-empty pizza box (or half-full, depending on your outlook, though today, indeed, my pizza box is half-empty) into the kitchen.

What do I want to do now?

I hardly finish the thought. I grab the phone and, from memory, dial Jason's childhood number. He picks up after half a ring. He does not say, "Hello?"

"Asha?"

"Wouldn't you have felt dumb if it was someone else?"

"I just did that to my aunt. She hung up on me. Thought she'd dialed the number wrong."

"What are you doing?"

"Honestly?"

"No, lie to me. Yes, honestly."

"Wondering why I left."

"Get over here."

"On my way."

I go into the bathroom, stare into the mirror. Makeup? Pretty dress? Lingerie? No, no, and no. Too much pressure. Too much everything. I settle for gray pajama pants and a sweatshirt, for brushing my teeth, getting the pizza off my breath. I gargle with Listerine. Twice. Run a brush over my hair. Consider masturbating, anything to ease the tension in my body. *No,* I scold myself. *It's been too long. Let it be what it'll be. Don't mess with that.*

I step out of the bathroom, pace around the kitchen. Walk down the hallway to the front door, peer out the small window at the side of the door. Pace back up the hallway. Get the champagne from earlier in the day. I'd forgotten to put it back in the fridge, and it's room temperature. I don't care. I pour myself a glass, down it in one swig, cough at the bubbles.

Pace down the hallway again. Peer out the window and jump back, as though a face in a bleeding clown mask is peering back at me. It's only Jason Kapaglia on my front stoop. He sees me looking. Waves.

I unlock the door. Open it. With two steps, he is inside my house. I grab his hand and pull him down the hall, up the stairs, practically running, into my bedroom.

SPRING (1998-99)

After the camping trip, Jason and I couldn't keep our hands to ourselves. The amount of time we spent together attached at the mouth was staggering. I think everyone we ever met caught us, at least once, wrapped around the other. I'm impressed we never broke the other's tongue.

I blame my make-out coma for not seeing what was happening to Jason until it all seemed to explode. In the midst of our love haze, Jason had started to pick fights. I use that phrase, "pick fights," in only the technical sense of the phrase. He'd never shout, but he'd casually bring up something that made him unhappy, and we'd discuss it, and he'd grow sadder and sadder, until he was a blubbering mess.

Everything about this new routine confounded me, but I know now none of it had anything to do with me. His dad had moved out that year, a few months after our camping trip. Mr. Kapaglia had answered the phone in his house one night, and, when another man had brazenly asked to speak to Trish, he'd said, *You mean Patricia?* He never called his wife "Trish." No one did. She wasn't a "Trish" kind of person. If it were possible to add even more syllables to "Patricia," she'd have insisted upon it.

After her husband left, Mrs. Kapaglia sort of disappeared into herself. Gaby always seemed to be at a friend's—she had a million—while Jason turned to me, and only me, for support. Looking back, I see that he was looking for the love and reassurance he should have received from his parents during that time, when they were both stuck in their own hells. I understand how he got a little swept under the rug, but I sometimes wish I could go back in time and tell off both of them, heartily. Not for splitting up—it happens, and not all marriages are supposed to last forever—but for completely forgetting about their ridiculously sensitive son in the midst of tearing up their lives and, by extension, their family. They should have borne some of his load. Instead, he dumped it on me. Pretty heavy for a fifteen-year-old navigating sophomore year.

To illustrate how that load looked, here is an incomplete list of things that might upset Jason:

(one)
Getting off the phone too soon, especially if I did so to talk to someone else. Once, when I had to hang up because Edward was on my other line to discuss a science project we were working on together, Jason showed up at Edward's doorstep twenty minutes later. *Just to hang out,* he said. He watched TV while Edward and I finished up the call. Just what Edward and I needed: a chaperone.

(two)
Having plans in place already when he'd want to hang out. A teenage couple, where neither party drives yet, doesn't have many options for dates. We tagged along with Gaby and her friends a lot, and sometimes one of our parents would drop us off at the movies or Kings Island. But if he invited me somewhere and I said, for example, *I can't. Bridget's spending the night,* he'd get all quiet and morose, then say, *Why don't you want to be with me?* Because you ask me inane shit like that.

(three)
Craig. Oh god, always Craig. Once, when my dad was at work, Jason snuck up to my bedroom. While we were in the middle of making out, he pulled away and pointed at my bulletin board. *Who's that?* In the photo, I am with two very similar-looking teenagers, a boy and a girl. We are on the beach. It was perfectly clear who was in the image with

me, but when I said, *Heather and Craig,* he murmured, *I wish you'd take that down.* I wanted to shove it up his ass.

(four)

Running. He'd joined the track team because of how much I loved to run. Unfortunately, what I loved about running was the solitude. I didn't want to join the team, too, and he took that as a personal affront. Never mind that he was a natural at it. Jason was built to run: long legs, lean muscle. It looked like he should trip over his own feet, like a fawn, but instead he seemed to fly, his feet hardly touching the ground. In his final meet that year, he set a new school record in the half mile. In the midst of all this, he was still a star. I may not have wanted to be on the team, but I bragged about him to anyone who'd listen. He never seemed to remember that part.

(five)

Nothing. Absolutely nothing. At least, that was what it seemed like to me. I'd call him in the evenings, and he'd have precisely zero to say. *I'll let you go,* I'd try, but he wouldn't want to hang up the phone. Nor would he want to start talking, nor would he want to tell me why he was being quiet. I watched a *lot* of TV that way that year, with the phone pressed to my ear, listening to my boyfriend breathe. I loathed it.

Because of that, this particular phone conversation on this particular day was nothing unique; we'd had it a hundred times before, and it wrapped up when he lamented that Edward and Daniel never called him anymore.

"When's the last time you called them?" I asked.

"I dunno."

"Call 'em now, see if they wanna hang out this weekend."

"It's OK if you don't want to talk to me anymore."

"I get you all the time," I said, trying to make a joke. "I can share."

"I don't know what I'd do without you." He paused. "Maybe when we hang up, you could call Craig." I sighed, and he continued, "You know. Your other boyfriend."

"I never dated Craig. We're just friends"—words that had left my mouth approximately a billion times.

"You still have his towel."

Jason *hated* my Miami Heat towel. He regularly asked me to throw it away.

Instead of taking the bait, I repeated, "Call them!"

"I'll call you right back."

He didn't. I didn't mind.

A few hours later, the phone rang.

"I'm coming to get you," Gaby said when I picked up the phone. "It's Jason."

"What's going on?" But she'd already hung up.

Gaby was in my driveway five minutes later, and she told me what happened: She'd been out with Dora, the friend from the camping trip. When she got home, the house was quiet; Mrs. Kapaglia was locked in her room, where she'd spent most of her days since their dad left, and Jason wasn't at his usual perch playing Nintendo 64 until Gaby screamed at him to get off and share the TV.

"Jay?" she called. Silence.

Then she heard a *thump* upstairs.

"Jay?" Gaby ran up the stairs two at a time. The bathroom door was cracked open. She swung the door wide to find Jason stooped over the sink. The small metal trash can was tipped over, its contents littered on the floor, like it had been kicked. An empty bottle of their mother's prescription depression meds lay on its side on the counter, empty.

"What did you do?" she shouted and grabbed her brother by the shoulders. The jostle bumped his hand against the counter, and a bottle's worth of pills fell from his palm all over the floor.

"Where is he now?" I asked, my body tense and trembling.

"Home. I told him I was picking you up, not to move. Got my mom out of her room. She screamed at him. Don't think *that* helped."

When we walked in the house, Jason and his mom were seated at the kitchen table. She looked exhausted, like she hadn't slept in a week.

Her hand was stretched out, holding tight to Jason's, whose fingers were limp.

"Hey, Jason," I said uncertainly, pulling the kitchen chair over, moving it as close as I could to his body.

His eyes were bloodshot and puffy, and he kept sniffling, wiping his nose with the hand his mother wasn't clutching like a flotation device in a hurricane.

My eyes darted from Jason to his mom, from his mom to Jason. I was certain she was mad at me, certain this was my fault, certain she knew it was my fault. I was curt with him. He heard my frustration when we talked on the phone. He hadn't wanted to call Daniel, and I insisted. *If I'd kept him on the phone, if I'd been my sweet, bubbly self, if I'd said "I love you" more, if I'd told him how handsome he was, how smart he was, how much I missed him when we weren't together, then maybe he wouldn't have thought of this. This wouldn't have happened, wouldn't have almost happened. His mother must blame me. She must hate me. It's all my fault. How can I ever speak to her again? How can I look her in the eye? She and his dad are fighting, and I know it, and she knows I know it, and she's embarrassed, and I'm embarrassed, and what am I doing here?*

Instead, Mrs. Kapaglia stood up, kissed Jason on the top of his head, then moved over to me and kissed the top of mine. She and Gaby left the kitchen, silent.

A few moments later, or maybe it was hours, Jason said, "I wasn't gonna do it." *Crack crack crackcrack.* His knuckles. "I wouldn't do that to you."

To you, he'd said. Not *to my mom* or *to my dad* or *to Gaby,* or, most importantly, *to myself.* But *to you.*

He reached out the hand that had refused to hold his mother's, and he grabbed mine from the table. He tugged on me until I stood up and lowered myself onto his lap. He wrapped his arms around me tightly. He didn't cry, but he held on to me, and I to him. We didn't talk.

I was about to be a junior in high school. I didn't know what depression was. It's only in retrospect that I see it. As far as I know,

Jason never was on any kind of medication. I don't think he had ever talked to a doctor. Can depression be an isolated incident? Something that happens only once, then fades away?

I don't think that's how it works, and I sure as hell didn't know what I was dealing with then.

SUMMER (2016)

Before Charlie's coma, I had been Mrs. Charlie Watters for three thousand, five hundred ninety-three days—just shy of ten years.

Being married was nothing like they told me.

It's hard work, they said.

You get what you put in, they warned.

The first year is the hardest, they swore.

Bullshit, bullshit, bullshit.

Being married to Charlie, to my Boy Scout, was cake, angel food, white and pure and fluffy and simple and sweet. It was heaven. It was the easiest goddamned thing I've ever done in my life.

The reason why is uncomplicated in its enormity: It's because he never wanted me to change. He never asked me to be less messy, to remember to buy toothpaste. When he was upset, he said so. He didn't point fingers or place blame.

One Sunday a month, I made it my sworn duty to bring him breakfast in bed. I even bought one of those trays with the handles and the short little legs that pop out and nestle on either side of the invalid. That was Charlie's word, not mine.

"I feel like an invalid," he said when I set the tray on his lap.

"Shut up. It's sweet."

"Where's yours?"

I ran out of the bedroom and came back clutching a plate with pancakes for me, too.

"Where will you eat?"

"On my lap."

"So I get the invalid tray and you get to eat like a normal person?"

"Shut up. It's sweet," I repeated.

He moved into the house I shared with Bridget, and for the first year of the marriage, Bridget lived there, too. When Charlie and I got back from our honeymoon, a week at a Mexican resort the first week of January, she'd thrown rose petals on our bed and lit about a dozen candles around the room. The following day, Charlie gave her a package wrapped with a huge bow.

"A thank-you for the flowers and candles," he said.

She tore into her gift, a girl on her fifth birthday, lifted the lid, stared at the box's contents for a moment, and broke into a grin.

"What is it?" I asked.

She lifted out a package of noise-canceling headphones.

"Just in case," Charlie said.

When Bridget decided to find a new place, I feigned excitement for the house to be ours, only ours, ever ours—and permanently, because we'd bought it from our landlord, Charlie's cousin—but I was devastated. I wanted us all to live together forever, but Bridget had decided it was time to leave. She bought a two-bedroom condo two miles away, making it the farthest we'd ever lived from each other since we met.

Her first night in the new place, I stayed the night. Her mattress had somehow not yet been delivered—when the moving truck showed up, the mattress was mysteriously missing, and it would never find its way home. Bridget took the opportunity to get the company to buy her a king-size pillow-top cloud, but that first night, all we had were blankets and throw pillows. We built ourselves a fort in front of her small TV, and I picked up Chinese from around the block.

I helped her unpack most of Saturday. When I left, she tried out her mailbox key for the first time. There, she met a man who lived downstairs, Alfie, a Brit eight years older than her who taught at UC's College of Medicine. They eloped six months later.

While she was meeting her future husband, I called Charlie from the parking lot. "The Chinese by Bridget's new place is awesome," I said. I was too sore, sweaty, and tired to cook. "Should I pick some up for dinner tonight?"

"I went to Kroger. Steak sound OK?"

"That's the sexiest thing you've ever said to me."

"Just wait," he said.

After dinner, he took me by the hand and led me upstairs.

"Hon, I never thought I'd say this, but not tonight? I'm exhausted."

Instead of responding, he stopped in front of the bathroom with TA-DA! arms. On the counter, he'd put a small basket of goodies— lavender bath salts, a candle that smelled like pineapple and coconut, a few fashion magazines, a shower cap, even though I'd never worn a shower cap in my life, and one of those foam pillows that suction to the end of the tub.

"Moving sucks," he said, and he gave me a peck on the cheek. "Enjoy your bath."

Being married rocks, I thought to myself.

I was only partly right; being married to my Boy Scout Charlie rocked, and it rocked for three thousand, five hundred ninety-three days.

On the three thousand, five hundred ninety-fourth day of marriage, Charlie woke up complaining of a headache.

"Want some ibuprofen?" I asked, moving to the drawer in the bathroom where we kept the pills.

He didn't answer, and I asked again, "Hon?"

He stood behind me in the bathroom, both of his palms pressing against his forehead, hard. He took his hands down and looked at me, squinting.

"What is wrong with you?"

"My vision's not right," he said, shaking his head and digging his palms into his eyes. "Everything's blurry."

"Call off work today?" I asked.

"I might go to the hospital."

"Christ, are you serious?" I was already getting dressed. Memories of our early relationship flashed through my brain. His father had been in the hospital because of a heart attack. He'd been fine since, to the point where I nearly forgot about it. But was this *that*? Charlie wasn't complaining of chest pains—his head hurt. Can a heart attack hurt your head?

When I pulled into the semicircle drop-off in front of the emergency room, Charlie had stopped talking. He could respond to me only with grunts, and I was convinced he was indeed having a heart attack like his dad. What else could it be? My Boy Scout was spectacularly healthy.

Of course he wasn't having a heart attack. What kind of complete fool would think he was having a heart attack?

He was having a brain aneurysm. Which led to a stroke. Which led to my husband, my love, my Charles James Watters, slipping into a coma, where he has resided for nearly a year.

Here's the thing about brain aneurysms: They're often hereditary, but Charlie had no family history. They're more common in women, but Charlie was a cis man. Black people are more likely to have them than white people, but Charlie's ancestors came from Scandinavia, land of the snow-white people, and Germany, Snow White's literal country of origin. Smoking can increase the chances of a brain aneurysm. He told me once, when he was sixteen, a friend peer pressured him into taking a puff off a Camel. He coughed so hard he vomited, and he felt so guilty he couldn't look his parents in the eye when he told them.

And? they said, waiting for the really bad news. Based on their son's behavior, he must have taken a puff and then put the cherry out in someone's eye. Maybe a little girl with cerebral palsy.

But no. That was it. Only that one puff.

Which is all to say, Charlie's brain aneurysm was as paradoxically unexpected as humanly, as medically, as physically possible. His chances of *dying* of one? They had to be about equal to the chances of him dying from a plane crash. Not being in a plane that crashed, mind you, but being the singular thing the plane crashed into.

I'm such a terrible human, such a terrible wife, that I don't remember learning that Charlie was in a coma a day later. I don't remember the doctor who told me—I'm assuming it was a doctor, maybe it was a nurse?—or the words they said. I don't remember my response, my reaction, my thoughts.

I've gone to a therapist sporadically over the last year. She called it a low form of dissociative, retrograde amnesia. Isn't that absurd? Like one of those damn fainting women who used to wear their corsets too tight. Modern, independent, adult me can't remember learning that her husband had slipped into a coma.

I hate that phrase, by the way. *Slipped into a coma.* It's too peaceful. Too easy. Slips are typically made of silk, wispy things that feel cool against your legs and look sexy when they peek from beneath the hem of your skirt. It'd feel more accurate to say Charlie detonated into a coma. Shattered into a coma. Nuclearized into a coma. Yes, that's it. He nuclearized, an atomic force capable of complete destruction, but worse, because there are people left, people who survived and don't know how to clean up after the onslaught, who aren't allowed to clean up because the nuclearization isn't complete, is it? Thanks to the machine that breathes for him and the tubes that feed him, Charlie is still technically alive. It is a technicality in only the most official, exact meaning of the word. *Alive.* A heart beats blood to a body's extremities, but it is no longer Charlie's heart or Charlie's body, because Charlie is not there anymore.

It is exactly what he never wanted. My Boy Scout deserved better, and I failed him. I will always feel that way. I remembered the conversation at the campfire a million times in the ensuing months, almost as though I had it on audio recording, a clunky cassette tape I could pop into the black, rectangular playback device in my brain. I replayed this audio so often and forced myself to be so thorough in my recollection that I don't even know if my memories are accurate anymore. Did he say *I would never want to be kept alive through tubes?* Or did he say *I don't want to get old and put on bed rest and force-fed medicine to stay alive?* Did he say *That's not living. That's not really alive?* Or *I'd hate to live like that?* Did he use those exact words in that exact order? I suppose it's the spirit of the sentiment that matters more than the precise words and phrasing, but I want to know the precision. The precision, to me, is precious.

When I think about the days and weeks right after Charlie nuclearized into his coma—and I don't like to do it, so don't ask me to explain it again—one memory replays, over and over. It's not of Charlie in the car as I drove him to the ER or seeing him in a hospital bed, hooked up to clear tubes and wires and beeping machines. It's not even of the first time I saw him at Pax, motionless and quiet, attached to all those tubes.

The memory is of me, alone at our kitchen table a few days after all that. Some part of me seemed to know from the beginning that my husband wasn't going to wake up, which is surprising—I am not an intuitive person. As a result, I don't know if this part of me is fatalistic or realistic, cruel or kind. I lean *kind* because this part of me kept its knowledge secret while I was in the midst of the blow. But once the dust settled, a thin blanket around my pale husband, my protective brain started to whisper to me gently.

I was alone in our house. In my house. My dad was on a flight back to Florida. He'd offered to stay longer, but I didn't want him around. I'd sent Bridget home because I didn't want her around, either. That either of these people let me shoo them out, I will never understand but always appreciate. Certain things, you need to do alone, to feel alone in order to fully absorb the scope of the heartbreak. Charlie deserved that—that I feel everything and numb nothing. It was a connection to him, however searing.

Every time I have this memory, I am transported there. It is not something of the past; it is something happening always, a crease in time to bring then-me to now-me and fold us together, eggs into batter, past into present.

I am at my kitchen table, breathing. In. And out. In. And out. In.

And out.

I'm breathing. I can breathe. I have the ability to draw air into my lungs, which powers my body. I press two fingers against the inside of my wrist and feel my pulse, the echo of my heart, which beats because my brain tells it to, because my brain is un-aneuritic.

The part of me that knows Charlie will not wake up, it is gentle with me. It says, *What if he's not better by Christmas?*

"Anything is possible," I hear the lady from Pax tell me, Maura, and Charlie's parents. We are in a small conference room down the hall from Charlie's room. The three of them ask questions. I do not.

What if he's not better by spring? asks the part of me that knows Charlie will not wake up.

The Pax lady is silent. I look up and realize she has said something to me. Charlie's parents hold one another. Maura glares at me. "I'm sorry," I say, and the Pax lady smiles. I will finally learn and remember her name in a few weeks. Josephine. I love her the way I imagine I might love an aunt, if I had any aunts. Josephine repeats, "Do you have any questions, Mrs. Watters?"

What if he never gets better? I do not think it at Pax because this piece of me with the knowledge is protective. It waits until I am in my kitchen before it whispers the words.

I am not going to get old with Charlie, I think. *We will not have kids. We will never set foot together on another continent.*

We will not hold hands again or make love again. He will never know what my body looks like wrinkled, my breasts sagging, my tannish complexion marred by the crags of age. We will not skinny-dip in the ocean. We will not buy a hot tub and play connect-the-dots with the stars or our limbs.

I listen to the clock on my wall, soft *ticks*, and I listen to the air conditioner kick on, whirling. I hear a quiet *tap tap* on the patio door, turn my head, watch a bumblebee bump into the glass.

Listen.

Drip drip.

Charlie taught me how to fix a leaky faucet the previous year. *I hope I remember how,* I think.

Drip drip.

My house is alive, speaking to me. I can hear it, but I will not hear my husband's voice again.

My eyes flicker to the clock once more, and I blink. I have been sitting at the kitchen table for twenty-two minutes, silent and listening, feeling my pulse in my wrist and breathing.

I draw a deep breath, deep, deep, filling my lungs with oxygen, delicious oxygen, full to bursting, tearing the seams, drawing in one more cubic centimeter of gas than my lungs are meant to hold. They stretch because they work, because they are healthy.

And I scream.

I imagine shattering the patio door, a shard of glass piercing the bumblebee. My noise is an extension of me, vibrating the drip right out of the sink. I imagine Charlie listening, because Josephine said his ears might still work, and he is stunned to hear my voice. How could he be hearing my voice? It is because I scream so loudly I cross barriers, I leap time, I break dimensions.

I imagine shredding my vocal cords, letting me spend the rest of my life in silence with my screams. My screams demand of the universe, *What am I supposed to do now?*

I imagine the universe knocking on the front door: *There, there, my dear, there, there.*

Grief is personal, a fingerprint or DNA cell. In my dad's eyes, it looked wistful, sadness tinged with love and memory. My grandmother cries every time she speaks of Papa. She hardly acknowledges her weeping and continues the conversation as though her eyes are not swimming, as though her tears are not overflowing down her soft face. I imagine other widows wear sweatpants forever or swear off romantic partners, who feel guilt every moment they are not actively missing their spouses, who question their existence and lose their sense of self and purpose.

Instead, three days later, I called Bridget.

"Let's go to Cujo's," I asked. No, not *asked*. Demanded.

We drank cheap beer and split nachos. It was the first food I remembered eating in a week.

At 9 p.m., the band came out.

"Shit," Bridget murmured.

I turned around to face the stage. Francis B. and his trio of boys, our wedding band.

While they fidgeted with their speakers, their mics, Bridget approached the stage. Francis saw her, recognition lighting up his grin, his wave. She whispered something in his ear, and his grin disappeared. His eyes searched the crowd, found me. He waved again and nodded to Bridget.

"Do you have to tell everyone?" I asked as she sat back down.

"Didn't want them playing anything from . . ." She shook her head. "Do you want to leave?"

I didn't. I wanted more nachos, and I wanted more beer, and I wanted to listen to music with my best friend and be sad.

During their break, Francis B. came up to our table. I surprised all three of us when I stood and gave him a hug.

"We play every Saturday," he said. "You should come back next week."

I did, without Bridget.

"Do you eat brunch?" he asked after their set that night, and I wrinkled my nose. "I know a place about ten minutes north that has a killer Bloody Mary bar."

Was this disgusting human being hitting on me?

I made plans to meet him the next afternoon.

"What the hell is wrong with me?" I asked Bridget that night at my kitchen table. I called her on the drive home, asked her to spend the night. She stared at me. "What?"

"I'm thinking," she said, and she stared at me longer.

"Well?"

"You should go."

"What?"

She shrugged. "Why not?"

"I can think of a few reasons."

"Don't tell Maura."

"God, no." I shuddered.

Maura had been calling me every day. *Where are you? When are you coming to visit? Let's plan our visits so someone is always there. Mom and Dad aren't going, either. What is wrong with everyone? Why aren't you helping? The Lord is caring for Charlie, and he simply has to rest. Our presence and prayers will make him strong. Where are you, Asha? Asha? Asha?*

I started to avoid her calls, and then I began to delete her voicemails without listening. I blocked her texts, too.

I went to brunch with Francis. I learned he had enrolled in school again. He was twenty-eight and had spent the last year in Spain—he told me the city, and I promptly forgot. He taught English to kids. He loved the country but decided a life of lesson plans was not for him, so he came home and enrolled somewhere locally for nursing. College was easy, he said. He couldn't believe how easy.

"It's like, coming back as an adult, you want to tell these kids in your class, calm down. Just do the work. You'll be fine."

These kids. His use of the phrase made me roll my eyes. Twenty-eight. What a baby. What a . . . wait . . . that's not actually that young, is it? However . . .

"Wait. If you're only twenty-eight, how old were you when you played . . ." I trailed off, counting on my fingers. "How did you play at my wedding?"

"You caught me." He gave me what, I could tell, he thought was a charming smile. "I had a fake ID to play gigs. Started the trio when I was eighteen. It was calling me, you know?"

I was only five years older than this guy, but I felt justified in looking down on him, righteous.

"I'm sorry about your man." He changed the subject abruptly, and I nodded. "Didn't know if it'd be weird to ask you out."

I nodded again. "It is," I confirmed. "But I'm here anyway."

"Have you been to Roux?" he asked. "It's a Cajun creole restaurant. Exquisite food."

"Cajun, like New Orleans–style?"

"Exactly."

Me and Charlie had been planning a trip to New Orleans. We wanted to go in the fall. I did not tell Francis B.

A few summers ago, Francis said, he and his brothers canoed down the Mississippi from the river's head.

"Lake Itasca," I said, and Francis lit up. He wore one of those newsboy caps, and he lifted it to run a hand through his hair. I started when I saw it—dark, longish, pulled in a tiny nub of a ponytail beneath his hat. Like Charlie's. Shorter, but close enough. A longing grew in my gut to touch such pretty hair, and I wondered if Francis would mind being my stand-in for a little bit.

"Had to cut it short after two hundred miles, though," he said.

What? I thought. *Two-hundred-mile-long hair? . . . Oh. The Mississippi.*

"We got a call that my great-grandma died. But we still wanna finish the trip. And not start from the beginning, that's the boring part. We'll start when it really gets good."

"How will you know?"

"What?"

"Without the boring part. How will you know when it gets really good if you don't do the beginning?"

He ignored my question and asked instead, "Would you ever do something like that? Take like a month and get on a river, camp out at night?"

"Not a chance," I said, thinking of my two forays into the woods. "I like beds."

He smiled like I'd said something dirty.

"I've been trying to figure out my next epic with my brothers. That's what we call them."

"Like the Appalachian Trail or the PCT?"

"The Pacific Crest Trail, yes!" He held up his fist to me.

I raised my eyebrow at him and bumped my fist against his. His smile did not falter, but a little voice in my head told me, *Leave*.

Instead, I asked him if he wanted to come home with me. On a Sunday at 2 p.m.

When we walked into my house, I watched my hand reach out and grab Francis's. I felt my body lead him over to our couch. I sat and pulled him down next to me. I watched him lift his hands, cup my face, lean close to me.

I felt his mouth against mine, dry. His lips were slightly chapped and thinner than Charlie's. He had a tongue ring.

My lips didn't respond. He pulled away and looked at me with such sorrow, as though he could possibly understand what was going on in my head, in my heart. Why was I doing this? Why did I want to do this?

"Baby, baby, baby," he whispered, like I was a toddler, like he was a dad.

I hugged Francis harder than I'd hugged anyone in years, even Charlie; my Charlie embraces were not full of desperation.

I didn't know what to do, so I pressed my lips to his cheek, to his mouth. It was not desire or lust that drove my fingers through his hair or pulled his body down on mine. It was a need to feel something else, anything else.

After, I lay back on the couch, staring up at the ceiling as Francis B., my wedding singer, spooned my side. We were both nude, our clothes kicked to the floor.

A few moments of silence passed, and I turned to look at Francis. He had his head propped on his fist. He stared at me, and I didn't know what to say.

So I pulled him toward me once again.

In retrospect, I wish I felt guilty about it. Or sad. Or . . . *something*. But I didn't feel anything. And feeling nothing in relation to sex—that had never happened to me before. Because sex had always been a joy for me, a thing done to feel good. Even when it was done in desperation, as my first time with Jason was, in part, that experience was . . . I wish I could come up with a better word than *wonderful*, but it's the most accurate, especially when you look at the parts of the word, as in *full of wonder*. Similarly: *awesome*, as in *full of awe*, and *terrific*, where the root is *terror*, because your first time can be scary. But that fear can highlight and underline a good experience to make it beyond anything you could imagine.

However, I did not feel good after Francis. I didn't feel worse, but that's probably because I couldn't feel worse. I was at my lowest. If I were to use a geologic analogy, I might say I was at the inner core, the center of the earth, where you can't go farther down without again going up.

When we finished the second time, I wanted to ask him to leave, but I didn't know how.

This was largely because he'd fallen asleep.

I lay on my back, half pinned under a naked man. I wanted to wake him up and get him out. But some batshit Midwestern politeness thing kicked in, like it'd be rude to rouse the sleeping man who'd just come inside me twice. (Don't get any ideas—I was on the pill, and Francis had a clean bill of health. This is not one of *those* stories. One life-altering misery at a time, please and thank you.)

So instead of waking him up nicely—*Get up, please*—or rudely—shoving him on the floor—either of which would have been better than this, I managed to wiggle the bottom half of my body out from under him. I slithered the rest of myself out but got caught at my head; he was lying on my hair. I gathered it in my hands and pulled slowly. It probably would have been easier if I'd have done it magician-style, like when Mr. Abracadabra yanks a tablecloth out from under a fully set table. But again, I was trying to not wake up Francis.

After I extricated myself, I got dressed and texted Bridget:

I brought Francis home and we fuc-

I stopped. That wasn't the right word. That word implies a fun time, at least in my experience, and I don't think that was *fun*, per se. I hit backspace three times and finished the text:

had sex and now he's asleep on my couch and how do I make him leave?

Immediately, the read receipt popped up and Bridget responded, WHAT?

As I started to type in my question again—How do I get him out of here???—I saw she was already responding again. Her message said, GET OUT.

Me: ?

Bridget: Get out of the house.

Me: But Francis is here.

Bridget: Right. But he'll wake up and you'll be gone and he'll just leave.

Me: Isn't that mean?

Bridget: OMG who cares?

Me: Let's call that Plan B.

Bridget: So what's Plan A?

Me: That's why I texted you.

Bridget: OK. What about this?

Her plan wasn't a bad one. So I turned on my ringer and flicked up the volume as loud as it could go. I left the phone on the floor near Francis's head and went upstairs. Bridget called. Even if I were in the shower, blaring Biggie Smalls, singing at the top of my lungs, I'd hear that damn ring. Francis, however, could apparently sleep through a firework display happening directly above his head.

The call went to voicemail. Bridget left me a message, and my phone chimed the alert. Seconds later, she called back. I clomped down the stairs as loudly as I could, jumping the last three steps so I thudded on the landing.

Francis, finally, stirred as I picked up my phone and said, loudly, "Hello?" Then "That's terrible, are you OK?" and "I'll be right there!"

I hung up, and Francis sat upright slowly, rubbing his eyes.

"Everything good?"

"I'm so sorry, I have to go," I said, trying to sound worried and hurried, but not quite distressed. "My best friend, Bridget, from last night, she got into a car wreck. I gotta go pick her up."

"Oh, that's the last thing you need right now, baby. Of course, go to her. Is she OK? I can go with you?"

"No," I said, probably too quickly. "No, you don't have to come. She's fine, just a little scared, I think. You should probably go."

He began to put on his boxers as slowly as possible, and I found myself staring at his crotch. *Get your damn nut sack off my couch* flashed through my brain.

"How about I just wait for you here?" he said, crawling into his T-shirt like a kid trying to put off bedtime. "Then I can be around when you get back."

"No, no, I—" I didn't know how to finish. "Francis, listen, I need you to go, OK?"

His face fell, and I found myself wanting to cushion the blow. But no—this man needed to get out of my house.

"I'll call you tomorrow," I said, lying. Anyone with a brain would have known I was lying. Right? *Right?*

Alas, Francis did not take the hint.

The next evening, he texted: How's your friend?

It took me a beat to figure out what he was talking about.

Good, I responded. Car should be OK.

Thank the stars!

Seriously. That's what he said. I did not respond. Ten minutes later: Have a good night, sweetheart. I'm thinking about you.

I snarled—Charlie called me "sweetheart." I did not like it coming from anyone else.

I thought for a moment, typed Thanks, then deleted it. OK, and deleted it. Why? and deleted. Could I respond with a thumbs-up? That felt cruel. After a few minutes of trying to figure this out, I saw his dots appear.

I hope that wasn't strange, he texted. Tho I had a beautiful time yesterday. I apologize if I made you feel something negative. That's the last thing I want, and he punctuated it with a little purple heart.

Thanks, I typed again, and this time, I sent it. Before I could put the phone away, the dots appeared again, then a trio of hearts: purple, red, purple.

I turned off my phone. Good Lord, what had I done? I was in no headspace to deal with this. I was in the throes of the kind of grief I'd only read about, and grief, apparently, can make you do ridiculous things. Today I look back at that girl going through the worst thing, and I feel compassion and grace for my 2016 self. In the moment, however, I had no room for grace. No grace, no Francis, no nothing.

Just Charlie. Only Charlie.

What do I do with myself now?

The room was much too quiet, and I didn't want a repeat of the conversation at the dinner table with my chatty house, so I watched, in order, all three *Lord of the Rings* movies. Nine-plus hours, with pauses only to pee and make popcorn.

The credits to *The Return of the King* started rolling around 1:30 a.m. The sun had been up when I first hit play, and I never bothered to turn on any lights, so I sat in the dark. I leaned over to turn on the lamp by the couch and would have laughed at what I saw if I was capable of laughter at that point. I was swaddled in a nest of blankets, used tissues scattered all over the couch and carpet. Not that *The Lord of the Rings* is particularly sad. But I periodically would start to sob, unrelated to

Sauron or the Orcs. *Charlie's impression of Gandalf . . . how it took us three times to get through* The Two Towers *together two months into dating because I couldn't keep my hands off Charlie . . . the way he loved Merry and Pippin . . . the way he loved Frodo's final triumph over evil . . . the way he loved . . .*

Instead of cleaning up, I fell asleep in my nest, and I dreamed of empty shires. I was lost, but none of the hobbits could hear me ask for him.

The next morning, I woke up shaking.

Specifically, Francis shaking me.

"What are you doing here?" I asked, meaning, *Why are you in my house?*

"You weren't answering," he said, his eyebrows knit together, anxiety painted on his face like van Gogh. "The back door was open."

"It's early," I said.

"Sweetheart, it's two in the afternoon."

Oh.

"What are you doing here?" I repeated.

"I had to make sure you were OK," he said.

"Francis, I can't do this right now."

"Of course, darling, of course. You just woke up. We don't have to talk now."

"No, I don't want to talk," I said. "Not at all."

He looked at me, seeming not to get it. I didn't know whether he was being purposely dense or whether he seriously lacked the ability to empathize with my situation.

"Listen, I'm in mourning right now," I told him, nearly disbelieving that it needed to be said. "I can't deal with any of this. I need to be alone. You know? Do you understand?"

"Sweetheart," he said again, his face falling, but comprehension crossed his features. "I'm such a . . . yes, yes, of course I understand. If my baby needs space, she'll get space."

My baby?

Francis left, and I took a forty-five-minute shower. When I got out, I finally turned my phone back on.

I had forty-two missed texts: one from my father, three from Bridget . . . and the rest were from Francis.

The next three weeks passed in a blur, but also whatever's the opposite of a blur. Because I don't really have chronological memories of that time so much as periodic spots of clarity, like

(one)
Bridget bringing a bag of groceries the first time.
(two)
Flashes of my movie marathons: The *Godfather* trilogy, four *Hunger Games* movies, eight *Harry Potter*s, ten *Halloween*s.
(three)
The timbre of my father's voice on the phone.
(four)
Bridget bringing a bag of groceries the second time, noticing I was in the same clothes from however many days prior, bathing me.
(five)
The texts from Maura, which I'd barely respond to, and
(six)
texts from Francis, which I'd never respond to.
(seven)
Masturbating daily, which brought grounding, brought gravity. The rest of the day, I floated six inches above my body.

After weeks of popcorn for dinner, coffee for breakfast, a few grapes or slices of American cheese for lunch, I promised Bridget that I'd make myself a real dinner. She offered to cook for me, and, in retrospect, I should have let her, if only to have another person around to serve as buffer for what was about to happen.

Bridget had brought me a T-bone, a bagged salad, and a bottle of cheap red wine. As the steak sizzled in the melted butter on the stovetop, I picked at pieces of lettuce from the bowl and opened the bottle of wine. In my search for a glass, I found, of course, our wedding glasses. *The way we kissed at midnight . . .* I slammed the cabinet door. The knot in my throat should have blocked the swig of wine from the bottle, but it ended up in my belly and not all over the counter.

Nope, I thought. *Steak. That's all you should think about right now. Steak.*

I started to hum it to myself, a little ditty of steak steak steak steak steak in tune to Rihanna's "Birthday Cake." Alone, in my kitchen, I sang a nonsense sex song to my dinner with a red wine mic: "I know you wanna bite this. It's so enticing. So rare and juicy. T-bone steaks are my bitch."

A knock interrupted my concert. I turned off the stove and answered the door.

Francis.

My first thought: *Why isn't he wearing a shirt?* I answered myself: *Because this is a guy who, sometimes, just doesn't wear a shirt.*

When I didn't say anything to him, a corner of his mouth lifted up, sheepish. He knew he shouldn't be here. I saw it on his face. Maybe that's why I let him come in when he asked, "Can we talk?"

We sat across from one another—Charlie had always sat next to me—at the kitchen table, and Francis said, "I know you're . . ." He trailed off, shook his head. "No. I can't know. What you're going through right now, I don't . . . I can't imagine . . . the sadness in your soul, I can hardly bear it. I hate to see you like this."

But you've hardly seen me at all, I did not say.

"I just want to heal you. I wish I could take you in my arms and love you and make it all better. Your poor heart." He reached over and covered my hand with his. "Your amazing, poor heart."

He stopped. I didn't respond. In the silence, a part of my brain registered a creaking in the hall, my house talking to me again, probably saying, *Jesus God, make him leave already.*

"That night we sat together at Cujo's, that was the best day of my life."

Me, unspoken: *You have* got *to be kidding me.*

"When I played at your wedding, you were the most beautiful bride I'd ever seen. I've seen a lot of girls in that bar. No one has ever been as lovely as you. This angel. This beautiful angel. When I taught in Murcia, the family I lived with? Their grandmother, their *abuela*, she read auras. She taught me how. I'm not too good at it, but you, your aura, it explodes at me. It's so fiery, completely red and orange, can you dig it?"

Would it be rude to stand up and get my wine?

"That means you're creative, and passionate, and sensual, and secure. It's the best combination, and so bright. Oh, baby, you are so bright. And I knew, I knew before I met you. Really met you. Since your wedding.

"Then you came back. I hadn't seen you in years. Years. Your friend came up to me. Told me what happened. Heartbreaking. The worst thing, baby. The very worst thing. But then I saw your face, saw you checking me out. And I thought, *Is this for real? Does this, this angel, this sensual, gorgeous, fluttering angel, does she want to be mine? It can't be. We'll only ever be friends. I'm not that lucky.*

"But the universe had other plans, didn't it? It had other plans, it sure did, can you dig it? And when you invited me back to your house, the universe asked me, *Are you ready for this, Francis? Are you really ready? Don't you mess around now, this is the real deal.* I know I can never be Charlie, baby, but I can be good to you."

He said my husband's name, and I recoiled. He held tighter to my hand, but it's like his speech was the magic potion to snap me out of my hypnosis.

"No, baby, no, I'm sorry, it's not like that. I mean, I still can't believe this could happen to you, my perfect sweetheart. My heart breaks in pieces for you, and they want to go to you, to wrap you up, to heal you. You've been through so much, and there's still so much to go through. But you have to know: Asha, *mi cielo*, my sky, I am here for you. Even if you're not ready for it yet, I came over to tell you, I can wait as long as you need, baby. I had to tell you. To your exquisite, ethereal face: I can wait for you. You can't lose me. Whatever you need, you got it. I want you to be happy, and what you have to go through, it breaks my heart. 'Cause I know what you have in you. I know what you could *be*. I *saw* it. I saw it when I was *inside you*."

Ugh, puke.

"And I'm gonna do everything I can. I pray for you every day, I'm gonna do everything I can to lift you up and bring you love. That's what I'm here for, baby. That's why I came here."

Then Maura stepped into the room.

SPRING (1999)

I never told my dad about the pills. When Gaby dropped me off that night, I said Jason was sad because of his parents, and Gaby thought I might be able to help. I did not say, *My boyfriend was thinking about suicide, and the only person he wanted to be around was me.*

The lie—which I told because I had no idea how to explain to my father what had actually happened, had no concept of "depression," let alone its actual manifestations—led to something unexpected.

Dad and I planned to visit my grandparents for a long weekend toward the end of summer, for my sixteenth birthday.

"How would you like to bring a friend?" my father asked me. Before I could say, *I'll call Bridget,* he continued, "Perhaps the trip will help Jason to feel better."

"Jason?"

He mistook my surprise for displeasure. "You do not wish to ask him? I only thought—"

"No, no, that's—Dad, really?"

"I thought maybe he would like to get out of his house for a few days. It sounds very . . . messy there. And I thought maybe you would like to show him your Florida."

When I called Jason to tell him, he immediately rattled off all he wanted to do there: "We can watch the sunrise on the ocean. Your grandmother can read my fortune. I can make dinner for everyone. We can go to the lighthouse at 26.26 degrees north, 80.08 degrees west."

I don't know why I was surprised he'd remembered my mystical boat trip with my mom to Western Sahara; Jason never forgot anything.

His excitement made me think that, maybe, this trip could cure him, that whatever was making him sad might dissipate in the Florida sunshine and salt water.

The night before we left, though, I had a knot in my stomach. What if moody Jason was the one who boarded the airplane? What if he met Craig and picked a fight? What if my grandparents didn't like him?

So I called Edward. I knew it was one of Jason's triggers, but I needed to talk to someone who cared for Jason, too, who might be able to help. Plus, I trusted him.

I didn't tell him about the pills, but I did want to know if he'd seen a difference in Jason since Mr. Kapaglia moved out, too.

"Jason's dad moved out?"

Crap. "I figured you knew."

"He doesn't talk to me like he talks to you."

"You're his best friend," I countered.

"Eh," he said. "The way he is with you, that's different. We both know Jason can be kind of intense. It's like you even him out. When your name is so much as mentioned, he sort of eases up a bit. It's like you relax him. Like you make him feel safe or something."

∽

The first night in Florida was perfect. Jason gushed over Nana's food, and he asked about the small garden my grandfather kept in the back. When my dad pointed out various herbs, plucking leaves from the ground and popping them straight into his mouth, Jason asked to try some, too.

That night, before bed, he asked my grandmother for an alarm clock for his basement bedroom, which had a futon, but not much else.

"I want to see the sunrise on the beach," he said, grinning over at me. Sure enough, before 7 a.m., I awoke to a soft "Ahh-sha. Ahhh-sha."

I opened my eyes on the living room couch—my dad slept in the spare room when we visited—and there was Jason, peering down at me.

Before I could get out of bed, Jason left a quick, sweet kiss on my mouth, and my lingering sleep dissipated like fog in the sunshine. I ducked quietly into the bathroom, brushed my teeth, changed into my swimsuit, some shorts, and a tee, and grabbed a towel from the hall closet in the dark.

We crept out the front door and were on the sand after a ten-minute walk. The dark beach was deserted and surprisingly cool. I cursed myself for forgetting a sweatshirt—my tee did little to keep me warm. Jason unzipped his hoodie and slipped it around my shoulders backward, like a blanket, after I spread out the beach towel. We cuddled and marveled at the vacant beach. The wind flapped our hair lightly, and Jason pulled me close and kissed me sweetly. I melted into him, and I felt myself pressing him back onto the sand. He laughed softly, taking my shoulders and sitting me up.

"We can't miss this," he said, but he slipped his hand under the hoodie, beneath my shirt and my bathing suit, and he stroked my breast.

I felt excitement for the sunrise, excitement at his hands on me, excitement to be there, on that morning, with this boy, in that precise square of sand.

As the fingernail sliver of molten pink crested the horizon over the Atlantic Ocean, I imagined stepping into the water with Jason, and I imagined making love to him there. I knew we were waiting until we were married for that, but the fantasy had been a favorite of mine for months. This is where my brain lived during the minutes it took the sun to fully bob into the sky: lost in the majesty of the sunrise and drowning in all that mental sex, enough that I didn't notice when Jason's hand stilled on my breast, then pulled gently, but swiftly, away.

"Wow," I exhaled. "I can't believe I've never seen that before. Thank you for waking me up. I—" I stopped talking. "What? What happened? Jason, what is it?"

His face had hardened, his lips pressed into a tight line. He looked straight into the middle distance, and when I tugged on his arm, he pulled it away from me.

"Jason, *what*?"

"Where did *this* come from?"

"Where did *what* come from?"

"This. The towel." He didn't move. He didn't budge.

I looked down, and dawning flooded my body with an icy-cold regret. Not wanting to wake anyone up this morning, I had pulled a towel blindly from the linen closet. Apparently the last time my dad and I visited my grandparents, the previous winter, I'd accidentally stolen Craig's faded Miami Heat towel. Jason and I were seated on it now.

"We must have picked it up by mistake."

"And when was that?"

"You remember. Dad and I were here in January."

"And you saw him." It was not a question.

"I saw them both. Craig *and* Heather." He cringed when I said *Craig*.

"Why didn't you tell me you saw him?"

"I always see them when we visit," I said, defensive, though he was right: I'd neglected to tell Jason about that afternoon on the beach with my friends. It was a purposeful decision.

"You lied."

"I never lied. Jason, I would never lie to you." I was having difficulty keeping my voice down. I wanted to scream, to shout at him, to ask him why he was ruining this amazing moment, to ask why he was always this impossible. I was trembling again, but not because I was cold. My hands clenched into fists, and I felt a pounding drum in my ears. I took a huge breath and let it all out in a rush. It felt like a roar. I muttered to myself, without meaning to, "I am so sick of this."

After a beat, Jason said quietly, "So you're sick of me."

Was I sick of Jason? I mean, I was sick of how sad he was all the time. I was sick of how much he cried, how little it took to set him off.

I was sick of him looking to me for *everything* and completely neglecting his friends. I was sick of him thinking he was awful at everything. As I list it out now, what was going on was so obvious. But sixteen-year-old me didn't have a clue. All that girl wanted was to have her smart, silly, wiggling boyfriend back. I hadn't seen him wiggle in ages.

"No. I am not sick of you," I said. "But I am sick of how you act. What do I have to say for you to trust me? What the *hell*, Jason?"

He was silent, and, again, the words came out of my mouth before I gave them permission: "I can't do this anymore."

Another pause. "And what does that mean?" His voice cracked on every word.

"This is too much. It's too much." I pulled away from him, to the farthest edge of the towel, and I looked at him. "It's too much. You're not happy, either."

At this, his watery eyes overflowed, and he pulled up a corner of the dreaded towel to wipe his nose. "No," he insisted. "No. I don't accept it."

"There's nothing to accept, Jason. It just is. Or isn't. Whatever. I can't do this."

"Say 'It's over.'"

"What?"

"You have to say 'It's over.'"

"I'm not going to say that."

"If you don't say it, you don't mean it. You have to say that."

"Jason, please." I had never begged for anything in my life, and here I was, begging.

"Say it."

"Stop."

"Say 'It's over.'"

I flashed for a moment to the last time I was on the beach, in January, with Heather and Craig. Heather went home early with cramps. After, without deciding to do so, Craig and I began to make a sandcastle. We snatched a bucket from a family down the beach, so our castle boasted a series of round, turreted towers. I worked on the moat while Craig used his pinkie finger to carve out small windows and doors on the towers. We didn't say much while we worked—hell, while we *played*; let's call it like it is—because we were too lost in the playing.

After, we stood up and admired our handiwork. Then, at the exact same time, we each kicked down a tower and jumped all over the castle, shrieking and giggling like four-year-olds. At one point we clutched hands and spun in circles until we flew apart, dizzy and gasping through laughter.

I've never wanted to date Craig, truly, but man, what I would have given for things with Jason to be half that effortless.

"Jason?"

"What?"

"It's over."

He stared at me for a moment before throwing his hands down onto the towel as hard as he could, making a dry *thwump* on the beach. He scrambled to his feet, and he took off along the shoreline.

I wanted to call out to him. I wanted to run to him, to pull him to me, to love him enough to fix whatever the hell was going on in his brain. But I couldn't, and I was sick of trying, so I watched him jog away. Before long he was a speck down the beach. I shrugged off his sweatshirt, my tee, and my shorts, and I waded into the ocean. It felt like I weighed nothing. I had the mass of a puff off a dandelion. It was delicious.

By the time I stepped from the water, the sun was much higher in the sky, and Jason stood on the beach, holding both his sweatshirt and the towel, which he handed to me. "I tried to brush off the sand so you can get dry," he said.

"Thank you." I wrapped the towel around myself and stared at him. He made it a point to look at anything but me.

When we got back to my grandparents', Jason took his portable CD player out on the deck, and he stayed there all day.

My grandparents and father didn't acknowledge his behavior until that evening, when, at dinner, Jason didn't say a single word. He ate quickly, cleared his plate, and disappeared into the basement. It was still daylight out.

"Asha," Dad said to me, quietly. I stared at him, unblinking, not knowing what to say.

The following day Jason stayed in bed until lunchtime. When he stepped into the kitchen, he found me at the table with Heather. I hadn't told her anything about the breakup, only that Jason was sleeping in. My dad and grandparents were at the hardware store.

"Jason, come say hi to Heather. Heather, this is Jason."

He gave a forced smile and a "Hey."

She didn't really notice. Instead, she said, "Craig told me to invite you guys to Rina's tonight. It'll probably be completely lame-o, but you can meet Wayne," who was Heather's current fling.

I should have made an excuse about why we couldn't go. Instead, I offered it up to Jason. Like a dummy. "What do you think, Jason? Wanna go?"

"Craig'll be there?" he asked, looking at his feet.

Before I could respond, Heather said, "Well, it *is* his girlfriend's. Where *else* would he be?"

He shrugged a shoulder, still not looking at us.

"Ohhhh kayyyy," Heather said, making a face at me. To this day, I've never met someone who could wear derision on her face as well as Heather Nilsen. "Well, Wayne's picking me up at seven. He can drive. He's a senior. You can ride with us. If you want. Or don't. Whatever." Jason either missed Heather's attitude entirely or he flat out didn't care. I suspected the latter.

I walked her to the door. She stepped onto the front porch and, not as softly as she should have, asked, "What's *his* problem?"

"Don't ask," I mouthed, then said aloud, "Well, see you at seven, I hope. If not, tell Craig hey. And sorry I missed Rina. Maybe I can meet her next time."

"Oh my god, if they're not *married* before then. They're together *all* the time. It's so gross."

I stepped back inside the house, closed the door, and turned around. Jason had disappeared again. "Where did you GO?" I shouted into the house. I found him back in the basement, tearing through his bag.

"Jason, come on, can't we be nice to each other or something? It's not like I don't love you anymore. I could never stop loving you." He didn't turn around but kept looking in his bag. "What are you *doing*? Look at me!"

He sat up with a small, wrapped package in his hands. He held it out quietly to me. I grabbed it and threw it against the wall behind him. I heard a shatter.

"What is going on? Jason, *what is going on?*" The more I asked, the louder I asked and the more he seemed to shrink. I felt myself reaching a point of mania, and I ran into the bathroom to throw water on my face. I took some deep breaths and glanced into the mirror. I looked deranged.

Back in the basement, I found Jason sitting on the floor, silent. I sighed and picked up the gift. I unwrapped the box and found what had been the blown-glass rose I'd recently pointed out to him at the mall. *A rose from you that wouldn't die,* I'd said, studying the soft folds in the petals and the delicate lines in the leaves. Now, it was in a hundred pieces, confettied shards and splinters, pinks and greens and purples.

I sat down next to him and laid my head on his shoulder. I felt him stiffen. Finally, tears started to pour down my face. "Jason," I said, my voice breaking, and he wrapped me in a hug. I held him tightly and sobbed into his chest. How much easier it would have been if I could've pressed my mouth to his, kissed it away, gotten lost inside his arms. But I knew that solution would have been as useful as a bandage on a chainsaw wound. What was broken here wasn't the rose, or me. It was him. And I didn't have a clue how to fix it.

That night, Dad asked me to go for a walk. I use the word *asked* loosely. What he said was, "Put on your shoes. We're going for a walk."

I didn't want to go, and we were both silent for a bit, while I counted the houses we passed, like I did when I ran. Finally, as we turned the corner, he said, "Asha, Jason is being very rude."

"I'm sorry."

"I do not know why *you* have to be sorry."

"It's my fault."

"I do not think so."

"We broke up yesterday." It was the first time I said it aloud, and I started to walk a little faster.

My father kept pace and, after a beat, said, "You were very excited to bring him here."

"I know."

"It must be very bad, then, to end your relationship here. This was not a mutual separation, I understand." I turned to look at my dad, and he continued, "Jason does not wish to end the relationship."

"I don't think so."

"He has hurt you?"

I stopped walking abruptly. I was determined not to cry standing out in the middle of the sidewalk. I shook my head. "He didn't hurt me. Not on purpose, anyway. But I hurt him. I think I hurt him all the time, but I don't know why. Or how. He's always *sad*. He gets really angry. Like about Craig. He doesn't trust me. Why doesn't he trust me?"

My dad put his arm around my shoulders, and I wrapped my arms around his waist. We walked this way for a bit.

"This is a youthful love?" he asked, and I looked at him, a question on my face. "A youthful love does not understand trust. It only understands possession and ownership, yes? You are *his* girlfriend, and he feels threatened when he has to share you."

"But what's to share? I don't want to go out with Craig, or anyone else."

"How would you feel if he was very good friends with a pretty girl?"

"A pretty girl in another state?" I asked, attempting a half smile. "I dunno. I mean, I wouldn't like it, but I wouldn't pick a fight about it all the time."

"His father has just left his mother. This is why he was sad when Gaby picked you up that night?" I didn't want to lie, but I didn't want to say anything about the pills, so I only nodded. "Maybe he is scared about that, and it is not about you at all."

"Maybe it's both."

"Maybe it's both." He was quiet for another block, and then he said one more thing. "Whatever is going on with your Jason, if you are not happy, you did the right thing. The right thing is not always easy. I'm proud of you, *bratti*."

Jason said little on the trip home. We shared a few forced laughs on the plane, though, and once, I think he forgot what happened: When we started our descent into Cincinnati, he pointed out the sprawling city as it appeared through the clouds. "Asha, look," he said, and he grabbed on to my hand. I held his back, and we didn't let go until the plane touched down.

Junior year started, and Jason and I didn't talk for a month. Then I got a belated sixteenth birthday card in the mail. After the generic sentiment—I'm sure it was not the one he had packed to give me in Florida—he'd carefully signed, "Love, Jason." He included a two-page letter. Here's the first page:

Dear Asha,
Your birthday card is late because it took me a long time to decide if I wanted to write to you. I started a few letters, then crumpled them up. Then I took them out of the trash and ripped them in little pieces to make sure no one found them, even though there were only a few words on them. I still wanted to be sure my words were for you only.

But I decided to write this, finally, because I need to apologize, and I think I know what to say now. I feel like I've tried to apologize before, but not enough. The last few months were bad. I was dependent on you, I know. I knew I could lean on you, and that meant so much to me. It still does. But you were the only person I felt like I could lean on, and that made me possessive. I know I'm a jealous person, and this didn't help. I wanted you for myself alone. I was self-ish, and I was scared to lose you.

It means I took you for granted, and I will forever be sorry about that. I'm sorry I didn't appreciate you more. I'm sorry I pushed you away. Even though that was never my intention, that is what I did. I'm sorry, from the bottom of my heart. I am sorry.

They say love is letting go. If that's the truth, then I suppose I love you truly because that is what I'm doing. That is what I have to do, and I understand that. I am still learning, I know, because I still wish we could have forever.

AUTUMN (2017)

Since my husband vacated his body a year ago, and since that out-of-body experience with Fucking Francis, there has been no one.

Until Jason.

The first time is quick. I'm not sure I will remember much about it—only that neither of us bother to take off all our clothes, and the bed is still made. I think, *Jason Kapaglia is inside me, and I'm wearing a sweatshirt.*

He rolls off me, panting. Our legs dangle from the foot of the mattress.

The second time, he starts by peeling off my sweatshirt. I answer by tugging off his crisp white T-shirt. Before he enters me, he does things with his hands, with his mouth. He hadn't done those kinds of things before. Before, we were teenagers. Before, we didn't know what we were doing, even though we thought we were grown-up. All I needed was the sight of a penis to want it. All he needed was a glimpse of my breast. Less. The thought of a glimpse of my breast.

This time, he takes his time. Makes sure I finish, too. This time, we make love.

After, we face each other on the properly messed bed, on our sides. He runs his fingertips down my chest, around my belly button, up my hip and side, to my shoulder, where he settles his whole hand. It feels nice. I don't know how to speak to this man in my bed, but his hands, at least, are right.

"Asha?"

"Yeah, Jay?"

"I've wanted to call you for years."

I think about that for a minute. What would have happened if he'd called sooner, when I was still married? And not just as a technicality, but as a woman who had a relationship with her husband.

I think about what we've just done, which wasn't to numb anything, like Fucking Francis. Quite the opposite—it was to feel something, something good, something wonderful. Throughout our lives, nearly since the moment we met, Jason and I have used each other for that good feeling. At its heart, in some nihilistic way, isn't that an aspect of all relationships? It's a necessity of life, an unintended—but sometimes intentional—output of loving another person. But think about it: When I was new to West Chester, I used Jason to figure out where and how I fit into my new life. When he was miserable over his parents' split, he used me to feel the love he didn't feel from them.

So when the first bits of unhappiness with Simone tapped his shoulder, if he had called me then—years ago, apparently—what would have happened?

"I'm glad you waited," I say.

"I wanted to be divorced."

"You knew it was coming."

"I knew. And I wanted it to be finished. Completely over. No residue, not like . . . Oh, what was her name . . . ?"

"Raya," I say immediately. I guess we used other people, too. And I never forgot the names of the women, the girls, he used to get over me. Well, to try to get over me, I suppose.

"Oh, man, Raya. Yes, not like Raya. You didn't deserve that. You deserved something, I don't know. Something clean." He studies me. "So what happened?"

"What happened?"

"Charlie."

"You know his name."

He looked sheepish. "Bridge's Facebook. I had to scroll back a long time."

"Oh."

"What happened?"

"Aneurysm."

"You said. What else?"

"It was a freak thing. Out of the blue. He woke up with a really bad headache. I took him to the hospital. He went into a coma. It's been a year."

"Jesus."

"Yeah."

"But this . . ." He trails off, points to his chest, to me, to his chest again.

"I don't feel married anymore," I whisper. I don't know if I am allowed to say that, but even after all these years, it feels like I don't have to hide anything from Jason. I know he won't judge me. He never has. It is the start of a mental checklist I don't even realize I'm making: *Things I Still Love Like Whatever about Jason Kapaglia.*

(one)

His lack of judgment after a year of Maura dumping guilt on me by the fistful is exactly what I want, what I need, right now.

"Will he . . . Can he . . . Do you think—"

"He's dying. Josephine, one of the ladies who takes care of him, she told me."

"Jesus," he says again. He studies me. "Before. Before it happened, before he . . . were you happy?"

I smile. "Oh, yes. So happy. I didn't know. I didn't know it could be that simple. You know?"

Jason looks sad. "I don't. It's never been simple for me. It's always such a fight. I got sick of working that hard. Simone and me, we worked hard. It worked for a while. Then it didn't."

"So you called me."

He shrugs, and I see a flash of the teen boy who used to make my heart beat. It is there, in the smile lines around his mouth. Deeper, more pronounced, but the same ones I loved then. "I always wondered what would have happened if we hadn't moved."

"Or if you hadn't gone and fallen for some other chick."

"'Some other chick.'"

"Well. We had other names for her."

"We?"

"Me and Bridge. Skank wad. Ho bag. Slut face. Cunt."

"I sense a theme."

"Did she hate me?"

"Yeah. The last time you and me . . . that's when I told her. It was the only time we talked about it. Because, mostly, I felt like I was cheating on *you* with *her*. Not the other way around. That last time we . . . at Edward's. That was the only time it felt wrong, like I was doing something bad to *her*. It's what made me choose her, I guess. That guilt, it meant something to me. That I loved her more."

(two)

He's achingly honest, even if it might sting a little. All these years later, the words that spring to my mouth are *Did you?* But I keep them in. It's tough. I imagine a curved needle threading sutures through my lips to keep them locked against the question I have no business asking. Oh, the question wants out so badly. But if Jason asked me to compare him and *Charlie*, could I? Of course not.

This struggle to keep from asking that unaskable question takes seconds, minutes. The silence extends. We stare at each other. Shouldn't I be able to think of *something* else? I mean, this man is here, in my bed, naked. He's been inside me. *Aren't women who've just orgasmed supposed to be at ease? Relaxed?*

The imaginary seams keeping my mouth shut burst, and "Want some popcorn?" falls out. *Where did that come from?*

"OK."

He stands up to put his boxers on, and I watch him shamelessly, all traces of inappropriate questions vanished. He catches me and pauses. "Again?"

"No. I mean, yes. But not this moment. Just looking."

He places his fists on his hips and poses for me, grinning. His grin falters for a beat, as though he's had an idea. Then, completely naked in my bedroom, Jason clenches his fists, holds them next to his face, and wiggles his entire body. Seriously . . . his *entire* body, ahem. I burst out laughing, and, for maybe the first time in my life, I see Jason Kapaglia look sheepish. He covers his face with his hands and says, muffled, "I cannot believe I just did that."

(three)

Playful, I think. I always loved that about Jason. And I know it's superficial, but

(four)

he's the kind of gorgeous that, in other men, tongue-ties me. But not with Jason.

Well. This visit notwithstanding.

I stare at his face, so handsome that I feel it in my blood. I let my eyes travel to his chest, covered sparsely with hair. His shoulders are broad, his arms slim—not scrawny, but not muscular, either. His belly pooches a bit, his hips, narrow. His, well, *that* is perfect. Strong thighs, long legs. I wonder if he still runs. He must have kept growing after I last saw him. He was six feet two inches then.

I stand up, and he whistles. God,

(five)

he's always made me feel good about myself.

"Shut up," I mutter and stand next to him. I don't even come up to his shoulders. We raise an eyebrow at one another. "Put your shorts on."

259

I grab my ratty gray robe from the back of the door, hold it in my hand for a second, and instead choose a silky one I haven't worn in a year.

It is 1 a.m., and, downstairs, Jason plops on my couch and flips through my channels. I pop two bags of popcorn and sprinkle chili powder over one bag and garlic salt over the other. "Beer?" I shout into the family room.

"Is that a question?" he shouts back, and I pull two bottles from my fridge.

"Look what I found," he announces, turning to look over the couch and watch me hop down the stairs. *The Matrix.* Of course.

"God, I don't think I've seen this since the theater." I put the popcorn on the table, hand him a beer, and curl up next to him. We eyeball each other, then simultaneously raise our bottles and click them together.

"Khoubakh," he says.

(six)

I can vividly pull up teaching that to Charlie, but the lesson with Jason is gone from my memory. Charlie never *was* able to pronounce it right, but of course Jason still remembers the Assyrian word for *cheers*. His memory—that brain—is the sexiest thing about him.

He takes a long swig, then points at the television. "I think I've seen it a hundred times since we saw it. Didn't you like it?"

"It's not that," I say, studying Laurence Fishburne and those weird, shiny glasses. "I didn't really pay attention to it. My memories from that movie are not of the movie, exactly."

He grins. "Well, yeah. But you never saw it again?"

Actually, I've actively avoided it. That night in the theater, on one of Jason's visits back to West Chester, about halfway through senior year, we'd sat in the back corner and gotten home covered in hickeys, my bra stuffed in my purse. On that trip, I'd still considered Simone a placeholder. It wasn't until the night of my graduation that I learned she was a little more important than that. So, no . . . I hadn't sought out the movie or the memories it evoked again, and I had turned the channel every time I accidentally came upon it.

"Come here." He leans over to place a loud, sucking kiss on my neck.

(seven)

I don't know whether touch is my love language because Jason is so affectionate and he got me used to it at the ripe ol' age of thirteen, or whether touch is my love language and Jason speaks it. But his physicality? Be still, my heart.

No. No . . . don't be still. Leap and hula and tap-dance it out, little darling.

For the second time in my life, I am unable to watch this exact movie because of Jason Kapaglia. It's not because we are horny teenagers—or, rather, horny middle-agers—but because my mind won't shut off. I keep looking over at him to make sure he is still there, if he was ever there at all. At one point, his arm, which had been draped over the top of the couch, encircles me, pulls me close, tucks me under his chin. The soft flutter of his heart grounds me. I don't have to keep questioning the reality of him; the reality is singing into my ear.

I spend the second half of the movie trying to figure out what I should say to him when the movie ends. It will be after 3 a.m. I should be tired. I should be falling asleep, but each of my body parts, each of my cells, each of my atoms, each of my protons and electrons are awake, alert, at attention. Sleep? What is sleep? Have I ever slept? I am vigilant, every moment of the years of my life spent asleep is forgotten. I have always been awake.

When the movie ends, Jason stands and walks to the mantel above my fireplace. I thought he'd been watching the movie, but no. He'd been elsewhere, too, in his head, studying my house, looking to learn me, to relearn me.

"Bridget was your maid of honor," he says, lifting up the photo from my wedding where I am giving her a messy, chocolaty kiss. He continues, softly, more to himself than to me, "She called me her friend-in-law once."

I say nothing, watch him stare at the photo. His eyes travel to the next photo, and he forgets all about Bridget and me, setting the frame down facing the wrong way. This eight-by-ten is the closest thing to a wedding portrait I have. Charlie and I are standing at the bar after he'd given a toast, thanking our friends and family and Cujo's and Fucking Francis—well, he was just *Francis* at that point—and the heavens. Our hands are clutched, fingers interwoven, and Charlie raises a glass of champagne with the other. His eyes squint shut in laughter while I stare at him, eyes wide open, a look of near reverence. Bridget hates this photo. Says I look like a choir girl worshipping an idol. But that's why I love it. It's nearly embarrassing to have been caught in a moment with such pure emotion and adoration on my face. It's the most honest photo I've ever seen of myself.

"Wow," Jason says.

"Yeah."

"Your face."

"Kinda crazy."

"No. It's not crazy. You never looked at me that way."

"Jay . . ."

"No, it's not that. I'm not . . . I'm not comparing. I always wondered if what I had with Simone, if it wasn't as good as what I would have had with you. I never stopped to think that, maybe, you found something better. Better than us."

"Jason, we were kids."

He looks at me, suddenly serious. "Don't."

"We were."

"No. Don't do that. Don't . . . don't try to diminish it." He stares at me. "Is that what you think?" He looks around the room, like he suddenly doesn't know where he is, doesn't know how he's gotten here.

"Shiiiiiit," I exhale softly, and I stand, go to him, clasp his hands in mine. "Jason, look at me. Look at me." I take his face in my right hand and jerk it toward me. "I said look at me. Charlie is the love of my life. He is the absolute best thing that has ever happened to me. When I realized that, when I realized what I had, I couldn't believe it. I didn't think that sort of thing existed. I thought it *couldn't* exist."

"What are you talking about?" He pulls his head away, and I see his youthful melancholy spread over his face. For a moment he is fifteen again.

"Sit," I demand, if for no other reason than to keep him from pacing around the room like a nervous tiger. He glares at me. I sigh. "Please, Jason. Please. Sit down?"

We sit side by side on the couch again.

"The reason I thought something like Charlie and me couldn't exist is because you and me didn't work out."

His eyes dart up to me from his lap.

"What we did, and what happened? It broke me, Jason. I was . . . I didn't know who I was anymore. We were kids when we met. I grew up because of you. I grew up with you, around you. I didn't know who I was without you because you'd always been there. You were my family. You were . . ." My voice breaks. "You were my heart.

"When you moved on, it was hard for me to get over it, the hardest thing I'd ever done, at that point. I had to tell myself that whole 'meant to be' garbage was bullshit. It didn't exist because it couldn't. Because if it did, then I found it too young, and I broke it, or I let it break, and I didn't fight enough for it, or something. As though I could've had any effect on what you did or what you chose. So if something that wonderful existed for me, it existed in you. And you were not mine anymore. Therefore, 'meant to be' could not exist. Because no twenty-year-old girl needs to think that she's already met and lost the love of her life.

"So Charlie . . . Charlie proved me wrong. He didn't . . . he doesn't negate you. He doesn't erase what I felt about you. But he proved me wrong because he taught me that, of course you and me weren't 'meant

263

to be.' Me and Charlie aren't, either. But me and Charlie were good. Jason, we were good. He made me better. And I didn't grow up around him and within him, like I did with you. We grew together. We clicked together. It wasn't about me and what he did for me—it's always been *us* with Charlie. Always us."

"We could have that," Jason whispers.

"Maybe. But don't you think that was a little much for a couple of kids? How strong could we have been if all it took was a move to break us?"

"It was more than the move."

"It was the move."

"In part. But it was me, too. I didn't realize it until last year. At couples' counseling. Me and Simone."

You went to couples' counseling and thought about me?

"After the third session, Dr. C pulled me aside and told me she didn't think it was going to work out. She goes, 'I have never said this to someone before. But your wife doesn't seem to want to fix things.'"

"Damn."

"She asked if I wanted to come back alone, though. I wasn't sure why, but I was curious. It turned out to be eye-opening. I didn't know there was a name for it."

"For what?"

"I was an incredibly depressed teen. Clinically so, I think. If Gaby hadn't come in that bathroom, I might have really . . ." He trails off. I am not moving a muscle, not blinking, hardly breathing. "That's not just 'normal teenage stuff,' like my mom said. It was more than that. Dr. C and I worked through it, a little. It's something that's always kind of been there, though never as bad as that summer. I realized, everything I put you through? That's what it was. I was depressed, and I was completely codependent on you. You were my anchor, and my safety net, too. I was terrified to lose that, so I held on to you too tight. I practically suffocated you.

"That summer was a mess. I felt like I didn't have control over anything. But you were steady. And if I seemed controlling . . ."

"Seemed?" I ask, a corner of my mouth twitching up.

"I was controlling," he corrects. "I didn't mean to be. I didn't know what I was doing. And thank god I never succeeded. Your freedom has always been beautiful, Asha. I loved it. If I'd have squashed that, I don't think I could have forgiven myself."

My heart quickens in my chest, thumps hard against my ribs. I didn't know it until this exact moment, but I needed Jason Kapaglia to acknowledge this.

"Do you want to go on a date?" he asks.

I can't help it—I snort, and he grins.

"Our timing sucks," I say through the guffaws. "Plus, we already kinda did it."

"Twice."

"Twice. Then we saw a movie. And now you're asking me out."

"Well?"

I don't want to date this beautiful man in my family room, this man in his boxers. I don't want to date and all that it implies—getting to know another person, gauging how we feel about each other, the nerves and the questions and the starting over. I don't want any of that.

But I do want him.

(eight)

My god, do I want him. I feel it in my finger bones. The insides of my mouth ache for him. The skin on the back of my ankles tingles.

His expression changes. "I know that look," he says softly, and he pulls me to him. He traces a dozen kisses across my face, hovering his mouth above mine. I press the tip of my tongue to his upper lip in return.

After we make love for the third time in one night, we are on the floor. I feel a contentedness I haven't felt in my spirit in an exceedingly long while.

This.

(nine)

This is why I loved Jason. This is why I have always loved Jason. With some people, there's just a *there* there, a drawing. It defies logic and explanation. It's a body's recognition of another.

My phone on the coffee table jingles. It's 4:30 a.m. The caller ID reads "Pax."

It can mean only one thing.

SUMMER (2016)

Maura was the image of fury. I saw her fists clenched at her sides. Her body trembled, almost as if she'd never be warm again. Her face flushed, and her eyes were wide, wild.

I asked, "What are you doing in my house?"

"You've barely answered my calls or my texts or my voicemails, so I came over." She held up the spare key Charlie gave her when we moved in. "Didn't even knock because I knew you wouldn't answer the door. Guess I know why." She pushed her chin forward as she spoke, her right arm slowly extending, her pointer finger thrusting with each word: "You. Are. Trash." She said "trash" as though it were four syllables long, her voice shaking.

"Hey, girl, that's no way to talk to—" Francis started, but we both cut him off, simultaneously.

"Shut up, Francis." That was me.

"Butt. Out." That was Maura, but she heard me, too. "*Francis*. Oh, he has a *name. Francis*, the ADULTERER, a biblical SINNER."

I blinked, stunned at her characterization, and noted that Francis looked equally as confused. This was the first time Maura spoke this way to me. I knew her family didn't love the fundamentalism she'd taken up over the years, but I'd never personally seen its cruelty. I wasn't sure if that was because this was new for her, or maybe it simply hadn't been directed at me before.

"Francis, I need you to leave," I said.

"I'm not going anywhere, baby."

"Francis, please. I will call you later."

"No, *mi cielo*, I won't leave you like this."

"I don't want to fight with you right now, but you need to leave this house." He blinked at me. I gritted my teeth and narrowed my eyes. "I need you to leave. Get out."

"OK, baby. I understand. You need your space. I dig it, I told you, I dig it. Don't you forget though, the universe loves you. I love you, baby, and I'll be waiting for you when the space gets too wide. I'll be here."

Maura was so scandalized she could only watch as Fucking Francis stood, dropped a kiss at the top of my head, and walked out the front door. As he passed her, she caught a glimpse of the enormous tattoo on his back: a huge cross that stretched across his shoulders and covered his spine. It was the final indignity. "*That* is a holy sign. Don't you know that? How dare you? How *dare you*?"

He eyeballed her. "Chill out, baby girl," he said. He disappeared around the corner, and we heard the door click behind him.

Maura stared at the space he had occupied for a beat before she whipped around to glare at me. "Well?" she asked.

"Well, what?"

"What do you have to say for yourself?"

"Want some dinner?"

"No, I don't want *dinner*. How could you do that to *your husband? To my brother?* What kind of *slut* does that?"

I stared at her, waiting for an appropriate response to come to me. Nothing. "Well, I'm going to eat."

"You will talk to me."

I plopped the T-bone, now cold, and a pile of salad on my plate. "You sure you don't want any?"

"ASHA."

I sat down at the kitchen table. "Sit and eat or get out," I told her.

"You *slut*," she tried again, angry tears threatening to overflow. "This is your fault. Charlie is in a coma because of *you*. This is our *punishment* because of *what you've done*."

I took a deep breath. Quietly, very quietly, I said, "Get the hell out of my house."

"What did you say to me?"

"Get the hell out of my house."

"*What* did you—"

I picked up my plate of food and hurled it at her. If she hadn't stepped aside, I'd have hit her square in the chest. Instead, the plate smashed against the wall. Glass shards exploded, and food flew everywhere. Two months after that, I found a crouton behind the liquor cabinet.

"Look what you made me do. Jesus Christ, Maura." She couldn't speak, and she looked at me with her eyebrows raised, mouth agape, top lip curled. "I can't believe you're going to make me throw you out of my house. Are you serious right now?"

I waited a beat, stood up, marched over to my sister-in-law, grabbed her by the upper arm—"Get your *disgusting* hands off me"—and dragged her to the front door. I threw it open, shoved her out, and put every bit of strength I had into slamming the door. I changed the locks the next day, firmly sealing this new, combative relationship. It, obviously, would never be repaired.

When I relayed the story to Bridget, her entire face was the letter *o*. Her eyes, her nostrils, her mouth—all *o*'s.

"That wasn't the worst part."

"How was that possibly *not* the worst part?"

After I shoved Maura out of my house, I left the food and broken plate on the floor and headed upstairs. I needed to run, to get out, to move, to clear my head; the last time I'd run was before Charlie's coma, more than a month ago.

My ritual of getting ready started with twisting my hair into a tight french braid and pulling on a sports bra, a T-shirt, old yoga pants, my hot-pink running shoes, and a ball cap.

I paused by the front door, holding on to the railing while I stretched my hamstrings and quads, waiting for the peace that always washed over me at that point in the ritual.

Nothing.

I stretched a little longer.

No peace.

I opened the front door, locked it behind me, slid the key in a small zipper pocket in my pants, and jogged in place in the front yard.

Co-ma. Co-ma. Co-ma, each echo of my foot slapping the pavement chanted to me.

This was not peaceful; this was hell.

I took the key back out of my pocket and opened the front door.

"I haven't run since."

"When was this?" Bridget asked.

"About a week ago."

"Sweetie." She took my hand and held.

I accepted her sympathy, but I didn't tell her that I'd told a fib: Not being able to run? That wasn't the worst part, either. No, the worst part was after I let myself back in my house, after I changed out of my running uniform and pulled my hair from its braid, I sat down on the kitchen floor. I thought I was going to clean up the food on the floor and the wall.

Instead, I ate it. I ate every bit.

"You ever hear back from Francis?" Bridget asked, and I grimaced. "That bad?"

"I had to block his number."

"Will he come back?" she asked, wrinkling her nose.

"He might. I was hoping you'd stay here for a little bit?"

"I was planning to stay here for a lot longer than that. But I wanted to give you your space . . . *sweetheart.*" It's a testament to my love for my BFF that she was able to make me smile, just a little.

The next day, I found a letter in my mailbox. No envelope, no stamp. Just a letter.

"My Sweet Baby," it started, and I crumpled it in my fist before I could read more, and I tossed it in the recycle bin on my way inside.

And that's the story of Francis B. He never came back, and I haven't spoken to him again. He was a bad decision I think I needed to make. That the *universe* needed me to make, baby, can you dig it?

SPRING (1999-2000)

Jason and I had a few classes together junior year, and it wasn't anything like when we'd broken up back in junior high: Instead of ignoring each other, we'd say hi, smile. We weren't friends, exactly, but we didn't act like we disliked each other, either. One day I saw him with his arm around a girl in our English class, Olivia. The next month, his arm pulled Ariana close. Two months after that it was Raya. Every girl shared my hair color, my olive complexion.

I dated new boys that year, too, but none of them were anything like Jason. Kyle was my height, and he had incredibly curly brown hair. He wore braces, and he had to take his glasses off when he kissed me. He always tasted of spearmint. Barring Charlie, Kyle remains the single *nicest* boy I've ever dated: He opened doors for me and helped me with my trigonometry without making me feel unintelligent.

Sometimes he'd come over after school and politely hold my hand. He asked my dad about work and cleared the table the one time he stayed for dinner.

I kept waiting for Kyle to make me feel that *oomph* that Jason made me feel, that longing and "No one can ever make me feel like this," and it never happened. So I didn't feel bad when Jason called one Thursday afternoon.

"What are you doing?"

"Nothing."

"Don't go anywhere."

Ten minutes later he pulled into my driveway. I'd had my license for a few months already, but I was nearly as excited for Jason, whooping as I ran down the stoop to his car.

"I passed!" he said.

"What about Raya?" I asked, grinning.

"What about Kyle?" he countered, returning my grin. "Get in."

I climbed in the front seat, held out my hand, and said, "Lemme see your license." He tugged a brand-new wallet from his back pocket.

"Fancy," I said, opening the trifold.

"Gift from my dad, to say 'congrats,'" he said.

"Your dad's back."

He shrugged. I pulled the ID from its clear pocket, eager to see the photo, knowing he would look handsome. He did. Behind it was the Michael Jordan basketball card I'd given him in my kitchen more than three years ago. At the time, it felt like a lifetime. Today, it sounds like a minute.

I looked at him, a question in my eyes.

"The wallet wasn't right until it was in there," he said. "I never took it out of my old one."

"Even when you dated Kendra Perkins?"

"Never."

He backed down my driveway, and we drove. We took back roads and side streets, winding two-lane roads into the country and lanes without street paint. We didn't go anywhere, and we held hands the whole way.

"You know you're my forever," he said.

I smiled to myself. *I know,* I thought. At a stop sign, he traced a kiss across my knuckles.

The next night I broke Kyle's heart at a chain Italian restaurant and, a week later, asked a kid named Derek to be my date to the Valentine's Day dance. Derek was a year behind me, skinny, with military-short hair. When we slow danced, he sang me a song I'd somehow never heard, about a man who played piano in a bar and fell in love with the patrons there. I fell in love a little, too.

But only a little. A few months later I was still waiting for anything Derek said to be half as exciting as Jason.

The last day of junior year, Jason ran up to my locker, skidding to a stop and crashing into the metal. "I just saw Derek kissing Lindsay."

"Huh. That didn't take long."

"So you're not together anymore?"

"No," I said, unable to hide my grin.

"Be my girlfriend?"

"Yeah," I said, and he kissed me, our third first kiss.

"Crap," he said. "Hold on." He raced down the hall. I watched his back as he retreated and realized, *That asshole hasn't dumped Raya yet.* I shook my head at my boyfriend as Bridget walked up to me and rolled her eyes.

"Again?" she asked, and I shrugged. "You two are gonna get married one day." I punched her on the arm as my mind raced back to my Turkish-coffee-grounds wish that summer evening with my grandma.

That night Jason and I drove out to those winding roads we'd driven around the day he got his license. He pulled off onto a gravel lane that disappeared into a cornfield. There wasn't a house around, not a car, not a sound, not a soul. He looked over at me, his eyes curious.

"Is this OK?" he asked, and I nodded. Oh, it was more than OK.

Isn't it weird how, when you're a kid, a teenager, there are so many *firsts*, and when they happen, and just before they happen, they feel momentous: first best friend, first kiss, first babysitting gig, first love, first period, first time driving a car alone, first time a boy puts his hands up your shirt, first summer job, first time you see a penis, first broken heart, first college acceptance letter. Every time I experienced one of these things, I kept waiting to feel different, older. Better, more worldly, somehow.

But I didn't. I felt like me.

That night in the corn, with the breeze blowing into my window, cooling my warm face, the rustle of the stalks, the night black but for the dashboard's blinking blue time that was never set right, I had another first: the first orgasm I didn't give myself. Kyle tried once or twice, but it was awkward, uncomfortable. It never, you know, *worked*. He didn't know what he was doing, and neither did Jason. But with Jason I had no problem teaching. Like that night at the abandoned fun house, I bossed him around: "Not so hard, that hurts. Don't poke. Rub. Up a little. Up. Up. There. Oh. Yup, yup there we go yup."

This first, like all the others, like the ones still to come, didn't change me. Individually, the events never held that much power, though I suppose that, grouped together, they wrote my history and helped me decide what I valued and who I wanted to be.

Later that summer, the world as I knew it shattered.

Summer was in full swing. The air was still, humid, the kind that carries weight. People either hate it or love it—they hate the feeling of suffocation, of melting, of not being able to inhale a full breath, to fill their lungs completely with sweet, cool air.

Me? I loved it. With the air so heavy, it felt like an intimate hug. When I opened a car door and slid inside, the heat was sexy somehow. I loved that it pressed against my skin, and I loved that I felt like I'd never be cold again.

It was that kind of night, and damp. Low, wispy clouds hung in the sky, obscuring the scads of stars we typically saw in the corn, as we came to call our spot. We'd returned there throughout the summer. We weren't always entwined in the seats; sometimes we got out and lay on the hood, flat on our backs, hands clasped. We'd look up into the nothing or talk about college: Did we want to go? Where? What would we study? Would it be far away? That was the only question we had answers to: We'd never be too far from the other.

Once he brought a constellation book he'd checked out of the library, and we looked for as many groupings of stars as we could find.

"The Big Dipper." I pointed, and he reached up to take my wrist gently, moving my hand in an arc, like its handle.

"See the really bright orange star? Right by the handle? It says Arcturus is a star that's in the Bible. It's part of a constellation called Boötes, a herdsman."

"Booties?" I asked. "The butt constellation?"

"No, wait, there's a pronunciation thing. It's boo-OH-tees."

We were silent for a few moments, and I whispered, "Booties."

On this night, it was too cloudy to see any stars, and we instead huddled in the back seat, kissing. Jason kept pulling away, which was odd—Jason *never* pulled away while we were in the corn. On the contrary, it was like he only wanted to perform experiments where we tried to wear the other's skin, to make our hearts expel blood to the rest of our bodies at the exact same millisecond, to blink our eyelids as one, to emit carbon dioxide in a single exhalation.

"What's the matter?" I asked, exasperated, my back flat against the passenger-side door, then tenderly, as I noticed the tears coming down his face. "Jay? What's going on? Talk to me."

His voice was completely monotone, completely flat, when he said, "My dad got a new job. We're moving to Washington, DC."

"Oh." It was all I could say. I couldn't even think extra words, let alone express them. A few beats passed, seconds that felt like days. Then, "When?"

"He starts in a few weeks. Gonna find a house for us. We'll move later. Maybe a month. Two. Maybe less." He paused. "My mom's staying here."

"Why don't you stay with her?" I asked. "Finish high school. Then we can go to college together."

"I want to stay here with you. I want to. But my mom is . . . and my dad . . . I'd rather live with my dad. I hate that I have to choose between you."

"But you can visit, right?" My voice cracked when I said "right." My instinct was to cry, and I felt the nerves in my body start to tremble.

But, no, I couldn't cry, not at this moment. Jason was barely holding it together, and if I lost it, too, we'd both be a mess, and what good would that do anyone? "Come here." I reached out, pulled him to me. I wrapped him up in my arms, and he buried his face in my shoulder, still trying not to sob. For not the first time, it struck me how big Jason was. He was nearly a foot taller than me, and yet I protected him, comforted him.

"It won't matter," I swore. "We can have senior years in different places. It doesn't matter. We'll figure it out. You know we will. We always do. We'll figure it out. You can visit. Maybe you could come back here for college. We can talk on the phone, all the time. We'll figure it out."

I wrapped my arms tighter around this man, this boy. His thick hair was damp, and I scratched my fingernails lightly over his scalp as I kissed him. I kissed his head and his ears and, before I knew it, he was kissing my chest and my neck.

Up until this point, nearly every sexual encounter the two of us had had seemed planned somehow. Even as I was lost in the moments, I kept my head enough to guide him, to ensure we didn't get too unchecked, too far into it. But this was different. I felt my body slide down beneath his and thought, *I don't want to think about this. I just want to feel it,* and I shut off my brain.

He shoved my tank top up, and I shimmied out of it. I pulled at his T-shirt, then laughed nervously when I heard a *riiiiip* as a piece of the front pocket tore away. Between how I'd been raking his scalp and the mess with the shirt and the heat of the night, he looked crazed, his hair sticking up in different directions. I barely noticed, fixated as I was on his belt.

We made love in the car and, for the life of me, I can't tell you how we managed, how we fit in the back seat. We were all knees and nails and lips, and I wondered, *When is he . . . ?* Then a brief, sharp pain made me inhale hard.

"Ash? Are you OK?" Jason raised up and looked down at me, and my insides swelled so I thought I might have a heart attack, teenage girl loved to death in the back seat of her boyfriend's mother's car in the middle of a rural Ohio cornfield, and, oh, what a sweet way to go.

"Come back here," I said, reaching for him.

A few moments later, he shuddered, and he dropped his weight half on me, half hanging off the seat. We lay together for a few more minutes before we spoke.

"Jay?"

"Yes?"

"I wanna do it again."

That weekend I stayed the night at Bridget's house. After she fell asleep, after everyone in the house was asleep, I tiptoed into her mom's office. I found the duffel bag Mrs. Casey had shown me two years prior and, true to her word, there were two boxes of condoms inside. One was opened already, and I slid out a row. They accordioned down. How many would we need? I checked inside the box and saw there were plenty left, so, what the hell, I took the whole row.

That summer, Jason and I filled ourselves with the other. When we weren't in the corn promising forever love, we were tangled up in movie theaters or my neighborhood pool. Jason's mom and dad weren't exactly present parents during those months, and a few times we snuck into his plaid-papered bedroom. One lazy Sunday, after we made love, we fell asleep for a short nap. I awoke in his arms with the sunlight across our faces, and I thought, *My life is perfect.*

It sounds like something from a Disney movie, I know, but is that really so bad? Any time period has its own toxicity for kids coming of age; for me, in the late nineties/early aughts, I was very familiar with sixteen-year-old Britney Spears in her sexed-up Catholic-schoolgirl outfit like an old man's wet dream, begging to get hit, baby, one more time. That my first experiences with sex dripped instead with songbirds and rose petals is probably not the worst thing.

The day Jason moved, he showed up at my house at ten in the morning, one long-stemmed rose in tow. He handed it to me, and I inhaled the scent. Why does a rose always smell romantic? My dad offered to make us breakfast, which broke my heart a little; he hadn't really known what to say to me when I told him Jason was moving, but he *wanted* to know. I saw it on his face and read it in his body language—he wanted to comfort and use the right words, but he wasn't sure what those words were.

"French toast? Omelet?" he offered.

"I can't stay long. My dad's anxious to leave," Jason said, cracking the knuckles on his left hand. "He wanted to be on the road by now."

"We'll miss you around here," my dad said. "I hope you like your new home. A move can be exciting, you know."

My father, ever the optimist.

Jason gave a small, tired smile, a smile much too old for his seventeen years. "Thanks, Mr. Khoury. And thanks for, I dunno, for everything. I'll miss you." Then Jason surprised all three people in the room—including himself, I think—by giving my dad a hug. My dad squeezed him in return, and I was struck by how tiny Jason looked—he was definitely taller than my dad, but he was lanky and slim. My dad, by no means a large man, looked positively imposing by comparison.

Dad gracefully left the kitchen, and I grabbed a small box next to the toaster. "I have something for you." As he opened the package, I fingered the new charm I'd slid onto my evil eye necklace. He pulled out his gift, a simple silver chain with a tiny key on the end. "It fits into mine," I said, resting the little silver heart against the pad of my thumb. A piece was missing, and Jason's key filled my heart perfectly.

"I'll never take it off," he said, slipping the necklace over his head, leaving it on the outside of his T-shirt. It was the same shirt from the first time we made love, the one with the torn pocket.

"I'll call you all the time," I said, stepping into him and wrapping my arms around his waist.

"Me too. And I'll come back. I'll see you. We'll see each other."

We held each other silently for a moment or two. Neither wanted to let go, but there wasn't anything else to say.

I walked him to the front door, then hopped on the bottom step so I could look at him without stretching up on my toes. He took his hands, those huge hands with the knobby knuckles, and he placed them on either side of my face. His thumbs reached under my eyes and wiped away the tears with a swoop. He gave me a soft, salty kiss, and I tried to record everything about it—the pressure and fullness of his lips, his flavor, his scent, faint from his deodorant, spicy and masculine.

I released him from my tight hug and placed my hand against his chest, atop the ripped pocket. I felt his heart beating as I studied my fingers.

"This is mine?"

"Forever."

I pinched the pocket and gave it a soft tug. A few more stitches pulled apart. He wrapped his hands around the pocket and the shirt anchored behind it and gave it a harder pull. The soft cotton tore away as the thread snapped, and he handed it to me. I balled it up in my fist as he gave me another soft kiss and pressed a slip of paper into my palm with the pocket.

"My address," he said. I read the city. *Del Ray.* "Outside DC."

I hated Del Ray with every inch of my body, with every breath I took. I hated the stupid letters in its stupid name and the way it sounded when someone said it aloud. I hated the stupid space between the words, its two capital letters. I hated its existence. I blamed it for everything, and I would for years.

I watched Jason's hand reach for the knob, watched him place his large palm atop it. He pulled, then stepped through the opening, stepped outside. I heard the latch as the door softly shut behind him. His car backed out of my driveway and disappeared from view.

I stood motionless until I felt a hand on my shoulder. Dad. I looked at him and let myself exhale the sob I'd been holding in for two months, since that night Jason told me in the corn. My dad sat on the step, and—the pocket and address still clutched in my hand—I cried into his lap the way I'd done as a girl when I would fall off my bike. But this wound, I felt instinctively, wouldn't heal as neatly as the scrapes. This wound would scar.

That night I sat cross-legged on my bed, weepy and futzing with Jason's pocket. I brought it to my nose—it smelled like him—and ran my fingers over the soft, overwashed fabric. On a whim, I reached for my old *Space Jam* pillow and laid the pocket atop its backside, flattened it with my palm, got an idea. I retrieved the sewing kit from the downstairs hall closet and went back to my room. I put on my Tony Rich Project single and let the various versions play through.

I used straight pins to tack the pocket in place in the center of the pillow, picked out a purple thread to match it, then changed my mind and opted for white to match the pocket instead. I threaded the needle and used a whipstitch to attach three sides of the pocket to the pillow.

As I stitched, every promise of the lyrics threaded through the fabric, too.

I finished, then slipped my hand inside the pocket. I closed my eyes, imagined holding Jason's hands.

Thinking of this moment always brings tears to my eyes. Not gushing sobs like my pop-up Charlie grief, but the sort that gathers at the corners of my eyes, little pools of memory for that heartbroken girl who imagined with every stitch that she was somehow sewing herself to Jason, connecting the two of them psychically. She had yet to even hear the term *poetic memory*, but if she had, she would recognize this craft project as something physical to represent what she knew in her bones: that Jason had written to hers.

That night I slept with my hand tucked inside that pocket. I slept that way for a lot of nights after, too.

AUTUMN (2017)

Jason stays the night. He offers to leave after the call from Pax, but I'd rather not be alone. It's not because of the sadness, though there's plenty of that; it's that I've been alone for a long time, and I don't want to be anymore.

We don't fall asleep until nearly 7 a.m. We get in bed after I receive the news about Charlie, but Jason keeps asking questions, and I keep talking.

"He was in a persistent vegetative state," I tell Jason. I pull out the drawer next to my bed and take out some pamphlets. Where vibrators and lube should go, I keep informational pieces on the long-term effects of a coma. I read aloud:

"Due to the use of a catheter, the patient may become prone to urinary tract infections, which can become generalized and poison the blood. Limbs may contract and become immovable as muscles deteriorate. Pneumonia may become common due to immobility and the patient's inability to prevent secretions in the lungs, which may eventually scar and even collapse."

"Did all that happen to Charlie?"

"He was never a big guy, but he wasn't scrawny. The last few months, I could hardly find him. His body, his face. He got so incredibly thin. Shadowed, almost, like he'd gone hollow. He had some bed sores, too."

"So how did you . . . ?" Jason pauses, and I put the pamphlets down on the nightstand. "Why did you think that now was the time? Why'd you think it was coming?"

He leans back on pillows he's propped up against the headboard. I nestle against his chest, and Jason wraps his arm around me. "His limbs were turning purple. He was dying from the bottom up. Well. Dying more."

"I can't believe I'm asking this, but you seem . . . not fine, but you're handling this better than . . . I don't know what. But better. How are you? Am I allowed to ask that?"

I nod, and I file through the range of emotions roiling inside my head. There are too many to name. I pick the two I'm most hesitant to voice; Jason has always made me want to be truthful.

I sit up so I can look at his face when I say, "Part of me is scared."

"To be alone?" he asks. "Makes sense."

"To see Charlie's parents. I haven't since right after the coma." I watch Jason furrow his brow. "What is it?"

He seems to choose his next words carefully. "I guess I find that unexpected. You're so warm. I'd think you'd all be leaning on each other." He stops talking and, to my surprise, blushes. "I'm sorry. I shouldn't have said that. Why do I feel like I still know you? We haven't known each other for a long time."

"You're not wrong," I say, and I reach over to take his hand. Mine disappears beneath his broad palm and long fingers. I think of why I don't want to see my in-laws—I think of Francis—and I say, "I made some bad decisions right after the coma. And I'm embarrassed."

In response, Jason brings my hand to his lips and places a kiss along the side of my pointer finger. The tenderness is too much at this moment when I'm already a shell, a Fabergé egg, and I start to cry.

Jason holds my hand to his mouth while I wipe my face with the other. I take a deep breath to say the second horrible truth I want to share. I whisper, "The other thing I'm feeling is . . . I'm relieved. Charlie would have hated this. All this. He told me once he never wanted to live on machines, and what do I do? I go and put him on machines. I didn't know how to tell them no. I didn't want to tell them no."

"Do you regret it?"

"I know Charlie would be mad at me. Or disappointed. But what's the point of regretting it? I didn't know what I was doing right after. Besides, after it was done, reversing it seemed so cruel. I did the best I could. I tried. I was wrong, but I tried."

Jason asks about my favorite vacation I ever took with Charlie, and he asks how we met. He asks if I ever spoke about him—Jason—and what Charlie said when I did. He wants to know what my dad is up to, and my grandparents. He asks how long I've lived in this house. What Bridget is doing these days. How I like my job.

I ask him about Gaby and his parents. Did his mom or dad ever remarry? Is he sad he and Simone never had kids? What did he like best about living in England? What did he miss about the United States? Is he going to stay in Ohio?

Here, for the first time in my line of questioning, Jason halts. He considers the question, then says, slowly, "That depends."

"On?"

He raises his eyebrows and tips his head toward me.

Oh.

"I'm not looking for a decision now. Or even soon. But for the time being, my plans are . . . let's say, they're flexible."

I sleep only a few hours, and then I go to Pax. I do this myself, promising Jason I will call him after everything is over.

"Should I come? To the funeral?"

"No." I am firm.

The planning isn't difficult. I've been prepared for a long time, and I need only call the right people. Pastor Mark, from our wedding, has agreed to lead the ceremony, if it can even be called a ceremony. In my head, this service is a compromise: I know Maura would want something deeply religious, but Charlie would not. I also know that if I suggested, even as a joke, that I wanted to dump Charlie on a mountain to let some birds of prey carry his body off to heaven, Maura might have an actual heart attack.

What happens is somewhere in the middle.

At the service, Bridget and my dad have strict instructions to flank me the entire time. I imagine it looks, to everyone else, that I am grief-stricken. They are correct, but they also don't know how much I hate this. I hate the ceremony of it all. I hate the people. I hate the tears and the clucking and the clutched tissues. I don't know three-quarters of the people here, and they do not deserve to clutch tissues. They do not love this man as I do. I am angry they are here.

Avoiding Maura throughout the ceremony is not hard—she never looks at me once—but there is one person who slips through my security detail. While Bridget and my dad speak to Alfie about picking up the fried chicken on the way home, I feel a tap on my shoulder. I turn around and stand face-to-face with Charlie's mother. I haven't seen her since one of my first visits to Pax; she never came to his planning meetings, and I never saw her or Charlie's dad at any of my weekly visits. I'm not even sure she knows about the after-party at my house. The after-event. After-mourning. After-the-ceremonial-goodbye-to-my-dead-husband.

Joanie was always a stout woman, with the kind of lap that looked soft and cozy. She had sparkly eyes that crinkled when she smiled, and she never left the house without lipstick. Today her face is devoid of makeup, and she looks as though she's lost twenty pounds. Her eyes are flat and glassy as she gazes at me.

I try to speak, but my mouth is frozen.

"Maura tells me you were there every week," she says. "I wanted to . . . I couldn't. I couldn't go. I'm sorry."

I had watched the back of her throughout the service, and she never once shuddered, never ducked her head or wiped her eyes. She sat nearly at attention, ready to salute a commanding officer should one pass. But now, here, in front of me, she collapses. I move to catch her so she doesn't fall to the floor. I wrap this woman, my mother-in-law, up in my arms, and I hold her as sobs rack her body. She heaves and gasps, and I squeeze her tighter and close my eyes, partly to avoid the stares from the rest of the room but mostly to ground myself. I focus on my breathing as I hold her, inhaling the Dior perfume Charlie and I bought her a few Christmases ago.

I smell so fancy! she had exclaimed after opening her gift and spritzing her wrists right there in her pajamas Christmas morning.

When she quiets, I whisper in her ear, "You smell beautiful, Joanie."

"Jim said it's inappropriate to wear perfume to your son's funeral, but I told him, I said, 'It's inappropriate to have to attend your son's funeral. I'll wear whatever I damn well please.'"

"I'm glad you did." I pull away and place my hands on her shoulders while she wipes her nose; she has an entire box of tissues in her purse. "Oh, Joanie, I missed you." I am not as close with my in-laws as I'd wanted to be. It's not because I dislike them. I like them very much, even as I've avoided them this last year or so.

Her eyes fill up again with tears, and I am afraid she will have another breakdown. "I'm sorry I never visited."

"That's OK. I—"

"It's not OK," she cuts me off. "I couldn't go there, to that place with all those *old* people. He shouldn't have been there. He wasn't an old man. He didn't belong there."

I understand.

"And I'm sorry about Maura. She was wrong to treat you as she did after she met that man."

I hear Bridget inhale sharply, and my world wobbles. My periphery darkens, closes in, and I'm dangerously close to passing out.

"She told you," I whisper.

"And I told her, honey, you just mind your business. You don't know what that girl is going through. You have no idea. 'Let he who is without sin cast the first stone.' She always hates it when I quote the Bible back at her to show her what a little blockhead she can be."

Her eyes shift over my shoulder, and she raises her finger to point. "Yes, I'm talking about you." I turn and see Maura standing behind me. "You have no idea what this woman has been through. You have no idea. Half of my heart is missing right now—I am never gonna get

287

it back—and I still can't put myself in her shoes. If I didn't have your father through all this . . ." She trails off, shaking her head, and then she says to me, "They say you never get over losing a child. I suspect they're right. But I imagine no young wife gets over losing a spouse, either. Whatever you needed to do to get through that, it's not wrong or bad." Now she turns back to Maura. There is an edge to her voice. "You hear that? We're all just doing our best."

I suspect the idea that I could ever be "doing my best" makes the clockwork that runs Maura hiccup and buckle. I turn, and Maura wears a look I recognize—she wears rage a lot—before she huffs out of the room, purposely slamming into people as she goes.

"She needs a friend," Joanie says sadly. "She's lost her only one." She pauses, and she looks at me. "Can't we go to breakfast sometime? You and me?"

I hug her tightly. "I'd like that." And I would. I invite her to my home after the service, and she thanks me. "I wasn't sure if I should go." This further breaks my broken heart.

Before we leave, Pastor Mark gives me Charlie's urn. I've chosen one in a dark aqua-blue marble. It has brown, black, and white veins and a thin metallic gold band near the top that reminds me of a wedding ring. Engraved along the bottom, the urn reads, "Charles James Watters, My Beloved." When I ordered it, the guy at the funeral home insisted I include Charlie's birthdate and death date, but I refused. I did not want or need the numeric reminder that my Charlie died too young. Besides, I couldn't control anything about the last year, but dammit, I could control his urn—and his ashes. I have big plans to put the vase on the mantel next to our wedding photo. I'm no longer certain I'll scatter him in Burnet Woods. Maybe one day I'll take him to Tibet and feed him to the vultures, and they can take him up to Buddhist monk heaven. He might like that.

I hug the urn to my chest as I walk out of the funeral home, Dad and Bridget back in their guard spots on either side of me.

There, seated on a wooden bench outside near the front door, is Jason.

"Don't be mad," Bridget says. "He called me last night. He sounded desperate."

Jason rushes to me. "How are you? Are you OK? Of course you're not. I'm sorry. Can I help? Here, I brought this. Here. I hope it's OK." He thrusts a package of pistachio halvah at me. Now I have my dead husband's ashes in one hand and a Middle Eastern confection in the other, and it flashes across my mind that the texture of one is not entirely unlike the other, and I don't know whether to hyena laugh or slam-your-thumb-in-the-car-door screech. Meanwhile, my dad stands there, silent, a fish gaping out of water, trying to figure out what the hell is going on.

"We're on our way back to Asha's," Bridget says for me. "Meet us there?"

I settle in the front seat next to Bridget in the car, still cradling Charlie in my arms, and my dad climbs into the back seat. We pull out of the parking lot. After five minutes I open the halvah. There's no knife, so I lift the entire brick and bite a corner. Crumbs fall back into the plastic container and litter my black dress.

"Want some?" I offer Bridget, holding the halvah toward her mouth.

"I'm good."

"Dad?"

"Jason is back," he says.

"Guess so," I say, taking another bite of the halvah brick.

"For good?"

"I dunno."

"I see."

I snort, and the quick exhalation further scatters halvah dust. "I don't."

Bridget, apparently, finds this hilarious. She laughs so hard she stops making any noise for a moment, and I reach over to grab the steering wheel so we don't careen off the road. After another honk, she says, "I think I just peed a little," which gets my dad going. He slaps the seat in front of him, popping my head off the headrest, scattering halvah crumbs all over the front seat. A year from now I'm certain Bridget is going to find halvah down by the seat belt buckle, in the crevices of the cupholder, in the folds of the material surrounding the gearshift.

Back at home I tuck the halvah in the pantry, then head to the family room to put Charlie on the mantel. I hesitate. Will people want to see him? Or say a prayer? Should I give his urn a place of honor for the afternoon? I am frozen to this spot, in front of the fireplace, and I cannot move my limbs. I don't know where to put the remains of my husband. I don't want to set him down anywhere. I want to carry him about for the day, or, better yet, I want to carry him up into our room—my room—and curl around him and go to sleep for a hundred years.

I'm not sure how long I stand there, stone still, tears streaming down my cheeks, before my dad places his hand on my shoulder. I turn, robotically, toward him.

"Bratti," he whispers, taking Charlie from me and setting him on the coffee table. He wraps me up in his arms, and, for the first time in a long time, I dissolve.

I clean up as best I can after in the guest bathroom. When I step out, my dad is waiting for me. "I put Charlie in the office," he says. "There's a door, if anyone wants privacy, but it's right by the kitchen, not too far away from you."

"Thank you." I try to smile.

Dad takes my hand and threads it through his arm so I cup the inside of his elbow, as I did when he walked me down the aisle to my future. He leads me into the kitchen, toward a very different kind of future.

The next two hours are a blur. All the people I successfully avoided at the service are now in my home. It's a collection of bursts and blurs, and later, the images will come back to me in flashes: Pastor Mark, Joanie, and Charlie's father speak quietly in the corner. Jason and

Alfie furrow their brows and nod in my family room. Charlie's friends from the Scouts fix plates of fried chicken and Skyline chili dip in the kitchen. I haven't yet poked my head in the office, and when I do, Maura is behind me.

"Privacy, please," she demands. I step away from the room, and she slams the door in my face. I wander into the dining room, where Bridget is messing with the buffet.

"I need something to do," I say.

Bridget hands me an empty platter. "There's a Tupperware of cookies in the kitchen. Your neighbor dropped them off."

I spend at least fifteen minutes arranging the cookies, one by one. It's not that I care what the cookies or the platter looks like, but I like that, when I appear busy, no one talks to me.

I return to the dining room and squeeze the tray onto the table. I look at what else is there—vegetables and dip, three different kinds of deviled eggs, an enormous thing of Skyline chili dip, and . . . oh. A tray of dates. From my dad, no doubt.

I reach for one and bite it in half. Like a waking dream, Charlie's face appears before mine, studying the half I'm holding to his mouth. He's naked, sweaty from the sex that happened over a decade ago. It would never happen again.

As I take in a breath to say I don't know what, a man I've never met introduces himself as Jermaine. I recognize the name—he works with Charlie at P&G. Worked. He says he's sorry, that Charlie was a great guy. I say "thank you" and "I know." Then he relays a story about my husband at work, a situation when their boss was being a particularly vile douchebag, and Charlie stood up to him. I know the story, but it still has me enraptured. At one point Jermaine makes me laugh, and the movement of the smile across my mouth feels like a deep, cleansing breath. As we talk, Jason catches my eye. He gives me a small grin and lifts his hand, as though to blow me a kiss, but thinks better of it and drops it to his side, returns to his conversation with Alfie. My heart accepts the kiss anyway and whispers *Thank you.*

When Jermaine leaves, I notice that the door to the office is open, and I see Maura standing, silent, next to her dad, her oversize purse clutched to her side like a life raft.

Charlie is alone in the office. My dad has arranged two vases of roses on either side of the urn. There's a plain gray rock with a simple black cross drawn on it. I recognize the rock from Maura's Instagram feed. She posted about it last week in her story: One of her followers sent it in response to Maura's plea for prayers. I am horrified that she shared her address with any followers, and I'm puzzled that Maura has decided to give away this gift. Maybe I'm supposed to give it back? I decide that I will simply consider the gesture to be sweet. Next to the rock, someone has added a small, framed quote. It reads, *Say not in grief, "He is no more," but live in thankfulness that he was. - Hebrew Proverb*

I don't know anything about Judaism, but the quote speaks to me. I'm holding the frame in my hands, reading and rereading the words, when Jason pokes his head in the room.

"I hope that's OK," he says. I hold up the frame, a question on my face, and he nods. "From Gaby, actually. She told me I'm nuts for coming—"

"You are," I interrupt, a small smile tugging up the corner of my mouth.

"Actually, she said, 'What kind of dumbass maniac goes to the funeral of the husband of the ex-girlfriend he just slept with again for the first time in a millennium?'"

"When you put it like that . . ." I say, then pause. "What are we doing?"

Jason shrugs. "What we always do: We're figuring it out."

"Figuring it out . . . figuring it out . . . figuring it out," I repeat, almost chanting. I set down the quote and reach for Charlie's urn. I lift it from the middle, and the lid topples off, rolling under the table. Well, that's weird. It was certainly secure when I had it near the mantel a few hours before. Maybe my dad loosened it. I put the urn back on the table so I can retrieve the lid.

"I got it," Jason says, dropping to his knees. He starts to stand too soon, and his head connects with the table, knocking over the urn.

"Charlie!" I gasp, reaching, but the urn topples to its side.

Nothing comes out.

"Oh, god," Jason says, standing up. "I thought he was actually in there."

"He was," I say. "We waited a few extra days to have his ceremony to give them time to cremate him."

"Did they forget?"

I try to remember what Pastor Mark said. Maybe it *did* take longer than it was supposed to. Maybe he told me, and in the fog of the last week—hell, of the last year—I forgot.

"No, look," I say. There are traces of small, hard, uneven pieces of ash on the pale-gray carpet. I pick up the chunks and place them in my palm.

Jason and I are standing close together, staring at my open hand, trying to figure out what this means, when from the hallway Maura says, "You really are a slut."

Jason looks up, stunned. "Excuse me? Who the hell are you—"

Maura cuts him off. "Charlie deserved better. He deserved so. Much. Better." At each word, her voice gets louder, until she nearly screams "better." She turns to bolt out the front door, and I watch her fly across my front lawn to her car. Something—maybe a loose stone or an uneven patch of grass—catches her foot, and she goes flying. I'm talking airborne. One shoe goes in one direction. Her purse goes in another. Jason and I rush outside to help. Maura tries to scramble up. Her black nylons have holes in the knees, and I see marks on her palms and elbows. I move to help her while Jason retrieves the shoe and purse.

"Give me that!" she shrieks.

"Hold on. Your stuff is everywhere. It . . ." He trails off, and he murmurs, "Jesus Christ." I see what's in his hand, and a blind rage drips over my vision.

"How dare you—" she says, certainly about to scold him for using the name of the Lord in vain, but I'm louder.

"How dare YOU?" I shriek. I'm having an out-of-body experience. I have no control over my words or my movements. Jason holds a large, zipper baggie of my husband's remains, and this baggie has fallen out of Maura's purse. I see it all as though through a tunnel; my peripheral vision seems broken. It's as though my sight has become crosshairs because my sister-in-law is trying to kidnap the ashes of my husband. "You jackass . . . goddamned . . . bitch-faced . . . HYPOCRITE!" I shove Maura as hard as I can.

What follows is a domino effect. She wears only one heel, and it's not hard to unbalance her. She stumbles back into Jason, who's not expecting to be crashed into. He drops her purse and, somehow, sends Charlie flying . . . right into a concrete birdbath. The baggie snags on the beak of a decorative bird, and the ashes of my dead husband go abso-goddamn-lutely everywhere.

Maura screams like she has been stabbed and drops to her knees to crawl on the grass. Anyone who missed the first part of the show runs outside to catch the second half. I float somewhere above this scene, watching with popcorn and fury. I do not place my hands around Maura's little garbage neck, and one day, surely, I will consider my restraint one of the miracles of my life.

It feels like a year, but it must be only seconds later when my in-laws drag their shrieking daughter toward the car, away from the base of the birdbath. She had been scooping handfuls of Charlie back in the baggie—no doubt mixed in with grass, dirt, and whatever else is in our front yard.

"Good thing we don't have a dog," I say to no one, and the laughter that had caught Bridget and my dad in the car touches my elbow.

Bridget runs out with a broom and dustpan because how the hell else are you supposed to pick up ashes from a front yard?

Before she can start, though, I say through a snicker, "Stop."

"I can take care of this. Asha, I got it. I can—"

I shake my head, trying not to laugh. "It's OK."

"Ash," Jason whispers, "he's in the birdbath."

I clap a hand to my mouth but cannot keep the guffaw inside. The pressure pushes out tears, and I stand there crying through laughter—or am I laughing through crying? I have no idea what I'm doing, but I know what I'm thinking: There aren't many vultures in the area, but even the possibility of them appeals to me.

SPRING (2000-05)

The night Jason and his dad arrived in Del Ray, Jason and I found ourselves on the phone, in the grass, sprawled out together but five hundred miles apart, stargazing.

"Can you see Orion's belt?" he asked.

I could.

"What about the Big Dipper?"

"Where's Booties, where's Booties, where's Booties?" I whispered into the phone, my eyes scanning the sky. "You find it already?"

Of course he had. He always found the stars before me. It took me longer to catch up, but I *did* catch up. Always.

I ran a lot that summer. Whenever I'd pass the house with the pond, I'd remember the fish, George and Gail. Eventually I started to think of it as our house, as mine and Jason's. Once, I even walked up to the pond to see for myself if there were any fish.

There weren't.

The next time I saw Jason was a month into the school year, our senior year. He showed up unannounced on my doorstep, red rose in hand. We both knew he already had a new girlfriend—someone he met when he went out for the track team—though neither of us cared; he ate dinner with my dad and me, then, under the guise of going to a party at Daniel's, we went back to the cornfield. I'd already stocked up from Mrs. Casey's closet.

It didn't feel like cheating. This girlfriend, whom he would eventually marry and divorce, was only a placeholder, I thought. Someone to pass the time with until the next time he and I saw each other. He didn't love her, I was certain, and he didn't make love to her.

This situation, this dismissal of a girlfriend, wouldn't be possible today, by the way. My senior year of high school fell in 2000–01, and it was easy to pretend Simone didn't exist, because I couldn't look her up on social media anytime I wanted. I never knew what she ate for breakfast or when she got a new haircut. I never saw photos of her laughing with her friends or under Jason's arm, his hand dangerously close to her breast. She only existed through what Jason told me, and when he talked about her, he never lit up like he did when he talked about me.

If social media *had* existed, though, maybe we'd have officially stayed together when he moved. We'd been on and off for so long, and even when we were off, we were kind of on, so it didn't seem important to establish "Are we together or aren't we?" What could it change? Without cell phones, we couldn't text one another when we couldn't sleep at 2 a.m. We couldn't take photos of our kissy faces or . . . Lord, I shudder to think about the sort of photos I'd have sent my teenage boyfriend. But I would have. Wouldn't have thought twice about it, either.

Instead, the photos we traded were printouts (and fully clothed). When he sent me a three-by-five of his senior picture, the boy in the image had proudly displayed the key necklace I gave him over his sweater. A note was tucked in with the photo:

I've been thinking about you lately. More than usual, I mean. I've been remembering everything—remember when we danced in your family room the day I met your dad? Snuck out to the pool? That time we went camping?

It's more than that, though. I've been thinking about YOU. The way you look, the way you act, the way you feel. It's probably not very healthy to think like this, having a girlfriend and all. Just know I'm still in love with you. I always will be.

I tucked the letter in the bottom of my mom's jewelry box, where I kept all my Jason memories: his other letters, the tiger's eye bracelet, the photo from the Christmas party where I did not say *I love you*, a petal from the rose he gave me the day he moved. And I still slept with my hand tucked inside my pocket pillow.

Over the years the petal would crumble. The bracelet would break, and I'd lose most of the beads. Eventually I'd take the heart with the missing piece off my evil eye necklace, and it, too, would get lost. When I realized it was gone, I tore my bedroom apart. I never found it. But the letters remained. And the pillow with the pocket—that even came to college with me that first year.

When I graduated from high school, Jason came to the graduation ceremony. He sat quietly with my father and my grandparents, who cheered loudly when they called my name and I walked across the stage: Asha Victoria Khoury, that's me, high school graduate.

My dad had an open-house party that afternoon, friends filing in and out as they attended as many parties as they could fit in the day. Neighbors stopped by for a hot dog or to drop off a hug and a card. Even Kyle, whom I'd stayed friends with, showed up. He'd gotten his braces removed earlier in the year, and he'd cut his curly mop close to his head. It somehow aged him a little, and I could see the man he would become.

When he arrived, Jason disappeared. I found him in my upstairs bathroom.

"You OK?" I asked, knocking.

"Go away."

"What's wrong?"

He opened the door, and his face read misery.

"What's wrong?" I repeated, alarmed, desperately thinking . . . *Please don't ruin my graduation party. Please don't ruin my graduation party.*

"I can't believe Kyle's here."

"Why not? We're friends. We're not dating or anything. And even if we were—"

He cut me off: "I know, I know, I have a girlfriend."

"Yes, you do. You and I are not together right now. Should we be?" It wasn't exactly the nicest way to see if Jason wanted to be my boyfriend again, even though I sort of wanted him to say, "OK."

"You're right. You're always right." He walked quietly past me and down the stairs. Five minutes later he grabbed Daniel, and they walked out the front door without saying goodbye.

That night, after everyone left and my dad and grandparents were in bed, Bridget and I stayed up, planning our summers and wondering about college. We'd both gotten into UC, where my dad taught.

"I think I want to be a decorator," she announced. "Or a party planner. I want to own my own business."

"That's amazing," I gushed, because it was, and because she was my best friend, and she could do or be anything. She could have said, *I'm going to be a janitor at a museum of fecal matter,* and I would have thought it was brilliant. That's what it's like, the days after you graduate from high school: Everything is possible, simultaneously. Every idea is a good idea, even if it's a terrible one. You don't even recognize it as "hope"—it's just the way things are. It's only life, and the idea that it could be fleeting is foreign, hieroglyphics in the dark corner of a cave you can't even see, let alone translate.

"What about *you?*" she pressed. "What the hell do you want to be when you grow up?"

I didn't know, and I loved it. I had enrolled in a little bit of everything at Cincinnati. It's what they do for undecided majors—here, taste it all, see what's sweet.

"Soooooo I brought something," she said, giving me an evil expression, pulling two bottles of beer and a bottle opener from her duffel bag.

"How'd you get those past your mom?"

Bridget shrugged. "I took them out of the garage. They're warm, but . . ." She shrugged again. "Does it matter?"

I didn't know—I had never had a drink of anything before. She started to open the bottle, and the *wshhhhh* noise seemed too loud. I snatched both bottles from her, slipped on some shoes, and stepped out onto the dark deck, not bothering to flip on the lights.

Bridget tiptoed out behind me, giggling. We crawled into the play fort my dad still hadn't taken down, and there, I opened my first beer.

"To us!" Bridget announced, smacking her bottle against mine with a cheery *dink*.

We each downed a huge gulp of warm beer. To our credit, neither of us spit out the gulp, but my god—was that awful.

"Why do people drink this?" I asked.

"It's fun?" Bridget responded, studying her beer in the dark before taking another, smaller sip. "Yeah, that's gross."

But we finished the bottles. After, we couldn't have been drunk, not really, but we acted like we were. It wasn't the alcohol but the night: We were drunk on possibility, on the future, on each other.

While we sat in the tree fort, gossiping, a rustle made us jump. I poked my head from the fort. "Hello?" I stage-whispered into the dark.

"Hey," I heard in sullen reply.

"Jason!" I greeted him, and repeated the obvious to Bridget, talking loud enough for Jason to hear, too. "It's Jason."

"No boys allowed!" Bridget replied, rolling onto her back. Jason's head peered into the fort. He saw the empty beer bottles, and he smiled sadly.

"Not much room for me up there," he said. He was being morose, but he was right—he was considerably taller than he'd been that early-summer afternoon we decided to date again before I took off for Florida.

"No, no, I'll go, I'll go, it's fine," Bridget huffed good-naturedly. She gave me a huge hug and whispered in my ear, "If you do him up here, I want all the details." Then she stuck her legs out the slide, said "Wheeee!" as she bumped down, and stood next to Jason. "Happy graduation, Jason!" she said, throwing her arms around his neck. He hugged her awkwardly. "Give me a real hug, you doofus! You've been my best friend-in-law for, like, ever."

That made him grin, and he wrapped his arms around my friend and lifted her in the air, giving her a little shake.

"Good boy!" she said, patting his cheek, perhaps a little harder than necessary, then sauntered back inside the house.

Jason crawled up into the fort with some difficulty. He sat next to me, and before he could say anything, I straddled him and kissed him hard. I moved against him and felt him respond. He returned the kiss for a moment, then settled his hands on my waist and pushed me back a little.

"What is it?" I asked.

"I'm sorry," he whispered.

"Don't worry about it. I didn't know Kyle was going to show up, it's fine." I tried to kiss him again.

"It's not that."

The last time I saw him look this miserable, we were seated at his kitchen table after Gaby had picked me up. I scrambled off his lap and sobered up immediately.

"What did you do? Did you take pills? Do we need to go to the hospital?"

"Nothing like that. I . . ."

"What?"

"IuhsewiSamoe."

Did he say what I think he said? Surely not. My Jason translator must have been broken.

"Jason, what?"

He took a deep breath, pop-pop-popped the knuckles on both of his hands, and he repeated, slowly: "I had sex with Simone."

I felt as though all my insides fell to the ground—heart, lungs, esophagus, stomach, kidneys, liver, brain, the whole lot of it, WHOOSH, toward the center of the earth.

"What?" My voice broke as I said it, and, as if in response to all of its internal organs migrating to my feet, my body started to shake like the temperature had dropped to below freezing; it was seventy-one degrees out, not a cloud in the sky.

"I'm sorry."

"What?"

"I didn't mean for it to happen."

"When?"

"A few months ago."

"A few months ago?"

"I didn't know how to tell you."

"Only the once?"

"What?"

"You only . . . you only did it . . . just the once?"

"Asha." His voice was tortured.

"More than that?"

He dropped his head, his chin against his chest.

"Why?" I asked, my voice rising.

"I'm sorry. I . . . I don't know. I didn't mean to. After . . . all I could think about was you."

Years later, after college, hell, even after I met Charlie and was happily married, I would sometimes think of that line—*All I could think about was you*—and feel terribly for Simone. What a horrible thing, to lose your virginity to a boy—Jason had told me months earlier that he was Simone's first boyfriend—who, in the afterglow, spent his time thinking about another girl.

"Why did you show me her picture?" I asked, my voice shrill.

"What do you mean?" he replied softly.

"You showed me her picture once. Why did you do that?"

"You asked to see her." He could only whisper.

"But now I know what she looks like," I shouted at him, pounding my fists on his chest. "I can picture it. I can picture it because I know what she looks like, and I know what *you* look like when . . . when you . . ." I couldn't form words anymore.

I curled into a ball, as tight as I could roll. I wanted to make myself tiny, tiny, insignificant while I thought of the pale girl with the plain face and too-close eyes and mousy hair. Nearly every other girl Jason had ever dated had looked a tiny bit like me—Kendra, Olivia, Raya—and here he was, falling for the exact opposite of the dark-haired ball sobbing at his feet.

"Asha," he said.

"Go away."

"Please don't—"

"Go away," I screamed at him. My head was still pressed against my knees, but my shout echoed in the small space. It's a wonder my dad didn't hear it. The neighbors. Maybe the police would show up, think I was being murdered, arrest this boy, drag him away.

I felt Jason press his hand atop my head, then heard him jump out of the fort. He landed with a soft *thwump* in the grass, and his footfalls faded as he walked away.

Now I know, of *course* Jason and Simone slept together. They were teenagers in love, and I knew what teenagers in love did. But I was naive. I trusted Jason stupidly, blindly, and thus I was stupidly blind-sided. He'd used to say he wanted to wait until he and I were married until we made love, but not waiting didn't matter since we were going to get married anyway. If we were always going to be each other's only, what did the "when" matter? And now he'd ruined it.

A few moments later, Bridget ran out.

"What happened?" she asked, climbing the ladder into the fort, now as sober as I was.

I looked up at her—god, what a pathetic sight I must have been—and somehow she knew.

"Damn," she breathed, and she sat down next to me, also stupidly blindsided. Still in my ball, I rolled over onto my other side and into her lap. She draped her body around me in as much of a hug as she could give in this position, and she held me as I sobbed, harder than I ever had before, even harder than I had the previous summer, when my dad held me after Jason left. Because even though Jason was moving, I was still *certain* I would be Jason's "forever." Because then I knew it didn't matter where we lived or who we dated—for the stuff that mattered, that *really mattered*, there was only me for him and him for me.

And now . . . I didn't know anything anymore.

Bridget blossomed at UC, a business major with a minor in entrepreneurship. We snuck beer into the dorms and brainstormed names for her business: B's Knees Events, Parties by Bridget, The Final Touch.

"That sounds like I give happy endings," she pointed out.

"Business will boom."

I did fine. I eventually chose to study marketing because it was easy. I went to class, did my homework, got As and Bs, went to some basketball games. But nothing felt right. Nothing excited me.

Jason went to college in DC with Simone, and we kept in touch sporadically freshman year. Usually I'd call him. At first he'd always sound hesitant, and by the end of the conversation he'd warmed up, sounded like the old Jason. Like my old Jason.

Once I called him after stumbling home post–Hairy Buffalo party. It was three in the morning. When Bridget and I opened our dorm room door, we fell inside, the booze in our plastic cups sloshing over the rim.

"I'm horny," I declared.

Bridget burst out laughing. "That Oliver kid couldn't stop staring at you."

I wrinkled my nose and pouted. "No! No, I don't want Oliver. I want Jason."

"You need to get over that asshole," Bridget said, finger wagging so close to my face she booped my nose. Then she spun around, grabbed the phone, and handed it to me. "I think Nikki and Lauren are still up. I'll head over there while you have *phone sex*." She shouted this last phrase so loudly girls up and down the hallway whooped and howled.

I dialed Jason's DC dorm number from memory, and he picked up on the fifth ring.

"Did I wake you?"

"You don't have to scream," Jason said softly, but I heard a chuckle exhale through his nose.

"I'm screaming?" I asked, and I stage-whispered, I think, "Is this better?"

"You're so cute," he said, and he paused. "I shouldn't have said that."

"Tell me how cute I am," I said, flopping down on the bottom bunk. "Tell me what you want to do to my cute little body."

"Asha," he said, his voice full of . . . what? Longing? Desperation? Misery? God, was it . . . pity?

"I love hearing you say my name. You used to like it when I said *Jason*. Remember?"

He didn't respond.

"What, is *she* over there or something?"

"Asha . . ." he repeated, and I sat bolt upright.

"Oh, god, she is, isn't she?"

"She's not here," Jason said, and I relaxed, but only for a moment. "I can't do this."

"Do what?" I asked, but I knew.

"Asha, I'm with Simone."

"Didn't used to stop you."

He didn't respond, and I didn't speak, either. We sat in silence for so long. I said his name again, "Jason," and was surprised to hear my voice break. I lifted a hand to my face. My cheek was wet. "You're picking her, aren't you? You're picking her."

It reminded me of that horrible conversation on the beach we'd had a few months after Jason almost took all those pills. Where I wanted to break things off but was too in love to say the words, where Jason begged me to say "It's over" until I finally acquiesced.

I refused to be that pathetic.

"Got it," I said, and I hung up.

I expected the phone to ring immediately after. Or a minute or two after. Or later that week. Or the following month.

It never did.

The next time I saw Jason was later that summer. Edward had a party, and I showed up without Bridget. I don't even remember why she wasn't there, but I distinctly remember feeling alone among the dozen people at the party. Jason was there. I didn't know he would be. He could hardly look at me most of the night.

After midnight, Edward opened up the hot tub in the backyard. No one had any swimsuits, and all the guys got in wearing their boxers. Me and Daniel's sister, the only other girl there, wore our bras and panties. She kept trying to give Edward a hand job under the water. I took it as my cue to jump out and run inside.

Our clothes were piled in heaps on the basement floor, and I grabbed my shorts and T-shirt and locked myself in the bathroom. I stripped out of my bra and undies and used a bath towel I found under the sink to dry off. When a soft knock tapped against the door, I wasn't surprised. I clutched the towel around myself and opened the door a crack.

"Hey," Jason said.

"Hey," I said.

"How are you?"

"I'm changing."

The look Jason gave me was nothing short of pained. I had a very real—and, it turned out, accurate—thought that this was going to be the final time I saw Jason Kapaglia.

"Is everyone still outside?" I asked.

"Yeah."

"Come on." I grabbed my clothes and his hand, and I pulled him into the spare bedroom on the other side of the basement, clutching the towel at my breast. I heard Edward whoop, "Asha ain't got no clothes on!" as I closed the door and pressed the lock. I looked up at Jason and, for a half a second, the expression on his face changed, and he was grinning, happy. I lost myself in the smile, and I reached up to kiss him. I felt his back stiffen and, worse, his lips. For the first time in my life, I kissed Jason Kapaglia, and his mouth did not immediately respond to mine.

I pulled away, and he grabbed on to my wrists. Not hard—he didn't hurt me—but firmly.

"No," he said. "I want to."

"Then kiss me like you love me."

It was like he'd needed permission to do so. He kissed me hard, and his hands pulled away my towel, roughly and awkwardly. He tried to feel every part of my body as quickly as he could. As though it were a race, as though he needed to cover the topography of me, every inch, one more time, and he was afraid he'd lose his nerve.

I pulled away from him, took his hand, and walked him to the bed. I pulled back the covers and got in, then watched him as he undressed and joined me.

"Like you love me," I said again, and we fell into it, slow, deliberate. When Jason moved against me, he never broke eye contact. That's how everything was with Jason—so serious, as though he wanted to infuse each moment with capital-*M Meaning*. Our whole relationship was like that, and I suppose it should come as no surprise that much of our youthful lovemaking was the same.

I started my sophomore year the following week, and within two months, I let my Fundamentals of Consumer Behavior prof seduce me. Oh, don't get grossed out—he was only twenty-six, and he was painfully hot. But I wanted someone like him—someone sexy, someone I would never fall in love with—for my second lover.

I didn't really date in college, and I didn't sleep around. I kept my head down, went to parties with Bridget, attended class. Sometimes I got antsy, and I'd find someone sweet and safe to take to bed. That's all it was. A lay. I enjoyed it the way any woman would, but I didn't have to feel anything monumental for the men. Life seemed easier that way. I know it sounds callous, but I needed that hardening during that time in my life.

Part of the lesson, at least, was a good one: Sex didn't have to be The Thing. It could just be A Thing. That didn't make it bad or unspecial or unimportant. But sex also didn't need to be so damn serious. And understanding that, in the long run, is a very good thing.

After graduation, Bridget and I rented a house together in Cincinnati. For New Year's Eve, we threw a party. I let her dress me. There, I met a beautiful man with long hair, whom I married one year, to the day, later.

AUTUMN (2017)

"What were you going to do with them?" Bridget asks the next day. My dad makes pancakes for us, and Bridget and I sit silently at the table.

I don't have to ask what she means.

"I figured I'd just keep him here. Or scatter him at Burnet Woods. I go there sometimes to talk to him. Or maybe that spot where we went camping, right after we started dating."

I cannot tell her I'm happy Charlie's in the front yard, that the thought of a bird taking him far away, to the treetops, to the clouds, to heaven and the gods, soothes me like a warm bath.

The three of us eat in companionable silence until Bridget, who scrolls on her phone, lets out a gasp and nearly chokes on a bite of pancakes. "Did you see this?" she asks. "Did you *see* this?"

"What is it?" my dad asks calmly.

Maura hasn't posted to @loveabides831 since Charlie died—I guess the stress of losing her brother, stealing his ashes from me, and dumping him all over the front yard wasn't conducive for creative social media content—but that's not to say the account has been silent.

No, it seems that, at some point yesterday, a @unicornlvr520, whose profile is mysteriously blank, left a public comment for Maura:

> Girl, you are sooooo fake. Why don't u tell everyone
> *why* you need those prayers? Why don't you say
> your hurting cause Charlie is IN A COMA? And instead

of surrounding yourself with family LIKE A NORMAL
PERSON, you made this fakeass account acting like a
little saint. But you are NO SAINT. I've known people
like you. I've been people like you. Instead of using
religion for all it's beautiful uses—to bring comfort
and ease the aches we all keep in our gut—u use it as
an excuse. Like everything has to happen fro a reason
just so nothing can ever be YOUR FAULT. Obvs this isnt
anyone's fault, not even yours. Stop blaming people.
STOP BLAMING PEOPLE.

"I don't know whether to slap you or kiss you," I say, unblinking,
unable to turn away from this train wreck.

"That's not me," Bridget says. "I wish I'd thought to do that."

"Who else would know she's blaming anyone?" I say, and we both
turn to my dad, who looks completely bewildered. "I guess you didn't
make a fake Instagram to chew out Maura, huh?"

"I did not chew out Maura," he says, slathering more butter on a
pancake. "But I'm happy someone did."

Later that afternoon, I have to stop by Pax to sign some papers
and pick up a few odds and ends—the framed photos I left around the
room, the blanket I brought from home, the candles. I don't recognize
the receptionist when I walk in, and I'm glad. I'm not sure what I'd say
to Madison today.

While I'm cleaning up, though, there's a knock on the doorframe.
Madison *is* here today, it seems.

People always feel like they have to say *something* after a tragedy,
especially an untimely death. *I'm so sorry* or *He's in a better place now.*
None of it actually helps the grieving party; it only makes the speaker
feel better, like they did something useful. But Madison knows there's
nothing to say; she simply steps in the room and hugs me.

In the year I've known her, it's the first time we've touched, and I'm
struck by how big she is. She always sat behind the desk when I would

visit, but standing next to her, I see she's nearly six feet tall, with broad shoulders and strong arms.

"My god, you give good hugs," I say, extending the embrace a beat or two longer.

"I wanted to let you know that you've been one of my favorites," she says. "I don't say that to everyone. Honestly, I don't even like most people. Dealing with all this, you see a lot of people's worst sides. But you don't seem to have a worst side."

"I know plenty of people who'd disagree with *that*," I say.

Madison cocks her head at me, as if about to say something, and her phone buzzes. She pulls it out of her pocket and flips a button to mute the buzzing. I study her phone.

"I've always loved your phone case. It's so youthful and . . ." I pause. "Wait. Unicorns?"

Her face flushes a deep crimson, and she cringes. "Please don't be mad. That was super unprofessional. But I couldn't take it. I couldn't take that stupid, smug face. Of all the awful sides of people I've seen here, she's the worst. And the last time you were here, I heard her screaming like a maniac, blaming you for everything. It's . . ." She trails off, shaking her head.

I can't seem to form any words in response to learning that Madison is @unicornlvr520, so I wrap her in another bear hug instead.

That night my dad and I tuck in to watch a movie. I fall asleep almost immediately. It's after 1 a.m. when my eyes flutter open.

"Dad?"

"Shh, shh, shh," he says. He covers me with an oversize blanket. I'm too tired, too cozy to go up to bed, so I let him. He shuts off the television and turns to leave the room.

I call him back. "Stay with me 'til I fall asleep."

He sits at the other end of the couch, lifting my feet up on his lap. There is a dim light coming from the kitchen, and I see his handsome, lined face. He is smiling.

"Recommencer," he says, the first *R* trilling.

"What's that?"

"It is French for 'to begin again.' This is where you are, *bratti*. You are beginning again. I have been there many times—when we moved to this country from Iran. When your mother died. When you and I moved to Ohio."

"How do I know it's time to *recommencer*?" I try to pronounce the word as beautifully as my father but fall far short.

"Things start when they must start. For strong people, they start sooner. They can handle more. They are impatient. They are ready."

Tears pour from my eyes. "I'm not ready."

He insists, "I think you believe you should not be ready for *recommencer*, but it comes when it must. There is no way to force it. Like the seasons. We believe we are not ready for the summertime to end, but then we remember the beauty in the falling leaves. There is sadness in *recommencer*, but there can be goodness, too. I swear on your life, there is goodness."

"It's too soon," I say.

"I read something the other day, and I want to read it to you," he says. He clicks on the lamp next to him and pulls his wallet from his pocket, then tugs out a newspaper clipping, an advice column from his local paper. "Listen, *bratti*:

> "When a loved one dies in our society, we expect to finish our grief stage before we move on to a new relationship. We feel that if we fall in love again, we are disloyal to our lost spouse, as if they never happened. But mourning and new love can come together. There is room in our hearts to miss one person and to love someone new. Our hearts can expand to hold much, and there is no manual or correct timeline to follow."

I study my father's face and see he is looking inward. "Dad? Who is that for?" He smiles sadly. I sit up, and we reach for one another's hands. "Celine? Dad, Mom died over thirty years ago. It's OK to have someone new. I'm happy you have someone new."

"I only loved your mother ever," he says. "This is very scary. But it is also very nice. Don't wait thirty years, *bratti*. Be happy today."

Then he pauses. He pauses for so long I wonder if he's drifted off to sleep. As my eyes start to feel heavy, he speaks again. "So . . . Jason."

"Jason," I agree.

"Does he make you happy today?"

Without meaning to, without deciding to, I feel my face break into a smile. Then my father mirrors something Bridget said to me . . . Wow, was it only a few days ago? He says, "I swear on your life, I missed that smile." He nods, as if confirming something that has not been said. "He is not a teenager anymore. Maybe this time, you two can be happy."

"Maybe," I agree.

I awake the next morning, in my bed. I don't even remember coming up here. Sunlight leaks in from around the curtain. I walk to the window and peek outside. It's bright out there, and I can hear birds through the closed glass.

For the first time in a year, I think it might be nice to be outside. *Hmm.* Tentatively, I pull a brush through my hair and put it in a greasy french braid. I trade Charlie's T-shirt for one of mine and a pair of yoga pants. Both are too big now, but they'll suffice. I get on my hands and knees to dig through the shoes in my closet and locate my running shoes, smashed in the back. While I'm digging them up, I find a pair of shoes I swear I haven't worn since high school, some clunky black Mary Janes I still have for some reason. I pull one from the closet and toss it across the room, and then the other.

My feet are going to kill, I think as I lace up my sneakers. Before I go downstairs, I grab those old Mary Janes to line up in front of the dresser. When I pick them up, something falls from inside one of them.

You have got to be kidding me. It's the small heart with a key-size hole I haven't seen since college. My Jason heart. *I found it.* I place it on my nightstand.

I go downstairs and stand by the front door, stretching. The motion, the ritual, causes a stirring, something like . . . what is that? It's hope. It's wanting. I try not to look at it head-on lest I scare it away.

I stretch for a full fifteen minutes. I'm out of practice, and I know it's not enough, but I'm antsy. What did Dad tell me last night? *Things start when they must start. For strong people, they start sooner. They can handle more. They are impatient.*

I am impatient.

As I open the door, my dad calls down the stairs to me.

"*Bratti*, where are you going?"

"Running," I say, and I see the pleasure on his face.

"Have fun," he calls as I close the door behind me.

I jog for a moment in the front yard, taking in the new day. It smells fresh, almost like camping. *Charlie,* I whisper in my mind.

I love you, the wind whispers back. At least, I think it does.

I last barely ten minutes before I am wheezing so hard I am afraid I will vomit. I limp slowly back home, but I am not defeated.

I'm just getting started.

SPRING (1998)

. . . and here's the second page of that letter Jason wrote me for my belated sixteenth birthday:

> The flip side of "love is letting go," then, is that if you never come back, you were never mine to begin with. I already came back to you, and it was the best thing I've ever done.
>
> And so I'll wait to see if you ever come back to me. Maybe in a week or a month. Maybe next year. Maybe—please don't make me wait this long, I don't think I could stand it—years and years from now, after you have lived life and had experiences without me. I hate to think of that, of you experiencing life without me. Because that means I will do the same, and I can't imagine it. But it's all part of growing up, I guess. Maybe those experiences can make us stronger, somehow, though I don't see how that is possible. Maybe I'm too young and selfish to understand how that could work.
>
> Please know that I'll always have a spot for you in my heart, now and forever. Know that, no matter what, I will be here for you. Even though you have other family and friends for support, you can always include me in that group. Don't ever be afraid to call

me, to reach out to me, for anything, whatever you need. I'll be there for you, always.

You were more to me than my girlfriend. I think you know that. You were my life, my friend, my love, my family. And when someone is so important, I don't think that ever goes away.

Even as I apologize to you, I also thank you. You've taught me so much—how to be strong, how to be loving, how to know who our friends are and how to value them. I am indebted to you.

If love is letting go, then I am truly in love with you. Maybe, one day, you'll come back, and I'll know: You're in love with me, too.

ACKNOWLEDGMENTS

True confession: I have no memory of wanting to be a novelist when I was a child.

A year or two ago my mom gave me this red spiral-bound book full of grade school photos, report cards, and favorites. Memories of the First Day of School and Best Friends. Favorite Activities and Favorite Sports. And, starting in fifth grade, Dreams or Ambitions.

In that space, in fifth grade, I wrote, in dark-red marker, with very perpendicular print, "I want to be become a children's book author." In sixth grade, I wrote, in black pen, with very perpendicular cursive, "book author, teacher, singer."

Truly, I don't remember wanting any of those things. In high school, after writing for *The Voice* newspaper for three years at Lakota West, I decided to become a journalist. It was the most logical way I could think of to get someone to pay me to write.

I wasn't wrong. But at some point in my thirties, I got an idea for a novel. I wrote it, edited it, gave it to friends to read, edited it again, sent it to agents, edited it some more, sent it to more agents. I wrote a really bad how-to/YA/memoir thing (don't ask). Followed the same process.

And then I wrote this. Followed the same process again, never expecting it to go anywhere but enjoying the journey. And here we are.

This book wouldn't exist without these people, the folks who helped and encouraged and cheered and edited and loved.

Jeff: You're first, babe. The amount of support you give is too great to measure. When I started on this whole "Maybe I want to get published and get a literary agent?" thing, you weren't surprised or all "Well, *that's* a longshot" about it. Instead, your attitude was so chill. So "of course you should do that." So "obviously you'll find representation. Duh." And that certainty—which is a certainty I've never had because, logically, doing all this is bonkers—has never wavered. It's one of the reasons I've been able to do this. I know that in my guts. Good god, I love you.

Mom and Dad: Mom, thanks for making me an empathetic, sensitive person who feels things way too deeply. It's the reason I want to figure it out on paper, the reason I want to write it down and hope maybe someone somewhere reads what I've written and says, *Oh wow. I thought I was the only one. I feel less lonely now.* Dad, thanks for making me roll my eyes—just a little!—at empathetic, sensitive people who feel things way too deeply. (Yes, that's a lot of self-eye-rolling. We contain multitudes.) And thanks for giving me the storytelling bug. You tell the world's best stories, and I strive to be just a fraction as successful at it as you are, to capture people just a sliver as much as you do. And both of you, thanks for that excellent weekend of dolma-making.

To my friends: My god, the pages and pages of crap you've read and helped me through over the years (and, in a few cases, decades). You've made me a better me. You're spectacular magic unicorns, and I love you so hard I could pop you: Brett, Dana, Emma, Erin, Jackie, Lindsay, Meghan, Rachel. You've had some sort of hand in this novel, in me as a writer. There is no way to properly tell you what your support, encouragement, and honesty mean to me. "Thank you" isn't enough, but I shriek it with my entire heart.

To Char: Thank you for letting me pick your brain over excellent Zianos about long-term rehab facilities. Truly, I couldn't have written this without your nursing insight. Readers, if anything related to Charlie's care doesn't ring true, that's on me, not her.

To Aja: For helping me decorate Asha's and Charlie's wedding so perfectly.

To Jake: For helping me understand why on earth anyone would want to run *for fun*. I think I get it now. Maybe.

To the Midwest Writers Workshop crew: Leah and Jama, MWW is my step number one. At pitch sessions and first-page critiques, I learned that maybe I should keep it up. Shout-out to those volunteers who shared an encouraging word along the way, especially Angela, Kelsey, and Matt. You boosted my confidence when I wasn't sure whether I should even have any.

To the women who've made these publishing dreams come true: Savannah, I couldn't have dreamed up a more perfect-for-me agent. You see what I mean and what I want to say, and you understand it better than I do. You make me so much better at this, and you make me even more excited to keep it up. I can't believe I get to live this life. I will feel gratitude about it—and to you—every day. Chantelle, I'm not sure I'll ever not be stunned that you decided to bring *Then, Again* to the Lake Union family, and I am grateful to have your expertise in ushering it into the world. You've got my best interests at heart—lucky, lucky me.

Finally, to you, to the readers: There's an intimacy that comes with spending time inside what another person writes, and I'm honored that you chose to spend your precious hours with me and in these pages. You, sweet reader, are a delight.

BOOK CLUB QUESTIONS

1. Music plays a large role in Asha's life, and two particular songs are representative in her mind of her two important romantic relationships: "SexyBack," with her husband, and "Nobody Knows," with Jason. Based on those songs, what can you glean about Asha's relationships with Charlie and Jason? What is a song you relate back to a relationship, romantic or otherwise? What does the song say about that relationship?

2. No one is the villain in their own mind. Had this story been told from Maura's point of view, she would be the protagonist—not the antagonist. For example, we'd be in her head listening to her frustration at Asha's refusal to join a prayer group (*Even if you don't believe it, what's the harm? And it could be something we could do together,* Maura might think) and walking through her impetuous decision to take Charlie's ashes (she didn't *mean* to dump them in the birdbath). In what ways do you relate to and understand Maura?

3. When a couple gets married, it's nearly impossible for them not to daydream or plan out what the rest of their lives might look like. Will their future center on growing their family? Or work? Or new experiences like travel? Will their extended families and/or friends factor into

day-to-day decisions, or will the marriage be more insular than that? And it's easy to feel like a couple has eons of time to achieve all their goals—certainly, Asha never imagined that her marriage to Charlie would have such a short countdown to its conclusion. What is something in your life that you never could have predicted? How did you react to it?

4. One of the themes of *Then, Again* is that we are more than the decisions we make when we are in the throes of grief. What is your take on Francis? Why do you think Asha made the choices she made in regard to him? In her mind, she doesn't define their tryst as unfaithful. Do you? Is fidelity black and white? Or is there room for gray area?

5. Asha's father's culture and experiences have a big influence in her life, which we largely see at mealtime. What other quieter ways do we see Adam's influence in his daughter's life?

6. Before Asha's grandmother reads Asha's fortune in her Turkish coffee grounds, Nana tells Asha to make a wish. When Asha asks if her wish will come true, Nana says it won't. If there was a way to know for certain how everything would turn out for us, would you want to know? Why or why not?

7. When Asha needs to clear her mind, she goes for a run. After Charlie's coma, however, she loses her motivation and energy to run. What do you do when you're feeling overwhelmed or anxious? Has that changed over time?

8. Asha's and Bridget's friendship is one defined by loyalty and trust. Do you have a Bridget? What traits define your friendship?

9. Sometimes when we experience intense emotions, we regulate them—without meaning to do so—by reacting in a way that is the opposite of what is expected. For

example, laughing hysterically when your dead husband's ashes end up in the birdbath. Has this happened to you? What were the circumstances? Were your reactions misinterpreted by others?

10. Finally, the number-one question of *Then, Again*: Are you allowed to date when your husband is in a coma and probably isn't going to wake up?

ABOUT THE AUTHOR

Photo © 2022 Emma Downs

Jaclyn Youhana Garver is the author of the poetry collection *The Men I Never*. Her poems have appeared in outlets including the *Oakland Review*, *Poets Reading the News*, *trampset*, and *Prometheus Dreaming*. She is a recovering journalist and works for the National Council for Marketing & Public Relations. Jaclyn lives in Fort Wayne, Indiana, with her spouse, Jeff. Find her on Instagram @jyogarver. For more information, visit www.jyogarver.com.